D0126109

LIPSHITZ SIX, OR

TWO ANGRY BLONDES

ALSO BY T COOPER

Some of the Parts

LIPSHITZ SIX, OR
TWO ANGRY BLONDES

T COOPER

DUTTON

DUTTON

Published by Penguin Group (USA) Inc., 375 Hudson Street, New York, New York 10014, USA
Penguin Group (Canada), 90 Eglinton Avenue East, Suite 700, Toronto, Ontario M4P 2Y3, Canada
(a division of Pearson Penguin Canada Inc.); Penguin Books Ltd., 80 Strand, London WC2R 0RL, England;
Penguin Ireland, 25 St. Stephen's Green, Dublin 2, Ireland (a division of Penguin Books Ltd.); Penguin
Group (Australia), 250 Camberwell Road, Camberwell, Victoria 3124, Australia (a division of Pearson
Australia Group Pty. Ltd.); Penguin Books India Pvt. Ltd., 11 Community Centre, Panchsheel Park, New
Delhi - 110 017, India; Penguin Group (NZ), cnr Airborne and Rosedale Roads, Albany, Auckland 1310,
New Zealand (a division of Pearson New Zealand Ltd.); Penguin Books (South Africa) (Pty.) Ltd.,
24 Sturdee Avenue, Rosebank, Johannesburg 2196, South Africa

Penguin Books Ltd., Registered Offices: 80 Strand, London WC2R 0RL, England

Published by Dutton, a member of Penguin Group (USA) Inc.

First printing, February 2006
1   3   5   7   9   10   8   6   4   2

Copyright © 2006 by T Cooper
All rights reserved

 registered trademark—marca registrada

LIBRARY OF CONGRESS CATALOGING-IN-PUBLICATION DATA
has been applied for.

ISBN 0-525-94933-X

Printed in the United States of America · Set in Classic Garamond · Designed by Amy Hill

Grateful acknowledgment is made for permission to print the following:
p. 201: "Along the Route of the Big Parade." Copyright © 1927. The New York Times Company. Reprinted
with permission.
p. 218: "The Man of the Year (Lindbergh)." Copyright © 1928. TIME Inc. Reprinted by permission.
Artwork on pp. 35, 140, 333, 374, 375, 376, and 394 by T Cooper. Reprinted with permission.

PUBLISHER'S NOTE: This book is a work of fiction. Names, characters, places, and incidents either are the
product of the author's imagination or are used fictitiously, and any resemblance to actual persons, living or
dead, business establishments, events, or locales is entirely coincidental.

Without limiting the rights under copyright reserved above, no part of this publication may be reproduced,
stored in or introduced into a retrieval system, or transmitted, in any form, or by any means (electronic,
mechanical, photocopying, recording, or otherwise), without the prior written permission of both the copyright owner and the above publisher of this book.

The scanning, uploading, and distribution of this book via the Internet or via any other means without the
permission of the publisher is illegal and punishable by law. Please purchase only authorized electronic edi-
tions, and do not participate in or encourage electronic piracy of copyrighted materials. Your support of the
author's rights is appreciated.

For family.

For Fi.

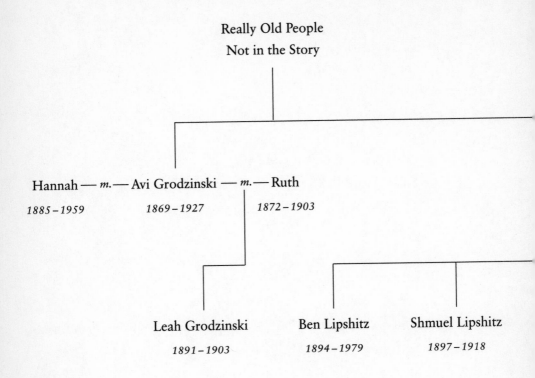

Really Old People
Not in the Story

Hannah — *m.* — Avi Grodzinski — *m.* — Ruth

1885–1959   1869–1927   1872–1903

Leah Grodzinski   Ben Lipshitz   Shmuel Lipshitz

1891–1903   1894–1979   1897–1918

LIPSHITZ FAMILY TREE

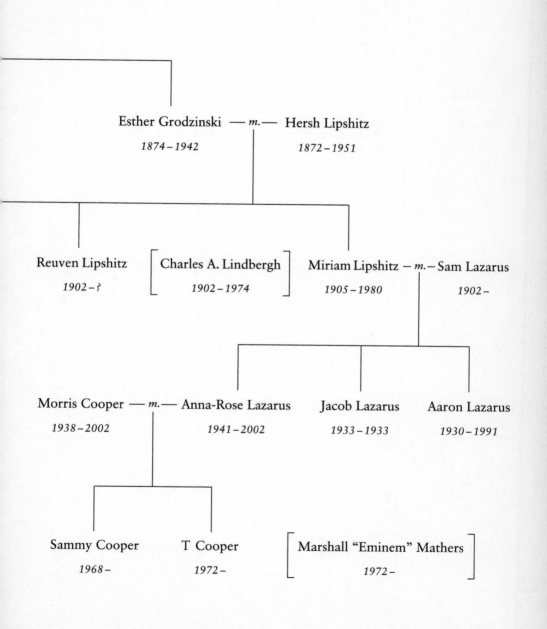

Lipshitz Six

A Novel

by T Cooper

(2002)

T Cooper
276 Murray Street
New York, NY 10007

PROLOGUE

1907

December 17, 1907

NEW YORK CITY

How do you lose a child?

It's not like a small piece of baggage or a head scarf, thinks Esther. *This is a child.*

This is a small blond child in a long wool jacket with a patch sewn twice over the left elbow. This is a jacket passed on from the small boy's older, decidedly less blond brothers who wore it before him. The jacket has four buttons on the front, and the boy in the jacket was securely attached to a hand not one minute before, Esther recalls as she is pushed from behind and trips over the suitcase that her oldest son Ben has left in her path.

She grabs onto Hersh's elbow to prevent a fall, and he looks at her. He has vomited for sixteen straight days, but he is her husband. He looks at her as though nothing is out of the ordinary, as though they are not standing on a plank over water that encircles a land on which they have never stepped foot. Hersh looks at her like all four of their children are present and accounted for. So it must be so.

Esther trusts Hersh, always has—he's an honest man, if nothing else—and so for a moment his look reassures her that all is well on the plank of

5

this ferry disgorging hundreds of tired people like herself onto this tiny island.

The line begins moving again, gently bouncing the plank, and all the people are milling about in front of a large brick building. Just to check again, Esther takes inventory of those related to her by blood: Tiny Miriam is coughing nonstop, wrapped around Esther's hip tight as a nag's saddle. Ben is ahead, next to his father, two bags slung over his shoulders, eyes wild every time he turns back, searching for his mother's eyes. Shmuel's wet hand squeezes Esther's left thumb. He has scarcely let go of it since leaving Kishinev almost one month before, and Esther thinks, the boy is getting too old to be clinging to his mother's hand in this manner. So, the two boys are present, as is the baby girl. But where is the blond boy Reuven?

Perhaps this is further proof of the fact that he was never hers in the first place, Esther thinks, as she considers when might be the right moment to tell Hersh that their youngest son is missing. But Esther does not want to ruin this moment, the moment they have debated for a very long time, the moment her brother Avi has described in his letters from Texas.

Now they are being funneled into another line in front of a building while a large country woman wails behind them, on and on in Polish, and her husband is trying to calm her, but she will not be quiet. The Polish woman's children look afraid. There are four of them. *There were four of mine,* Esther thinks, *but now just three.*

With this, Esther is reminded that she must notify her husband that she has lost their youngest son, certainly the blondest, most blue-eyed Jew in all of Bessarabia—and of course now in America. A hot, soaked Miriam is clamped onto Esther's neck and hips so tightly, Esther can scarcely breathe. Miriam has pulled out and untwined each of Esther's braids from under her head scarf, which she had put together so carefully as they waited on the ship out in the bay, before the ferry finally came to take them to the island. *They will surely not let me into this country now, not with this crazy hair and red-faced, feverish baby,* Esther thinks, but takes the words back so as not to curse her family any more than it has already been cursed.

They are waiting in a long line underneath a canopy in front of the building. Windows in the roof make it so that you can see the sky, which is gray. Esther had somehow thought it would always be sunshine and warmth in this new country, but it is decidedly cold in America—though not as biting as home. There are men yelling at them in English from either side of the line. Esther can tell from the conversations around her in Yiddish and Russian that the men are offering train fares to other parts of the country, American money, rooms to stay cheap in New York City.

Her children will not stop with the questions, so how could Esther get a word in to tell her husband that their youngest son has disappeared?

Shmuel: "Mama, what is that?"

Ben: "Papa, why are those men shouting?"

Shmuel: "Is this America?"

Ben: "Papa, will I be a partner with you and Uncle in the shop?"

Shmuel: "Is this Texas?"

And the baby Miriam crying and crying so loud in her ear. There is simply nothing to be done about the baby.

And then Hersh must get in on the conversation: "Esther?"

And what does my husband want now? Esther wonders. *What now?* Why they didn't go with Avi in the summer to Texas, Esther didn't understand. If her husband was so frightened of the spirits and rioting, why didn't they just leave with Avi then? Or before? If they had left before, they would be there now. In Texas, America, with all four Lipshitz children, including the blond one, and no screaming Polish lady behind her and the baby constantly crying wet and hot in her ear.

Esther is so angry now at Hersh for saying her name in that pleading way, like he is going to ask her a question she's supposed to know the answer to without him asking the question in the first place. He does it all the time. And usually Hersh is Mr. Know-Everything, but not now. For

7

once Esther is welcoming his pretending to have all the answers even if he doesn't.

"Reuven is gone," Esther blurts then.

"Yes," Hersh replies. He has not heard her. He and Ben pick up the two heaviest suitcases and push them forward in line. A Jewish man is translating in Yiddish what the American man in the uniform is saying. The people are to leave their baggage and then go upstairs for inspection.

"Hersh, did you hear?" Esther says louder, over the heads of their three children between them.

"Yes," Hersh says to his wife. "We will be separate for medical inspection, but we will meet on the other side."

"No," Esther insists, "Reuven."

Hersh looks at her, then at the three remaining children. "Reuven!" he exclaims in a voice so loud the people in line start looking at the Lipshitzes, and the Yiddish man momentarily stops translating what the American man is saying. "Where is Reuven?"

Esther looks behind her at the Polish woman, who is now sitting on two suitcases and being fanned by her husband. Her children still cling to her, and Esther knows just what this Polish woman needs: no more hot hands and wet coughs and red faces all over her. Just a five-minute break maybe would help this woman.

Esther cannot stand to look at her husband's confused face. *Do something.* But Hersh just stands there, lips cracked and parted. Esther scans the crowd behind them for a blond head among a sea of black. There is nothing, no blond hair except for one of the men in uniform. His hair is damp and slicked back over his head. *Reuven will most likely wear his hair like that one day,* Esther thinks, *because he will be a handsome man, quite possibly one of the handsomest. The kind that draws attention, longing looks, maybe even love.* She looks again at the Polish woman, who is panicking and presently gaining attention from the guards. Esther thinks she could do an impression of a hysterical woman like the Polish lady, though one who is even more hysterical because she has lost her youngest son.

But Esther knows Reuven must be behind them somewhere, holding onto another woman's hand, and soon this temporary mother will look down and see that Reuven—while perfectly beautiful and blond—is not her son, and then they will ask the little boy his name, and the name of his parents, and then they will call, "Hersh and Esther Lipshitz?" and in this manner they will find the parents of the lost boy.

But, Esther thinks, *Reuven is just a boy of five and does not understand any other language.* Esther is sure Reuven does not know his last name, or the names Esther and Hersh, just Mama and Papa. And with all the blond hair, he certainly does not look like the son of Jews. Now the hysterical woman impression is coming to her, but slowly. Esther starts inhaling in short gasps. She says in Yiddish to the man who was speaking Yiddish and English with the guard, "My son, my blond son is gone."

"Esther," Hersh interrupts, whispering. "Do not make such a commotion."

"Mister, sir," she continues, ignoring her husband. "We have lost one of our children. We just arrived, and now he's lost."

The interpreter comes over toward Hersh. "Sir?"

Hersh responds, because it is clear the man does not want to speak to a potentially hysterical woman like the one behind them, just to her husband. "Uh, yes, sir," Hersh begins, taking off his hat. "We just disembarked from the *New Amsterdam* and after that this ferry, and the next thing I know, I'm looking back at my wife, and she tells me our child is gone. He is just five, a blond boy of five." *Of course, it is her fault.*

"Okay sir, please wait here," the man says, but he does not go anywhere, just talks to more people in the crowd around them.

"Hersh, tell him we are going to Texas, tell him we must find Reuven before we go," Esther prods.

"We must be calm," Hersh says. He seems to know what he is speaking of, and for a moment, it makes sense to Esther to be what Hersh says, calm. Miriam has fallen asleep around her neck, still heavy on her mother's hip, but at least the girl has let go of Esther's braids. Shmuel is still latched to Esther's thumb. Ben stands looking between his parents' faces. Of the three remaining Lipshitz children, only he seems to understand what has happened with the youngest boy.

"You don't want to make too much commotion with these people," Hersh adds.

"And you know this because you have been here before," Esther says. "*These* people? Hersh, Reuven is gone."

"Calm down," Hersh says, forcefully. "He is not gone, he is just missing."

"Mama, I can go back and find him," Ben says, and Esther looks at him, knowing he will never find Reuven in this mass of people and baggage and children and so many men and women looking so tired with traces of vomit all over their shirtsleeves and shoes. She does not want to lose Ben too.

"Go," Esther says anyway.

"You stay right here," Hersh demands.

"Papa, please, I can run back to the ferry very quickly and see if maybe Reuven has been found by somebody there."

"No, you'll do nothing like this," Hersh says. Ben looks at his mother, but she doesn't know any longer what the right thing is.

The man who speaks Yiddish is just ahead now, with an American in a too-small uniform who is walking backward down the line, looking at each of the cards pinned to the people's coats, and staring closely at each person's face and eyes. Esther checks that all the remaining members of her family still have their tags pinned to them, and they do. Miriam's tag is so large it is jabbing into her cheek as she sleeps on her mother's shoulder. Shmuel has his tag pinned to the top of his hat. The man is getting closer now. On some people he is writing something in white on their jackets, and when he does this, the person is sad. Esther can see this much. One woman with a baby in each arm is crying because she has the white writing on her coat.

The man stops in front of Hersh. "This is my family, my wife and three children," he says.

"*Four* children!" Esther yells. "Hersh, tell the man about Reuven." But Hersh does not say anything. The man looks at Hersh and Ben closely, and then Shmuel. He approaches Esther and Miriam.

"Ma'am, please wake your child so the inspector can look in her eyes," the translator says. Esther is still stunned that Hersh has just said that there are just three Lipshitz children, not four. She shakes Miriam awake, and the little girl blinks several times, whining softly into her mother's neck. The American man in the uniform has a very hard look on his face, and this clearly frightens Miriam when she first spots him. He touches her chin and then pulls it toward him forcefully. Miriam turns away just as he is satisfied with something in her eyes. Hersh steps forward.

"Sir, excuse me," he begins, again taking off his hat and holding it to his chest. "I have a minor problem here, and that is our fourth child, our son Reuven, is missing. He was on the ferry with us, but in the rush with all of the people into this line, he seems to have gotten lost." Hersh chuckles nervously as the translator tells the American what Hersh just said.

The American says something back, and the translator says, "Please go upstairs for your medical inspection, and when you are waiting for the legal inspection downstairs, you will be met by somebody from the Hebrew Immigrant Aid Society."

The American and the translator move on to the Polish family behind them. The smallest child receives a chalk mark on his lapel, and this starts the Polish woman's wailing again. Esther wants this lady to shut up. She wants everyone to shut up. The nervousness around her, she can smell it stuck to the people's bodies and scalps, sour like the stench of a cow's teat. She looks back at her stupid husband, the usual blank look splashed across his face.

"This is what you are going to do for our son?" she asks him. "This is what you do?"

"Esther, we have to wait," he says. "You see how this is."

Esther does not see how this is. She jerks her thumb out of Shmuel's hand and peels Miriam off her neck and dangles the baby out in the air in front of her father. Hersh replaces his hat and takes Miriam, because if he doesn't, Esther swears she will drop the baby. Esther steps out of line then and walks toward the American man in the uniform, and soon she is tugging at his elbow. "Sir, please, please help us," she says in Yiddish. The American is confused and certainly doesn't recognize Esther. "Sir, you just visited me and my family. We are from Russia and we are the ones who lost the son, the blond boy about five years old."

The American looks at her and takes his elbow out from Esther's grip. The translator tells the man something in English. He says back, "No," and this is one English word Esther recognizes.

"Ma'am, you must stay in line and take your other children through medical inspection before anything can be done," the translator says.

Esther wants to cry, but she hasn't in about four years, since her brother Avi stopped speaking. She had certainly cried many times before that, but not once since. Esther wants to be a hysterical woman who has just lost her child, but she cannot.

"And where are you from in Russia?" the translator asks while the American guard moves on to inspect another family.

"What?" Esther asks. "*What?*"

"You come from which city in Russia?"

"Kishinev," she says.

"Oh, yes," he says, letting the sadness settle momentarily, and placing a hand on Esther's shoulder to guide her back to where her family waits in line. "I hail from Barafka, near Odessa. You know it?"

"No," Esther says. She does not want to go ahead in line. She wants to go back to the ferry to find Reuven. "Please, I have a very blond son, sir. You would recognize him the moment you saw him."

"Ma'am, you must go in the line upstairs," he says. "I give you my word, somebody will come with the Hebrew Immigrant Aid Society and they will help you find the boy."

"He does not look like a Jew," Esther says. "Surely someone will mistake him for something else."

"Please, Mrs.—," he says, searching the card on her coat, "Lipshitz. You will be so much better here in New York than in Kishinev. Please just do as you are told."

"But we are not going to New York," Esther protests. "We are going to Texas."

"No ma'am. This is New York."

We will get to Texas. Esther doesn't know who this man thinks he is to suggest otherwise. Because Esther wants more than anything to be reunited with her brother Avi, who had somehow managed to find both his words and laughter again in Texas, maybe thanks to this lady, this American Jew named Hannah he writes of in his letters. Esther pictures Avi there with the American Jewish lady, and cowboys, and Indians, and jagged wire fences all around them. She wants to see her brother like this almost more than she wants to find Reuven at this very minute—though it is a horrible thing to admit. The translator takes his hand off of Esther's shoulder then, and she steps back into line, silently taking Miriam from Hersh and hugging the child to her breast. Miriam had finally stopped crying while she was with her father.

"What did he say?" Hersh asks.

"Mama?" Ben adds, when Esther doesn't immediately answer.

"We must wait in line, and then some people who help the Hebrews will come to find Reuven." Esther pictures a tall American holding Reuven's hand and taking him back to his parents. A nice, helpful American taking care of the little blond boy who is lost.

An American doctor in a mask is peeling Miriam from Esther's arms. Miriam has started to cry again and she will not be quiet. She is worse than the Polish lady who, thank God, was taken to a different room. The doctor is having to pry each of the baby's hot fingers from Esther's braids and shirtwaist.

"I lost my son," Esther says in Yiddish. "My son."

"Yes, ma'am, your daughter will be just fine."

The translator says something to the doctor.

"This is your daughter, and she will be fine," the doctor says. The translator relays this to Esther.

"My *son*," she repeats. "My son is missing, he is a blond boy, the only blond Jew from Bessarabia province."

The doctor shakes his head and sticks a small piece of metal under the rim of Miriam's eyelid and flips it up to look underneath. Miriam screams, but Esther can't bring herself to care. At least she's here. The doctor repeats the procedure in Miriam's other eye, and then does the same to Shmuel. Ben and Hersh have gone into a different line where they are taking the men and older boys. There is a long line of women and their children behind Esther. Nobody has white writing on their clothes here, but there is crying, mostly muted, and peppered with sporadic, frighteningly loud gasps.

"The doctor wants to know how old your girl is," the translator says to Esther.

"She is just two."

"Has she been sick on the boat?" he asks.

"Yes, she and her father have been vomiting the whole time."

The doctor looks into Miriam's mouth and back into her throat. He squints and holds Miriam's jaw in his big hands. He looks for a very long time, writes something on her card and then pins this card to Miriam's jacket again.

Esther waits with her eyes closed as the doctor puts a cold metal disk to her chest and listens to her heart. He can listen as long as he wants, Esther knows, but he's not going to hear anything.

"Ma'am, can you put the little girl down so the doctor can hear your heart?" the translator asks.

She puts Miriam on the ground and holds her hand. Now the doctor seems to be hearing Esther's heart. Or at least pretends that he is. His hands are on her head, and she closes her eyes as he roughly rakes through her scalp. He then pulls Miriam's head toward him, repeats the search, and finally moves on to Shmuel. He writes the same symbol on all of their cards, and pins Shmuel's back on his hat. The translator helps out by pinning Esther's card to her dress.

"Sir?" Esther asks the translator, "the doctor understands there is one more boy he will have to look at?"

"Yes, ma'am," he says. "We can take care of that later."

"My boy is missing," she says to the doctor, and he ignores her, waving his hand at the next woman in line, with her two children in tow. Esther hesitates at the doorway.

"You must go downstairs to join your husband now," the translator says.

"Okay, but we can come back up when we find the boy?"

"Yes, but you must go now."

Hersh and Ben are waiting in the big hall downstairs, and Esther is led by two Americans in uniforms to the penned-in area where her husband and oldest son sit. There are hard wooden benches, with white metal, hip-level fences around them. There are maybe thirty other people in the closed-off area, all from the *New Amsterdam,* and Esther doesn't know how she is supposed to fit in with her two children. But the guard stops in front of the pen, lifts up a bar and motions that Esther is to go in. There are mostly men, and maybe five other women with children. Everybody has a big card attached to a jacket or hat, and it is very cold and damp in this large room.

Esther places Miriam on her father's lap and sits in a small space on a bench where two men have moved aside to make room for her. It is much closer than she wants to be to these strange men. They do not smell very good. There is a general odor of rotten herring and vomit, plus the faint greasy scent of the boat's engines still clinging to the fibers of everybody's clothing.

"We all passed," Hersh sighs. "Now the Hebrew Society man will come, and we will find Reuven." Hersh says this to make it so, but Esther knows it is not true. The first part may be true, the Hebrew Society man may come, but he will not find Reuven, not after this.

There is a large American flag over their heads. It is very large, and the white stripes are yellowed in many places. The flag is snagged on some sort of hook, splitting it down the middle, and it hangs from the railing of the balcony overlooking this big room. There are guards looking at all the people from the upstairs balcony. They are leaning their elbows on the railing, bored.

All the people are talking softly, all the different languages, but mostly Russian, Polish, Yiddish, and German. The collective effect is a cold hum that fills the room. Sometimes a person's name is called, and he or she jumps up, collects children if there are any, and the guard lets them out of the pen by lifting the metal bar.

This happens for maybe four or five hours before their pen is practically emptied out; it is just the Lipshitz family and four other people now on the hard benches. Miriam is asleep on a sweater beside Esther, and Shmuel is curled up against his father on the bench. Ben is sitting at the other end of the pen, looking toward the windows as though he is a young man who might be on this journey alone, without his family, eager to get into America and start his new life.

Esther has repeatedly checked each doorway that leads into this massive hall for Reuven's blond head. She has twisted her head toward each door for all of these hours, over and over—a nervous pigeon. But she fears she will not see Reuven again, not in this hall, not in America.

Esther supposes that she has always treated Reuven as though he were a mistake. This must rub off on a child, she thinks. Though, was it any different from the way she treated all of the children? Reuven was supposed to be a girl, have hair as black as her other two boys', as black as Hersh's and hers. Her bulging belly was unexpected, as she and Hersh did not make love very much after Shmuel was born. This was shortly after they moved in with her brother Avi and his wife. Things were simply different after that. Hersh had, after seeing Reuven's white head, half seriously accused Esther of infidelity. *Esther, infidelity! Ha!* Hersh had even let something slip about Esther and Avi, how this freakish boy is what can happen when a grown brother and sister, with husbands and wives of their own, live together in the same house.

Esther looks once more at each of the doors, and decides she will no longer strain her neck. She closes her eyes then, not for sleep, just to rest them like mothers do. But minutes later Esther's eyes rip open when a guard slams shut the gate to an adjacent pen. It is a horrible metallic shriek that echoes throughout the cavernous hall. This is her punishment for thinking Reuven was a mistake. Esther's lips are cracking, and she licks the corners, picking up a distant trace of blood on the tip of her tongue. Her three remaining children are within eyesight, and her husband is chatting on the bench across the pen, his less-than-broad back facing her. She thinks of Reuven again but wills herself not to look toward the doors. Maybe if she doesn't look, that's when he'll come, and then they will be on their way to Texas like nothing—none of this—ever happened.

Hersh has struck up a conversation with a man from the adjacent pen. He is from a village outside Minsk. He knows of Texas, says his relatives are in a state nearby called Tennessee, and he will go there one day with his family. He wishes to work and make money in New York before he can send tickets for them to come from Minsk. He says the Lipshitzes will be happy in Texas, but Esther doesn't see how the man can possibly know something like this.

"Hersh," Esther calls.

"Excuse me," he says to the man from Minsk politely, then turns to his wife. "Yes?"

"Why aren't you worried?"

"Is this what you wanted to say?" Hersh asks.

"I think we should speak to the man about the Hebrew Society people again. We are almost the last ones here."

"Yes," Hersh says, and turns to say one last thing to the man from outside Minsk before reluctantly attracting the attention of a guard strolling by. The guard doesn't understand. Miraculously, a tired-looking man from the Hebrew Immigrant Aid Society arrives shortly after, opening the bar to the pen and sitting beside Hersh on the bench opposite Esther and the kids.

"You have lost your child?" the man asks in Yiddish.

"Yes, sometime on the ferry, right after we docked here on the island," Hersh replies.

The man records some information in his notebook. "And the boy?" he asks.

Esther bursts in, "A blond boy of five. His name is Reuven, and he was wearing a black coat and a hat."

"Much like every boy that has arrived here today," the man says curtly. To Hersh he asks, "Are there any other identifying characteristics on this boy?"

"Like his mother said, he is just very blond, almost white hair," Hersh explains, looking at Esther, confused. "He does not look like a Jew."

"Of course not," the man says.

"Do you think you can find him?" Esther asks, but the man does not acknowledge her. So she adds, "Or is there a special room where they put the blond boys who come to America?"

Hersh interrupts: "Sir, we are on our way to Texas, we have the tickets already."

"Oh," the man says.

"What is this, 'Oh'?" Esther asks, but it is as though her words are disappearing into an empty barrel.

Now a woman from the Hebrew Society arrives. The guard lifts the bar for her and she comes to sit next to Esther. She has very strange clothing, but a kind, almost familiar face. "You have very beautiful children," the woman says to Esther.

"Yes, thank you," Esther replies, trying to listen to Hersh's conversation with the man.

"We must get you through the inspection process first, and then you'll stay here overnight," the man begins. "You cannot go to Texas until we find this boy, of course."

"Of course," echoes Hersh.

"Do you have any relatives in New York?" the woman asks.

Esther can't think. Hersh says nothing.

"How much money do you have?" the man asks. "You may stay with us at the HIAS building for a short time, but after that—"

"We have enough money," Hersh says. Esther knows her husband does not want to tell the man how much money they have, nor show him where it is hidden. This is how he is. She wants to tell them—if it will help get Reuven back—that there is some in each bag, her brassiere, inside a pouch sewn into Shmuel's pants, tucked into Ben's boots. There had been some sewn inside Reuven's coat.

"Raina!" Esther remembers, blurting the name out loud. "My cousin Raina lives here in New York."

"Where does she live?" the woman asks.

"On a street with an S."

"Suffolk? Stanton?" the woman asks.

"Could be Stanton," Esther says, "or maybe Suffolk."

"This is very important," the man says. "If we can get them to come here to greet you, it will be much better for the immigration officer."

"I don't know her husband's last name," Esther adds, "but his first is Isaac, and he's a tailor."

"Surely there are not many of these in New York," the man says, cutting dark eyes toward Esther.

"Where are they from?" the woman asks, seemingly to interrupt the rude man from interacting with Esther any longer.

"She is from a small village east of Kishinev, but I don't know about the husband. Raina went to America as a young girl," Esther recalls. Only Hersh, she thinks, would let this strange, Jewish, American man treat his wife so meanly.

"We'll find her and ask her to come meet you tomorrow," the man says. "Now, when we go into the interrogation room, I will do much of the talking. If I ask you a question, answer me and I will tell the man. You might need to show him your money, so please tell me it was the truth when you said you had enough."

"I have what they say is the equivalent of maybe twenty dollars for each of us, plus a little more," Hersh says.

"And please, tell your wife she is not to talk unless I ask her a question from the officer."

"I am right here," Esther says, "you can tell me this yourself."

"Ma'am," the man says, turning to her. "Please do not speak unless I ask you a question. I will apprise the officer of the special circumstance of the lost boy."

"Okay, I understand," Esther says. "Thank you."

"Mama, are we not going to Texas?" Ben asks.

"Not yet," Hersh answers.

"We will call your name momentarily," the man says, and then he and the woman from the Society get up to leave the pen. The woman smiles at Esther and visibly admires Miriam, who is still asleep at Esther's side.

Two hours later they are called into the interrogation room. The floors are made of dirty white tile—small shapes with six sides each, cracked in every direction and very black in the spaces in between. A man in a tight uniform sits across from the Lipshitzes at a large wooden table. Another man in a suit stands by the door, some sort of soldier.

The same rude man from the Hebrew Society enters and sits next to Hersh. Esther studies the floor, with Miriam in her arms and Shmuel sitting by her side. Ben is in a chair by himself, closer to the guard by the door, again looking like he already belongs here. His shirt is neatly tucked into his trousers; there are very few wrinkles in his shirt and coat. His hat rests neatly in the center of his lap. Esther watches him brush some lint off of his lapel and straighten the card that is pinned there; Ben notices his mother watching him and he smiles, eyes wet under long lashes. *What a pretty boy,* Esther thinks.

Then she remembers Reuven, and hates herself for having forgotten him yet again. In just ten or eleven hours, she had forgotten him countless times. Esther thinks she must be the worst person in the world—Old or New. The men are talking—the inspector, Hersh, the man from the Hebrew Aid Society. *What a difficult man,* Esther thinks. She feels sorry for his wife. *If this is what all the Jews are like in New York, I'm happy I came with my own.*

Esther studies the grimy floor as Reuven slips from her mind once again. She is thinking of her brother Avi in Texas. She supposes that sitting here in this office and enduring the rude American Jew is just what she must do in order to bring about a reunion. Her beautiful brother, Avi. Then Hersh is asking her for something, holding out his hand. He is pointing to her bosom, and Esther realizes he wants the money. She looks around her and sees that nobody is looking at her because the inspector and the Hebrew Society man are talking loudly in English, and so she reaches in and pulls out the worn bills and puts them in Hersh's hand. Ben is carefully rolling up his pant leg and doing the same. She sees Hersh stacking all of their rubles on the table in front of the inspector, and Esther thinks they will for certain be stolen like what happened on the train when the two young men came and took the money from the young German girl who was traveling alone to meet her brother in America.

Esther tries to meet Hersh's eyes, but he will not look at her. He is sitting on the front of his chair, left knee almost touching the Hebrew Society man's. Her husband the lapdog. Esther hears something about a building on a street called East Broadway. So many times the man says "East Broadway" and so does the inspector. They repeat Raina's and Isaac's names too.

Esther wants to go to Texas now and send for Reuven later. She does not want to go to New York and go to this office on East Broadway each day to inquire about Reuven, as they are suggesting. She has accepted that she is the worst person in both the Old World and the New, so she feels no need to pretend to be otherwise. This is probably why the man from the Hebrew Society is so mean to Esther; he knows she has lost her child, and yet she is not hollering and crying and requiring to be fanned by her husband. The man can see that Esther just wants to get to Texas with or without Reuven, that she knows it is just one of many sacrifices a person makes to get here. Like the fine dresser Avi had built for Esther and Hersh on the occasion of their wedding. This dresser, like Reuven, is just one of many beautiful things that must be left behind.

* * *

```
1907 DEC 17=
AVI GRODZINSKI=
WOLF'S DRY GOODS=
WHARTON TEX=

DEAREST AVI STOP=
REUVEN LOST STOP CANNOT COME TO TEXAS UNTIL WE
FIND STOP STAYING WITH COUSIN RAINA IN NEW YORK
STOP SEND ALL CORRESPONDENCE HERSH LIPSHITZ STOP
IN C/OF HEBREW IMMIGRANT AID SOCIETY STOP EAST
BROADWAY STOP NEW YORK CITY STOP= YOUR LOVING
ESTHER STOP=

=
```

* * *

In the women's sleeping quarters, Esther is tucked into a tiny creaking cot with Shmuel and Miriam on either side of her, and the muffled cries of strangers all around. Wet, hacking coughs seem to be the only thing interrupting the sobbing, and Esther cannot believe that all these women and their children actually passed the doctor's medical inspection as she and her own children had. It had been the most terrifying part of the day. Well, besides the obvious. Esther inhales deeply and feels the beginnings of a rattle deep in her own chest, and Miriam's cheek sits in a puddle of thick mucus on the dirty canvas of the cot beneath them. Esther finally sleeps.

"Where are your parents, young man?"

"I don't know, sir."

"Does your father work here?"

"He is a doctor, sir."

"Oh, well then, let me see if we can find him in delousing." The guard brings the small blond boy past several hundred filthy people standing in several lines. They carry blankets and suitcases and hatboxes; large white letters are painted across their jackets, front and back. Another boy the same age as the blond boy, though with black hair, scowls as the guard passes, the blond boy's hand in the guard's own. The dark-haired boy clutches a jar to his chest with holes poked in the cap. Inside there is a tiny gray mouse. The blond boy thinks he recognizes the dark-haired boy from the ship. The boy holds out the jar with the mouse, and the blond boy takes it with his left hand, secretly tucking it under his jacket. He looks for his father as he passes by the lines, settling on a slight bearded man in a hat with a large tag pinned to his shoulder. This is his father, but the man's eyes are filled with smoke and sadness, and he does not recognize the blond boy as his son. The guard pulls the blond boy away from the man. Everyone in these lines looks the same.

Upstairs in the delousing room, a blond doctor with hair neatly slicked back on his head looks up from the dark head of hair he is examining.

"Son!"

"Papa!"

"Son!"

"Papa!"

"I'm just finishing up, my boy," the doctor says, pushing the black head of hair away from him forcefully. "We'll catch the last boat back for supper with Mummy soon." The Jew attached to the head stands up uncertainly and shuffles away. This is the same man from the line, the one with the smoke in his eyes.

"Next," the doctor says, straightening the stethoscope around his neck. Another tired Jew comes; he too is the same man as before. "Thank you for your trouble. My boy, he wanders."

"Certainly, sir," the guard says. He clicks his heels twice and exits the room. He is a Cossack.

"Richard, what is this?" the doctor asks, opening the blond boy's jacket and revealing the gray mouse in the jar. "Where did you get this? You know you are not to play with these children."

"I'm sorry, Papa."

"I work very hard to make them clean, and I don't need my own son wandering off and picking up diseases."

"Yes, Papa," the blond boy says, eyes turning to the floor. "But can I keep him?"

The doctor sticks a long metal needle into the cloudy eye of the Jew in front of him.

"Sure, but let's not tell Mother," the doctor says in between pricking the Jew's other eye, and the blond boy smiles very wide. "Who's my boy?"

"I am."

"Who's my boy?"

"I am!"

In the morning, Esther barely recognizes Hersh and her oldest boy hunching over some sort of porridge at the end of a long table in the massive dining hall.

"There's Papa," Esther says to Shmuel, who had been upset from the moment he opened his eyes earlier that morning. Shmuel would not speak, nor would he stop touching his mother in some form or another. "Go surprise your Papa and brother. They'll be so happy to see you."

"No," Shmuel says. *At least he's speaking,* Esther thinks, looking at him, the large card from the ship still pinned to his hat. *What is it we are doing?* Esther wonders, as she approaches Hersh with his curved, small frame perched on the edge of the wooden bench. He looks up from his meal and smiles weakly at her, and she can tell her husband is wondering the very same thing.

"The Hebrew Society man said Raina and Isaac are coming on the ferry this morning, in maybe one hour," he says. "And good morning to you, my little bean," Hersh exclaims, scooping up Shmuel and setting him on the bench next to him. Esther puts Miriam down, and the little girl toddles unsteadily around the edge of the table to sit next to her brother

Ben, who offers her a spoon. A sign over Ben's head reads in six languages, including Hebrew at the bottom: "No charge for meals here."

"It was the second candle of Hanukkah last night," Esther says.

"I didn't even know," Hersh replies, finishing the last bit of soup and handing a small corner of bread to Shmuel.

Waddling toward her, Raina looks nothing like what Esther remembered, but they had been just girls when Raina's father, Esther's uncle, left for America, sending for his wife and two girls exactly one year later. This was during the pogroms of 1881 and 1882.

Raina is an ox, Esther thinks. There was no indication of future hips this vast when the girls would play naked under Esther's parents' bedsheets in the summer, when everybody else was outside working hard. Esther remembered running her hands along Raina's small hipbones, around her bottom, squeezing her close, and smelling her neck. They would sweat this way for hours, touching everywhere on each other's bodies—behind ears, inside armpits and belly buttons, under folded knees and elbows, and finally, just once, between Raina's skinny legs. It was soft and dry there, and quite nice, but Esther never touched Raina there again. The next thing she knew, Raina and her sister were gone, with two or three letters from America each year in their stead.

"Oh, thank *god,*" Raina yells, moving toward Esther, arms open wide. She grabs Esther's face between her hands and kisses her on both cheeks. "You haven't changed one bit. And this must be the beautiful Miriam."

"Thank you so much for coming," is all Esther can manage. *And you have certainly changed,* she thinks, but does not say it.

Introductions all around: Raina's husband Isaac is a man much like Hersh, though beardless and thus more handsome, Esther observes. He looks kind, if slight, and seemingly honest. They do not speak much on the ferry ride over from Ellis Island to the Battery. The wind is loud in their ears, a steady drumbeat. Upon landing, Isaac, Hersh, and Ben carry most of the Lipshitzes' bags. Esther holds on to Miriam while Shmuel totes a small satchel and stays close by his mother's side. He does not answer any of the questions Raina asks of him, even those requiring a simple *yes* or *no*.

Raina points things out to Esther and the children along the way, but Esther cannot recall even one of these places and things, even a moment after Raina mentions them. She does look up when Raina points to the Hebrew Immigrant Aid Society building on East Broadway as they walk by. Esther scans the massive building, and, for the first time that day, thinks of Reuven. *How can this—it must not be the first? But it is.*

"They will find the boy," Raina says. "They are very smart there."

"Yes," Esther replies.

She looks at her three remaining children. Miriam and Shmuel seem positively horrified walking through the streets of New York. Only Ben is strutting with his head up, eyes wide, taking in the massive city around him. He trips several times because he isn't watching where he's going. Hersh and Isaac are talking a few paces behind.

The streets are packed with horses and carriages, people speaking Italian, Yiddish, Russian, even some Chinese. Some motorcars sputter by, trailing thin threads of black smoke behind them. There are so many goods laid out on the street, in carts, on the ground, around people's necks. So many people walking by, going in so many directions, each building taller than the last. Soon the signs are in both English and Yiddish, and Raina says, "We're almost home."

"We won't stay very long," Esther assures her. "We'll find Reuven and go to Texas to meet Avi very soon."

"Please, we're family," Raina says. "You were my favorite girl, Esther, and I missed you terribly when we left."

"Oh, no—"

"Please," Raina interrupts, "you'll stay as long as you need in our home."

At Thirty-eight Suffolk Street, Raina ceremonially announces, "Here we are," and opens the front door at the top of five brown stairs. An entire baker's store is contained in the space beneath the stairway, and Esther inhales deeply, taking in the yeasty warm scent. But soon the familiar warmth is decimated by a smell so completely animal that Esther imagines she knows what the ark must have smelled like after forty days. This is an odor Esther had sensed in patches on the way up from what was called the Battery, where the ferry from Ellis Island dropped them off in New York. It is a smell that Esther immediately knows will never be eliminated from her clothes until she incinerates them—somewhere in a fireplace in Texas, in a town called Wharton, which might as well be one million versts from New York, Kishinev, everywhere.

The building's vestibule is dark, and there is an unlit gas lamp beside the archway above the stairs. Paint chips the size of Miriam's hands flake off the wall, the banister, the tiny stairs. Burlap covers the walls where the wood paneling stops, and on it is painted a bucolic scene with dark green trees and a brook, what is supposed to be sunlight through the leaves—though this scene, too, is crumbling beneath the varnish that is supposed to protect it. Esther begins dragging her baby girl and two small bags up the four flights of narrow stairs. She hears the loud shuffling of her husband's and sons' feet echoing behind her, as the stairs and hallway grow darker and darker the farther they move away from the vestibule. The smell in the hallway is even stronger now, made worse by the steam from somebody's dinner being prepared. They pass by an open closet with a dirty toilet in it, a tiny mirror on one wall, a small basin in the corner, insects scattering. Each door they pass is marked with a tilted mezuzah, Esther can see this much, and Raina's is no exception. When she unlocks the door to the apartment, Raina encourages Esther in first, propping the door open after it bangs hard against the wall, sending plaster crumbling.

There are three small rooms partitioned by two half walls with empty window frames in them. Two windows with glass face the street, and one next to the sink looks into darkness, at dingy clothing strung up inside some sort of shaft. Esther peels Miriam off of her neck one last time and puts her down. Usually Miriam takes off running when her feet hit the ground, but this time, there is nowhere to go. Fabric and cuttings and clothing lay everywhere in the apartment. Jars with buttons, boxes with spools of thread, a couple of Singer sewing machines on rickety tables. There are two cots in the living room, Esther notices, and a large bed in the other, which is filled with more clothing and bolts of fabrics. A small wire crib is pushed up against the bed in the tiny bedroom, but it is slanted severely, head down toward the window because the floor is so uneven. One of the wooden slats in the floor is missing, and Esther immediately thinks of Miriam snapping a leg if she were to run into that part of the apartment. Where would she fall?

I am a good mother, Esther thinks, *doing things like worrying about my children's well-being, potential pitfalls, and other types of danger.*

Esther knows Reuven will never see this apartment, or any other the Lipshitzes will occupy. She hopes that wherever Reuven is, it is better than this place. She heard in letters from Raina and so many others how much prosperity there was in America, and in New York especially. But this is not a dream.

"Is this the other room?" Esther asks, pointing to a locked door.

"Oh, no," Raina says. "That is the neighbor's apartment. Don't use that unless there's a fire."

"Okay," Esther says as she watches Miriam get too close to the stove and realize that it's hot. There are black stains on the wall behind it, wallpaper peeling and curling off the ceiling above.

Hersh bursts in the door then, breathless from the climb, and drops the suitcases ceremoniously on the floor on either side of him. "Beautiful," he exclaims. "Isaac, Raina, you are so kind to let us stay in your home."

"You're family," Isaac says. "Raina? How about you prepare some dinner so these people can rest." Raina hugs Esther to her breast one more time

29

and pats Miriam on the head before turning her attention to various pots and pans in the sink. She works on a slab of wood placed over a large tub next to the sink. *This must be the bathtub,* Esther thinks.

Esther finally sits down on one of the cots in the living room. It groans and stretches under her weight, and she thinks it might rip. But it doesn't. Esther does not yet understand how nine people will live in three small rooms (Isaac and Raina have a boy and a girl of their own). But Esther doesn't care about that right now, for this cot is the most comfortable piece of furniture Esther has enjoyed in over a month since leaving home.

Surely someone is to blame for this, thinks Esther. *Reuven, the mistake of a boy. Where did he go? I held his hand, we stepped onto the gangway, and then he was gone. Perhaps if Shmuel weren't being such a baby demanding his mother's attention, or Miriam so clingy and loud . . .*

But no, this is Hersh's fault, to be sure. He should've been helping with Reuven instead of chattering with Ben about the shop they will open with Uncle Avi in Texas. Or he should've taken the family to America when Avi left in the first place. Sitting in this tiny apartment with her family swirling around her—a concentration of bodies not unlike those of strangers on the ship for all those days—it comes to Esther: *Because of my stupid husband, I will never see my beautiful brother again.*

When a man does one thing right in his whole lifetime—just one thing—but this thing is the only thing that matters, do you forgive everything else? Esther wondered about this all of the time since Passover five years before. There never seemed to be a satisfactory answer. And so in the meantime, she waits.

Esther stands and looks out of one of the apartment windows. Dark smoke fills the sky over the dirty brick buildings. Striped mattresses hang over balconies, rugs are spread on the metal stairs clinging to the fronts of the buildings, clothing on lines running everywhere back and forth. This high up, Esther can see many roofs; some people seem to be living in small wooden shacks on top of them. She presses her cheek up against the window and looks right, following the street. In the distance she can see a stone structure, with cables that disappear behind another building and a tiny American flag twisting in the wind on top. She feels too tired to ask Raina what it is now, but there will be time to ask this kind of question later.

"Can I help with dinner?" Esther calls into the kitchen, because she feels like she should.

"Oh no," Raina replies, "there will be enough to do later for Hanukkah supper. Just rest now."

I

1903–1942

March 4, 1903

KISHINEV, RUSSIA

"Do eagles have two heads, Papa?" Ben asked his father.

Hersh looked down at the crumpled piece of paper in his oldest boy's hand. He recognized the emblem on the front of the pamphlet, and inside:

SAVE RUSSIA FROM THE JEWS

BEAT THE JEWS!

"Where did you get this?" Hersh snapped. His tone brought fear to Ben's face, and Hersh saw a tear forming in the crusty corner of his sensitive son's left eye. He did not answer his father.

"Hersh, leave him alone. They're all over town, these pamphlets," said Avi, from the other side of the tiny shop. He was covered in sawdust. "They rioted in Tumanovo yesterday at the market. Someone said the dead Christian boy's blood was used for some Jew's Passover matzos."

"This is becoming serious. We should leave," Hersh said.

"Where are we going, Papa?" Ben asked, recovering from his father's brief betrayal. He surveyed the small table that his uncle Avi was crafting. The dry scent of warm, burning wood filled the air around them.

"Nowhere, son," Hersh said. "We're going nowhere. Go see if your mother needs help upstairs with the baby."

"But I am trying to learn the trade from Uncle, like you said."

"Go."

Ben ran to the back of the store and up the stairs, taking them two at a time, and calling, "Mama!"

Hersh had asked Avi to start letting Ben apprentice in his cabinetmaking shop. Hersh didn't want his oldest son to be a lender like his father. Unlike Hersh, Avi had a *real* business—he sold items to the Russians, and for the most part they left him alone when they saw he did solid work that cost less. In Hersh's business, there was nothing but rancor and mistrust. On most days Hersh believed Avi was a good man, if a little cocksure. When Hersh married Esther, Avi was kind enough to allow Hersh to conduct his bookkeeping and lending business out of the back of the cabinetmaking shop.

"I think we should leave town for Passover," Hersh said.

"Oh, you are such a worry-for-nothing."

"Look at this, it says the tsar is asking the people to beat the Jews on Easter. That we suck the little children's blood for our religious practice."

"But Hersh," Avi asked, very seriously, "does it say we must have *Christian* children's blood?"

Hersh looked up at him. He held the pamphlet high, so Avi could see the crude drawing, but Avi just ducked his head into the cabinet and blew very hard so that sawdust flew all around him in a cloud.

"Avi?"

"I just don't see why they think the Jews suck the blood, when the Christians are always eating the body and blood of Christ," Avi said, chuckling.

"You think I don't know what I'm talking about? Trust me, this is how it happens," Hersh insisted. "It's not funny."

"I know, this is not a funny matter. Just think, Hersh. They must carry a great deal of guilt over eating his blood and body all the time, no?"

Hersh sighed audibly and turned to look at the ledger on the desk in front of him. He needed to collect on a loan across town. Hersh pulled on his dark overcoat and grabbed his hat down from the nail over his desk.

"Every year, it's the same rumors about the Jews sucking the children's blood," Avi said. "Why is this different? So this time they found a real dead boy. So the peasants will have a little too much vodka and steal a Jew's hat in the street, break a couple of windows."

Hersh looked at Avi and fit his hat snugly on his head. "I'll be back before supper, tell Esther for me."

"Don't worry, old man," Avi called as Hersh pulled the door shut behind him. "You act like a man twice your age!" Avi yelled after the door slammed.

"What was that, my love?" Avi's wife Ruth asked as she came down from the upstairs apartment.

"Oh nothing, I was just telling Hersh he's an old man," he said, getting up to find an awl.

"You mean the gray hair?" she asked, looking over Hersh's work on the back table.

"No, something else," Avi said. "But that too, come to think of it." Avi looked up at his wife, the curve of her neck sliding into the dark dress that hung so loosely down around her chest. He could make love to her every night, any time he wanted. And she would comply, and he loved her for this, and she loved him back for the very same thing. No more babies, not since their daughter Leah eleven years before. They could do this all the time (which they did), and still nothing grew in Ruth's stomach. It was as though her body didn't want to make another, not after how perfect Leah came out.

Ruth didn't know Avi was watching her as she wrapped the four fingers on her right hand around the back of her neck and gently squeezed. Avi felt this between his legs, and also in his throat. He dropped the tools and crossed quickly to his wife, grabbing her roughly and bending her playfully over the back of Hersh's chair.

"Avi!" she yelled. "Hersh will be back." But she didn't want him to stop.

Avi nuzzled the back of her neck and then turned her around to face him. "He's across town."

"What's he worried about now?" Ruth asked.

"Oh, nothing," Avi said, trying to kiss her into silence.

Ruth noticed the crumpled paper on the floor next to Hersh's desk. "What is this?" she asked, ducking Avi and picking it up.

"This is his worry, the tsar telling the peasants to make more pogroms."

"When?" Ruth asked, pulling away from Avi.

"Easter, they say, but who knows with this kind of thing," Avi said. He went back to his work. "And look at that picture. Not even a good drawing of a Jew—like a child's work, don't you think?"

"This is for the boy they found dead?" she asked.

"The nose is much too small, don't you think? Look," Avi said, pointing to the pamphlet, but Ruth would not.

"Is it that dead boy?" she asked again.

"Yes, but the paper said the doctors ruled it wasn't a killing for blood, and the friends of the boy, they said they didn't see him go into a Jewish shop before he died after all. On and on, all these made-up facts and it all adds up to nothing, you see? Go upstairs, don't worry, we'll be fine. They have known me here for years, and my father for years before that. Everything is fine."

Ruth looked over her shoulder at Avi as she walked upstairs to help her sister-in-law prepare supper for their two families. Avi knew that later he would make love to her the way she liked, from behind, many times over, until they were drenched and tired and no longer trying to be quiet, and she would fall asleep across his chest, her soft hair stuck to his neck.

April 6, 1903

Hersh awoke to a loud banging noise emanating from the wood shop downstairs. Esther stirred next to him in bed, her scent strong and sour in the mornings.

"What is it?"

Hersh ignored his wife. He jumped out of bed and pulled his overcoat around his shoulders, heading down the hallway toward Avi and Ruth's room. His right arm stuck halfway into its sleeve, and Hersh struggled with it, finally forcing his arm through with a loud ripping noise. He looked down and noticed that the lining of his coat was torn and hanging under the armpit. "*A chorbn!*" he hissed.

He tapped on Avi's door. "This is it, Avi," Hersh whispered. Then louder, "Avi, get up. We have to make a plan." He banged on the door harder, the noises downstairs growing louder.

Avi stumbled to the door and opened it a crack. "Is it not obvious we're still sleeping?" he asked Hersh, who could see the beautiful Ruth over Avi's right shoulder. She sat up in bed, clutching a white sheet to her chest to conceal her breasts.

"You hear that banging downstairs? They're coming today," Hersh insisted, but tried to keep quiet so Ruth wouldn't hear. Avi just stared at him silently, so Hersh turned and hurried down the hall toward Avi's shop alone. Along the way, he picked up the cane that had belonged to his father; it hung on the coatrack at the top of the stairs. It was the only thing he had from his father. Well, the cane and the tooth, but the cane was the only true *possession* of his father's, not something god-given like a tooth.

Hersh took the stairs quietly, gripping the cane in two fists above his right shoulder. At the bottom, he crept slowly around the corner by his desk, peering into the darkened and empty workshop. The banging was still audible, but there was nobody, nothing there.

He looked outside. Through the dirty glass, Hersh saw a few families heading to church for Easter. The sun, which hadn't been out much in the last few weeks, was filtering in through the haze in the windows, refracting small squares and circular patterns of light on the sawdusted floor.

Hersh approached Avi's large worktable, where a massive cabinet awaited some final touches. Avi does good work, he admitted to himself, and then he thought of Avi making love to Ruth in the shop. Hersh had walked in on them once, just after Hersh and Esther's first child Ben was born. He'd never imagined anything like it: Avi behind Ruth with his trousers down and she with her dress up over her hips, the top of the dress hanging down around her waist. She had both hands on the table—there was sawdust between her fingers and a little in her dark red, curly hair. Avi cupping Ruth's right breast in his right hand. They'd stopped when Hersh came in—Avi's member bouncing and glistening purple—but Hersh rushed back out the front door of the shop anyway and didn't come home until well after supper, his cheeks still flushed warm and red from what he saw. Hersh could almost feel what it was to have a soft, white breast in your hand like that, very gentle; you support it weightlessly, and this makes you feel as though it is your job to make sure that nothing bad ever happens to it.

Hersh had tried to do something like this with Esther once after seeing Avi and Ruth in the shop, but Esther laughed at him and made grunting noises like barn animals do. He wished he could've said to her that she might change her mind if she knew her brother made love that way, but Hersh kept it to himself, his little secret pictures in his head when he indulged himself.

Hersh's thoughts were interrupted by more banging, or tapping now, as it was quieter than before. Hersh lifted the cane up higher as soon as he sensed the breath of another creature in the room. He was frightened. The image of Avi pushing into Ruth disappeared entirely as Hersh peeked further around the side of the cabinet and prepared to bring the cane down hard, if need be.

"Papa?"

"Ben!" Hersh was angry. "What are you doing here?"

"I'm helping Uncle with this box. Do you like it? It's very pretty."

Hersh sighed and lowered the cane.

"Papa," Ben asked, "don't you think the box is pretty?"

—

"Papa?"

"Boxes aren't pretty, Ben. They are sturdy, useful, hardy, well made. But they are not pretty."

"Oh," Ben said, dropping the hammer he was using to bang on some scraps of wood.

Hersh looked at his oldest son. He was wearing his mother's apron. "What are you making?" Hersh asked him.

Ben's eyes grew bright. "Well, this is a beautiful little decoration for the top."

"Can you finish it later?" Hersh asked.

"Yes, Papa."

Hersh looked outside to see another large family heading toward the church. He could hear the mother yelling at her son to hold his sister's hand. "You are my little bean, yes?"

"I'm a bean," Ben agreed.

Hersh picked up his son and threw him over his shoulder like a half-empty sack of potatoes. Ben giggled and kicked the whole way up the stairs. At the top, Avi was waiting, leaning against the wall with his arms folded across his chest, smiling.

"Good morning, Uncle," Ben said to Avi. "I'm finishing the box for you like we said."

"Thank you so much for the help," Avi replied, though he looked at Hersh. "So it's back to sleep now?"

"I'm not very tired," Ben said.

"Well, it's quite early to do so much work in the shop, don't you think?" Avi said.

"He was just going to get back into bed with his brother," Hersh said then, sliding Ben down his own body and onto his feet.

"So, Ben is the pogrom?" Avi asked Hersh.

"It sounded like they were breaking into the shop."

"It's the last day of Passover, so we made it through, yes?" Avi said. "Now you can relax a little. I'm afraid you'll have no more black hair left after tomorrow."

Ben hugged his father's knees before skipping down the hall toward the boys' room. Avi chuckled as the two men turned to rejoin their wives in bed. Hersh stood in the hallway until the door to Avi and Ruth's bedroom quietly clicked closed behind him. He shrugged off his coat and slipped back into his own room, where Esther was waiting for him in their warm, dry bed.

Just before noon, Hersh took leave of his family and sat down in Avi's shop with his father's cane across his knees. He sat where his eyes were just level with the windows and street. Many Christians and their families streamed by the window, dozens upon dozens of them, plus some Moldavians, all heading toward Chuflinskii Square for an Easter celebration.

Hersh didn't like the sound of the people, or the way the men and older boys were walking, many of them drunk and loud. Hersh did not like this very much at all. He didn't want to bring it up to Avi again either, nor worry Esther or Ruth needlessly, but Hersh decided he would sit and wait and see for himself how this would go.

Hersh watched Old Man Nachman from across the street approach the corner and look both ways at the peasants around him. His movements were twitchy, his shoulders hunched around him like a cloak. This was not a leisurely stroll for the good man, Hersh could tell. It appeared as though a noisy, bothersome spirit were following him, a dark shadow against the crisp blue sky. This man is not usually trailed by dark spirits, Hersh knew, and yet there they were. Nachman looked up toward the sky when he reached the middle of the street, turning left and right, then spinning his body around to face what surely he felt behind him.

"It's right there," Hersh whispered, pointing at the spirit and standing up as his father's cane fell noisily to the ground beside him. But it was too late. Two drunken youths came at Nachman from both sides, pushing him to the ground. The old man bounced twice on his behind and landed on his back in the street. The smaller of the boys kicked dirt into the old man's face, scraping the inside of his shoe along the ground like he was kicking an old dog out of the yard. The bigger boy stood laughing, and finally the smaller one stopped scraping the ground and spit on Nachman before running away.

For a moment, Hersh considered going outside to help his neighbor. But instead, he went upstairs and found Esther in their bedroom, folding sheets on the bed. Their baby Reuven lay sleeping in a basket on the ground beside her. She stopped when Hersh entered the room.

"What?" Esther asked.

"Please, no questions," Hersh pleaded, fighting the impulse to crawl into his wife's arms and ask her to smooth the hair against his head very gently like she did sometimes. "Get a bag and put some clothing for the children into it. Maybe some honey cakes too, and we'll go very soon. Do not tell the children anything. Say we are going to visit your mother."

"Hersh, no," Esther said. She wondered when her husband had grown so old. And crazy. Ruth had said that Avi said that it would come to this. She pleaded: "Please don't make us leave our home."

"You mean don't make you leave *Avi*."

"Hersh, *no*."

"Pack now," he said. "I have to speak to your brother."

Esther began to sob, but no tears came until after Hersh left the room. She looked at her little blond boy Reuven, asleep in his basket. Sometimes she couldn't believe he'd come from Hersh and herself—so much blond hair it was almost white, the joke of the Jews. Esther's tears slowed then, and her lips curled up a bit when she thought of the way Avi and Ruth would tease her whenever Hersh was away after Reuven was born: "Which one of the peasant men did you go with to make this child?" they asked, laughing and pointing out various big, square Christian men with hands like rocks, carrying large sacks back and forth on the street in front of Avi's shop.

Her tears began again though, as she pulled a small suitcase from under the bed and placed some undergarments into it for her husband. Her generous and kind husband who is habitually so troubled, but nobody knows all the reasons why. Only him.

Or perhaps not even he knows.

Hersh found Avi and his wife and their daughter Leah sitting together reading. "Where are the boys?" he asked. Leah looked up at him, shook her head. "Avi, I'm sorry, but I have to talk to you," Hersh said.

"Okay," Avi said, setting the book down on his lap.

"Alone, maybe," Hersh suggested, nodding toward Ruth and Leah.

"No, they can hear."

Hersh was not happy about this, but he spoke anyway. "Avi, I saw Nachman pushed down by peasants in the street. They are all drunken, and it's just no good outside today."

Avi put his hand on his wife's knee, Hersh noticed. He continued, "So I'm leaving, and I want you to come with us."

"And where will you go?" Avi asked.

"I don't know, but I have the nag prepared with the cart, and Esther is packing a bag and some food." Hersh could tell he was not convincing his stubborn brother-in-law. "We can go now, Avi, just leave Kishinev and go. We will come back in a day, no more."

"And who will finish the work I have to do on that cabinet downstairs?" Avi asked. "I have to deliver this to the police station tomorrow."

"You can still do this," Hersh pleaded. "I would just like us to leave tonight."

"And how will I deliver this if you are taking the cart?"

"Avi, please—"

Avi looked at Ruth. Hersh thought the look in Ruth's eyes was that of ridicule, as though husband and wife had discussed this very possibility before it came about.

"We're family," Hersh added. "We should do this together."

"We're staying, Hersh," Avi said. "I'm sorry."

"There is nothing I can say to change this?"

"I don't think so," Avi said, standing up. "But I'll watch the house while you are gone. Somebody should."

Hersh shook his head and turned toward the boys' room, where Shmuel and Ben were stacking pieces of wood from Avi's shop into a miniature village. "Boys, we're going on a short trip. Get your coats. Ben, help your brother."

"Yes, Papa."

Hersh went back down the hall, past where Avi and Ruth sat whispering. Leah had gone. The couple stopped whispering when Hersh walked by. He remembered the look in his sister-in-law's eyes, that of mockery, he had originally assumed. But then he decided, *No, this woman is frightened, and if she were my wife, I would protect her with every last drop of blood in my tired body.*

Avi lifted Shmuel onto the cart and Ben after. He helped Esther up front and then passed her the basket with Reuven inside. The little boy cried incessantly.

"Where's Hersh now?" Esther asked her brother.

"I don't know," Avi said. "You'd think he'd be the first one out nere." He stepped up onto the cart and kissed his sister very softly between the eyes.

Ruth came out to say good-bye as well. Leah was playing a game on the back of the cart, slapping Ben's feet as the boy jumped around, finally knocking his little brother over in the process. Shmuel yelled out.

"Ben, don't hurt your brother," Esther said. Then, to Avi and Ruth: "You're not coming with us? Maybe just in case Hersh is right?"

"I have to watch the shop," Avi said. "They know me. I sell to the police. Nothing will happen to us."

Just then, Hersh came out the door of the shop with a small step stool in one hand. He set it in front of the door and walked up the two steps, terribly unbalanced. He pulled a large Christian icon out from his overcoat and placed it above the door. He stepped down and looked at the icon, but then climbed up the stairs again and resituated it exactly in the center of the doorway.

"I think they know we are Jews by now," Avi yelled to Hersh.

"This is for the people from out of town." Hersh folded the stool and carried it back inside Avi's shop.

Hersh came out brushing the sawdust from his coat. He stood in front of Avi and looked at him with his most serious face possible. Many more carousing Christians streamed in the direction of Chuflinskii Square.

They were throwing rocks, pushing one another drunkenly, as a scattering of pamphlets and dust tumbled in the street.

Hersh hugged Avi, and Avi hugged him back. Hersh then pulled Ruth to him awkwardly, sort of half hugging her too. His ear brushed her cheek, and Hersh was immediately aware of how soft Ruth was. The image of her right breast in Avi's hand came over Hersh once again. This happened, now that the families lived together, at least three or four times a week. He took one more sniff of Ruth before releasing her, and then Hersh climbed onto the cart and whipped the old nag, setting the whole lot of them creaking into motion.

"Boys, sit down," Hersh said. "Leah, good-bye, my dear. Be good for your mother."

"Good-bye, Uncle," Leah said, very politely and making a funny, teasing face at Ben. She stuck out her tongue at him as the cart rattled away. Hersh looked at his wife and saw that her head was turned back toward her brother and sister-in-law. He willed her to look at him, but she would not.

Hersh knew Esther had always been a little in love with her brother, and he could tell she didn't want to leave him now. Avi was probably a little in love with Esther too. They didn't speak much, but there was something there between brother and sister that never would be between Hersh and his wife, Hersh and anybody. Hersh worried that he *was* crazy, that Avi was right, even as the cart pulled away. Hersh knew Avi was a good man though, one of the best. Handsome and kind, agile and strong, but also a big kidder—yet entirely responsible, too. He had vowed to his parents always to take care of his sister, and he did, even after Esther had married Hersh. Avi was respectful of Hersh's domain, yes, but he still quietly made sure everything was okay for his baby sister. Avi was for certain the better man of the two, Hersh knew it was true. But it still chagrined him.

This is why Avi got the most beautiful woman in Bessarabia province. Hersh's Esther was a beauty in her own way, but Ruth, she was something else entirely. Ruth was the only woman Hersh had ever seen who seemed like her body was made for the sole purpose of making love. He would've thought this even if he hadn't walked in on Avi and her in the shop that day.

And he sort of hated her for it, but also wanted her very much. Hersh knew he could never have Ruth or even do something like this to Esther, but the way Ruth's lips were—very full and red, like she was pushing them out all the time on purpose. Her eyes also big and dark, always wet. She sent messages through her eyes and lips, and they were both just advertisements for something else, somewhere else on her body, Hersh always thought. He hated how she moved, how she looked at him, how she looked at her own husband.

Ruth's beauty was so prodigious it was almost grotesque. All the elements of her face put together comprised such a beautiful whole, but when Hersh dissected her face and considered each feature (which he often did while seated across from her at supper), he couldn't help but hate each individual part of her. Especially her lips, and her angular cheeks, which for some terrible reason glowed pink all of the time, winter and summer, morning and night.

Hersh thought for certain that Esther and Ruth talked about him and the private matters between husband and wife all the time. He couldn't prove it, but he knew they discussed things Hersh believed should remain between him and Esther alone. He both wanted this and didn't want this. For if Esther suddenly became the kind of woman Ruth was, he would have to hate her too. But he didn't ever want to hate Esther that way. That way where you want to go inside and push and push and maybe put your hands around her neck and squeeze just a little too hard because she likes it but doesn't tell you so.

"Hersh?" Esther said.

"Yes?"

"Didn't you hear me?" Esther asked. "I said to tell Ben to sit down; he won't listen to me."

"Ben—"

"Yes, Papa?"

"Listen to your mother."

Esther reached over and put a hand on Hersh's knee. This was what it felt like to have a woman like Esther put her hand on your knee, he thought. Yes, for once he had made a decision without Avi's opinion or approval. Right or wrong, it would be like this from now on, Hersh decided.

He looked around him, at the masses of carousing boys filling the streets. There was something in Kishinev, something not right. He looked behind him toward the square and saw black and gray spirits circling everywhere. They swirled above certain buildings, and one even spun like a screw down the chimney of a house on Aleksandrov Street. A wave of cold rushed through Hersh then.

"Did you feel that?" he asked Esther.

"What?" She pulled her hand away from his knee.

"Nothing," he said, and whipped the nag once more to speed him up. Reuven had finally stopped shrieking and was asleep under the blanket in his basket, safe between mother and father.

*   *   *

Avi told his wife and daughter to go into their bedroom and wait for him there. The look on his daughter's face was a queer one, Avi thought, almost like an old woman. Leah was the wisest child he'd ever met, and he didn't think this just because she was his. Ruth's countenance was different though, Avi noticed. He kissed her on the forehead and took in her scent, then told her again to go down the hall and stay there until he came to get them for supper.

Avi climbed up onto the roof just as the sun was setting orange in the sky beyond the cathedral spires. He could hear the distant growl of a crowd coming from the square, and saw a glow that could've been fire in a building. But the police were nowhere, so Avi assumed this light was from the celebration. He knew how much the peasants liked their drink.

Soon a group of Jews came down the street, three of them huddled together and carrying canes and sticks by their sides. Avi yelled down to them. He recognized two of the men as neighbors. One called up to Avi, "They're coming now, breaking windows and stealing."

"Who?" Avi yelled, but the pack kept moving, eventually disappearing into one of the stores on the corner.

Avi climbed off the roof and went into the bedroom, where his wife and daughter were cuddled in bed together. He thought they were both asleep, but when he walked around the other side of the bed, he saw that Ruth's eyes were open, and she was looking toward the open window even though the curtains were closed.

"Do you hear?" Ruth whispered.

"It's okay," Avi assured her.

"It is happening like the pamphlets and posters said."

"The police are out; they're not going to let anything happen to so many Jews," he assured her.

Ruth held her hand out to Avi, but it floated in the air for a few moments before Avi took it. Ruth pulled Avi close to her and pushed the back of his hand against her cheek emphatically. Avi was forced to sit down on the bed, very close to Ruth's stomach.

"I have to stay downstairs," Avi said.

"I'll come with you," Ruth suggested. "She's asleep."

"No, please," Avi said, more forcefully than he'd intended. "Stay."

Avi took his hand back from his wife's cheek and stood to leave. He saw how Leah was wrapped around her mother from behind like that, and noticed that she was just a fraction smaller than her mother, but they were the same proportion and shape. That even though half of him was in Leah, she was basically to be an exact replica of her mother. Avi had always thought Ruth was one of a kind, but now there was hope for future generations—another undeserving boy like he had been would be so lucky as to one day know such a love with a woman just like Ruth. Avi smiled as he locked the bedroom door behind him and went down to protect his shop.

Avi saw that Hersh's cane was on the ground beside a chair pushed in front of the door. He found a crowbar on his worktable and took his place in the chair, facing the window. Some families were walking home now, away from the square, but these were mostly women and children, older men. Avi knew it was no good that many of the young men did not accompany their families.

He stood to put out the lamp and sat back down in the chair, the crowbar resting across his knees. He sat this way for who knows how long. Soon he was asleep with his head hanging at a violent angle over the back of the chair, and Avi could not see the spirit that spun like a cyclone outside his shop door. It knocked the icon Hersh had placed above the door onto the ground. Avi awoke from the noise, but didn't discern the cause. As he looked about him and realized he had fallen asleep in his shop and not in bed with Ruth as he had been imagining, he saw a flame growing in size through the murky window in his shop door.

Glass broke, and a rock bounced to a stop on the floor beside him. Then there was silence. Avi rose to his feet and clutched the crowbar in his right hand very tightly. He opened the door slowly to a group of drunken Christian boys, but again, he did not see the spirit that rushed into the house over their heads and past him, all the way to the back of the shop, swirling around Hersh's desk and finally up the stairs into their apartment. The young drunken Christians carried clothing, shoes, clubs, and canes. One even had a small table hooked around his elbow. Avi thought it was possibly one that he had made a few years earlier for the shoemaker on Aleksandrov Street.

Avi recognized the young man with the table. He was the son of a policeman, for whom Avi did much work. This boy had helped Avi carry a large cabinet for his father one time. A different young man then yelled in Russian, "Beat the Yid!" and threw a rock at Avi's head. He ducked, and the rock broke another small pane of glass behind him.

"I can make you another table just like this," Avi said to the boy with the table, very calmly. He gripped the crowbar tighter in his hand.

"You are a stupid Jew," the other young man said. He held a small torch in front of him, waving the flame at Avi before tossing it through the open door of the shop. Avi looked behind him at the fire skidding across the floor. He knew he had a few moments before the flames caught. He looked back into the eyes of the boy with the table.

Just then a woman across the street screamed, and all the boys but the policeman's son turned to look at a couple that was being harassed by a bunch of boys on the street. The husband was trying to protect his wife, but he couldn't.

The policeman's boy with the table leaned to another boy and whispered something in Russian that Avi could not hear. Then for some reason the whole group turned to leave. They joined the smaller group that was harassing the couple on the street. After staring at Avi for a few more seconds, the boy with the table ran and jumped on the Jew's back, tackling him to the ground while the others kicked his wife and pulled at her dress. The table broke when the boy and the Jew rolled on the ground, and then the boy took one of the legs from the broken table and beat upon the Jew with it. After three strikes, he again looked at Avi, who had come back outside after throwing a blanket over the flames on his floor, quietly extinguishing them.

The policeman's boy pulled the Jew's overcoat over his head and then off his body. He tried on the coat as the Jew lay on the ground beneath him, holding his head and crying, "Please" in Russian, over and over. The boy held his arms out to his sides, observing each one as if in front of a mirror at the tailor's shop. He brushed off the front of his new coat, and dust clouded around him before settling back onto the street.

April 7, 1903

At six a.m. Avi came upstairs to wake his wife.

"Ruth, Ruth," he whispered, gently touching a soft shoulder. Leah stirred and turned over next to her mother. "Ruth, wake up."

Ruth opened her eyes. Avi almost felt as though he didn't recognize her. This was maybe the first time since they were married that they hadn't slept in the same bed.

"I am going with some of the men to the police," he said.

"Don't go," she said, rubbing her left eye. "Stay out of this."

"I have to talk to them, they'll listen to me," he said. "I'll be back in a few hours for dinner. Stay with Leah up here. But if you hear anything downstairs, I want you to go into the closet in Hersh and Esther's room and lock yourself in."

"Avi, no."

"Please Ruth, please, for me."

"If it is over, then why are you going?" she asked.

"Because what if it is not over?" Avi replied. He patted Ruth on the shoulder and leaned across her to kiss Leah on the back of her neck as she began to wake. She smelled so sweetly of a little girl smell. Avi wondered if all little girls smelled this way, or just Leah.

Ruth watched him go.

Avi and Schlomo Barsky decided that they would speak for the group of shopkeepers who assembled to ward off further riots and confront the police. They walked toward the New Marketplace with canes and sticks, crowbars, and anything else they could find to serve as weapons. Jews were not allowed to own firearms by tsarist decree, but Avi knew a few of the men concealed guns under their coats anyhow. He felt proud as the group of Jews walked down the block toward the square. More joined along the way, and Avi thought there were maybe one hundred by the time they stopped and assembled: A massive pack of them in black overcoats and hats, their jaws set tight and determined under full, wiry beards. They looked menacing.

The men stood together silently as Kishinev's Christians awoke to the beautiful morning. Many filled in around them, and some of the rioters from the day before returned, circling the men and periodically yelling, "Beat the Jews!" But they dare not face one hundred angry ones. Soon Avi spotted the police carriage coming toward them, and he was filled with relief.

Avi and Schlomo approached the carriage. "Avi, hello," the officer said, nodding his head calmly and surveying the scene over Avi's shoulder. It was the father of the boy with the chair.

"How are you, sir?" Avi responded. "I know you see what's been happening to our businesses."

"I do, but you men must leave here before you make it worse."

"We're simply trying to defend ourselves because you would not," Barsky said, stepping around Avi, who tapped him on the shoulder, indicating that he should be the one to speak to his friend.

"They have destroyed eight of our shops and two houses in this quarter alone. They're stealing things and scaring the women and children," Avi said. "What have you done to stop this?"

"We dispersed the crowds and arrested over fifty men yesterday," the policeman said. "All this was just a strange occurrence because of Easter. I think the worst is over."

"I don't know," Avi said, leaning against the policeman's carriage.

"I know," yelled Barsky. "I know they are just preparing more for today, you've seen it for months in the pamphlets."

"They think you want it to happen because you don't do anything to stop it," Avi added, very calmly.

"You think I don't know this?" the policeman asked, suddenly angered. "Now, go. All of you, I want you to go home or I'll arrest you too."

Some of the Jews started yelling at the police, at which point the police acquaintance of Avi's said, "Tell them to go. Now."

"I cannot," Avi said.

The policeman motioned with his hand, and soon many officers came from the carriage and the street and started arresting the loudest of the Jews. Barsky pushed an officer and was clubbed on the head by another. He was arrested and thrown in the carriage.

"Go," the officer repeated.

Avi whispered to a few of the men that they should go before more were arrested. "Come to my shop in one hour," he told them.

Avi turned and headed back toward home. The streets were strangely still. After several blocks, he noticed a few of the rioters were tracking him—foxes stalking the stray chicken who escapes a coop. As soon as they were well out of sight of the police, three men encircled Avi, each with a club in his hand.

"You think you are friends with the police?" one of them asked in Russian. "They don't care about you Jews." Avi didn't respond. He looked around for a house or shop to escape into, but doors and windows were shutting all around.

Avi heard a crisp, cracking sound then. He watched the lips of the young man who was speaking to him. He was saying something about bloodsuckers, but soon the words did not match with his lips. Avi stood through two blows to the head from behind. He felt warm, and he saw the man's lips moving through a smaller and smaller black hole. The third blow to his head forced Avi to the ground, and he landed on his cheek in the dirt. There was blood there, but Avi did not know it was his until he saw the three men walking away with the clubs at their sides. The one who was talking, his club was darkened with blood. Avi reached up with two fingers and felt the warmth all over his head.

He brought the fingers in front of his eyes and through the black hole of vision he saw the red, brighter now that it was closer and not on the man's club. Avi rolled onto his stomach and pushed up with his hands but he could not lift his own weight. He reached up with the same fingers and pushed a little harder on the warm spot on his head, and there were small, sharp pieces of something in the depression where the warm blood was.

Avi rolled onto his side and watched as more peasants emerged from their houses onto the street. They were yelling and carrying things down the street, into their homes, out of others'. Soon after, a small, orange fire quietly licked at the second story of a house down the block. But the flames grew smaller and smaller through Avi's strange view, and then the fire was gone, the peasants were gone, and Avi's vision closed up so that he saw only a blackness so deep that he felt certain there would never be anything but it.

It was white when Avi opened his eyes. *Snow, after Passover?* He could not see very well, and so Avi reached up and rubbed his eyes. When he pulled his hands away, they were covered in white feathers stuck to his skin in dark, crusted blood.

Avi's head throbbed, and it was so heavy he could not lift it from the ground. There were feathers blowing all around him, and a dog barking nonstop, just barking and barking in rhythm with the throbbing in Avi's head. He could not see the sky through the feathers, or the dog, just bits of blue and pink and more white, maybe clouds? He did not know where he was, or when. He thought of Ruth and Leah curled together in bed, but didn't remember why he wasn't with them.

I must sit up, Avi thought. *I am going to pick up my head and make this horrible cur stop barking. And then I am going to see about these feathers.*

Avi placed his hands on either side of his head and squeezed. He felt something loose and clicking. There were more feathers stuck to his face, and fresh blood oozed down from his hair, he could feel it. Avi sat up in the street amidst an endless storm of blowing feathers.

They are slaughtering geese? Please, the barking.

The dog came closer to Avi then, whimpering, and he saw that it, too, was covered in feathers and blood. Avi's head was pierced by a spear of pain, and he noticed he had no shirt, no coat or hat. He was just covered, his chest and arms, in caked blood and white feathers. The dog licked Avi's head, and he tried to shoo it. "Away!" he thought he might be saying, but Avi couldn't produce sound in his throat.

Now, sitting up, Avi began to see through the feathers that many homes were ransacked, and a couple half burned; there was furniture, clothing, sheets and shoes on the street. Ripped up mattresses and pillows, drained feather beds, cooking utensils, tools, a side of meat, pamphlets, vegetables, pots, a doll, a wooden leg with a man's shoe still on, books, an empty violin case. And everything, all of this, blanketed in feathers.

The dog finally trotted off, and Avi felt like he might try to stand up. But then he heard the horrible creature again, this time barking at another man on the ground in the yard of a house near where Avi sat. Avi thought to go aid the man, and this helped him get to his feet.

He followed the barking and eventually offered a hand to the man. But he did not take it. Avi saw then that the man was twisted so badly, his spine was bent all the way backward, and the man was dead, his mouth propped open with feathers stuck to the inside. The dog kept barking at the man, and Avi tried to kick it away, but he could just barely keep his balance.

It was growing dark outside, Avi could tell this much. He did not know why this man was dead. Avi did not know why the dog would not stop barking, or why it was so hard to put his feet one in front of the other to go home. He looked for someone on the street, but nobody came. Avi didn't know which way was toward his home. Or was he home? He knocked on the door of the house with the dead man in the yard, but all he could hear on the other side of the door was a woman crying.

"Ruth?" Avi yelled. "Ruth?"

Just more crying.

*　*　*

This is a bedroom.

This is my sister Esther and her husband's bedroom.

Her husband is okay, a so-so guy.

He is somewhat of a goose, but overall honest and kind and provides for his wife and children.

He cannot provide a baby girl, but that is the only thing my sister wants that he cannot provide.

The only baby I provided for my wife is a baby girl.

This is my sister and her husband's bedroom.

On my sister and her husband's bed is the only baby I provided, a girl.

This is Leah.

Beautiful Leah.

Her legs are pried open the way her mother's were when Leah was born.

There is blood on the bed.

There is blood on the bed my sister and her husband share.

There are feathers all over the place, all over.

They cover the dresser I made for my sister's wedding present.

They are in the bed.

They are even stuffed into the circle of blood between my daughter Leah's legs.

They are stuffed into her, inside her.

These are white feathers from the pillows and the bed that are stuffed into my Leah.

I have not yet looked at her face.

I am afraid it will be worse to look at her face than it is to look between her legs.

But now I am looking at her face.

Her lips are misshapen.

There is something wrong with her lips.

They are much bigger than I remember.

There are more feathers stuffed into my baby girl's mouth, between her red lips.

This is a girl of eleven and one-half years.

I was afraid the face would be worse than between her legs.

But it is not so bad.

Just her lips are different, and I must get used to it. We'll all get used to it.

I have been in this room that my sister shares with her husband just one other time.

This was when I helped Hersh carry the dresser I made as a present for their wedding.

It was a nice dresser, and my sister loved it.

There are many feathers in many of the drawers of the dresser now.

They are all open but the top, which is locked.

What was in the drawers is now on the floor, and feathers have replaced what was in the drawers.

There is breathing in the room that is not my own.

This means Leah can breathe through all of those feathers.

This is a relief.

But there is my wife in the closet.

My wife is the one who is breathing loudly, and her eyes are red and wide.

She is just crouching there, wheezing in the closet.

I am now trying to open the locked drawer in the dresser, but it is a good lock.

I started installing these heavy locks in the dressers and nobody, they can't open them without the key.

I am trying to pry open the locked drawer with a crowbar that is covered in feathers and blood and was on the floor.

I can't seem to pry open the drawer because my hands keep slipping in the blood covering the crowbar.

I don't know why my wife insists on sitting there in the closet.

April 10, 1903

Dr. Slutskii rewrapped the bandages around Avi's head. Some blood and yellow cranial fluid continued to seep through, but the doctor knew it was good, and Avi—like most of those who had survived through the last few days—would be saved.

"He can go with you now," the doctor told Hersh. "We need to make space."

"Avi?" Hersh said loudly and slowly. "Did you hear? Dr. Slutskii said you can come home now. Avi?"

"There should be nothing wrong with his hearing," the doctor said. "You don't need to talk that way."

"Oh, well, thank you, doctor," Hersh replied. He sat down gingerly on the edge of Avi's bed. "You hear that, Avi? Now I know you're listening. We are going home now. Esther fixed up the house very beautiful, almost like normal, and you will be very comfortable."

Hersh looked down the row of beds in the Jewish Hospital. They were stacked side by side, some on top of others, all containing men and women with white bandages around their heads. Some bandages covered parts of their faces and eyes and torsos, their arms, a few elevated legs.

"Avi, the doctor did a good surgery for you," Hersh continued mindlessly. "Everything will be okay now."

Hersh didn't know what to do with Avi, and he started to panic. He couldn't remember what the doctor had said about getting him home. A nurse whirred by, rushing toward another patient who was moaning in the corner, thick blood seeping through the yellowed bandage over his eye. Hersh spotted an empty wheelchair on the other side of the room; he maneuvered it through the tight maze of beds and medical equipment and then parked it next to Avi's bed.

"You need to get into this," Hersh said.

Avi opened his eyes, blinked a few times very slowly and looked at Hersh. A wave of cold surged through Hersh then, and through the look in Avi's eyes he recalled how he'd sensed the same kind of chill when he and Esther and the boys left Kishinev the Sunday before. The spirits swirling around the city as all the restless Christian peasants streamed into town, in the opposite direction Hersh was taking his family. Reuven had cried wildly in the back of the cart, a terrible, ripping wail. Esther's hand heavy as an anvil on Hersh's knee.

"Avi, you need to get up."

After about five minutes of staring at the ward's pockmarked, peeling ceiling, Avi slowly sat up, and Hersh rushed to offer him a hand. But Avi did not take it. He kept looking up, hands on his thighs. Hersh noticed his hands and fingers and arms were crisscrossed with cuts, some deep and stitched, others more superficial. Avi blinked a few more times and looked down the row of injured and near dead next to him.

"You are lucky the doctor could fix your head," Hersh said, but he immediately regretted the words. Avi slowly turned his gaze back toward Hersh, but didn't look at him. "I'm sorry," Hersh added nervously.

Avi put a hand on the wheelchair as Hersh held onto the handles to steady it. Avi pulled himself into the chair and tapped both hands on the armrests to let Hersh know that he was ready. Hersh wheeled Avi down the hall then, past the room where the corpses were stacked in rows, side by side on the wood floor. Candles burned around them, and family members cried softly next to some of the bodies. Avi did not turn to look into the room, but Hersh did. He caught six or seven white faces in a row against the wall. Mouths open with hollowed cheeks, sticky bearded chins jutting up toward the ceiling, eyes sunken and gaping.

Hersh pushed Avi outside into a blast of white sunlight. He wheeled Avi across the square and down Gostinnii Street. Tiny threads of dark smoke crept up into the sky on either side. Some Jews were repairing their homes and shops, others were packing their remaining possessions and loading carts to leave the city. Clothing and shoes littered the street, darkened patches of blood soaked the road in some spots.

"The feathers," Avi said softly, as a small cloud of them swirled across their path in a gust. These were the first words Avi had spoken since Hersh found him, Ruth, and Leah in Hersh's bedroom on Monday night when he, Esther, and the children returned.

"It is difficult to clean up so many feathers," Hersh said. "They will maybe never get all of the feathers."

"Most likely not," Avi agreed. He did not speak again for the rest of the walk home.

When they reached the stairs in the back of Avi's shop, Hersh supported his brother-in-law up to his bedroom. Ruth was in bed, where she had been for the last three days. Avi's heart pumped palpably when he saw her, and for a brief moment he forgot about Leah. But when Ruth turned to him with dark red eyes, he remembered the red circles of blood filled with feathers on his beautiful daughter's face and in the space between her legs, and he knew he would never make love to his wife again. He tried to recall the last time they had, but couldn't. He wondered how it might've been different if he'd known it was to be their last.

Hersh stood behind Avi in the doorway, and Esther joined him with the tiny Reuven on her hip. They stared at Avi and Ruth, but Avi couldn't imagine what they expected. In all the years of sharing a home, never had the two couples been as intimate as this, one looking in through the open door of the others' bedroom.

"Can you leave us alone?" Avi asked, and Hersh quickly pulled the door shut behind them.

"I am pleased you're alive," Ruth said to Avi, as soon as Hersh and Esther had gone.

"I'm not," he replied, limping toward the bed.

"You know I can't love you any longer," she said, her back to Avi.

"Oh, I know. I was just thinking this on the way home." Avi slowly lowered himself onto the other side of the bed beside her.

"But where will you sleep?" she asked.

Avi spoke on four occasions in four years.

1. April 11, 1903

Occasion: Finding Ruth dead in a bathtub filled with her blood and now-cold water.

She announced to the family that she was preparing to take a bath, boiled copious amounts of water, and then locked herself in the washroom. Water could be heard splashing for hours. After knocking for some time with no response or splashing, Hersh helped Avi to the door and then at Avi's behest, knocked the door off its hinges with a firm butt of his shoulder.

Ruth lay in the tub with open slices in the flesh of her forearms. Her body and head were submerged in the water, up to the bottom lids of her open eyes, and when Esther came in to see why her husband had broken a door down in the house, she let out a short scream that awoke Reuven and started him crying for twelve hours straight.

What Avi said: "Bury her next to Leah."

2. March 28, 1904

Occasion: Hersh deciding one year was too long for a grown man to go without speaking, so he sat down with Avi to tell him a story he had never told anybody else, even his wife.

"It was 1881, and the tsar had just been murdered, you might recall," Hersh began, as Avi worked silently, sanding a piece of furniture, the same piece he had been working on before that Passover. "I was maybe eight or nine, and I remember my mother pulling me, just dragging me by the arm is all I can remember. My mother had my sister by the other hand, and we were running through the shtetl, past the synagogue, past my uncle's house. I don't know where we were going.

"I just remember my mother moving faster than I'd ever seen, my sister and myself being dragged behind on either side of her. And then we stopped, and there were dead men all around us, dark heaps littering the ground behind the synagogue. The peasants were so angry, they thought the Jews had killed the tsar. So they came and they did just like they did in Kishinev last year, and there was nobody to help, and we had no warning, nothing.

"So I see the Torah scrolls from the synagogue, and they're just ripped into shreds on the street, and I'm thinking this is the worst thing that could ever possibly happen, and I let go of my mother's hand because I see my father sitting against the rabbi's house way over there, next to a few other men lying in the dirt. I'm thinking the men are upset because of the Torah scrolls, you know, they're mourning them. My father's back is facing me in his dark coat, and he looks like he's just sitting there against the wall, resting a little and sad about the Torah, but then I get in front of him and I see his knees folded very tight against his chest and one arm is no longer on his body, and his mouth is gone, there's just blood there now.

"There are teeth on the ground in front of my father, maybe three of

67

them, and I pick up one and look at it, and it smells like the trees and horses maybe. And so I wipe off the blood with my fingers and put the tooth in my pocket.

"This is when the spirits came to me, and they never went. So Avi, maybe this is why I left Kishinev last year, because I saw this. There was no way for you to know, you see?"

What Avi said: "And you are certain this was the tooth of your father, and not some other man?"

3. August 14, 1905

Occasion: Esther giving birth to a baby girl—Miriam—who came into the world silently in the same bed where Avi's only daughter had died.

Avi was trying to sleep with a pillow over his head down the hall, attempting to drown out his sister's wailing. Since there was no sound of a baby crying, Avi half hoped that the child had been born dead. But soon, Esther's screams ceased, and Avi could hear Hersh in the hallway, loudly thanking god for giving him a baby girl, but then reassuring the three boys looking in on their mother that he would've been just as happy with four sons instead.

In the morning, after Avi dressed for work and before he went down to the shop, he knocked twice on his sister's bedroom door before poking his head in to see her holding the tiny and red Miriam in bed, suckling her mother's right breast.

What Avi said: "Now you will know what it is to lose a girl, Esther."

4. July 18, 1907

Occasion: A flyer being dropped off in Avi's shop. Within:

THE JEWISH EMIGRATION SOCIETY OF KIEV is looking for skilled workers and laborers under the age of forty years to begin a new life in the New World. Please be proficient as the following tradesmen: carpenters, iron workers, cabinetmakers, joiners, butchers, tinsmiths, painters, paperhangers, shoemakers, tailors, masons, plumbers, machinists, and many others. It shall be necessary to work on the Sabbath, which is an American tradition.

The Great American West welcomes Jews to its wide-open spaces and land of opportunity. Already, Russian Jews are making between seven and eighteen dollars a week in several of the above trades. Many of your co-religionists in America are wishing to employ their brothers from the Old World.

You will wish to send for your family soon after you taste the freedom of the American West. Approximately 85 rubles includes all required documents for emigration, plus rail passage to Bremen, Germany, and steamship passage to Galveston, Texas. Next steamer departs the port of Bremen, Germany, for Galveston, Texas, America, on ____1 August 1907____, via North German Lloyd Shipping Company.

Inquire with local ITO representative in _____Kishinev___:
____Chaim Tchernowitz____, _____1181 Bratslav

Avi crumpled up this flyer and tossed it into the wastebasket under Hersh's desk. He went upstairs and found his sister stuffing a carp in the kitchen.

What Avi said: "Tomorrow I am leaving for America."

Galveston, Tex.

August 26, 1907

My Dear Esther:

I know it has been a long time, but I have been punished for my crimes and now believe I can begin anew. Some may say I don't deserve this. I just hope you have not forgotten your adoring brother.

You must come to Texas. It is a wide-open land of opportunity here. I have arrived safely in Galveston, despite an uncomfortable sail from Bremen. The accommodations were more suited to cattle. Worms in the bread, plus rotten herring, rotten meat, and rotten potatoes for twenty-four days on a very slow boat. The Germans, especially the sailors, would beat some of us passengers, for no reason other than our asking for a bit of hot water. When it was so warm in the bottom of the boat, a few of us would go to the decks upstairs for some fresh air, and the sailors would throw cold water on us from above, the officers encouraging them in this endeavor. Thus, we could not remain upon the deck to avoid the sickness below.

This is no matter now, as Rabbi Cohen and the others at the JIIB in Galveston are finding work for myself and all of the other men in towns throughout the American West. I have been told that I will be assisting a German-Jewish cabinetmaker for possibly twelve dollars a week, which is very good for a man in America, especially a greenhorn such as myself. I am told I will be in a town close to the larger city of Houston. I shall send you another letter as soon as I secure a place of residence.

I will soon be saving money and already, after just two days, I am filled with certainty that I shall be very comfortable here. I believe you and Hersh should come to Texas. All the children appear happy here.

Inquire with the ITO headquarters in Kiev, the Jewish Emigration Society, for passage to Galveston. There is also perhaps a bureau in Kishinev or Odessa. They can help arrange documents. I suggest you find another route to Galveston, because the German ships are so hostile to our people. Once you land in New York, Philadelphia, or maybe Baltimore, there are many railroads that lead to Texas.

Please show this part of the letter to Hersh: Hersh, please sell the shop for train and steamer passage. We shall never wish to live in Kishinev again. There is ample work for you here.

I think Texas is very possibly the next best thing to the promised land.

Please send my regards to the boys. And to Miriam, who does not know her uncle very well, I'm afraid. I hope to correct this situation soon. I have sent a letter to Mother and Father.

Lovingly,
Avi

Wharton, Tex.

September 15, 1907

My Dear Esther:

I write now from a new town in Texas. The job with the cabinetmaker did not work as expected. But the JIIB has found me another position in a packing plant. My duties include stacking oxen on a rack, and I have been earning nine dollars per week. The manager has promised a one-dollar-a-week raise in one months' time, plus one more dollar after two months' time. As you know, this is not my desired occupation, but I believe I will soon find a position in which I can put to use my skills.

I believe it is a perfect time for you and Hersh to bring the children. The Yiddish papers have described the dire situation in the Kiev region, and I believe it is time to leave Russia altogether. There are some Jews here in Wharton and many more in the larger city of Houston. A very forward-thinking synagogue. I believe I can find Hersh work at a similar wage to my own. This will be sufficient to support our family once again.

Some news: I have met a woman, Hannah, a beautiful American-born Jewish girl—almost blond hair, like Reuven! I know you will like her. But Mama, I'm not so sure. Hannah's father owns a dry-goods store in Wharton and some elsewhere in Texas, and I have been letting a room above the store since arriving here. I believe when I can save up some money I shall ask her to marry me. I have shaved my beard. All the Jews do this here, and Hannah believes I am quite handsome! Esther, you will for certain not recognize your brother!

Please send all correspondence in c/o Wolf Dry Goods, Wharton, Texas.

Lovingly,

Avi

Kishinev

October 16, 1907

Dear Avi:

I am so happy that you are communicating with me again. What you report of the journey across the ocean is truly terrible, and a tear came to my eye as I read your words.

I have sad news for you, and that is Mama has died. We have been sitting shivah now for three days. She was very uncomfortable in the end. Hersh carried her into your old bedroom for the last days of her life, and Dr. Slutskii attended to her needs until the final breath. Papa sat beside her the whole time. She said your name on the night before she passed. I told her you were very happy and rich in America, soon to open another cabinetmaking shop with the money you are earning now. I did not mention anything about the oxen. This seemed to make her happy, and perhaps soon it will be true, and I will not have stretched the truth so much to our dear mother during the last days of her life?

Avi, I miss you terribly. I am pressing Hersh on the subject of joining you in Texas soon, but he is not very fond of the idea. I have even begun inquiring in town—there is an office here in Kishinev that deals solely with the trip to Galveston. They have said that if we have a family member already in Texas, they wish us to find a different way there, as they wish to send those with no contacts already in America, Texas or elsewhere. But they are quite helpful with information about the journey.

I am trying. Hersh is stubborn, but sensible. I don't need to tell you this.

It fills me with happiness to hear you are well in Texas. You have committed no crimes, you need not be forgiven by anybody, except perhaps by Avi himself.

And this Hannah lady? I am eager to meet her, though very jealous she is the first to touch your smooth cheek with no beard upon it. Just like when we were children.

Your loving Esther

Kishinev

Dear Avi:

Since we have not heard back from you, and we are preparing to embark for America, I am sending you another letter.

Hersh has decided to take us to Texas to join you. The entire village of Rovkow has been burned down, sparing just one Jewish house and the tall tree in its yard. Hersh's work is filled with constant complaints and threats from his customers. Bookkeeping work is becoming more scarce. We will buy rail passage to Rotterdam, where we will catch the steamship to New York. An agent in Rotterdam is said to be able to offer rail tickets from New York to Houston. Hersh has collected on all of his remaining loans and we will have enough to assure the Americans that we can support ourselves in their country.

Hersh will not sell the shop. He believes we might come back after a while in America, once the world outcry begins to tame the tsar, or eliminate the pale. Already we have heard about demands from Western newspapers and politicians—have you seen these?

Papa remains as stubborn as Hersh was. He says he will not leave, that this is his home. I have tried to entreat him to come with us, but he does not seem to understand. He gets very confused since Mama died. He will stay with Aunt in Perchkov. He seems happiest when near his sister.

We are leaving in two days' time. If you have left your present station, please leave word with this Mr. Wolf, so that we can find you as soon as we arrive in Texas. I am frightened of this journey, but I believe when you say it is a land of opportunity.

There are too many memories on the streets of Kishinev, and in all of the buildings. If I go to the grocery and feel the sun on my forehead, I may think that it is a nice day without sadness, but then the man who makes change for me has one arm missing and his blind son sits on a stool in the corner, and then it's not such a lovely day after all.

I fear it will grow worse before it grows better. But what do I know of these matters?

I know I miss you, dear brother. I await eagerly the time when you will hug me to you, and I can feel your sweet breath in my hair.

Your loving Esther

November 13, 1907

Hersh had heard of agents who specialized in helping Russians cross the borders without the expensive government permits. And so here he was, packing his wife and four children onto the cart Avi left him, readying the nag for the long journey. Hersh filled the feed bag full of oats and slung it behind the old boy's twitching ears. He also left a large bucket of fresh water by the nag's feet all day before they were to leave. He drank copiously.

At about eleven in the night, Hersh took Miriam out of her bed, waking the little girl in the process. "I'm sorry, my little darling," he half whispered in a singsong voice, "but we have to leave now, or the cowboys in Texas will miss you."

The three boys awoke when they heard Miriam begin to cry. "Papa," Ben asked, "are we going now?"

"Yes. Please help Shmuel and Reuven get dressed and ready," Hersh said, pulling a dress over Miriam's head as the little girl's sobs wound down into a wide yawn. "Mama has some food for you to eat."

"But I'm not hungry," Ben said.

"Me neither," added Shmuel.

Reuven was silent, as usual, allowing his brothers' words to stand in for his own.

"Put some food in your stomachs," Hersh said. "I don't know when we'll get another proper meal."

Hersh went back downstairs to load the remaining bags onto the cart. Ben appeared shortly after and started helping with the last of them. Hersh climbed back upstairs to check on Shmuel and Reuven and to retrieve the feather bed, so the children could sleep through the night. Hersh doubted this might happen, but it was worth the try. With the bed slung over his shoulder, Hersh pulled Reuven by the hand and pushed Shmuel gently from behind, down the stairs, past his old desk, and through Avi's tiny shop. Reuven cried and protested the whole way.

Hersh recalled all of the times his own father had forced him and the rest of his family to rush and hide in the middle of the night in the shtetl. They had been lucky to be passed over by the Cossacks on so many occasions—they paid their Christian neighbors well not to betray the Lipshitzes' secret hiding spot in their barn. Well, they'd been lucky right up until the last time the Cossacks came, when Hersh's father never came back. Hersh thought he should explain something about this to his own boys now, but he didn't know what he might say. Their eyes seemed to comprehend, even if their brains did not. Children like these didn't seem to have many questions about the dead.

His oldest was outside, loading the suitcases onto the cart; Ben turned around when Hersh came out the door to Avi's shop, a hesitant smile across his face, as though he was excited but didn't think he was supposed to be when a family is sneaking out of its home under the cover of darkness. Of all the Lipshitzes, Ben seemed most eager to go to America. Esther had been pestering Hersh for months now to go, but this was for a different reason from Ben's. Esther wanted to be with Avi once again, and nothing was going to stop her—not even the length of Germany or the massive Atlantic Ocean.

But Ben seemed to want America for America's sake. He read all about it in the Yiddish and Russian newspapers, offering little facts and tidbits about life there from time to time. Just two days before, when Hersh announced to the family that they would be leaving, Ben had started wearing his hair differently, slicked back on his head with wax under his cap. At supper the night before, he described the train that runs underground in New York City, which he said one could ride for a price of five cents, at the speed of forty miles per hour beneath the city's buildings and streets. Hersh had asked if Ben knew what a mile was, and the boy shrugged and speculated, "probably something like a verst."

Hersh picked up Reuven and set him in the middle of the feather bed in the back of the cart, wedged between suitcases—his own mini berth. It was a cool night, the stars out and the moon just beginning to peek over the Orthodox church at the end of the block. Shmuel climbed up onto the cart by himself, and Hersh went back inside to search for any remaining items that were supposed to come with them. In the kitchen he found Esther with Miriam on her hip, staring into an open cabinet.

"Esther?" Hersh asked quietly, sensing he should be gentle. "Are you ready? The boys are downstairs and the cart is packed."

Esther didn't say anything. She looked at Hersh and then back into the cabinet. Hersh stepped around his wife and pulled Miriam off her hip, peering into the cabinet himself. It was empty except for a jar of pickles.

"I don't know if we shall need this," Esther said.

"I think we can leave it," Hersh said, bouncing Miriam in his arms. She giggled.

"I don't have—well, there is no more room in the food basket," Esther said.

"I think we will be fine without the pickles."

"I don't know."

"I'm pretty sure." Hersh touched his wife's shoulder. Nothing. "Esther? Can you look at me?"

She turned to him while slowly closing the cabinet door. Miriam reached for her mother, and Hersh lifted the child back onto Esther's side. Miriam clung to her mother's neck with one hand and sucked the thumb of the other, a strange little monkey.

"We must go now. This is what you wanted, right?" Hersh asked.

"Certainly, yes."

Hersh slowly guided his wife down the hallway, toward the stairs and then into Avi's shop. Sawdust still covered the floor, but less so than when Avi used to work full-time. The same large cabinet Avi had been working on in 1903 sat on the worktable. It seemed to take up all of the available space in the shop, even the air. Hersh pushed Esther on by the cabinet, but she hesitated in front of it, running her palm along its soft flank.

"Perhaps if Avi were still here this would have been reduced to dust by now," Hersh said with a chuckle. Sometimes he was unsure of his joking around his wife. Avi was always the funny man—enough for everybody in the family—but in the few months since his departure, Hersh felt less self-conscious about choosing his words, more free with letting what was in his head fly out of his mouth.

"This is a horrible thing to say," Esther said, now patting the cabinet like it was the kind of dog that you would allow into the house.

"Esther, I just meant to say—" Hersh started, but then decided against it. And then his wife of fourteen years looked at Hersh as though he'd just sold their youngest boy into slave labor. He added, "We're all just a little nervous now. Let's get on the road, and then this will be behind us and everything will be clear once again."

"Maybe we can take this with us," Esther suggested. "Or what about the dresser upstairs?"

"This is entirely not possible," Hersh said, putting his hand to the small of Esther's back and pressuring her gently toward the door. She would not budge though. Hersh noticed his father's cane leaning up against the wall by his desk. He went to pick it up.

"If you are bringing that old thing, then certainly I get to bring one item of importance to me," Esther said. "I think we should bring either this cabinet or the dresser Avi made for our wedding. Whichever is lighter."

"Esther, no," Hersh said, being the man of the house, even if it was a house they were about to leave. "They do not take large pieces of furniture onto trains and ships. People don't bring these kinds of things to America."

"Some people do," she said. Esther looked sad. Miriam was groggy and heavy in her mother's arms, her neck loose like a chicken's.

"Avi can make all the dressers and cabinets you want when we see him in America. You will have all of the dressers you would like for your new home there."

"But these are special."

"The new ones will be special too."

"It's different."

"Esther, please," Hersh said, and he was growing somewhat impatient. "I can certainly return the tickets and go put the baby back into bed upstairs. It will be like we never thought of leaving in the first place."

Esther retracted her hand from the cabinet as though it had become a wild creature, poised to bite. She turned on a heel and exited the shop with Miriam, the door slamming shut behind them. Hersh now put his hand to the softness of the cabinet. It really was smaller now for all of Avi's work on it over the last four years, the wood thinned in spots, almost to a finger's width. This cabinet would be useless to the customer who originally ordered it, Hersh thought, whoever that was. He couldn't help but smile—the one job Avi never finished.

Hersh inhaled the dry, earthy scent of the shop one last time, left hand on the doorknob, the right clutching his father's cane. He put out the lamp by the door and pulled the shade down in front of the window. He thought he saw the spirit that usually hovered over his desk settling in and around the open spaces in Avi's overworked cabinet then, but he couldn't be sure. There were so many. At least they would have the house to themselves now. Hersh closed the door and joined his family on the cart.

Hersh climbed up and whipped the nag harder than he'd intended. He felt sorry for the old boy, anticipating the trip ahead. The crystal stillness shattered then, like the split second before a train leaves the station. The ramshackle cart plaintively squeaked into motion beneath them, and all of the Lipshitzes remained silent for the moment, even the baby Miriam. This old chariot would—at least for the time being—bear the untold burden of everything Hersh possessed in this world.

November 16, 1907

ROMANIAN BORDER

The Russian took Hersh's money and tucked it into the breast pocket of his coat like some sort of agent for the Secret Police in Kiev. He was a damp-looking soul, and Hersh thought the man would still look this way even if it hadn't been raining for the last three days straight since leaving Kishinev. The man then instructed Hersh to pull his cart behind a farmhouse across the road, and promised to come retrieve the family sometime before midnight to cross the border.

"Is there someplace we might find something to eat for the children?" Hersh inquired.

"My wife feeds your people in the barn." He coughed and looked past Hersh, over his shoulder at the cart, up and down the length of Esther, it seemed to Hersh.

"This is kosher food?" he asked the man.

"Ha!"

"Well, thank you," Hersh said, deciding then that he didn't like entrusting this man with anything, much less getting his family out of the country safely. But what else was there?

They ate a very reasonably priced meal of meat and potatoes in a barn.

The man's wife was a portly woman with a warm smile, but she didn't speak. She offered milk to the three youngest children, skipping Ben. Hersh realized that to other people, Ben must look like a miniature grown man now, having just been passed over for a serving of milk. Hersh didn't recall noticing Ben's broadening shoulders, crackling voice, the soft black hair creeping down his upper lip. All this seemed to have happened in a month's time. He watched Ben eating across the table, filling up on everything in sight in preparation for the New World he was to be entering. It seemed to Hersh that there wasn't even a sliver of regret in Ben, or if there was, Hersh hadn't seen it. Even Esther faltered for a moment, Hersh thought, thinking of the lone jar of pickles in the cabinet.

After dinner, the man's wife motioned that the six Lipshitzes could stay in the barn until her husband called upon them to cross the border. Soon, another man poked his head into the barn, asking for food. He said he had two others with him, and the wife waved them all in, seating them at the table and bringing out more food shortly after.

Hersh felt so tired, but he did not want to sleep. Shmuel and Reuven were asleep on a hay-filled mattress in the corner of the barn. A stove kept the area warm, and Hersh was happy for it, seeing his children's eyes closed in some sort of repose. He wondered when the man was going to come to take them across. He figured it was coming up on midnight.

Hersh turned to Esther, who was sitting on a barrel holding Miriam in her arms. He and Esther had barely looked at each other since leaving Kishinev the night before. They had spoken about necessary issues only, almost always prefacing their words with one another's name:

"Hersh, we must stop so that Shmuel can relieve himself."

"Esther, do you think this tree over here is a nice place to rest and prepare something to eat?"

"Hersh, how much longer do you think it will be until we reach the border?"

"Esther, since it is raining and I would like to keep our documents dry, would you like me to transfer them into my trousers for safekeeping?"

"You do not think I can keep some papers dry?"

"No, Esther, I just thought I might alleviate you of this burden, since I am driving the cart and you must attend to the children."

Hersh so disliked when they communicated in this manner.

The three men finished their meals and came to sit by the stove where the Lipshitzes rested. "Where are you going?" one asked Hersh in Russian.

"Rotterdam," he replied. "You?"

"Bremerhaven."

"Is that your nag out there?" the other man asked.

"Yes," Hersh said.

"Do you have room for three of us, one small suitcase each?" he asked. "We can pay you what, three or four rubles each to the train station?"

"Oh, that is not in order," Hersh said. "I'm not sure the old nag can take much more. It'll slow us down, but if there's no other way, then you can come."

"I insist we pay."

"Okay," Hersh said, looking at Esther, who rolled her eyes at him.

"You are traveling to New York?" the first man asked.

"Texas," Hersh said.

"Texas? Ha!" the man exclaimed, and this was the second time in a few hours that a Russian had said "Ha!" to Hersh. He wasn't sure he liked it very much.

"You are going to New York?" Hersh asked.

"No, Philadelphia," he said, "and then Chicago. I have a brother there."

"And you?"

"Also Chicago."

"What about your friend?" Hersh asked, nodding to the third man, who didn't look into anybody's eyes or say one word even. He seemed a gentle man, almost like a woman in the way he sat and ate so delicately.

"He's coming with us."

Hersh glanced up at Esther again, but she looked away. She watched the agent man's wife clearing the table, the odd glass or plate clinking and breaking the silence in the warm barn.

The third, quiet Russian sat next to Ben by the heat of the stove, and soon the two were clearly communicating, though wordlessly. With a worn deck of cards, the man was entertaining Ben, and the boy smiled very wide, his dark eyes gleaming with two pinpoints from the lamp light. Sporadic, muted laughter came from both of them when the man pulled a card from Ben's pocket, or pulled the very card that Ben had just picked out of the deck from behind his ear. The way the two bent their heads into each other, Hersh saw, they could almost be brothers. This was the kind of man Ben would grow into, Hersh thought. There are women who like these men. They are sensitive and birdlike. They don't drink much, they have few friends, they just give their wives maybe one or two children, and then work at something with their brains to support the children. Perhaps Ben would go to university in America. Then he might meet the kind of woman who would want a man like he would become.

Suddenly the agent man burst into the barn, making a great deal of noise to announce his presence. He whispered something into his wife's ear, and then told everybody gathered around the stove that it was time to leave.

"You can take these three men just across the border on your cart?" he asked Hersh, but it didn't seem to be a question.

"We are all set with this," he replied, and Esther again made eyes at him. "What?" he whispered to her, but this only seemed to make her more angry.

Silently they loaded onto the cart, Ben passing Reuven up to his silent Russian friend. Miriam slept across Esther's lap. Hersh looked back to check that everybody was safely seated before whipping the nag. He saw that Shmuel gripped Ben's elbow tightly, while Reuven sat on his lap. It seemed that Ben was able to comfort Hersh's children in a way Hersh was never able to do. Hersh tried smiling at the two youngest boys clinging to his oldest, but it was too dark for them to see.

He steered the nag around the other side of the barn, where the agent man waited beside the road, half-obscured in shadow. He walked alongside the cart as they slowly headed to the border. A large striped barricade was lifted in the open position, and two guards in fine uniforms stood to the side, rifles slung around their shoulders. One went into the small shack emitting a thin stream of smoke from a metal chimney as the cart approached, but the other, a tall man with a clean-shaven, pale and pointy face, stared at Hersh as he guided the cart under the barricade. Hersh looked away, busying himself with the reins, but when he looked back at the severe guard, his eyes were still fixed on Hersh's.

"Stop!" the guard yelled in Yiddish, and Hersh pulled back hard on the nag. Miriam whined, and Hersh's chest filled with tight ropes. The agent man scurried over to the guard, and they spoke softly in a language Hersh thought was Romanian, but he couldn't hear very well. Back and forth they went, the guard's voice erupting in tiny, periodic explosions. Esther placed a hand on Hersh's knee, damp and heavy. This was the first unnecessary contact they'd had in so long Hersh couldn't remember. The agent man came back to the cart.

"He didn't know there was to be so much baggage," he said, but he would not look in Hersh's eyes as he spoke.

"Well?" Hersh said.

"He needs something else."

"Like what?"

"What can you offer?"

"More money?" Hersh tried to control his anger. He looked at Esther, who stared straight ahead into what seemed to be all of Moldavia. A few lights twinkled in a village not five versts west of them. A breeze with a hint of warmth to it settled around them, rattling some trees, freeing a few twisted leaves into the night sky. It was warmer now that the rain had stopped.

"Do you want more from us?" one of the Russian men offered, reaching into his jacket for his pocketbook.

"No, he wants something from the father."

Hersh didn't know what to do.

He bought some time by reaching into the pouch in his coat's inner pocket. The nag kicked at the wet ground, shaking the cart. The poor soul needs some more oats with all this added weight, Hersh thought, as he fumbled clumsily through the papers in the pouch. There was the deed to the building.

"I can sign over these papers for a shop and apartment in Kishinev," Hersh said then.

The man looked at him. "What else?" he asked, hoping—Hersh knew—for something that might be split more evenly. Perhaps you could live upstairs with your lovely, personable wife, and the guard could run the shop downstairs, Hersh wanted to say, but restrained himself.

"There are many valuable tools there, fine furniture, almost a full house," Hersh said. "Even food in the kitchen cabinets. He could sell this building for a good amount of money." Hersh held out the deed in front of the man.

The agent man took the paper and sighed, shaking his head as he walked over to the guard. They spoke for a few more minutes, the guard lighting a cigarette and quickly smoking it halfway down before the agent man came back over.

"Okay." He clutched a fountain pen and handed it to Hersh, who signed the deed over to the guard. As Hersh handed both back, the agent added, "Plus he would like one extra ruble per piece of baggage."

"Certainly," Hersh said, counting out six rubles. One of the Russians passed three more rubles forward, and Hersh gave the whole lot to the agent. Hersh knew these nine rubles would never reach the greedy hands of the guard, having first landed in slightly greedier hands in transit.

"Go," the guard said, waving the hand that was not caressing his rifle. He stared at Hersh while the cart rattled by, and as they crossed the first of many borders to come, Esther replaced her hand on Hersh's knee, even heavier this time. Silently they bounced through the night, the only sporadic sound coming from Ben and his mute friend, giggling softly as they played with the deck of cards on the back of the cart.

The next day, Hersh approached a peddler on the street in front of the train station. His family waited next to their baggage on the platform. Hersh could hear the wail of the train approaching the small town in the distance, arriving from the west.

"Sir, excuse me, but I am trying to sell this nag and cart," he said in Yiddish to the peddler.

"And why does this concern me?" the man replied.

"Well, mine may be tired, but yours is positively one step away from becoming a fine piece of leather," Hersh said with a smile.

"I don't need another."

"Well, do you know where I might be able to get a few rubles for this one?"

"Why should I tell you this?"

"Because you seem to be a nice man," Hersh said. He noticed the man's nag's hindquarters were shaking, literally a few short steps away from toppling completely, sure to take the entire cart with him. "Are you certain you don't want to talk about making a deal for this fine creature of mine?"

"I am certain," the peddler said. "Now leave me alone."

"Your business will improve threefold," Hersh said.

"No."

"It seems—if you don't mind my saying—that your nag is on, what they call, its 'last legs,'" Hersh said.

"Oh, really?"

"I think so."

"Well, it seems to me—if you don't mind my saying—that the train has whistled two times now, and you will be what they call 'out of luck' when your family boards the train and it departs without you."

"Indeed," Hersh agreed. He liked the old Jew, but even more so because Hersh was certain that people like him would never exist in America. They didn't leave.

"What will stop me from taking the old boy when you leave him here in front of the station to catch the train?" the old man asked after a moment.

"Probably the very same thing that will stop me from putting the creature out of his misery before I go," Hersh said, but he couldn't imagine killing this old nag, or anything else really.

The peddler surveyed Hersh's horse, walked around its rear and ran his hand over its ribs. White smoke billowed in the sky above them from the locomotive.

"I'll take five rubles for him," Hersh added.

"I'll give you three."

"Only because I'm in a hurry, I'll take four."

"Three."

"Sold."

The peddler took a few rubles out of a pouch in his pocket and slid them into Hersh's palm. "Good luck over there," the old man said.

Hersh smiled and patted the man gently on the shoulder. He then leaned in and stroked his nag on the neck, down to his wet shoulder. "I hope you like being a Moldavian now," he whispered, and turned toward the platform.

Hersh watched his children's faces transform over the course of the week on the trains: through Iasi, Chernivtsi, L'viv, Cracow, and then finally Germany. The children seemed to age before his eyes, and Hersh found himself hoping they got to Rotterdam soon, or he might miss his children's youth entirely. Maybe it wasn't exactly that they were aging, just that he was noticing things about them he'd never noticed before. He'd never looked at them for so many hours, days, nights in a row, all at once, nonstop. He was used to seeing them come and go, or at least used to himself coming and going, reacquainting himself with his children and wife practically every time he sat down for supper.

Hersh tried explaining something like this to Esther, but she didn't even nod her head or seem to want to comprehend. Unless tending to one of the children, Esther just stared out the window at the passing countryside, declining to talk with the other passengers in the third-class berth, even when Hersh struck up a conversation and introduced his wife to whomever he was speaking. In fact, Hersh thought, Esther was being quite rude.

Finally in Berlin, they had to wait two more days for the next engine to Rotterdam. Hersh worried they would miss the ship to New York. They found a boardinghouse that catered to immigrant Jews especially, with a kosher restaurant in the same quarters in the basement. The prices were at least four or five times that of nonkosher restaurants.

"I don't care how much," Esther said to Hersh on the first night, when the children were so hungry that Miriam and Reuven were whimpering. They stood in front of a door with a small sign in Yiddish: "Kosher food here."

"At this point, what does it matter?" Hersh asked her, because he knew that it didn't. The Lipshitzes had probably consumed their last kosher meal during the supper before they left Kishinev, Hersh thought.

"Save the money," Esther conceded, standing very still. Her hair hung in strange, flat curls underneath her kerchief. It seemed to Hersh that Esther looked as though she had misplaced something. It had been like this since her beloved Avi left. Hersh picked up Reuven then, and they waited as a very loud motorbus passed before crossing the street toward the restaurant inside the train station. Esther carried Miriam, Ben and Shmuel trailing behind.

"I'm sorry," Esther said, though Hersh didn't know what she was referring to.

"What? Why?" he asked, because this sort of thing made him acutely nervous. "Come on, Ben. Help your brother cross the street."

"Hersh—" Esther continued, very soft and serious.

"It's nothing," Hersh interrupted. "Ben!"

The boy was absolutely mesmerized by the city around him. He studied each person as they passed by on the sidewalk, tried to read every sign and look into every window, falling behind the rest of his family on numerous occasions. He wanted to separate himself already, Hersh could tell by his puffed-up posture, but he was no man yet. Hersh clipped Ben on the back of the head as soon as he caught up. Ben's hat fell to the ground.

"Papa?" he said, bending to pick up his hat. "What?"

"You know," Hersh said. "Help your mother."

Ben brushed off his hat and placed it perfectly back on his head. He looked at himself in a store window and frowned at his father.

"Did you hear me?" Hersh asked him.

"Yes."

"Then do it."

They ate a total of four nonkosher meals at the restaurant in the train station, and for two nights, slept in one room at the boardinghouse, three to a bed. The children fought. He and Esther still didn't speak. Hersh checked every few hours to see whether the train schedule had shifted, but it never did. There was this, at least, to be thankful for, Hersh thought.

November 28, 1907

GERMANY

Finally the Amsterdam/Rotterdam train showed up at the station, and it was packed full of America-bound travelers from all over Eastern Europe. They took up nearly all of the seats. The Lipshitzes squeezed into a third-class car, finding three seats together and another three across the aisle. Unlike some of the other trains, Hersh wasn't entirely trustful of the whereabouts of their baggage on this one. There were long benches with wooden slats for seating instead of the usual individual seats, and children were splayed on the floor on blankets between their parents' feet.

Somewhere east of Hannover, the train stopped cold on the tracks, nowhere near a station. A conductor announced in German that there were mechanical problems (somebody translated this). Hersh looked at Esther across the aisle, who was sitting with Miriam in her arms, Shmuel and Reuven on either side of her. A large man's elbow hovered over Reuven's head as he gestured while speaking to another man, and Hersh worried his boy would be hit inadvertently. Reuven didn't seem to notice though, as he slumped into his mother, his fine blond hair clinging to her coat in a mess like a bird's nest. A Russian woman's generous hips pressed up against his other side.

After about four hours of stillness, the conductor came through again, announcing something in German that was not translated this time by anybody in their car. Hersh raised his eyebrows at Ben, who, Hersh thought, was just about at the age where he could confide in him about the worries of life. He was actually looking forward to this with Ben. He wanted another man around the house, besides his brother-in-law Avi. Finally, Hersh thought, there would be another opinion, and we won't always defer to Avi. Maybe now when both her son and husband say something, Esther will listen. She'll see that Avi doesn't always make the best decisions. It was funny that Avi had made perhaps the worst decision a man can make in this world, and yet still Esther is running to him all the way across the world. Hersh chuckled to himself, though in truth, it wasn't very funny at all.

The sun was sinking, and many passengers dozed off in the stillness. Hersh hoped they were actually fixing the train. A young girl directly across the car from him seemed to be traveling alone. He had noticed her a few times before, but this was the first time Hersh really studied the girl. She looked to be about Ben's age, or perhaps a bit older. She spoke to nobody, never ate or drank, even when mothers around her spread out food on their laps and fed their families. She was a homely looking girl, Hersh thought. And very shy, making eye contact with nobody.

As two more hours passed, darkness enveloped the car completely, as well as the countryside around it. Out the window, Hersh could see a fire-place flickering inside a tiny farmhouse far off the left side of the train. There were no stars, just fast-moving, dark clouds that raced and over-lapped one another in the purple sky. Inside the car, only the men kept their eyes open, Hersh noticed. They seemed, like Hersh, to be watching over their wives and children as they slept, or tried to achieve the closest thing to it.

Hersh heard the train-car door open behind him, and two German boys' voices. The boys, about seventeen, eighteen years old, entered the car quietly, and Hersh could tell they were seeking some sort of trouble.

The larger boy walked down the aisle, surveying the sleeping passengers, staring boldly into the men's eyes. He turned back to his friend, who had stopped in front of the little German girl; she was sleeping curled around her bag, with her head folded impossibly onto her shoulder. The boy flicked the girl on an arm, but she did not wake.

The other boy came back, and pushed the girl's shoulder a little harder. This woke her up, and she looked up at the boys, startled. She wiped a bit of drool from her chin with a palm, and the boys started speaking to her in German. At first it was a normal conversation, but quiet. She answered their questions with short sentences. One boy pulled gently on the front of her shirt, where breasts had probably only recently started to grow underneath. She pushed his hand away.

Hersh looked around; there were about six or seven other men who were awake. They all looked out the windows, or at the floor, their laps. Hersh wondered why nobody—himself included—was saying anything to stop this.

The girl repeated, *"Nein, nein,"* slapping the boys' greedy hands away. Hersh wanted to get up to stop them, but he looked at his sleeping family and understood completely why he couldn't. One of the boys reached under the girl's skirt then, and she screamed. The men in the cabin shifted nervously in their seats, turning backs on the scene. Hersh stared at her, though. He thought it was the least he could do.

The other boy reached into her shirt and revealed a money pouch. This, you could tell, had been carefully sewn into place by the girl's mother or grandmother, or maybe an older sister. The boy ripped the pouch from the girl's shirt, and she started crying. He unfolded a wad of German marks, held them up in front of his friend, and stuck them into his vest pocket. His friend kept touching the girl, but the boy who took the money grabbed his arm away from underneath the girl's skirt, and they exited the train quickly. Nobody moved. Most still slept. The German girl let out a few sobs, but they were muffled.

As soon as he saw the boys' heads bobbing toward the next car in the train, Hersh gently lifted Shmuel's head and arm from his lap and placed him on the seat on which Hersh had been sitting. Shmuel pulled himself toward Ben, who pushed the younger boy aside in his sleep.

"Are you okay?" he asked the German girl, but she did not understand. She just cried softly, looking at the empty pouch, up at Hersh. The other men in the car watched.

Hersh stood to search through Esther's basket for a honey cake to give the girl. When he found one, he held it in his palm to her. At first she refused, but when Hersh nodded to her that it was okay, she took the cake and consumed the whole of it in three bites.

Her tears stopped as she chewed. Hersh pulled down on her skirt then, which had been hiked up over her left thigh. He straightened the fabric over her knees and patted her on the shoulder. Hersh reached into his pocketbook and took out a bunch of rubles, folding them tightly and tucking them into the little girl's pouch. "You have your steamship ticket?" he asked.

Hersh pulled his own family's tickets out of the pocketbook inside his jacket and showed them to the girl. She nodded her head and fumbled through her bag until she produced her own ticket. Hersh could see it was from Antwerp to Boston. He smiled at the girl and put the ticket back into her bag, patting it for safety.

Suddenly the car jolted backward, and the train began slowly padding through the darkness. Hersh sat quietly next to the girl until the train reached full speed. He stood to go, but the girl reached a hand around Hersh's wrist, pulling him toward her. He sat back down next to her, putting his arm behind her neck, and the girl leaned in close to Hersh, resting her head heavily against his chest.

Hersh looked up to see if anybody was watching, but by now the men had grown tired of being watchmen of a crippled train, and many slept. Movement was safety, and they could rest until the next stop, planned or otherwise. Only Esther was watching Hersh now. It was clear she had been watching the whole time. The look in her eyes, on her whole face, was as confusing and disorienting to Hersh as this entire trip had been thus far.

In one look, an entire lifetime. There was love in Esther's eyes, there had to be, right? But there was also a little hatred, rage, disgust, and perhaps if he was lucky, begrudging admiration. But what else? Hersh wondered, as he held the strange German girl in his arms and she drifted to sleep, twitching sporadically. Hersh raised his eyebrows at Esther, and she managed to curl the sides of her lips upward a bit. At least there's this, he thought, a half-smile from Esther.

December 1, 1907

The Lipshitzes lined up to board the *New Amsterdam,* which was surely the largest vessel any of them had ever seen. A tall, thin, bespectacled Dutch doctor observed them closely as passengers crept forward in the long line leading to the massive ship. He stopped in front of Esther and Miriam, stooping to place his hand over Miriam's left eye and pull down her lower lid. She jerked away, shaking her head violently. The doctor moved on to Esther, looking right into her face, and Hersh saw his wife smile in a way he never saw before. It was a coy, almost sexual smile, one Hersh associated with the two old prostitutes who always teased him as he crossed the square on his way back home for supper each evening.

The doctor pulled back from Esther and looked at Hersh. He held out his hand, palm up, and Hersh realized this was where he came in. Hersh produced the six documents the Holland America Line worker had filled out for his family, and the doctor put six identical marks on the cards and gave them back to Hersh. He tucked these back into his pocketbook as the doctor went to the next family in line, another bunch of Jews from Ukraine.

After this family, Hersh saw the doctor pull somebody from the line, a short man with red eyes and a horrible open sore on his neck—it was black around the edges, oozing a yellowish fluid mixed with thin streaks of blood. Hersh had stood directly behind the man in the line for rail tickets from New York to other points in America, and had watched a stream of murky fluid slowly saturate the man's otherwise white shirt collar as he haggled over a rail ticket. He kept pulling his coat and collar up over the wound, but every time he moved, the sore revealed itself.

The man screamed something in Polish at the doctor, growing increasingly angry with each word he yelled, but then two of the doctor's assistants came and guided the man out of line, gripping his shoulders tightly. Hersh watched his children watch the man being dragged away—even Ben looked frightened for the first time since leaving Kishinev—and wondered if he should say something to quell their fears. But what would he say?

"Reuven, how many decks are on this ship?" he asked his youngest boy, tilting his head back to take in the great vessel before them. Reuven looked at his father as though Hersh were speaking English. "Can you count for me?"

Reuven shook his head at his father as if *he* were the strange man with the gaping wound on his neck, and buried his blond head in his mother's coat. Esther looked at Hersh.

"What?" he asked.

She didn't respond, placing a hand on Reuven's soft head.

"Well, we made it," Hersh said then, exhaling loudly through his nose.

"Not yet," Esther said, shifting Miriam from one hip to the other.

Hundreds of first- and second-class passengers lined the upper decks and waved at friends and family bunched onto the dock. It was a cold winter day, gray and punctuated with sprays of rain. A young man and woman on the second deck from the top kissed openly as waving, jumping passengers pushed in on all sides of them. It was a long, passionate kiss, Hersh couldn't help but notice, and also couldn't keep from watching. And for the first time in a long time, he allowed himself his old secret fantasy—the one of Ruth. It felt even more forbidden now—she had been dead four years, her husband already having replaced her with some American girl in Texas. *But if it were me,* Hersh thought, *there would never be another after Ruth.*

He watched the couple continue kissing up on the deck as his family inched forward in line. The man slowly moved his right hand onto his lady's cheek, covering her ear and pulling her even closer toward him. Hersh looked around him to see if anybody else was watching this display, but there was too much commotion, too many people. And then finally, after a far-too-long absence, it came to Hersh, and he closed his eyes. Ruth is bent over the chair in front of Hersh's desk, with her dress bunched over her hips, two pale breasts completely bare and swinging gently. Avi is not there this time, and as Hersh steps into the quiet shop and approaches, Ruth glances back at him over her right shoulder, smiling with those dark lips closed, eyes moist.

But then the second part comes as it always has since that day. Ruth bathing in her own blood, submerged to the lashes. She is folded into herself, filleted arms hugging her knees to breasts—though this is of course not the way they actually found her. This is more like Hersh assumes we all die, going back to the way it is in the mother's belly. He found his father doing this up against the rabbi's house in the shtetl, tucking his knees to chest as tightly as he could with only one arm to hold them. And Hersh knew he too would curl up this way some day, albeit in a different place than he'd ever assumed it would happen.

In Texas. All for Esther, which was ultimately for Avi, who didn't have any idea about exactly how much—or how many—people sacrificed for him. Hersh being one, his children being four more. Ruth and Leah having made the ultimate sacrifice for this man who doesn't even know it.

In the afternoon on the sixteenth day, Hersh and his two youngest sons lay on their cots in one of the four massive steerage compartments of the *New Amsterdam*. Shmuel and Reuven slept. A bucket of vomit sat on the floor by Hersh's side, filled primarily by himself, Miriam, and Shmuel. It swished gently as the ship rolled along. Compared with all the other smells contained in this compartment, the bucket of vomit was nothing; at least it was fresh and hadn't been sitting there for days like most of the other bodily emissions that scented the air. Esther entered the distant end of the compartment then and walked the many rows toward Hersh with Miriam on her side. Always that little child clinging to Esther's hip, Hersh thought, unable to recall the last time he himself had been allowed the same opportunity.

"They say we are approaching New York," Esther said, sitting on the cot and softly rubbing Reuven's blond head as he slept.

"Where's Ben?"

"On the deck with that Austrian boy."

Hersh rolled over to look at his wife. She was gaunt, with dark patches under the eyes, and dull, stringy hair where normally it was thick and shiny, full of motion. There had been horrible food on the ship the whole time, and what had been passable, both he and Esther gave to the children.

"Do you want to try to get some air?" Esther asked, tugging on Hersh's pant leg.

"Maybe soon," he said, and turned to vomit once more into the bucket. Dried spittle clung to Hersh's beard, but by now it was just thin strings of bile he was adding to the bucket's contents.

"Shall I empty this again?" Esther asked.

"No, I'll do it."

They sat for another hour like this, Miriam eventually falling asleep on the cot next to her brothers. Timid cheers began on the upper decks, then became thunderous waves as all the tired people began funneling through the tiny oval doors. Many accented variations on the words "New York" coursed along in the putrid, electric air of the compartment, and Hersh lifted his head from the hard mattress when he heard the commotion. Sitting upright, he retched again, but nothing came out.

"Let's go up," Esther said, gently shaking the three children from sleep. "Do you want to see America?"

Hersh steadied himself for a moment before trying to stand. He didn't want to look into his children's faces, not yet. He wanted nothing more than a moment to himself. Just a moment, he asked, and then promised to be patient, smiling, and strong enough to pick up the small boy one more time and tell him everything would be okay. Reuven climbed onto his father then, terrified, and apparently ignorant of Hersh's silent bargain.

"You want to see?" Hersh asked, but Reuven had already begun to cry. "Come on, my little bean," Hersh said, summoning the last bit of strength in his knees and thighs to bring himself and his boy to a standing position.

"Please stop crying, just this once," Hersh said softly. Reuven quieted some in his arms then, and Hersh followed Esther, Miriam, and Shmuel through several rows of disarray and up the narrow stairs to the tiny steerage deck.

Women wept, a few men too. Esther looked back at Hersh, but she would not cry, he knew. Not anymore. Strangers hugged strangers; they all smelled horrible, so human, Hersh thought, and knew he was no exception. He was embarrassed, but there was nothing to do about it. People were packed side by side, covering every inch of the deck. Hersh actually felt some of his weight supported by the people around him— quite a relief. He looked above him and saw part of the second- or first-class deck filled with more smiling passengers, in decidedly better condition than those surrounding Hersh.

"Can you see it?" Esther yelled back to him. Or maybe it was, "Reuven, see it?" Then she pointed out something off to the side of the boat. She squeezed Shmuel's calf beside her, which was eye level as it dangled off the shoulder of the stranger who generously lifted the boy so that he could see over the heads in the crowd.

Hersh hoisted Reuven above his head too, setting the boy on his shoulder. Reuven kept crying, and the weight of him was practically breaking Hersh's neck. His head was forced down so that he could see nothing but the deck beneath his feet. Reuven's sobbing increased. Hersh could feel the spasms reverberating through his own body. Hersh bounced up and down slightly to try to cheer the boy. "Can you see it?" he called up. "It's a lady with her arm up in the air," Hersh explained, but he couldn't actually see it himself. They were too far back on the deck, and the ship too far away, slowing now as several other smaller ferries and tugs darted by.

"Put me down, Papa," Reuven said, and Hersh slid the impossible boy down his neck, shoulder, and finally his side, and held him close to his legs. Reuven's small feet rested on Hersh's shoes. They were completely separated from Esther now, but Hersh could see her head among the sea of black hair, hats, and scarves. "Mama?" Reuven whined.

Hersh stood on the tips of his toes as his legs shot sharp pains directly into his back. He tried to reach between a few men to get Esther's attention, but she was too far away to touch. "Mama is just over there," Hersh said to the boy, but also to himself. "Stay with your Papa now."

Hersh felt he might vomit again, so he looked up at the sky and tried to breathe air that had not already cycled through the people around him. He saw a boy swinging from a pole above and ahead of where he and Reuven stood. It was Ben, holding onto the wooden rail with both hands and one foot loose, swaying above all the people's heads beside another boy about his size. He pointed toward whatever was visible on either side of the ship, though Hersh could not see for himself what Ben obviously could. The sun had just disappeared behind him, but some of the last remaining light illuminated Ben's face.

Hersh's gaze crept farther up the ship, where the first- and second-class passengers milled about on the decks above. He saw what he thought was the same man who had been kissing the lady so exuberantly back in Rotterdam. But he was alone now, and looking out over the water with a blank expression on his face. Hersh wondered where she went, what happened to the girl.

The ship slowed to a stop in the middle of the harbor, and it rocked there for some time. After about thirty minutes, a small ferry docked beside the boat and began receiving the passengers from the upper decks onto its own.

The steerage passengers began pushing back downstairs then, in many cases shoving the very same strangers they had minutes before been hugging in celebration. They all surged back down into the sleeping compartments to bundle up their belongings and maybe splash a little water on their faces in preparation for disembarkation. A little boy in the cot across from the Lipshitzes' fished a tiny brown herring out of a can and held it to his mouth. His mother slapped his hand and pulled the herring away before the boy could slip it between his lips. Perhaps in anticipation of all the good food awaiting them on land, Hersh thought. His stomach turned at the idea of putting anything into it—ever.

All of these people, including the Lipshitz six, sat quietly on their cots waiting with their coats on, hats tipped just so on their heads, blankets folded over forearms, bags slung across shoulders, crying children on laps. Ready just like this for quite some time before they received further instructions from a crew member about disembarking. It was twelve hours before another, larger ferry came to take these passengers to Ellis Island for their inspection.

December 31, 1907

Esther thought it must be Hersh at the door of Raina's apartment. Instead, it was Ben, hat in hand, returning from the HIAS office on East Broadway.

"Anything new?" she asked, imitating a mother who doesn't lose hope that her lost boy will be found—even after two weeks of nothing.

"No. Can I go out now?"

"Where are you going?"

"Out."

"It's snowing."

Ben shrugged "So?" the way men do at the women in their lives.

Esther wondered how she had missed the moment when this boy turned into a man, and she thanked the heavens that Ben did not inherit Hersh's weak chin. "Be back for dinner," she conceded.

"I was going to get something."

"What? Where?" Esther asked. "And with what money?"

"I earned some of my own. I can get a knish."

"Then you'll be back for supper?"

"Yes."

There are many ways to lose a child, Esther thought, as she watched her oldest button his coat and replace a brown hat on his head. Walking behind him on the street, she would assume she was following a handsome man of twenty. Ben opened the door, but just before leaving asked, "Do you want me to go back this afternoon?"

"No, I'll go," Esther said.

After dinner Esther scrubbed the dishes. She tried to do what she could. She never was very good at sewing—a veritable disaster on the Singer—so at least she could do this, prepare food for Isaac and Raina and their family. Hersh had come back for dinner, too, still jobless.

Raina was working on a pair of trousers when Isaac came to touch her gently on the shoulder before returning to the small shop he shared with a few other tailors in the neighborhood. When Hersh saw this, he came into the kitchen to do something similar with Esther, but she pulled back from his touch. In truth, she didn't know why she did this, but it had something to do with the dumb look on her husband's face every time he came back to the apartment with no work. Men were losing jobs by the hundreds—they read it in the Yiddish newspapers. It was a bad time to come to America with the depression everybody was talking about. Esther expected Hersh to rise above it somehow. Their money was running out, for god's sake, and it was embarrassing.

"He needs to get a job," Hersh said of Ben, continuing an earlier conversation from dinner.

"He said he's making money working with a friend," Esther offered, but she didn't believe it herself.

"I don't like how that sounds," Hersh said, pulling at his long thin beard.

"Well, at least he's making *something*," Esther said, but she chuckled as she said it, padding any harshness toward her husband when in front of Raina. This was the only time she felt bad for it, though.

"He should be in school then," Hersh said, ignoring Esther.

Esther dried a plate on her apron. "We'll be leaving soon."

"I don't know, Esther."

"What is this, 'I don't know'?"

"I don't know," he repeated, and Esther wanted to fling the pot she had just scrubbed at Hersh's head. She would just like to nick him on the forehead with it, leave a red, raised bump for him to remember how stupid he could be. It would be gone by morning. Hersh went to sit in Isaac's chair and read through last week's list of job possibilities from the HIAS.

Raina came into the kitchen, where Isaac had left a pile of fabric over the back of a chair for her. "Oh, Esther, I have so much work today; I can look after Miriam and Shmuel this afternoon if you want to go to the office alone."

It was as though Raina had just offered Esther one thousand rubles. She hoped Hersh hadn't heard. Oh, to have an hour alone—no Hersh, no children, no crowded apartment. Just one child on the mind, but it's the best kind—one who's not present. There is such enchanting freedom in a child who needs no care, no potatoes, no milk, no scrubbing in the tub, no answering question after question after question.

I am a terrible mother.

"I can come with you if you'd like," Hersh called into the kitchen, innocently enough. "Everybody seems to be closing up since it is the New Year. Nobody wants to speak to me about work today."

"Oh, how nice for you two to be alone together," Raina said. Esther wondered if Raina ever, just once in her life, wanted to be alone.

"Esther?" Hersh asked.

A shrill scream swirled in Esther's belly then, shooting up through her insides, her intestines, cycling through every organ, but especially the spleen. It curled in and around her lungs, gaining strength there before shooting through all the valves in her heart. Finally, her throat, the back of her mouth, around her teeth, her tongue. She opened her mouth and heard herself letting it out, the highest decibel ever recorded on either side of the Atlantic. And yet when she parted her lips, nothing came out.

"Esther?" Hersh asked. "Did you hear me?"

"What did you say?"

"I said, I can't really look for work right now because of the New Year. Maybe I can accompany you to the HIAS office to inquire about Reuven."

"Okay."

At about three-thirty, Esther began readying herself for the walk down to the Hebrew Immigrant Aid Society. She had made this walk at least once a day in the two weeks since they had arrived in New York. Every day, she went with Miriam and often Shmuel, a few times with Ben, and of course with Hersh. Always Hersh. But never alone. Ben sometimes went alone in the mornings, Esther taking the afternoon shifts.

Today is my only day, and my husband has ruined it, Esther thought, pulling a scarf over her head and looking out the window into the street below. The snow was accumulating now, maybe an inch or two of it on everything, the fire escapes, the clothes hanging over them—all frozen stiff by now.

"Ready?" Hersh asked, rising from the chair where he was reading *The Daily Forward,* grunting or laughing or sighing through each article. Esther didn't understand why Hersh thought she wanted to hear these noises. She hated hearing them even more than she hated when he recited aloud interesting little facts or political questions from the papers every day.

"I am perfectly happy going alone," Esther tried, one last time, but she knew it was useless.

"Oh, no, you shouldn't go alone."

"You need to rest," she suggested.

"What if they need me for something?"

"What could they possibly need that they don't already have, Hersh?"

"I don't know," he conceded, "but I'd still like to accompany my wife."

Esther thought she should've thrown the pot when she had the chance. It was a missed opportunity. "Okay," she said. "Let's go."

On the street, the city seemed quieter than Esther thought it could ever be. And yet there was also a hum of excitement, all the people preparing for the last day of 1907. This had not been a particularly good year, Esther thought, and didn't understand what there was to celebrate. Perhaps that 1907 was over? But it looked like it would get worse still in 1908.

In one stinking year she had lost a brother and a son, and now the latter was keeping her from getting back the former. And worse, Hersh was presently trailing behind Esther on the street, dragging his feet through the dirty snow and asking, "Why are you walking so fast?" He stopped in front of the pickle store after Esther finally gave in and slowed down. Hersh leaned his head over the barrels as though he considered dipping a toe in the freezing water for a swim. Esther observed the angle of his head as it bent so seriously toward the task of finding the perfect pickle and, briefly, she hated herself for hating him so much. But when Hersh directed the man to fish out certain pickles for him, one after the other, she glimpsed an opportunity.

Esther turned on a heel in the snow and took off down Orchard Street, fading into the bustle on Hester. She walked so fast, her feet cold and growing wetter with each snowy block. But they were glorious blocks indeed. She was not carrying a child, nor dragging one by the hand behind her; she was just going, going. Every time she looked back, Hersh was nowhere to be found, and she felt better and better. She could go any direction she wanted. She could take any route to the HIAS office. She could even go one or two blocks out of the way. Or not at all.

For this one shimmering moment in the snow, she could relax. *I am being a good mother; I am going to inquire about my lost boy, like I do two times each day in hopes that someone has found him and he will be safely returned to his parents.*

Esther knew Reuven would never be returned to his parents, safely or otherwise.

But this was okay now, Esther thought, because she was alone and she was in the process of being a good mother, doing what anybody, as a good mother, would do if one of her four children were lost.

She just kept going, plowing her own trail in the snow and paying no mind to the street signs. Soon there was an enormous steel structure in front of her, and Esther stopped to watch the men hanging off of it like fruit. They were building another bridge, putting it up so close to where the Brooklyn one was. It was so close and tall—maybe taller—and yet she couldn't see this new bridge from Raina's apartment like they could see the tip of the Brooklyn Bridge, always with the flag whipping in the wind.

Raina had been here in New York when they opened the Brooklyn Bridge. Oh, the fireworks they shot off the bridge that night. All the families hungry, but oh, the colors in the sky! Raina was just a child, five at most. But it was the first thing she remembered about America. And apparently the last, Esther thought, since she could practically set her internal clock by it: Every time Raina would catch Esther staring out the apartment window in the bridge's direction, Raina would launch into the same silly story about the grand opening. The fireworks, on and on, and how her father took her halfway across the bridge the very next day. It had been packed with people, mostly the curious like they were.

Esther always wondered why Raina's father had taken her only halfway across the bridge. It made no sense. If Esther had the chance, she would walk across it, all the way across it to the other side. Which was the real reason for bridges in the first place, to get from one side of something to another side of something else. It was not to go halfway across and then turn back.

Esther looked behind her to see whether Hersh had caught up. There was nothing, just bundled black figures rushing places, zigzagging across streets, and cutting streaks of black into the snow. Carts lining the block, horses kicking their hooves in the muddy slush and jingling their reins. People were brushing off their goods, packing them up, and pulling them into storefronts. Some shoveled the sidewalks, others smoked, quietly watching.

She fancied she might walk across this bridge when it was completed. Or if she wanted to go sooner, she could take the Brooklyn Bridge instead. Right now. She could just button up her coat and tighten the scarf over her head and go across. It would be windy. She would start over. She didn't know where. She knew from Hersh's interesting facts about New York that as soon as she had gone as far as she could go after crossing the bridge, she would hit water again where the land ran out, and she would be as close as you could be to Russia, on a long finger of land sticking out from America and pointing toward home.

Perhaps when she got to the end, a steamer would be there waiting to take her back. Just one small- to medium-sized steamer waiting for her at the end of America, with a large bed and clean, private toilet just for Esther, and fresh hot food served in her cabin during the trip. There would be no buckets of vomit. She would have no children. If you don't *have* children, you cannot *lose* children.

She would live in Odessa all alone. Or Kiev. Or heck, she could learn Dutch and stay in Rotterdam, Amsterdam, something like this. She would learn to sew and mend and live in a room in a women's boardinghouse with other young women like her, but much younger. She would speculate and twitter with them about what childbirth and sex with a man was like, but she would know for sure four times over about the first, and many more about the second. She would humor the ugly women who couldn't find husbands. Give them extra attention because nobody else ever did, not even their fathers.

She thought of Reuven. If they never found him she would be as happy as if they did. This made her a horrible person. But this was a horrible place. Texas would be better. Esther knew Avi could fill this hole, even if there is the problem of his new girl Hannah. Esther wanted to leave New York as soon as they found Reuven. Maybe before.

Esther's thoughts were interrupted by a man's voice calling, muffled through the snow, and she was certain the man said her name. *It's all over.* But when she turned around to face what she assumed would be Hersh trudging up the street toward her, confused, another man was raising his hand and waving at a woman on the opposite corner. She watched the man cross the middle of the intersection in front of an oncoming motor bus and hug the woman tightly. *It's not Hersh*. Esther felt the kind of relief that accompanies the realization that rioters have mercifully passed by your house. You have hidden in the space beneath the warped wooden slats in the kitchen floor, and your father's rough hand has covered your mouth to assure silence, but as soon as he lets go and your lips are free, you know you will be okay.

Esther's gaze drifted back up at the men dangling from the bridge, and she waited as one lowered himself to the ground and disconnected himself from the ropes that bound him to the girder. She turned down East Broadway and toward the HIAS office, glancing over a shoulder every few minutes to check for Hersh. When Esther entered the building and climbed the stairway, she fit her shoes into the familiar grooves worn into the center of each stair. She held onto the right railing, sliding her palm along the cool, smooth surface in case she started to fall backward, feeling her weight being pulled back down the stairs and toward the snowy street. Sometimes it happened.

She recognized almost all of the men and women working in the office. Some smiled at her, others said hello and addressed Esther by name. She could not remember any of these people's names if Reuven's life depended on it. They were nice, well-meaning. Too bad they didn't know that they would never find Reuven, that he was gone, either dead and mutilated, or living among goyim.

"Anything?" Esther asked the man who had been managing their case since the day after they had landed on Ellis Island. Esther was happy that the rude man who had helped them on the first day was not assigned to their case permanently. In fact, Esther had seen him just twice in passing during the two weeks of coming to the office, and she never spoke to him; he never spoke to her, never asked about Reuven, nothing a normal human being would do. He just seemed to stare at Esther coldly.

"Nothing new," the man said. "But we have been approved to purchase a little space in about four different newspapers. We'll run the photograph of Reuven with a description, and hopefully someone will remember him from that day."

"Which newspapers?" Esther asked.

"The Yiddish ones."

"Why?"

He looked confused.

"A blond boy like this is not going to be taken by Jews, returned to Jews, found by them, nothing," Esther insisted.

"Please, Mrs. Lipshitz," the man said. "We're putting many resources into this case."

"You people say you understand how blond this boy is, but I don't think you really comprehend."

"Yes, Mrs. Lipshitz, we know this from the photograph."

"This is a very blond boy," she continued.

"Yes."

"Very blond, and does not look like you, me, like anyone here in this office."

"No, of course not."

"What do you think happens to a blond boy?" she asked. "Surely he hasn't been taken by Jews who read the Yiddish newspapers!"

"Yes, ma'am." The man stared at her across the desk, and Esther felt self-conscious. She didn't even know what she was arguing for. Perhaps the half hour of freedom had gone to her head. The boy was gone, these people had no idea how to get him back, and this was a useless endeavor, coming to this office twice a day. And worse still, Hersh would probably be showing up any minute now.

"Can I get you a cup of tea or some water?" he asked.

"No, thank you."

"Let me get the rest of the file so I can run this advertisement by you."

"Okay," Esther said, and she watched the man carry the file containing all that remained of her youngest son and walk out the door.

In a moment, a man stuck his clean-shaven face into the office where Esther was waiting, and she immediately recognized him as the rude man from Ellis Island. Esther felt her own face heat up when she saw him, and he started to pull his head back out of the office but stopped as soon as he recognized Esther and saw that she was alone. The man entered then, standing next to the desk and shuffling through some files in front of him.

"And have you had any luck locating the boy?" he asked very awkwardly.

Esther was shocked. "No, nothing yet."

He turned to face her now, and she could see that his cheeks were red, with streaks of white in them like some people get out in the cold. "I'm sorry to hear that."

"Thank you."

"Mrs. Lipshitz, right?" he asked, offering Esther a hand. "I never introduced myself properly. It's Jonathan. Jonathan Steinman."

She took his hand. She didn't know what else to say, so she looked over her shoulder at the door for the other man to come back with the advertisement.

"How are you finding New York?" Jonathan asked.

"Oh, it's fine," Esther said, "just fine."

"You don't like it very much."

"Not so much," Esther admitted.

"It must be hard with the lost boy."

"Yes," Esther said, but she didn't know if that was the reason.

"Have you seen much of the city?"

"Not really, no."

"Oh, you need to explore the city," he said, "and then you will fall in love with it for sure."

"I don't know," Esther said.

"Have you ever had Italian food?"

"No, my *god* no," Esther said, holding a hand to her heart. "You don't keep kosher?"

"It is not very easy in my life."

"Are you not married?" Esther asked, but she couldn't believe she was being so forward.

"She died of consumption last year."

"I'm sorry."

"Thank you."

They were silent for a moment. A very uncomfortable moment. She felt for the man, but at the same time she also wondered what it would be like to eat food prepared by an Italian.

"Maybe one day when you come to the office to check on the boy, I can take you for some food. A wonderful restaurant is just a few blocks away, and I know the owner, Mr. Guerrieri, well."

Esther didn't know what to say, so she didn't say anything at all.

"Or maybe some tea then," he added nervously. "Of course your husband would surely enjoy—"

Just then, Esther felt weight of some sort descend upon her, the pressure in the room suddenly growing heavy. Seconds later, Hersh stepped through the door, a burst of cold air preceding him, and snow dusting his hat and jacket, melting in his messy beard.

"Esther, what happened?" he demanded.

"Oh, Hersh," Esther said, standing. "You remember Mr. Steinman from Ellis Island?"

"Yes," Hersh said, shaking Mr. Steinman's hand. "Yes, how do you do?"

"I am well. Please, call me Jonathan."

"Well, okay then, Jonathan," Hersh said, looking back and forth between Jonathan and Esther.

"We are waiting for the man to bring the advertisement they will be running in the Yiddish newspapers," Esther reported. Hersh didn't speak. He removed his hat and coat, hanging them both on the hooks behind the office door.

"Well, I'll be leaving now," Jonathan said. "Happy New Year to you both."

"Happy New Year to you," Esther said, but she wished he would stay.

"Yes, good-bye," Hersh said, and then Jonathan was gone, and Hersh was the only man in the room.

"What happened out there?" he asked again.

"I don't know," Esther said. "I was walking and walking and then I looked back and didn't see you."

"I told you I was stopping for pickles."

"I didn't hear you."

"Well, perhaps if you were walking at a normal pace, you might've heard your husband when he spoke to you."

"I didn't. I'm sorry."

"Why didn't you come back for me?"

"I didn't know where you were," Esther lied. "It was cold and I knew we'd meet here and I didn't want to waste any more time in case they were going to be closing the office early for the New Year."

Hersh looked at her and grunted. She hated this noise more than anything.

"In any case, we found each other, and that is all that matters," Esther added.

"I get the feeling you don't want to be with me," Hersh said. "And now I see you with this Jonathan man. What were you talking about?"

"Reuven, of course," Esther lied.

"Well, I don't think he's even assigned to the case any longer," Hersh said. "He shouldn't be talking to a woman when her husband is not present."

"Oh, Hersh, don't be ridiculous."

"He was very rude to you before, and now he is so nice and concerned?" Hersh asked, his voice rising. "I was a boy once, I know how this is."

Esther laughed at Hersh, and she knew this bothered him to no end. Thankfully, the man came in with the proposed advertisement, and Hersh and he shook hands. "Mr. Lipshitz, hello. Your wife didn't say you'd be coming in this afternoon."

"I was just passing by the office and thought I might catch her."

"Oh, well, nice to see you," he said, spreading out some papers in front of Esther and Hersh on the cluttered desk. "Any luck finding work?"

"Not yet," Hersh admitted.

"Well, I know it's difficult now, but employment services downstairs can certainly help you find something temporary."

"You are doing too much for us already," Hersh said, sitting down in the chair next to Esther. "I think I can find something on my own."

"But you should let us help you. This is what we're here for, Mr. Lipshitz."

"Yes, thank you, I know," Hersh said.

Esther studied her husband. He looked strange to her, as though from another land, while she was from America. The beard on Hersh's face looked grotesque to Esther. She wanted it gone, didn't want to walk the streets on the arm of a man who looked like that. It wasn't right anymore, she knew that much.

Esther glanced at the advertisement placed in front of them while Hersh bent over it, scrutinizing every detail. There was Reuven, looking up at his parents from a tiny blurred photograph among a sea of other missing persons Esther was certain would never again see the family members who sought them. When Hersh was satisfied (*was he* ever *satisfied*? Esther wondered), they thanked the man and went back down to the street, Hersh holding the door for his wife before following her back out into the cold. Turning up Orchard Street, Hersh pulled Esther's hand through his elbow and held it there. Darkness was coming, the streets slightly calmer now than before.

"I think this advertisement might bring us something," Hersh said.

"No it won't," Esther replied.

"Why do you say this?"

"Because you're being ridiculous."

"Don't tell me I'm ridiculous," he said, pulling his arm away from her.

"Well, you are being ridiculous."

"You act like you don't want to find Reuven," he said, stopping abruptly on the sidewalk. A man walking quickly behind them almost bumped into Hersh.

"You act like *you* don't want to find him!" Esther said, but she knew it wasn't true.

"Esther, what are you saying?"

"I don't know. What are we doing here?"

"We lost a boy."

"And now everyone has to pay. The boys, Miriam, me, you," Esther said. "There's no work here, what are you going to do?"

"I'll find something."

"We can't live with Raina any longer."

"Well, we can't afford to live anywhere else until I find some work."

"What are you going to do?"

"Stop badgering me, Esther. I'll find something."

"You keep saying that. Why don't you see what the people at the HIAS can find for you?"

"I don't want their help."

Esther didn't say anything further. She started walking again, though didn't speed up like she had on the way to the office. Hersh grunted again and followed. They passed several shuttered stores, some still in the process of closing up for the night. Hersh nodded his head at those who acknowledged him. Esther's feet were wet and cold. The snow on the ground was dirty and black, more slush now than snow.

She kept her eyes on the sidewalk as they rounded Suffolk. Hersh may or may not have spoken to her after that—Esther shut him out. Her gaze was fixed on the snow, dirt, and garbage on the sidewalk below them, and if she squinted her eyes a bit, all of the different shapes and shades between black and white blended together, like when the train passes by the shtetl in the night. If you are lucky, the train might make an unscheduled stop—just slow enough for you to hop aboard—because you will go wherever the train goes, slicing into the night and leaving everything else behind. You might be lulled to sleep as it rocks along, picking up speed slowly but steadily. And you might imagine something else for yourself at that point. Something bold and different, something that might make you a mere witness to somebody else's nightmares instead of your own.

A man and woman stroll in the park by the river. It is nighttime, and the moon is a small glowing dot in the snowy sky. They are in love, but it is forbidden. The man's wife has died, leaving him with two small children. The woman is married with three of her own. The two lovers have seen parts of the city that most people they know avoid. They do this partly to escape the gaze of those who know them, but it is also thrilling to plumb the dark corners and alleyways of this massive, strange city, to test unfamiliar realms belonging to people who come from countries and continents thousands of miles away, across oceans. A salty film from a spicy yet sweet noodle dish the woman cannot pronounce the name of coats the tongues of the man and woman, the backs of their throats buzzing with the sting of foreign flavors.

They stop and embrace passionately, the woman pressing her own cheek against the smooth, beardless cheek of the man. This is shocking sweetness the woman is certain she will pay dearly for one day—and there, over the man's strong, broad shoulder, the woman sees something hanging down over the water, snagged on the bank. It cannot be what it appears to be, she thinks. Like so many things.

She lets go of the man and he looks at her, crestfallen, because he believes this means she is not feeling the strong feelings he feels for her. He never wants to be without her, but he knows he cannot be with her because of her husband, her children.

She lets out a small yelp, and will not look him in the eye, but instead she gazes just past him, over his shoulder. And now he knows for certain he has just lost her forever. (He tends to be dramatic—yet passionate, which is why the woman loves him like she's never loved, nor ever will love, her middling husband.)

"It's a child," she says.

"You are with child?" he asks, suddenly horrified.

"No, look, a child," she repeats, pointing toward the water.

He looks. There, hooked by a jacket on a dead branch that sticks out over the water's surface is a small child, four or five years of age. It appears to be a boy, though in the dark, they cannot tell for sure. The child is submerged up to its waist in the water.

The woman worries that when the police come, she will have to give her name, and she knows her husband will surely discover her infidelity. The man decides he will do most of the talking, and he holds her to him tightly while they wait for a beat officer on the busy street above the park. It is suddenly colder, or they notice that it is cold, where they hadn't paid attention before.

When the first policeman arrives, the man takes him down to the river's edge and points to where the child is. The child cannot be reached from the bank. The woman follows a few paces behind; she does not want to stay on the street alone. People will look at her suspiciously, she thinks. Surely she will be judged for giving up on her family so quickly.

Later two more policemen come in a small horse-drawn wagon, and one of them jumps out holding a long stick with a hook on the end. He descends into the park and wades into the water up to his knees, but he does not get wet because he wears high boots. The snow has stopped.

The policeman pokes at the child with the stick and sees that it is snugly hooked onto the branch. After three tries, the other policeman throws a rope around the child's neck, and then the first one pokes some more at the child, harder, harder, and then he has hooked the child by the coat, loosened it, and is pulling it toward land with the stick. The rope tightens around the child's neck, in case the policeman with the stick loses his grip on the child, but luckily, the woman thinks as she grips her man's elbow and watches, they did not have to pull that child in by the neck.

It is obvious the child is a boy now, as he is undressed from the waist down.

"Dirty bastard," a policeman says.

The two men pull the boy, dripping wet, onto the grass beside the river. He has a full head of blond hair, the woman notices, and there are leaves and other river debris stuck in it. He would be quite beautiful, she thinks, if he weren't dead. She is happy to know her three children are safe at home with her husband—though it is the last place she wishes to be herself. A policeman listens to the boy's mouth and heart, even starts pressing on the boy's chest for a moment, but it is obvious that he is long dead.

The policeman covers the boy's lower half with a heavy horse blanket, but before he does, the woman notices that the boy is circumcised. The policeman begins searching through the inner pockets of the boy's coat and finds a pouch sewn into the inside of his jacket. He opens it up and finds money inside.

"Rubles," he says, holding up the bills to the policeman, who says that whoever did this to the boy was a "dirty bastard."

"Can we go now?" the man asks the policemen.

"Go ahead. Thank you for calling this to our attention. You two have a nice night if you can."

Even the policeman thinks the man and the woman should be going home together.

They were back in front of Raina's building, Esther stalled at the base of the stoop. Hersh's beard was dusted with a layer of snow, with crusted red lips flickering underneath; he had been speaking to her the whole way home, but Esther hadn't registered even a single word. She remembered then that upstairs they were to celebrate in the New Year with the family, yet she didn't understand how any of them could possibly think there was anything to celebrate.

April 8, 1908

NEW YORK CITY

Ben ditched school early with Max Ross—his best friend in the world. That night, the block fights would happen: Max's and Ben's block of Suffolk against the one between Rivington and Stanton. Max wanted to gather as many bottles and cans and rocks as he could, and then stockpile them under his building in preparation for the fight.

"Let's ride the subway," Ben suggested, fingering two nickels deep in his pocket.

"Why?" Max asked, stuffing cans from the garbage into his half-buttoned coat. "Here, help me."

"Why not?" Ben did not understand Max's fascination with fighting nor his lack of interest in the subway, but he believed Max to be a very handsome boy. He had dark olive skin, always smudged with dirt. Ben watched the ropy muscles in Max's arms as he carried armfuls of bottles and other garbage they were to use for the fight later.

On Max's neck was a thick, raised scar that traveled from behind his right earlobe down to his collarbone. Ben never asked what it was from, and Max never said. Ben found himself thinking about this scar all of the time, staring at it, making up stories about what might've happened to

Max before Ben knew him. He wanted to share some of these hypotheses with Max, but it never seemed the right time.

"Come on, why don't you help?" Max prodded. "I'll take a ride with you some other time. Now we have to get ready."

"Okay," Ben said, but he didn't like dirtying his shirt with the messy bottles and cans, the remnants of various rotten liquids and foods dribbling out. Because he knew it made Max happy though, Ben began collecting and carrying as many as he could.

They carefully piled the ammunition under the stoop of Max's building. It took at least an hour, maybe more. The man who owned the fabric store in the building's basement chased the boys away once, but he didn't see their stockpile, so it was safe, their mission accomplished. The boys went home for the obligatory supper with their respective families.

At a quarter to eleven, Ben peeled himself away from his brother Shmuel's wet sleep in the cot beside him, and slipped out of the apartment to meet Max at the stoop. Several other boys from their block huddled around him while Max delineated the battle plan. He didn't look at Ben when he showed up, just stopped talking briefly and then continued gesturing with his hands and pointing out various locations on the block.

Max, Ben, and another boy named Stephen were to stay under Max's stoop and attack from there. Several other boys had other stoops on the block covered. Some boys would go onto the roofs and work from there. The boys from north of Delancey would show up in about fifteen minutes, and as soon as Max yelled the word, they were to bombard the boys with debris all at once.

Ben tried to listen to Max's plan, but he couldn't concentrate. He just watched Max's red lips moving. He wiped his left cheek several times, leaving dark smudges of dirt across it. Ben liked how this looked on Max, like he was some kind of fearless Indian chief. The boys broke their huddle, and Stephen began lining up bottles and rocks in their stoop, according to size and weight. Max stepped into the middle of the street to check in both directions, while Ben tried to busy himself by imitating Stephen's intricate and, to Ben, totally incomprehensible preparations.

"I think they're going to come from both ways this time," Max said, jumping back down the stairs, two at a time.

"Probably," Stephen replied, very seriously. He looked at Ben. "What are you doing?"

"I'm getting these things ready," Ben replied, speeding up his movements and managing to topple the pile of ammunition.

"Shit," Stephen said, pushing Ben out of the way and restacking rocks and cans. "Why does he have to be here?"

"Leave him alone," Max said. "He can throw."

"As long as he stays out of the way," Stephen said. Ben didn't respond, as though Max and Stephen were talking about somebody who wasn't there. Max looked at him and smiled like it was going to be okay, and so Ben chose to believe this and started to prepare his pile again.

A boy on the roof across the street screamed, "They're here!" and then Max popped his head around the staircase and said, "Damn it, they're early. Come on."

Ben grabbed a milk bottle and held it up behind his head. When the pack of boys stopped in the middle of the block, cans and bottles and rocks and anything and everything rained down upon them from above. They tried to take cover, but Stephen and Max and the other sets of boys from different stoops began hurling things at them from the side, so Ben joined in. His first three cans missed his intended targets entirely, but when he switched to a rock, he pegged one boy between the shoulder blades, and the boy fell to his knees. Ben felt horrible, but when he looked at the warrior face Max was making beside him, he felt spurred on.

"Nice one," Max hissed. Now Ben wanted to drop as many boys as he could.

This went on for some time, the fight punctuated by breaking glass, and men sliding up heavy windows in the tenement buildings above and shouting down to the boys to stop fighting or they would fetch the police.

Usually this meant they had another half hour or so before the police would come, and the boys would disperse.

While Ben was turned around and gathering more ammunition, a boy came close to the stoop and rolled a garbage can down into the stairwell where Ben, Stephen, and Max were protected from view of the street. Its rotting contents tumbled out all over them. "Hey, is that Stephen Black down there?" the boy asked, laughing. "Hey, Abe, come over here and show Stephen your hand."

Another boy came over with a wide grin across his face. The first boy grabbed his hand and pushed it toward Stephen's face. "Smell this," he said. "I think you might recognize your sister there on his fingers."

Stephen jumped up the stairs, pushing aside the second boy wiggling his fingers, and wrapped both hands around the neck of the first boy. They fell to the ground, rolling around a few times before Stephen sat on the boy's chest with his knees pinning down arms and began punching him in the face over and over. The back of the boy's head pounded the street with each blow.

"Oh my god," Max said, "look at this, Ben. He's beating the crap out of that guy."

Ben didn't want to look, but he did anyway. He had overheard his father telling his mother that something like this had happened to Uncle Avi the time they left town that Easter in Kishinev. One night after Aunt Ruth died, Ben snuck into his uncle's room while he was sleeping and touched a fingertip to the blood seeping through the bandage around Avi's head. When he brought the finger to his nose, Ben remembered gagging on his tongue and spitting up a burning flavor in his throat. There was hollering down the block then, and Ben noticed a few other sets of boys were locked in pairs fighting a few buildings over. He looked back at Stephen and saw that the boy he was punching wasn't fighting back anymore.

"Come on, Stephen," Max yelled. "Enough."

But Stephen wouldn't stop. Finally a couple of boys from the other block pulled Stephen off the boy, and when they let him go, he sprinted down the block toward his family's apartment. The boys kneeled down to the badly beaten boy, and Ben watched Max watching them.

His eyes fell again upon the scar on Max's neck, now covered in dirt and a little blood from somewhere, but Ben couldn't locate a fresh cut on Max's face. Max was breathing heavily, his chest visibly expanding and contracting as he gripped two dripping bottles, one in each hand. The fight wasn't over by any stretch—the police hadn't shown up yet—but there seemed to be a mutual lull in deference to the downed boy.

Ben moved closer to Max as though he were trying to see the hurt boy, but really he was taking in the scent from Max's body. It was not like that of a younger boy, say his brother Shmuel, but not quite his father's odor either. Suddenly, quietly, while all attention was on the injured, bleeding boy, Ben leaned over and put his lips to Max's neck just beside the scar. The taste of Max's skin was of salt and vinegar—with a faint trace of how Uncle Avi's blood had tasted.

Max pushed Ben away, and he fell backward, stepping onto the pile of remaining rocks and bottles. They heard more yelling, another window break upstairs when a rock broke through it, cans rattling against brick. But to Ben, this space under the stoop was dead quiet. He looked at Max.

"You're a fairy, aren't you?"

Something in Ben's chest snapped. "No, no, Max—" And then a rock cracked Ben in the head, and he fell to the ground at the bottom of the stairs, surrounded by garbage. At first he thought Max might've thrown the rock, but when he looked up, he saw Max defending their fort against a new group of boys who had just ambushed them from across the street. A couple of policemen rounded the corner of Delancey.

"You're bleeding," Max said.

"What?" Ben asked, propping himself up on an elbow. His leg was bent impossibly behind him. He struggled to straighten it.

"Your head is bleeding," Max repeated, pointing. "And the cops are here, you have to get up." Max looked at Ben one last time before running up the stairs above them. Ben heard the door to Max's building slam shut above him, and all the boys scattering down the block.

Ben picked himself up, though he was incredibly dizzy. For a moment, he couldn't remember which direction Isaac and Raina's apartment was, but then he saw the sign for the hat shop at the end of the block and headed for it. He held a palm to his head as blood ran down his face, pooling in the wells between his fingers. He could taste it on his lips.

"What happened?" Esther yelled as soon as Ben came through the door. Everyone was asleep but her.

"I fell," he said. Blood soaked his shirt.

"Oh my god," she exclaimed, running to him. "Hersh, wake up."

"What, Esther, what?"

"Look at your son," Esther said, gathering some rags and soaking them in a pot of water.

Ben gave in to the dizziness and collapsed on the floor with a thud. The room spun around him.

Isaac appeared at the bedroom door. "What's going on?"

"Oh my," Esther said, kneeling beside Ben and propping his head up on her knees. Blood seeped through Esther's nightgown.

"What did you do, boy?" Hersh asked.

"He needs to see a doctor," Esther said, wiping Ben's face with the damp towel, pressing another to the wound. Shmuel woke up and started crying when he saw his brother on the floor. Miriam slept still, but Raina and her two kids now appeared at the bedroom door behind Isaac.

"Let me see," Isaac said, crossing to Ben and kneeling beside him. He pulled off the bloody towel Esther held to Ben's forehead. "He just needs some stitches."

"I should say so," Hersh said.

"We need to go to the doctor," Esther said, shooting Hersh a look. "Now."

"Actually I think I can get Mr. Kohler, the pharmacist, to do this. He'll sew up the boy, and we don't have to go to the hospital."

"Does he know how to do this kind of thing?" Esther asked.

"Esther, please," Hersh said.

"Please, what? You have a job now, we can call the doctor."

"Esther," Isaac started, "if you don't mind my saying, this isn't a major cut, and Mr. Kohler has been sewing up the whole neighborhood for years. I think you'll be happy with his work."

Esther looked at Hersh, who nodded some sort of approval. Isaac went into his bedroom and got dressed. "I'll go to his house and wake him," Isaac said, putting a hat onto his head. "Meet us at Kohler's near the corner of Orchard and Rivington."

"Are you sure?" Esther asked.

"Certainly, the boy will be fine," Isaac assured her, touching Ben on the shoulder. "Oh, and Hersh, bring cash."

Esther propped Ben up and placed his hand on the towel that covered the cut. He wondered why everyone was calling him "the boy," when he was sitting right there. Esther and Hersh got dressed quickly, Esther quietly assuring Shmuel everything would be okay, and asking him to take care of Miriam while they were gone. Ben sat against the wall, pressing the towel to his head. The blood wouldn't stop dribbling through his hands though, warm fingers tickling his face.

At the pharmacy, Mr. Kohler squirted the needle in front of Ben's face, and the drips of clear fluid glistened on the black-and-white tile floor beside Ben's feet. The pharmacist gave him the shot right into the cut on his head. The pain seared through him at first, but soon it was gone. When Mr. Kohler tugged on the curved needle and dark thread in front of Ben's eyes, his head jerked with the motion, and he could even feel the skin tenting, but there was nothing else—no searing stabs any longer. The jerking motion repeated about ten times, Ben counted, and then the pharmacist made a twisted tie with both hands and cut the needle from the thread.

"Young man," Mr. Kohler said, "you are the proud owner of twelve new stitches."

"Will it make a scar?" Ben asked.

"Shouldn't be too bad in a few month's time."

"There won't be a bump?"

"Shouldn't be," the pharmacist said, cleaning up the area and placing all of the sharp silver instruments in a small tub of alcohol.

"So you won't even be able to see a line?" Ben asked again.

"Ben!" Esther yelled. "Stop it."

"What?" he asked.

"Thank the man so we can let him get back to his family."

"Thank you," Ben said, reaching up to touch the jagged thorns on his forehead, just below his hairline.

"Don't touch," Mr. Kohler said. "It needs to stay clean, or you *will* get a scar."

Hersh handed Mr. Kohler a folded bunch of bills, and the old man slipped them into his vest pocket. He turned off the light in the store, muttering to himself, "I'll just have my boy clean this up tomorrow."

He waited as Hersh, Esther, Isaac, and Ben exited the store, and then pulled shut the heavy, beveled glass door to the pharmacy and locked it behind them. Kohler headed north on Orchard—taking short, quick steps—and the others headed down Rivington toward their apartment.

"If I find out you were fighting with those boys," Hersh said.

"Leave it until the morning," Esther said. "Do you feel okay, Ben?"

"I feel fine, Mama," he said. "I'm just tired."

"Shmuel will sleep with us so you can get some rest," Esther said.

"Why do you baby him?" Hersh asked.

"Oh Hersh, you're just jealous," Isaac said, and Esther laughed a bit too loudly.

Isaac opened the front door to their building and held it for Esther. Hersh took the weight of the door then, and Isaac entered. Hersh let the door close in front of Ben, who stopped just before walking into the door.

It seemed to Ben that Hersh would clap him on the back of the head or something like that. He thought his father might be angry, but Ben couldn't recall a time when his father was ever extremely angry. He seemed more frustrated. But then, his father always seemed frustrated. The two stood silently on the stoop for a moment. The street was dark and empty, though a few lone figures walked the sidewalks. Two black dogs nosed a pile of garbage in the middle of the damp street, partially lit in the glow from the few functional streetlamps on the block.

"What is it with you?" Hersh asked.

"Honestly, nothing, Papa," Ben said, picturing Max's neck then, followed by the sight and sound of Stephen pounding that boy's face and head into the sidewalk.

"Really?" Hersh said, shaking his head and opening the door for his oldest. Ben skulked by his father and started the long, dark climb up four flights of stairs.

In the apartment Ben stripped out of his bloody clothes and Esther put them into a laundry bag out on the fire escape. Esther boiled him some water and Ben went into the bathroom down the hall and rinsed some of the blood off his skin. There was a tiny cracked and clouded sliver of a mirror above the toilet in the bathroom, and Ben leaned over to look at his face in it. Blood caked all over his cheek and neck. It matted his hair. The smell of it loosening in the warm water made Ben gag and spit up a bit into the toilet. He kept scrubbing, slowly and gently.

When his face was clean, the wound was more visible. He studied it closely and wondered about Max, whether he was worried about Ben at that moment. Ben pictured Max after the fight: out of breath, silently letting himself into his family's apartment, stripping to his underwear and undershirt and slipping into bed beside his two younger brothers. Max would be lying on his back awake, hands laced behind his head, studying the ceiling with a slight frown in his thick eyebrows.

Ben was no fairy. Max would see in the morning.

Ben studied the crooked caterpillar on his head and rubbed his thumb along the stitches. He didn't care what Mr. Kohler said. Ben decided he would rub dirt into his cut tomorrow, and would do so every day thereafter until it healed. This would surely raise a nasty scar when the stitches were removed, he thought, and then Max and he would make quite a pair. Very tough boys you wouldn't want to mess with if you came across them on the block. Because they had seen and done things—and even had the battle scars to prove it.

July 14, 1908

NEW YORK CITY

Hersh pried open his locker at the end of the shift. A small slip of paper fell out in front of him, rocking through the air before spinning twice and finally settling on the linoleum floor. He picked it up and studied the English writing; there was a lot of it, six or seven typed lines. He could pick out many of the words thanks to the night classes he and Esther were taking, but just in case, below the English, someone had scribbled in Yiddish:

Basically, you're fired. Factory's losing money— shutting down the card-stock division . Empty your locker, and go to the office to collect your last wages. Don't forget your uniform and key or no check .

Hersh turned to the burly man who was opening the locker next to him. A paper fluttered from his locker too. He picked it up in his massive, fat hands and whispered "Fuck!" to himself before crumpling up the paper and throwing it into his locker. Hersh thought the man quite brash, and looked around to see if anybody was watching them. He thought the man might be Irish, but Hersh had never really spoken to him before.

"You get one too?" the man asked in heavily accented English.

Hersh nodded his head.

"Fuck!" the man said again, louder this time. He pulled off his suspenders and stepped out of his bulky uniform. Hersh did the same.

So, he lost another job. He could live with it, though he dreaded telling Esther. Every time, it was further proof to her that they should go to Texas, and also, in Hersh's mind, abandon all hope of finding Reuven.

Hersh pocketed his check and exited the factory into a blast of heat from the street. He stepped onto the back of a trolley and let the air blow his sweaty hair. His beard was trimmed because they made him do so in the factory. He could feel the wind sifting through it, cooling his cheeks and chin. He would not miss cutting three-by-five cards. Nor would he miss the bloody layers upon layers of blisters on his outer palms.

When Hersh walked into Raina and Isaac's apartment, Esther knew what had happened before he said anything. She stared at him from the couch, where she was working on a pair of trousers by hand. "What now?" she asked.

"What?"

"Hersh—"

"So, I lost another job," he admitted, hanging his hat on the nail above their tiny bed. "They cut out my division."

Esther didn't say anything.

"Nobody else's wife I know gives her husband so much grief," Hersh said, feigning anger.

—

"This is a man's business, so don't you trouble yourself."

—

"Where's Raina?"

—

"I'll find something else."

131

"What? What will you find, Hersh?" she finally asked, putting down the sewing beside her. "You like cutting paper?"

"It fed us all right."

"Yes, as well as the job slaughtering chickens you lost last month."

Not this again, Hersh thought.

"I did not marry a chicken slaughterer, Hersh Lipshitz!"

Here we go.

"The most base of all jobs, and you manage to lose it!"

"I don't understand," Hersh said calmly, washing his hands in the kitchen sink. "So is it worse that I *had* the job as a chicken slaughterer, or worse that I lost it?"

—

"Ach, the silence. I'm so tired of it."

She stared at him, one of the gravest looks he'd seen on his wife (and there had been some pretty grave moments up until this point). "I'm taking the children to Texas; you can come with us if you'd like."

"And exactly how do you intend to live if I don't send money?"

"I'll get a job, and Avi will take care of us."

"Avi, Avi, Avi," Hersh yelled. "Always Avi, why didn't you marry your brother then?"

"Hersh, please!"

"If you think it's bad for work here, it's one hundred times worse in Texas. Go read about the depression in the papers."

"Avi says it's better in his letters. He has a job waiting for you."

"Oh wonderful, he'll have me peddling bananas."

"Now Mr. Big Man won't sell fruit," Esther said, "but he'll slaughter chickens and come home with stolen chicken parts in his pockets to feed his family?"

"What about Reuven?"

"HIAS will wire if anything happens. And Isaac and Raina are here."

"Fine," Hersh said, but he didn't know if he meant it. He could admit that he was growing tired of the blank looks on the tired HIAS employees' faces, pretending to be busy working on the case when there was no sign of Reuven after more than half a year of looking for him. And all the advertisements produced nothing but one lady with no husband and too many children who wanted to unload one of them. This, he didn't need any more of. But, Hersh had to admit, he was even more sick and tired of Esther nagging him all the time about Texas.

At supper that night, Esther announced to the family that they would be leaving in a week. Raina and Isaac looked surprised, Hersh thought, but ultimately relieved. He'd helped some with monthly rent, and paid for much of the food since they had moved in, but still, the family needed their apartment back—Isaac needed space to work again, his kids a place to sleep.

Shmuel seemed oblivious to the news, and Miriam just sat there, forcing a too large wedge of potato into her mouth and swinging her legs to and fro under the chair.

"I think this is a fine idea," Isaac pronounced.

"But we will miss you," Raina whined. At this, Hersh saw Esther roll her eyes the way she does. He was happy they weren't directed at him for once.

Only Ben appeared distressed. He looked back and forth between his mother and father. "No!" he yelled suddenly. "I'm not going."

"What do you mean?" Esther asked him.

"I'm not leaving New York."

"Oh yes you are," Hersh said.

"No, I'm not."

"Remember how much you wanted to work in the wood shop with your uncle Avi?" Esther asked.

"I changed my mind; it happens."

"Don't speak to your mother that way," Hersh snapped.

"What about school?" Ben asked.

"They have school in Texas, probably better," Esther replied.

"What about Reuven?" he asked then. It was the question nobody at the table was willing to ask, but everyone was most likely thinking. Esther looked to Hersh, and he realized she expected him to say something. But how was he supposed to say something when he was asking himself the very same question?

"You're just going to leave him?" Ben asked. Nobody responded. "I'll stay here then, and look for Reuven."

"You're coming with us," Hersh said.

"No, I'm not."

"This sounds like a good idea," Esther said quietly after a moment, almost to herself.

"Mr. Kohler said he'd hire me at the pharmacy," Ben added when he heard his mother.

"Yes, this makes sense," Esther said, tapping the table in front of her plate before leaning down to pick up Miriam's spoon from the floor.

Hersh couldn't believe what he was hearing. "Are you crazy?" he asked.

"You heard him," Esther said. "He doesn't want to go, and he's practically a man now, he can make his own decisions."

"So now you want to sacrifice *two* of our children for your brother?"

"Now, let's just wait a minute here," Isaac interrupted. *Thank god for Isaac,* Hersh thought, because he was certain Esther was preparing to leap from her seat and strangle Hersh at that minute. "The boy is welcome to stay with us."

"We would *love* to have him," Raina added.

"I'll pay my share," Ben offered.

"Of course," Isaac said.

"And I'll go to the office three times a week, checking on Reuven," Ben continued. He seemed to have thought this out before. He was all wound up, already contemplating and savoring his freedom, Hersh could tell. Hersh would miss Ben, but he was actually a little jealous of him. "And who knows, I should be in New York in case—what if I'm walking down the street one day, and I recognize him walking with some woman?"

"Oh yes, this is very likely to happen," Hersh said, picturing what this might look like, Reuven following some strange blonde lady down the block, holding her hand, prattling away with her in English like he'd never known Yiddish. Before he allowed himself to go too far with the fantasy though, Hersh noticed Esther glaring at him from across the table. He didn't recognize his wife any longer. Quite possibly never did.

And now his one potential ally against Esther and her glower was abandoning him for a chance at something Hersh would never know. This sort of opportunity was of course what you hoped for for your children, but perhaps just not like this.

July 23, 1908

NEW YORK CITY

Hersh looked at himself in the tiny shard of a mirror in the bathroom down the hall. This would be the last time he was in here, and despite his overall effort to appear completely against the move to Texas, Hersh found himself happy to be leaving behind the splashes of excrement covering the commode, the hole in the floor, the damp and crumbling wall behind it. While he was on the subject, he wouldn't miss the fetid stench, broken basin, the rodents so large they acted like it was you who was interrupting them.

Hersh tugged on his beard with his left hand, pulled it very hard until it stung. Then he took the scissors he'd borrowed from Isaac's kit and started chopping at the hair. It was thick, though nowhere near as long as he used to wear it in Russia. He hacked at it in this manner for maybe five minutes, the balls of wiry black hair piling up in small bunches in and around the sink. When his face was a patchy mess, Hersh opened the razor he'd bought from the peddler on the corner and set it on the cracked basin. The dull light from the lamp in the hallway reflected yellow in the shiny blade. He splashed his hands in the pan of warm water he'd prepared in the kitchen, wetting his short beard and face. He dug a squat brush's bristles into a new, round, white bar of shaving soap—also from the peddler, free with the razor and brush—and circled his face until only his dark eyes peeked out above the creamy foam.

Hersh could hear Esther and Ben moving suitcases out into the hallway, Raina's voice fluttering with questions and crying sporadically. Hersh had never shaved before. His hands shook. He'd thought of asking Isaac for help, but he was embarrassed. Hersh dipped the razor in the warm water and put it against his face. He was amazed at how easily the hair came off—this thing was sharp. Ruth had used one just like it on her arms in the tub.

He did two strokes and then rinsed the blade in the water again. Hersh could barely see himself in the tiny clouded mirror, but he moved to the other cheek then, which was dark because it was on the opposite side from the lamp. He watched the silver blade slide across the skin, so smooth, just a soft scraping sound, almost like he could hear it from the inside of his ears louder than from the outside. He moved down to his chin and completed a few bumpy strokes before noticing some blood on the blade. He couldn't see where it was coming from though, because there was still so much hair.

"Hersh?" It was Esther, yelling for him down the hallway. "He must be sick." Then he heard Esther's quick, little "We're going to Texas" footsteps and then three hard knocks on the door to the bathroom. This nudged the door open some, but Hersh slammed it shut with his behind.

"Don't come in," he yelled through the door. "I'll just be one second."

"I can't find the tickets," she said.

Hersh's hands were soapy, but he searched his inner jacket pocket for the train tickets. They were there, the same ones he'd bought in Rotterdam for the trip all the way through to Texas from Ellis Island. The train company said they were still valid.

"I have them," he yelled to Esther. "Just give me a few minutes."

"Are you feeling okay?"

"My stomach."

"Do you need anything?"

"No, just leave me alone," he said, dipping the razor in the water and washing away the cloudy red smear from the blade. Now a few small beads of his blood crept through the hair that remained beneath his chin. He heard Esther's footsteps heading back to the apartment, and then her say to Miriam, "Go get your dolly."

Hersh finished up in about ten more minutes. He cut himself a few more times, but all except one stopped bleeding by the time he was done. He ripped a small corner of newspaper from the pile of it behind the toilet, and stuck it to the worst cut on his chin. He held it there for a few seconds before enough blood soaked through, sticking the paper to his face.

Hersh stepped back and moved his head side to side so he could get a full view of himself in the mirror. He opened the bathroom door to let more light in the room. He could really see himself then, or at least half of his face at a time. He truly didn't recognize the man in there, but it felt about right, considering everything.

He heard Esther down the hall again: "What's keeping Hersh?" And then he knew it was his cue to come out and meet his wife for the first time as a beardless man. Hersh scooped the hair out of the sink and brushed it into the toilet. He dried the razor on his pant leg, folded it up and slipped it into his jacket pocket. Then he wrapped the soap up in the paper it came with, and put that into the other pocket with Isaac's scissors.

He opened the door slowly and stood in the hallway. Esther was bending over a valise, but stood up erect when she saw him. She looked at him for a few seconds before her face changed from being occupied and irritated to something else entirely. One thing he loved about her was that when Esther's face changed, it did so completely.

She cocked her head to the side, blinked a few times with a crooked, closed-mouth smile on her lips. She dropped Miriam's dolly by her side; it bounced on the valise before sliding off and hitting the hallway floor. Then Esther moved toward Hersh slowly, her steps much slower than the usual rushing-around Esther gait.

She reached up to Hersh's face with the back of her right hand, hesitating for a moment before touching there. Her knuckles were soft and warm against Hersh's cheek. He realized then he hadn't completely dried his face yet, and needed a towel to finish the job. This was the first time Esther had touched the skin on this part of her husband's body, Hersh realized.

She turned her hand around and felt his face with her palm then, bringing the left hand up in the same way. She cupped his face in her hands, unsticking the blood-spotted paper from his skin and sending it spinning to the ground between them.

"You don't have a sick stomach," she said.

"No," Hersh admitted. "I feel fine."

Esther brought her face right up to Hersh's then, and for a moment he thought she would kiss him on the lips, something they had not done in . . . Hersh couldn't remember how long. Instead, Esther gently put her lips to the right side of Hersh's face. She didn't really kiss him then either, more just rested her soft lips against his cheek, slightly parted. *Sometimes I forget how Esther is a woman,* Hersh thought to himself, smiling. His wife felt good to him. Almost nothing else did, but for once in a very long time, Esther made some sort of sense.

"Yeeow!" Ben screamed from inside the apartment. Esther pulled her hands away from Hersh's face when Ben burst into the hallway, saying, "Come on, you don't want to miss the train—whoa, what have you done with my papa, mister?" Hersh thought his son must be making fun of him in some way, but he couldn't tell exactly how.

"Ready?" Hersh whispered to Esther then. She nodded to him, that crooked smile still on her face, and turned to go down the hall. Hersh watched his wife from behind and remembered all the things he used to want to do to her when they were first married.

July 10, 1913

AMARILLO, TEXAS

Esther kissed Avi good-bye on the cheek and spread the newspaper he left for her across the kitchen table. She loved that he'd always stop by to see her at break time after eating with his wife Hannah a few doors down. Esther and her dear brother sharing an after-dinner coffee—this was all she could ever ask for. Esther sipped the last of her coffee and scanned the columns on the paper in front of her. Directly under and slightly left of the "Panhandle fed, Amarillo killed—Fresh meats at Griffith Grocery" advertisement, Esther's eyes snagged on the little drawing:

[advertisement]

Call on PROF. STEVENS,

The renowned Palmist and Hypnotist at Suite 124, Hotel Amarillo, without delay. He can tell you many things about yourself which you are not aware of, and which may contribute materially to your happiness.

Prof. Stevens reads your entire life's prospects from the lines in your hands. His work is scientific and is recognized as such by all intelligent people. He is one of the greatest and most successful practitioners of Palmistry of the present day. Do not fail to call on him. Appointments can be made by telephone. All consultations strictly private. Satisfaction guaranteed or no charge.

What was this "hypnotist" and "satisfaction"? Esther decided she would ask Shmuel to translate the words for her, to be sure this sign was what she thought it was.

She busied herself with the washing until she could take the waiting no longer. The newspaper sat opened to the advertisement on the kitchen table, and Esther returned to it, running her fingers over the letters in Professor Stevens's name. She had a good feeling about this. Maybe not a good one, but a feeling. The front door slammed open then, and her boy Shmuel yelled "Mama!" He started up the steps. "Mama, Miriam hurt herself!"

Esther folded the newspaper and pressed her palms onto the crease, smoothing it. She wiped her hands on her apron and took a very deep, almost painful breath. Esther imagined the air bringing with it concern for her daughter's safety and well-being. At least, Esther thought, as the new air filled her lungs and they in turn pressed up against her rib cage, it would by necessity also place pressure on her heart—the location where you are supposed to feel these sorts of things such as worry and love and concern for a maimed child, or even a pathetic husband.

As four feet clambered noisily up the stairs to their half of the house, Esther told herself that whatever it was, it couldn't be too bad because here they were, her two remaining children, both alive and ascending on all four legs, this very moment.

She greeted them at the top of the stairs then, and her awkwardly mannish son held the hand of her strangely beautiful, though dark and wild-haired daughter, who did not start crying until precisely the moment her eyes met those of her mother.

Why does she always seem to know when I am not caring enough? Esther wondered upon meeting Miriam's dark little eyes.

"Darling, come here," Esther said. Miriam's knee was bleeding, and Esther could see a small metal shard sticking out of it.

"She fell off a bench," Shmuel said, looking down.

Esther picked Miriam up and sat her on the kitchen table. In bending her knee, a fresh line of dark blood sprang from the wound and sifted through the baby hairs on Miriam's shin. She let out a loud wail when she saw this.

"Shh, shh," Esther said, placing a damp kerchief onto the wound and wiping away some of the blood.

"Mama, no!" Miriam yelled, leaning back and resting her hand on the newspaper behind her. Before Esther could say anything, Miriam had crumpled the paper in her fist.

"So am I to believe she was sitting on a bench and she just fell off it onto the ground?" Esther asked.

"Yes," Shmuel said. Miriam stopped crying long enough to look at her brother as he said this. Esther understood this brother-sister protective dynamic all too implicitly; she and Avi had been the same way when they were young.

Esther didn't say anything. Instead she gently pressed the kerchief to Miriam's knee, rinsed and repeated several times, adding a little soap each time. She could smell the perspiration coming off Shmuel standing next to her—a disgusting bitter scent she could sometimes trace in his underwear on laundry days—especially during these hot summer months. His brow was damp, with stringy black hair stuck to it in wavy lines. He shifted his weight from leg to leg, breathing in through his nostrils and out through his mouth loudly. She wondered why Shmuel had turned into such an awkward man-child when her other boy had been so perfect.

Ben was practically a man by the time they left him in New York five years earlier—and at fourteen, he had been two years younger then than Shmuel was now. Beautiful Ben. Esther again inhaled the scent of the boy standing next to her, and took in the sight of the bloody knee in front of her—but in her head she pictured Ben as he must be now, dressed in a tidy brown suit and strolling with a handsome young lady on his arm, down East Broadway or Hester Street.

Esther removed the kerchief from Miriam's knee and looked closely. "Shut your eyes," she said, and then just as Miriam complied, Esther grasped the metal shard and wrenched it from Miriam's knee.

"Mama!" Miriam cried, as Esther tossed the offending, bloody nail into the sink. It slid noisily to a stop near the drain, and Shmuel raced over to get a closer look. Esther rinsed the kerchief and lathered some soap onto it before returning to Miriam's knee.

"Look how long that is," Shmuel said, poking at the nail in the sink.

"Yes, it's very strange that she got this so far into her knee by falling off a bench," Esther said.

"Very strange," Shmuel said.

Esther boiled some water to put in the tub. "We're going to soak that leg for a little bit, okay?"

Miriam did not answer.

Later, while Miriam soaked in the pickle barrel, Esther and Shmuel sat at the kitchen table. Shmuel hadn't uttered a word since "very strange."

"Read this for me," Esther said as though she didn't really care, uncrinkling the newspaper and sliding it across the table toward Shmuel. "What's this word?"

"Hype-know-tist," he sounded out. "I don't know."

"What about this one?" she continued, pointing to "satisfaction."

He read for a moment. "Oh, this means if you don't get what you want, then you don't have to pay."

Esther nodded her head.

"Why? What is this for?" Shmuel asked.

"Nothing," Esther said, folding the paper. "I was just wondering."

"When's Papa coming home?"

"Why?" Esther asked. She stood to check on Miriam, who was looking out the kitchen window and swinging the leg that wasn't soaking in the tub.

Shmuel shrugged his shoulders. "I don't know."

Esther lifted Miriam's leg up for a closer look. Water diluted blood, and the skin around the dark purple hole was white and pink. "Five more minutes," Esther said.

"Mama—" Shmuel started then, guiltily.

"No," Miriam piped in.

"No what?" Esther asked.

"Mama," Shmuel repeated, silencing his sister with a look.

"Yes?"

"I took Miriam to the Gem Lake pool with me. When we were waiting in line outside, some of us were balance walking on the back of the benches, and . . ."

"And what?"

"And Miriam wanted to try, so I helped her up there and I promise I was holding her hand, but at the end she fell off and there must've been a nail sticking out of the bench."

"You were at the pool?"

"We didn't get in."

"But you were in line to go into the pool?"

"Yes, but we didn't get in."

"It says 'No Jews,' Shmuel," Esther yelled. "And she can't even swim anyway!"

"I was going to hold her."

"Like you held her on the bench?"

"Yes?"

"They let Jews in for free on Wednesdays."

"They let *everybody* in for free on Wednesdays!" Esther hollered. "It doesn't mean all the other rules disappear too."

"David went in last Wednesday."

"I don't care!" Esther said. "I don't care what David did last week, or any week."

"I'm sorry."

"I will tell your father what you did when he gets home and we'll see what he has to say about it." Esther wished it were true, but in reality, both Shmuel and Esther, and even Miriam to some extent, knew that Hersh would not have much to say about the pool. Or anything else really.

A couple hours later Miriam was in bed, Shmuel read at the kitchen table, and Hersh's cart rattled up the driveway in front of the house. Esther felt her chest tighten to the point of mild discomfort—the way it did about ninety-five percent of the times she first saw her husband after any length of time away from him. She would not tell Hersh about this Professor Mr. Stevens from the newspaper, she decided right then, and the tightness relented slightly. Because if he was not correct about your questions, you did not have to pay the man, and there would be no harm done. Esther decided she would take some money out of Hersh's secret tin behind the stove and put it back if the man was wrong. And if he was right, well, in this case, Hersh wouldn't care about the money because Mr. Stevens would have been right, and then they would know for sure, and everything—absolutely everything, and not just the money—would have been worth it.

Hersh came in the door, his face a caked-on, dark brown-red from the dusty roads on the outside of town. There must be three layers of dirt on his cheeks, Esther presumed. He came over to wash his hands in the sink, but before he did, Hersh ruffled one of them through Shmuel's head of hair.

"Papa!" Shmuel whined, pulling his head from Hersh's touch. Esther decided then that she would be, for this evening at least, the only one who would not express annoyance at her husband. She might feel it, but Esther decided that for the rest of the night—and possibly even the next morning—she would not show it.

"I had a good day out there," Hersh said, soaping his hands up to his elbows. "Sold thirteen bags of feed."

"You would be doing even better if you worked for Avi and Mr. Wolf," Esther said. *Oh well, I tried.*

"I just told you, I did very well today," Hersh insisted.

Esther would not respond as she normally did in this discussion—the same one they had at least once a month since arriving in Texas—due to her resolution to be kind to Hersh for the evening. She shouldn't have started it in the first place. It just slipped out.

"You know I think it's better if we keep the family and business separate for now. I still don't trust his father-in-law one bit." Hersh added, taking advantage of Esther's rare silence on the persistent matter of Avi's trying to take care of Hersh's family in addition to his own. He wiped his hands on the kitchen towel. "Whose blood?"

"It seems that we have a little fish in the family who wanted to go swimming and took his little sister with him," Esther answered.

"What did you do?" Hersh asked of what was, for all intents and purposes, his only remaining son.

—

"Tell him," Esther insisted.

"What?" Hersh asked. There was more silence. Esther shot Shmuel her fiercest eyeball.

"I took Miriam to the pool for a swim, but it didn't matter because we didn't get in."

"She was hurt at the pool?"

"Outside the pool."

"But you're not supposed to go to the pool," Hersh said, removing cash and coins from his crumpled old pocketbook and dumping them on the table.

"It was very hot today," Shmuel said.

"Yes, it was," Hersh agreed mindlessly.

"That's it?" Esther shrieked, but once again remembered her promise and changed her tone. "I mean, wouldn't you like to tell your son something more, considering he caused a very long metal object to be lodged in your only daughter's knee?"

Hersh looked at his wife, clearly confused by her kindness. "Um, yes, Shmuel," he started. "Do not go to the pool anymore."

Shmuel looked at his father. "Yes, sir," he agreed, but he too was confused. Of the three, Esther was the only one who knew she would soon be in possession of all the knowledge, thanks to Professor Mr. Stevens at the Hotel Amarillo.

"What's this?" Hersh asked, sitting down for supper. "You didn't open this letter from Ben?"

"I know there is no news," Esther said as she went down the hall to see if Miriam was still asleep. She decided not to wake the girl for supper.

"He says he has found work in the kitchen of a cafeteria on Delancey," Hersh read from Ben's letter when Esther returned to the kitchen. "Shmuel, did you hear that? Your brother is making two times what he was making at the newsstand."

"That's good," Shmuel said, remotely lifting an eyelid.

"I think he has a girl," Hersh said as Esther served their supper: a kugel and potato soup.

"And why do you think this?" Esther asked.

"Because he doesn't speak of a girl, and when a fellow makes an effort to leave the girl out, then there's always a girl."

Esther fought to stem annoyance, because here it was again. For some reason, even though she often pondered the same thought, this theory of

Hersh's about Ben's nonexistent girl enraged Esther. The way he thinks he knows everything. The way he tells you as much. The way he fills up all the spaces with absolutely nothing.

It was two days before Esther could manage to break away and call on this Mr. Stevens at the Hotel Amarillo. When she stepped off the streetcar downtown, Esther realized this was the first time she had been downtown without Hersh or one of the kids. In five years. A busy day was afoot for all the laborers, and many more who weren't working milled about on the sidewalk in front of the dry-goods store looking for work. Esther ducked into the hotel lobby and strode up to the gentleman at the front desk.

"I'd like to leave a message for Professor Mr. Stevens."

"The circus fellow?" the clerk responded.

"Oh no. This advertisement in the paper?"

"Let me see," the clerk said, taking the clipping and holding it close to his face. "Yeah, the circus guy, he's in room 124. I think he's there. Want me to call him for you?"

"Oh no, no," Esther demurred. "I just thought I could leave a message for him so we might set up an appointment."

"An *appointment*?"

Esther looked at him. "Yes."

"I don't think you need an appointment."

"Well . . ."

"Just a moment."

When the clerk returned, he told Esther that Professor Stevens would see her in fifteen minutes if she liked. Esther wondered what she would do for fifteen minutes. By the time she decided upon sitting in the lobby by the window, a young gentleman in a porter's cap approached her. "I'll take you to the suite, ma'am."

"Thank you."

Esther clutched her bag to her chest as she followed the young man down the carpeted hallway to the left of the front desk. She noticed it was cooler in the hallway than in the lobby or outside, and quite dark.

"Here we are," the young man said, and knocked twice on the door.

"Welcome, Mrs.—"

"Lipshitz."

"Welcome, Mrs. Lipshitz," the man who opened the door said with a flourish and wave of his outstretched hand. He was heavy, with a thin, black, and well-waxed mustache seeming to tickle his nose. He wore a tattered deep-purple cape around his neck that fell off the right side of his body. As he directed Esther to one of the two seats at a small wooden table by the window, Mr. Stevens futzed with the tie for his cape. "Please, have a seat."

"I do apologize if I have surprised you with my visit," Esther began. "I wanted to leave a message for you, but the boy at the desk said it was—"

"Oh no, please," he interrupted, lowering himself into the chair opposite Esther's. "I knew you were coming."

"You knew, *how*?"

"I just knew an important customer would be arriving today to visit with me."

"Oh!" Esther was impressed.

"Now, what can I help you with today?" he asked. She could smell rum on his humid breath. "I can do a standard analysis of your palm, but I'm feeling strongly that you have a pressing matter that you wish to discuss with me."

"I do, I do."

"Please, tell me."

"I don't know what to tell."

"Just start at the beginning."

"The beginning? Really? I don't know . . ."

"Please," he urged her, brushing crumbs off the table between them.

"Well, we came here from Russia approximately six years ago—my husband, myself, my sons Ben, Shmuel, Reuven, and my daughter Miriam . . . I don't know if you need to hear all of this."

"No, no. Please, go on."

"Yes, so when we came to Ellis Island in New York, the youngest boy, Reuven, see, he was supposed to be with his father, and his father, well, Hersh believed the boy was with me, and then, you see, it was very, very crowded with all the people, and we never saw the boy again after that point."

"He just disappeared?" the professor asked, shaking his head slightly.

"I don't know."

"You just, what, *lost* him?"

"Maybe. I don't know . . ."

"Please, continue."

"Well, that's it. We stayed to look for the boy in New York with my cousin Raina and her husband—he's a very nice man who let us live with his family there—but we couldn't find Reuven, and the men at the Hebrew Society couldn't find him, and my oldest son Ben, he's in New York still, looking for Reuven every day, but he cannot find him either."

"I see."

"He was—he is—a very beautiful blond boy."

"I see, yes." There was a long silence then, maybe two or three full minutes. Esther was nervous. She looked out the window onto Polk Street as a ranch man passed by pushing a large stack of dark coveralls on a cart in front of him. It reminded Esther of the massive piles of men's trousers and jackets, and boys' coats, all stacked from the floor practically to the ceiling in Isaac and Raina's apartment. How for a few weeks over the New Year, they had to wade through scraps and fabric that were knee-high covering the floor.

Esther was startled when Professor Mr. Stevens grasped her forearm and then her left hand, turning it over, palm up. His hands, contrary to what she'd expected, were quite soft and fleshy—no calluses or dry spots.

Esther could feel a rush of warmth travel the length of her arm and swell in her chest. It was quite queer to have a man other than her husband touch her in this manner. The last one to do so before this strange and not too pleasantly scented man was Jonathan from the Hebrew Immigrant Aid Society in New York.

On the day before Esther and Hersh boarded the train for Texas, Esther had paid a visit to Jonathan one last time. His eyes were dark, wet, and full of a curious sort of sorrow when she told him they would be leaving for Texas. Esther found herself wanting to hold him close to her in that office, but instead she offered her hand in the wide space between them. "But what about the boy?" he'd asked, and this angered Esther, as though he were suggesting—as Hersh did quite frequently—that she was a bad mother for leaving her lost boy somewhere in the strange city. She began to withdraw, but before she could, Jonathan quickly clasped Esther's hand in both of his and held it against his soft cheek for a few seconds before gently kissing the base of her palm. Then he let go of her, for good. Esther had never felt a man's cheek so soft—she could remember this softness still, in her neck, chest, stomach, even lower than that. Her sons had cheeks this soft, yes, but they were not men. And Hersh's cheek, forget about it. The very next day after her visit with Jonathan, Hersh had surprised Esther by shaving his own beard just before they left for the train station. It surprised and delighted her more than she'd thought possible. But sure enough, after just a few days on the train, Hersh's cheeks and chin grew even pricklier than they had been when he wore a full beard.

"Oh my," the professor said, interrupting Esther's reminiscence. He sounded very concerned. "Yes, I can see this great sorrow was written from the beginning."

"How?" Esther looked at the line on her palm where he was pointing. He gently rubbed his second finger up and down the line.

"Can you see this major break?" he asked, tapping one spot on Esther's palm. There were so many crisscrossing lines, she could not tell which one he was referring to. "Yes, this gap here represents crossing the Atlantic, and you see here, this is a major sorrow at the end of the gap, before the line continues on for a very long time."

"Oh my."

"Mmmm. Yes, I see," he continued. Esther could feel the flush that had started in her chest traveling up into her neck and face now. "Okay, okay, can you do something for me? I'd like to compare this to your other hand, just to make sure of what I'm seeing here."

Esther lifted her right hand onto the table and turned the palm up. She felt like one of those tramps she'd see hopping off the boxcars when they stopped in town for the night, begging for a scrap of bread or a penny. The professor leaned back in his chair and stared intently at Esther's upturned palms.

"Yes, yes," he repeated.

"What? Sir, you must tell me," Esther insisted. For a flash second, as the large man's body resettled into a reclining, slouched position in his chair, Esther wondered if she weren't in some sort of danger, alone in a room at the Hotel Amarillo where nobody but the boys at the front desk knew she was. The girls who visit single men in hotel rooms in the middle of the day are not the kind Esther wanted to be associated with. But the bolt of fear disappeared as quickly as it had come when the man leaned forward, bringing his forehead within inches of Esther's.

"This is going to be difficult to hear, but please listen to me," he began, the sweet stench of liquor thick in the small space between them. But Esther leaned in, too, because to be fair, she had endured stenches much worse than this one. "This Reuven boy, he is still alive."

"*Alive*? Where?"

"Well, I cannot confirm that, but I can tell without a doubt that this boy is going to be a famous man some day. Very, very famous, and everybody is going to be watching this young man and wondering at his fate."

"Oh, this is wonderful news!" Esther exclaimed, but the man's countenance was severe. "There is more?"

"I'm afraid that with such joy there must be further sorrow," he began.

"As I said, many, many people will care for this young man and send him well wishes, but I have to tell you that there is another of these large gaps ahead in this man's life. A very sorrowful event to follow the joyous one."

"Oh no," Esther said, pulling her hands away from the professor's. "There must be something I can do to help Reuven."

"There is nothing. I cannot see a scenario in which you will be reunited with this boy as you knew him."

"I don't understand."

"You can't change this," he pronounced. "But know for certain that after the sorrowful gap in the young man's life, there will be a long, fulfilling life to follow."

"But how will I find him and tell him?"

"You will know when it is time to know."

Esther sat back in her chair. She wanted to leave this man immediately, though she believed he knew even more than he had already told her. Mindlessly, the hand he had first touched drifted into her bag in her lap, fishing for the money she had brought.

"Would you like to know more about your own life?" he asked.

"No, I think this is enough," Esther said. "I would like to pay you for your help with Reuven."

"Okay then. That'll be five dollars, thank you so much. And if you have any friends who wish to partake of my services, I will be in Amarillo for exactly one more week. Or if you yourself wish to come back . . . I can offer you half price on another reading."

"Okay, well, thank you," Esther managed. She gave the man five dollar bills and stood to leave.

"The sorrow is the same type of sorrow you and your husband endured," Professor Mr. Stevens said as Esther approached the door. "I am speaking, of course, of the kind of sorrow that one can survive."

"Thank you," Esther said, and soon she was in the dusty bright Polk Street sunlight in front of the hotel, and a cable car was clicking down the block toward her. Esther stepped onto the car and dropped her coin into the box. She wondered about exactly what kind of sorrow there was that one could not survive.

Back at their home, Esther could tell before opening the front door and ascending the stairs that something was wrong. *What now?*

Shmuel was at the kitchen table, holding a dripping wet cloth over his eyes. He could tell it was her without seeing. They could always tell. "Mama?" he whined.

"What happened to you?" she asked, pulling the cloth from his eyes. Two purple, red, and orange circles spun out around both of them. "Oh my!" She almost wanted to laugh at her masked son.

"Two guys beat me up."

"At work?"

"After."

"Where?"

"In town."

"Where in town?"

"I don't know."

"Shmuel Lipshitz, if you went to that Gem Lake pool again, I'm going to beat you myself."

"I didn't go."

"Where did this happen then?"

"After work."

"Where?"

Shmuel stood up, though wobbly, and slowly made his way down the hall to his bed on the couch. He practically fell onto the cushions, letting out a moan that sounded dangerously similar to Hersh's.

Esther followed him into the living room with her hands on her hips. She wondered whether Professor Mr. Stevens saw this coming and just neglected to tell her. "I have to go collect your sister at the Resnicks'.

We'll discuss this when I get back." Esther paused. "Do you need anything?" Shmuel shook his head slowly and let out another Hersh-moan.

When the father of all moaners came home later that evening from peddling way out on the eastern outskirts of Amarillo, father and son sat at the kitchen table after Esther cleaned up. Esther worked on repairing Hersh's suspenders in the living room, Miriam playing with a doll on the floor beside her. Straining, she could just hear when they started to converse.

After a long silence, Shmuel admitted softly, "I was at the pool."

"What happened?"

"I took my clothes off to change into the bathing suit, and two guys looked at me naked and said I was a Jewsie, and no Jews allowed."

"For this they beat you?"

"They said Mama was a whore and you were a Jewsie Christ-killer."

Esther could hear Hersh exhaling loudly, and imagined him rubbing his hand over his face and pushing thumbs into eyes.

"Is this somehow new information to you?" Hersh asked.

"I had to fight them."

Silence.

And then: "Did you at least get to take a swim?"

"No."

Esther accidentally pricked herself with the sewing needle and instinctively sucked on the fingertip.

July 24, 1913

Ben removed his hat from the peg behind the kitchen storage door and placed it just so on his head before stepping out into the damp heat of the late morning. The stench of just-past-turned meat in his hair made Ben want to take a trip out to Coney Island for a swim. But he hadn't been to the HIAS office in a month, and he'd been promising himself for at least a week that he'd go there after work at the cafeteria that day. Plus, he didn't want to be accused of not caring. Which he did. Care, that is. But he did know in both his head and heart they'd never see Reuven again, living or dead.

The fairies had been in again last night, yakking it up and simpering away, teasing Ben any time he'd pass by with a load of dishes or potatoes from the basement. Ben admitted to himself that he'd made three extra nonessential trips just to pass by their table. This one fairy everyone called Misha, with powder and rouge on his face like a woman, was especially relentless, asking Ben questions he didn't know the answers to. And then everyone would laugh when he couldn't answer. Half of Ben wanted to sit down and joke with them, but the other half wanted to join some of the other customers in frowning at the fairies who came there a couple of nights a week and chattered late into the morning hours. They were indeed shameless, embarrassing, and frightening degenerates. But they were also beautiful creatures, Ben thought—especially Misha with his ropy thin body, dark skin, oiled-back wavy hair.

Ben pushed the idea of Misha's shirtless torso out of his mind even though he could feel the thought trapped and swirling somewhere between his legs. The more he tried to push the image out, the more persistently it surged as he waded through the thick lines of shoppers and pushcarts on Willet Street. His head firmly planted elsewhere, Ben promptly tripped over a heavy sack of something on the ground beside a cartful of fish. Lying there with a better view of it, Ben realized the sack was actually a drunken tramp who'd grabbed his leg and was begging for money. He scooted away from the tramp, now crawling toward Ben through a fetid puddle of water fed by the cart of rotting fish above them. The man looked at Ben with a slightly opened mouth and expressionless eyes, and Ben recognized him from the saloon on First Avenue, but the man didn't recognize Ben. He fished through the front pocket of his vest and found a couple pennies for the man, who reached out his hand in front of him. But he couldn't hold it up off the ground for very long, and so the outstretched arm rested on the ground between them. Ben dropped the pennies into the man's palm, which he noticed was crisscrossed with deep red lines and scabbed all over. When the man closed his fist around the pennies, Ben saw that two of the nails on the four visible fingers were completely missing—oozing yellow pus and crusted blood from the places the nails should've been.

Ben stood up and brushed off his pants. He made a right on East Broadway and continued down to the Hebrew Society building, climbing the stairs to the office yet another useless time. He knew his mother and father didn't really expect him to come here each week anymore, but in some ways it felt like disrespecting Reuven not to.

"Hello, son, how are you doing?" Jonathan asked when Ben reached his office and stood respectfully outside the door with his hat in his hand behind him.

"Fine, thank you, sir," he replied.

"It's good to see you," Jonathan said. "It's been a long time, no?"

"Yes, well," Ben managed.

"You're looking well."

"Thank you," Ben said, embarrassed. "Has there been anything new I might report to my parents?"

Jonathan shook his head in that barely traceable way he did. It seemed like he never actually wanted to say "no," and so tried not tempting fate by refusing to acknowledge the negative with this almost imperceptible shake of his head.

"How's the new job?" he asked then.

"Oh, just great," Ben said, remembering the lisping fairies and then standing a little taller and puffing his chest out a bit more. "I'm making a great wage. Thank you so much for the letter."

"No problem. It is both my job and my pleasure," Jonathan said, moving a stack of paper from one side of his desk to the other. "And your mother? Any news from Texas?"

"She's doing well. Both she and my father," Ben said. He knew that what Jonathan really wanted to ask was, "Did your mother mention me in a letter?" or something like that. And she had, in almost every letter she'd written since the day the Lipshitzes arrived at Uncle Avi's house in Texas. She'd told Ben to thank Jonathan profusely and send him her wishes every time Ben went to the HIAS building. What kind of wishes she never specified, but Ben did as his mother asked that first time. There was something a little too ardent in Jonathan's response to that first message, though, that made Ben promise himself never to pass along his mother's greetings again. He added then, "It seems my brother Shmuel has become quite the student at the high school in Amarillo."

"That's wonderful. Just wonderful," Jonathan said.

"And he has a job for the summer," Ben added.

"Yes, wonderful to pitch in." Jonathan's hands drifted to flipping through some of the piles of paper.

"Well, thank you again for everything," Ben added.

"Sure, yes, thank you for coming in," he said, standing quickly and walking Ben to his office door. "There's a couple of leads we might have with a new fellow who works with records on Ellis Island."

"It's okay," Ben said, knowing what this was.

"See you then. What, another month or so?" he asked, but this only served to underscore how futile these visits actually were. "Please tell your mother—and father of course—that I send them my best wishes in your next letter, and that we're still working hard on the boy's case."

"I will tell them," Ben agreed, putting his hat back on his head. "Thank you."

"'Sunday, after attempt after attempt to save me had failed, I began to lose confidence. I prayed and prayed continuously. Sometimes I would be in a stupor. I could hear people coming in, but they seemed far away. I could hear voices, but I do not remember what was said. Sunday night I slept some. I dreamed of angels and I awoke praying.'"

Esther held her hand to her heart. "Oh my, Avi. This poor boy."

"Wait, he goes on," Avi said, folding the front page of *The Amarillo Daily Sun* in half and then halving it again. "'Tuesday morning I thought to myself, "Four days down here in this cave and no nearer freedom than I was the first day. How will it end? Will I get out or—" I couldn't think of it. It doesn't frighten me. I have faced death before. It doesn't frighten me, but O God, be merciful! I keep on praying. I say, "O Lord, dear Lord, gracious Lord Jesus Christ all-powerful, get me out if it is Thy will, but Thy will be done." I know I am going to get out. I feel it. Something tells me to be brave, and I am going to be.'"

"Oh, may Jesus bless you, Floyd Collins," Esther exclaimed, and tears were pouring from her eyes.

"What?" Avi asked sharply.

"This poor, poor boy."

" 'May Jesus bless you'?" Avi asked through one of his faces, causing Esther to feel insignificant in the way that only an older brother can.

"Well, this is what he believes in, Jesus," Esther said.

"And he's asking Jesus to save him, but not if Jesus doesn't want to?" Avi asked.

"I don't know. This poor, poor boy," Esther repeated, blotting the corners of her eyes with one of Hersh's kerchiefs. She stood and wiped the kitchen countertop with the kerchief when she was done wiping herself. "He's not going to get out of there, is he?"

"I don't believe so," Avi responded, shaking his head. He wanted to add, *And I don't care,* Esther knew, but in deference to his sensitive sister, he decided against it. Avi could most likely think of a fate—many fates in fact—worse than being trapped in Sand Cave in the middle of Kentucky. Esther could too, if she thought about it for a short moment.

"What is this, 'spelunking'?" Esther asked, composing herself.

"Going in and out of the caves," Avi replied.

"But why?"

"I don't know. The men, they go in the caves for money."

"You mean there's money in the caves?"

"No."

Esther looked at him. "What then? Is there gold or diamonds down there?"

"I don't know. No," he said, exasperated. "People want to go into the caves and so when you find a cave and it's your cave, then you can make the people pay—or something like this."

"Oh," Esther said, but she still didn't see why anybody would pay to go inside a cave. Avi could be like a husband sometimes, Esther thought, not a brother at all. He might be the kindest one living, but Avi was still a man, one with all the frustrations that are their birthrights. "Well, I just don't understand this," she added, hoping to end the conversation.

"The goyim," Avi said after a moment, sneaking a peek at his sister above the newspaper.

Esther finally laughed, and Avi laughed with her. And then Esther remembered why she asked her brother over on these evenings when the house was so still and empty, Hersh staying late in the country on deliveries way up in the panhandle, Miriam at work downtown and then joining friends afterward for a late picture show.

Just Esther and Avi again, if even for a moment, like when they were kids in Russia, and she would look into her brother's sweet brown eyes and feel like everything would be okay—that she would one day marry a boy just like Avi. Who would then turn into the kind of man who would take whatever wasn't okay and make it so.

Avi turned back to the folded newspaper in his hands and continued reading about Collins, the man who stopped the whole country when he got his foot stuck under some rock in a cave in Kentucky. With his back to her like that, his shirtsleeves rolled up under a vest, head tilted forward so she couldn't entirely see the tan spot of skin that had appeared in the thinning swirl of his crown over the course of almost eighteen years in Texas, Avi wasn't quite Avi.

If Esther blurred her eyes, Avi might as well be Hersh there at her kitchen table, sipping coffee just the way he liked it. Sometimes she confused how each of them took it—two sugars and no milk for one of them; one sugar, a splash of milk for the other. It could almost be an entire lifetime spent together and ending up in this, her second kitchen in Texas—third in America. Their children all dead or grown. Avi's angel Leah vanished in the tsar's smoke. Shmuel taken from them, once when the Jewish Welfare Board came to town and charmed him away to the war. And a second time, when the war was over, after Esther received a preprinted "I've arrived" postcard signed with his name and saying he was safe and due home in a few weeks. It was just two weeks after the postcard arrived that another letter from the army appeared in the mailbox, saying Shmuel had passed away from influenza at Camp Dix in New Jersey.

And Reuven, Esther must have whispered aloud then, because Avi looked up at her. Truth was, she didn't think of him as much anymore. Nobody uttered his name.

Now Esther wasn't certain whether she'd actually spoken the name or not, but the way her brother looked at her told Esther Avi knew exactly what she had been thinking—about them together like this, practically husband and wife, somehow outliving most of their kids and never asking why. Women of fifty don't blush, but what blood there was left in Esther for these sorts of frivolous things rushed into her face and filled her cheeks then, pulsated in the skin under her eyes, and she could not look into her brother's face.

"You know the strangest thing with the Collins situation," Avi began again, looking down at the paper. "This reporter fellow who goes into the cave every day and talks to Collins for his newspaper articles."

Esther emptied a pot that was soaking in the sink. She watched the water pour out. Not really the water, but rather what she could see through it—the scratched white porcelain of the sink, stained a brownish-red in the nicks on the surface. Through the water, the gashes seemed larger, more grotesque in some way. But soon the water ran out, and the sink was just the sink again.

"You know what I'm saying?" Avi continued. "He is stuck there and this little man, Skeets Something, he wiggles down there every day—maybe he could get stuck also—and brings Collins food, water, a blanket. And just talks to him and writes down what the boy says. But he can't do anything to get him out."

Esther turned to Avi, placing her wet palms on the counter behind her.

"Listen," Avi said, tapping the newspaper and reading: "'Now, fellow [this is what he calls me]' the reporter Skeets writes this, you know, telling us that Floyd calls him 'fellow,'" Avi explained. "'You better go out and get warm. But come back,' this is Floyd telling the Skeets man. 'You are small and I believe you are going to get me out. I want you to tell everybody outside that I love every one of them, and I'm happy because so many are trying to get me out. You go out now, but don't leave me too long. I want you with me and I'll keep helping all I can to move some of this rock.'" Avi shook his head and sighed, noisily tossing the paper onto the kitchen table and settling into one of his coughing fits.

"Oh my god, Avi," Esther exclaimed. Avi stopped hacking when a small saucer fell into the sink, shattering to pieces. "This is him."

"What?"

"This Floyd boy, this is him, I know it is," she continued.

"What did you break?" Avi asked, standing and joining his sister at the sink.

"This is Reuven," Esther insisted. Her gaze drifted out the kitchen window at Avi's dusty Model T, which was parked in the driveway, the "Wolf's Dry Goods and Supplies" sign affixed to the driver's-side door.

"What are you talking about?" Avi asked.

"The man, the professor said he would be very famous and then something very bad would follow," Esther explained quickly. "Yes, I'm quite certain of it."

Avi placed his hand on Esther's shoulder and pulled her into an embrace. Esther pushed him off and went to the newspaper on the table. She flipped back to the front page, where there was a photo of a hole in the ground and many men standing around it with their hands on their hips, but nothing of this Floyd Collins boy's face.

She skimmed the article as fast as she could. "Help me," she said to Avi.

"Help you what?"

"Help me see what this boy looks like," she insisted, but the words were blurring in front of her eyes as she attempted to read and comprehend them.

"Esther," Avi said forcefully. "Tell me what you are doing."

"Sandy-haired," she exclaimed, pointing at the paper. "He is a sandy-haired boy. Many blond boys get sandy-colored hair when they grow."

"Esther?"

She sat back down on one of the kitchen table chairs. Her hands began to shake, and Esther thought she might vomit. Avi sat next to her.

"Esther?" Avi repeated, pushing the paper beyond Esther's reach. "Please, what's happening?"

"Avi, you must not tell anyone," Esther began, "not Hersh, Hannah, nobody, please."

"Okay."

"Promise me."

"Yes, yes, I promise. What?"

"Well, I visited this man who knows things about the future, he was at the Hotel Amarillo, and I paid him and he told me this was Reuven, that I would know when it was Reuven. He said my boy was still alive and going to be very famous and spoken about by many, many people, but that a great sorrow would follow."

Avi sat silently. He looked concerned.

"This is Reuven," Esther insisted.

Avi didn't seem to know what to say.

"I am his mother and he said I'd know, and now I know, this is my boy."

"This is not Reuven," Avi said finally.

"Oh, it is," Esther said. "I am certain of it."

"When did you go see this man?"

"This is my boy. This is our Reuven."

"Esther, when?" Avi repeated. "When did you visit this man?"

"I don't know, maybe ten years now."

"This is not Reuven," Avi insisted. "This man at the hotel is a con artist. And besides, this Floyd, he's a grown man, and Reuven, he would still be a young man of what? Twenty years now?"

"How old is Floyd?" she asked, grasping for the paper. Avi grabbed it from her before she reached it.

"Let me look," Avi said. "This is no good for you to get yourself so upset."

"Look then," Esther said, crossing her hands on her lap calmly, though she could still feel them trembling.

"This is not him."

"Read."

"I will," Avi said, folding back the paper so he could view the front page. "But this is not him." Avi silently and slowly skimmed the many columns about Floyd. Though he'd been here longer than his sister, Avi hadn't picked up written English as quickly as Esther. She shifted audibly in her chair several times as she waited for him to finish.

"Well?" Esther prodded after another few minutes.

"Please."

Esther stood up again, went to the sink, picked up the pieces of shattered saucer, and dropped them into the garbage pail. She returned to the table and sat again. "So?"

"Ah, yes, here," Avi said, and he looked proud of himself. "Here, the man is thirty-six years old."

"Where?"

"Right here, you see?" Avi pointed to the third article on the page about Floyd and his previous life on the Collins family farm.

"This is a mistake then," Esther said.

"No, there is no mistake," Avi insisted, rising and dropping the newspaper into the garbage on top of the saucer.

"What are you doing?" Esther asked.

"Leave it be."

"No, a mother knows," she insisted. "Mothers know."

"No, Esther."

"The professor said it would be so."

Avi shook his head and leaned up against the kitchen sink, staring at Esther, who remained seated at the table. The uncontrollable trembling in her hands began to subside, but she knew she needed to remain calm on the outside if she was going to convince Avi this was his nephew. They must do something to help save the boy.

The two sat in silence for some time before hearing Hersh pull into the driveway in the Wolf's delivery truck. Brother and sister made eye contact, and though she could tell he was concerned about her, Esther knew Avi wouldn't dare betray her to Hersh.

Soon Hersh opened the front door, smiling idiotically. "Avi, good to see you," he said. "And good evening, my lovely bride." He kissed Esther on the forehead.

"How was the drive?" Avi asked.

"Great," Hersh said, taking off his coat and washing his hands in the sink. "Though I can tell you my back aches all over, the whole thing."

Esther rose and put an already prepared plate of food on the table. She then bent to retrieve the paper out of the garbage.

"Thank you," Hersh said, sitting down before the food and tucking a napkin into his shirt. "Smells good."

Esther tucked the newspaper behind the mixing bowls and sat back down next to Hersh as he began eating. She remained silent, staring out the window into the dark sky. Avi too, silent.

After swallowing a few bites, Hersh looked up from his food, then back and forth between his wife and brother-in-law. He rose and poured himself a glass of water before sitting down to resume eating.

A few more bites, Hersh's chewing audible. He looked again at Esther and Avi, neither of whom had moved. "What is it?" he asked.

Avi coughed, shook his head, and raised his shoulders simultaneously. Esther said nothing.

"Is there something I need to know?" he repeated. "Esther?"

"No," she said.

Hersh looked at Avi. And everybody knew what Hersh was thinking. Again with the secrets between Esther and Avi—something between them that Hersh never, in over thirty years, ever had with his own wife. Ten thousand miles they came, and still, Hersh playing second to Avi. Hell, Hersh finally caving in and working for his brother-in-law when it became crazy not to. Esther heard it all the time, even if it wasn't actually audible. They all did.

"No problems with the deliveries?" Avi asked then, believing himself to be changing the subject.

"No, nothing," Hersh said. "I collected from Smith and Johnson, made it all the way up to Dumas with the hardware."

"Did Campo settle up?" Avi asked.

"I didn't get it from him, no."

"What?" Avi asked. "You didn't get the cash from Campo?"

"No."

"Mr. Wolf has cut off his credit, you know that?"

"I know, I know," Hersh said.

"Well, what?"

"How's he supposed to make any profit to pay us if he doesn't have anything to sell?"

"I can't believe you screwed this up," Avi said. "Mr. Wolf is going to be so upset with me."

"I'll go back there Friday," Hersh offered. "He said he'll have it by Friday."

"He always says he'll have it on Friday. And we don't have any more deliveries up north on Friday," Avi said, rubbing the back of his neck with a palm. "We need you in town Friday, and we can't afford to give up the truck all day just for that asshole Campo."

"I don't know what to tell you," Hersh said.

Avi sighed loudly.

Esther interjected, "I'm not feeling very well. I'm going to lie down."

"What's the matter?" Hersh demanded, as Esther disappeared down the hall. Then to Avi, "Is she okay?"

"She's fine," Avi said. "What about Campo?"

"I don't care about Campo!" Hersh scraped the remains from his plate into the garbage pail and noisily deposited the dishes into the sink. "I'm going to check on my wife."

"Hersh, wait."

"I don't care, Avi," he said. "Tell Wolf to take it from my pay until I can collect from Campo."

"You don't have to do that," Avi conceded.

"Then what?"

"I don't know, but just don't do this again."

"Dock my pay."

"I won't do that," Avi said.

The radio Avi bought for Hersh and Esther then crackled in the living room, the volume having just been turned up considerably: " . . . *following the Collins case, I have some sad news to report from Cave City, Kentucky,*" the announcer began. *"After a final futile attempt at tunneling down to him from above, the fearless young man has finally perished—way too prematurely in his sandy grave, I might add."*

When the radio's volume was turned down, both Avi and Hersh heard Esther sobbing in that way women do.

"And in other news, the sudden deaths of those two Ohio State students appear to be the work of a murderer. According to university officials, strychnine was apparently mixed into capsules that were administered to the now dead students at the university dispensary. A lunatic's work is feared in the two deaths, as well as a host of other illnesses in several other students who also received the capsules issued for treatments of colds over the last five days."

Esther knew Avi would live—of course she did—and yet when Hannah opened the door to their home and led Esther back to look into her brother's sickroom, she couldn't help but also peek briefly into a world she'd yet to occupy: one with Avi not in it.

"Hi, my boy," she said to him. He had gotten so bad over the last year.

Esther wished Avi's silly wife Hannah weren't standing so desperately close. And she found herself smiling inside that Hannah could not make a child during the last few years with her husband. Avi didn't want another—not after Leah—but he agreed to try for Hannah. Esther stepped in front of Hannah then, cutting off her view of Avi through the doorway, and carefully padded over to the bed and placed a hand on the scratchy wool blanket over her brother's legs. They were thin as pitchforks.

"I brought the paper again," Esther said with exaggerated enthusiasm, lowering herself onto the chair beside the bed. Avi smiled weakly.

"Okay if I go to the grocery?" Hannah asked. "You can stay awhile?"

"I can stay all night," Esther said.

"Oh, there's no need for that. I'll be back soon," Hannah assured Esther, smiling. She pulled the door shut behind her.

"How are you feeling?" Esther asked. The bumpy ridges around his sunken eyes were now yellowish-green.

"I'm dying."

"No you're not," Esther said, "don't be silly."

"This is the time."

"No, it's not. Let me read you some of the newspaper."

"You prefer it here to home, right?" he asked.

"Of course, of course I do. Why are you talking about this crazy thing?"

"I wish I could stay," he said, trailing off and punctuating a short silence with a loud, seemingly painful gulp in his throat.

"Oh, don't be so severe. Water?"

Avi shook his head.

"Shall I read?" Esther asked, but Avi didn't respond.

"Okay, here: 'Radio fans of Amarillo and the Plains had the pleasure yesterday at noon and again at six-thirty last night of hearing Harry M. Snodgrass, acclaimed by thousands all over the world as King of the Ivories, over local station KGRS.' Did you hear this? I must've missed it," Esther said.

"'Telephone calls flooded the station while the pianist played on the air and telegrams were received for several hours afterward.' Okay, this is rather boring . . ." Esther scanned the paper.

"'Youth drowned in creek near Higgins'? Oh, look here, the Lindbergh boy took off in his plane from New York yesterday, and with only a couple hours of sleep in the last sixty," Esther started. "I don't know how wise that is since he has to fly so far, but . . . Look here, they say he is noted for his practical jokes. Would you like to hear about his practical jokes?"

Avi nodded.

"'One of Lindbergh's favorite tricks was to put a cricket in another pilot's bed and when it was discovered, to tell the poor frightened soul it was a scorpion.' That doesn't sound very fun. Let's see . . . 'According to one of his financial backers, Lindbergh does not like to smoke, chew, drink—even coffee, nor does he enjoy the movies. He does not stay up late at night and hasn't any use for dancing or girls.' Well, what on earth *does* he do, I wonder?" Esther asked.

"Hopefully fly," Avi said softly.

Esther looked at her brother then. "Yes, hopefully he can fly," she said.

Avi closed his eyes and seemed to fall asleep in mere seconds. The sun was low in the sky, slowly pushing shadows across the headboard behind Avi's head. Esther put her hand on his chest; it rose and fell for two labored cycles before she pulled away. Esther then folded the newspaper and dropped it to the floor. She removed her shoes and carefully climbed into bed next to her brother. Avi tried to move over to accommodate Esther, but she whispered, "Shh," and his body went limp. She watched his chest some more.

Esther curled into herself and pressed up against her brother's side. There was no warmth in him. None. She refused to believe this was a sign of anything other than the draft coming in from the open window. Esther closed her eyes and concentrated on Avi's breathing, trying to time her own with the rhythm of his. But she couldn't, because it was too slow, and Esther found herself gasping for air after three or four attempts at taking Avi-sized breaths.

Esther fell asleep then, for who knows how long. She was abruptly awakened by shouts and hollers, car horns, cowbells, sirens, and an infinite number of other peculiar noises coming from the streets outside. Esther shot up in the darkened room. The racket crescendoed. She was certain it was a military attack of some sort, an accidental explosion, or a celebratory parade—or perhaps some bizarre combination of all three. Since Avi did not budge beside her, Esther assumed she was having another one of her dreams. So when the ceiling silently cracked open above them, and the roof shingles peeled back, exposing Avi's bedroom to the sky, Esther thought nothing of it.

The fire siren relentlessly screamed at its highest pitch, practically drowning out all of the other commotion. Some stars twinkled expectantly in the purple sky above her and Avi's bed. She checked again to see if her brother was awake and observing this as well, but he wasn't anything close to conscious.

A cloudy spirit swirled in the air above the opened roof then, and at first Esther was frightened, but when she realized it was just God, she grew calmer. Maybe He was upset with her for not being observant during all these years in America. But what else was she supposed to have done? A coughing, mechanical purring almost like laughter began to drown out the din, and soon after, Esther saw a small biplane sputtering by overhead. It circled above the opened roof a couple of times before chugging off in the direction of downtown. Esther hoped the plane didn't spray those chemicals they used for crops on Avi and her.

In a rare tender moment between them, Hersh had once told Esther that he constantly saw things like this in the sky or on the streets in Russia—the "swirling spirits," he called them. She didn't believe him, and he never mentioned it again. This, now, was obviously what Hersh had been talking about then, but she would never admit it. Esther wanted to wake Avi to show him, but he needed his rest. They were beautiful, the swirly spirits. The sounds from town were still so thunderous, but now there was a sort of whispering emerging over all of the competing noise. Esther decided it was just God again, telling her that He understood who was her first, last, and only love, but that she would need to find a way to let him go.

The sirens rose and fell so many more times as Esther slid back down next to Avi on the hard mattress. She pulled the covers up over his shoulders and returned a hand to his chest. It rose and fell, almost in time with the sirens' wailing. Esther still sensed the frenetic buzzing of all the people in the streets outside—even after she wedged herself up against her brother's body until she could hear only his mucous breaths beside her ear. There was something electric in the hairs on her arms, the back of her neck. She closed her eyes once more.

"Esther, Esther." It was Hersh, tapping her shoulder. "Esther, we have to go home now."

"What?" Esther opened her eyes. The room was now lit by a small, bare bulb on the ceiling, and the roof was mended as though it had never split apart. Esther searched above her for any telltale seams, but there were none. Hersh pulled his wife up to a sitting position on the edge of the bed.

She looked back at her brother, who had not moved. "I can stay the night," Esther offered sleepily.

"No, thank you so much," she heard Hannah's voice say, but she could not yet see from where.

"Thank you for coming to get me," Hersh said to Hannah.

"We'll see you tomorrow," Hannah said, and now Esther could see the shrew there, seated on the chair by Avi's bed, the one Esther had occupied earlier. Had Esther just referred to her sister-in-law as a "shrew"? She hoped she hadn't said it out loud. Perhaps she too was running a cancerous fever like her brother. Hersh held Esther's elbow as he guided her toward the bedroom door.

"Thank you," Hersh said.

Sporadic shouts burst out of the darkness as Hersh put Esther in the passenger seat of Avi's car and shut the door behind her. After he went around to the driver's side and started up the engine, Hersh ardently reported: "Lindbergh did it, he made it," and proceeded to tap the horn every few seconds as they drove by bunches of revelers on the street.

The Amarillo Daily Sun landed facedown, first thing in the morning, on the far edge of Esther's and Hersh's driveway. Before Esther even bent to pick it up, she knew that there would be a large photograph on the front page of Charles Lindbergh. Before confirming this, Esther read: "Lindbergh Does It! The 'Flying Fool' Lands in Paris after 33½ Hours of Constant Flight," across the top fold of the paper. *Thirty-three and sixty is ninety-three, minus three. The boy had no sleep in ninety hours,* Esther calculated. She flipped the paper over.

And then there it was: his serious face, the first time she'd ever seen it. Like this at least. The shape of the head, the hairline, the ears. It was partially in profile, this photo, with the boy looking slightly upward and into the distance with his brow set sternly, seemingly focused on different shores even then. The otherwise constant fluttering sensation in Esther's chest subsided momentarily.

Esther took the newspaper, still folded, into the kitchen, where Hersh was enjoying a cup of coffee. Because Hersh could do things like that, enjoy a cup of coffee.

"Come with me to Avi and Hannah's," she said.

"I think they would like some time alone," Hersh replied. "Maybe we could visit a bit later?"

"Take me now, please."

Esther didn't wait for Hannah to come to the door. She let herself in through the back and went directly to Avi's room. Hersh followed behind, apologizing loudly into empty rooms before Hannah emerged from the rear bedroom, startled by the commotion.

"I'm sorry, so sorry," Hersh said to her.

Esther planted herself on her knees next to Avi's bed. Avi opened his eyes slowly as soon as he felt his sister's hands on him. Hersh and Hannah stood in the doorway watching.

Esther recoiled when she saw the dead look in Avi's eyes. It seemed her entire body began perspiring from every pore then. But just for one chilling second—before she remembered the photo of the boy in the paper.

"Hello," Avi said softly.

"Please, may I have one simple moment alone with my brother?" Esther asked. She had brought Hersh along to occupy Hannah, and now he wasn't even doing that much.

"He needs to rest," Hannah insisted.

"Yes, Esther, let's have a cup of coffee and visit with Hannah," Hersh echoed, "and then we shall visit Avi when he's had a chance to rest some more."

"Come to read me the news again?" Avi asked Esther. "About the flying boy?"

"Please?" Esther shrieked, and it came out louder than she'd intended. She didn't wish to startle Avi, but she did want more than anything for the two audience members behind her to disappear. Hersh and Hannah finally stepped back from the doorway and receded into the hallway. Esther rose to close the door and returned to Avi's bedside.

"How are you feeling, my love?" she cooed, but in truth, she didn't have time for an answer. Nor did she necessarily want to hear what that answer would be.

"I think somewhat improved from yesterday."

"Please, listen," Esther said, unfolding the paper.

"Yes, read to me about Paris."

"No, Avi, listen, please try to listen," Esther said, now whispering. "Look at this photograph." Esther held the front page up to Avi as if she were trying to sell him a copy on the street.

"Closer," he said, trying to focus his dazed eyes. "Oh yes, I see, what a handsome fellow."

"No. This is *him*," Esther said even softer. "This is for certain him."

Avi looked at Esther for a moment as though he didn't understand. She nodded her head spastically, holding his gaze, and soon Avi coughed wildly. "Now I don't feel so good," he said.

"Do you need some water?" she asked, but Avi shook his head, still coughing.

After the fit subsided, Avi tried to sit up against the pillows but abandoned the idea after a few failed attempts. Esther watched him struggle, waiting for him to catch on. If he could only see, he would know. And then he couldn't die.

"What about it?" she prompted. "Do you see it? It's him. It's uncanny, it's *him*."

"Esther, no," Avi said then. "No, please—"

"Yes, this time it is for certain. You see, right here: He is a 'sandy-haired son of the Midwest,'" she insisted.

"No, no, please," Avi pleaded.

"Maybe this family, they couldn't make a baby and they maybe bought him from a disreputable person at Ellis Island, you know these things happen, and—"

"Esther," Avi interrupted.

"You see this, right?"

"Esther," he continued, "please try to love Hannah for me."

"How old does this boy look—maybe twenty-five years? This is Reuven's age exactly."

"Please, no."

"I must warn him," Esther continued. "He must know that a great tragedy will befall him soon."

"Esther, please. Let him go."

"I have to find out his precise age."

"No, you have to let him go."

"They'll know at the newspaper office. I'll go downtown and be right back with this information to prove to you."

"Please," Avi repeated again. "Let the boy go." But Esther did not hear, because she was out the front door and down the block, climbing onto the streetcar before Hersh or Hannah or anybody else would be able to catch her.

At the newspaper, all the men were running around the office, and papers were literally flying with details of the transatlantic journey. Esther refused to leave until the receptionist allowed her to speak with one of the reporters. She sat for two hours before a man came out, shirtsleeves rolled up and without a necktie.

Esther recognized him from Shmuel's old school. He wasn't supposed to do this sort of thing, but the boy—well, really a man now—told Esther he'd try to get the information she requested. He probably felt guilty that Shmuel had died after the war, while he was returned relatively intact to his own mother. The boy disappeared back into the mad shuffle.

Because there were several copies of it, Esther read the entire Sunday paper, front to back, and started to reread the front-page story about flooding in Louisiana: "Hundreds of families, too stubborn to evacuate, may be drowned." The *Sun* hadn't gotten the news of Lindbergh in time to get it in the morning paper. Everything else seemed positively tedious and obsolete in comparison. Esther stared at the receptionist pecking at her typewriter, but the girl would not return Esther's look. Finally a different, younger boy Esther did not recognize returned to the front office and handed her a small piece of paper with some handwriting scribbled on it:

C, Lindbrg = Feb 4 1902
Sorry it took so long — V. busy today

*   *   *

Before she saw the Wolf's delivery truck parked in front of Avi's house. Before she saw Hannah already draped in black, tiny and folded into the vise of her father's long arms. Before Hersh came scuttling toward Esther with his arms outstretched, palms shaking back and forth. Before all this, and thanks to a tiny scrap of paper folded into her palm (ink running now in perspiration), Esther had been overcome with the most satisfying and peaceful knowledge she had ever thought possible. The kind of knowledge she believed would sustain her for the rest of her days.

But on the other hand, and before the sustaining, lifelong peace and satisfaction could begin, there was this, her generally well-meaning, but often useless husband running to intercept her before she reached Avi and

Hannah's house. That look on his face. That of a child who has lost hold of his mother's hand in a busy market, only to reach up for a hand that he soon discovers is not his mother's. This, Esther finally realized at that very moment, is what her husband looked like ninety-nine percent of the time. Here he was, looking up at her once again, with nothing to say, because when it came down to it, he really didn't know who this woman at the end of his outstretched arms was.

"Esther, where did you run to? We've been looking all over," he said. And then, "I'm so, so sorry."

So if I am so calm and peaceful, she asked herself, then why am I collapsing into my husband and beating upon his chest, periodically his face, and screaming, "No, no, no!" loud enough so that the entire neighborhood can hear?

Why?

God said He knew who was Esther's first, last, and only, that's what he said. But nobody, not even God, really knows. She was sorry for not being observant any longer. Really, she was. But it was nearly impossible. "Why?" she screamed, and Hersh held her. He didn't tell her to be quiet, though everyone was looking at them. Mr. Wolf approached. "Why, why, why?" she wailed.

"Shall we go inside?" Mr. Wolf suggested softly.

"Take Hersh, Miriam, anybody else, please. But not my Avi," she continued wailing.

"Maybe you can give us a moment," Hersh said to his boss, Mr. Wolf, and Esther liked him for this—especially in light of the last thing that had slipped from her lips. It had been entirely true. Hersh held her tight, and it felt good to give her weight to him, but soon Esther slid through his arms to the dirt.

"We have to let him go," Hersh said softly. "He was suffering so."

Hannah approached, the lucky black widow, and echoed what was—after "Lindbergh did it!"—rapidly becoming the chorus of the day: "Let him go."

```
1927 MAY 23=
CHARLES LINDBERGH=
IN C/O AMBASSADOR MYRON T. HERRICK=
PARIS, FRANCE=

MY DEAR BOY STOP=
IN TEARS AS I SEND THIS STOP YOU HAVE MADE
SO PROUD STOP PLEASE BE CAREFUL STOP=
MRS STOP HERSH LIPSHITZ STOP=
=
=
```

Detroit, Michigan

May 23, 1927

Dear Mrs. Evangeline Lodge Lindbergh:

How proud you must be of your boy. Though in many ways, he isn't your boy any longer, is he? He belongs to the world now, to the sky. In a sense, he is all of ours. Yours, mine.

You should be proud, as I know you are. I wonder if you have seen this photo (enclosed) of your son, from the Amarillo Daily Sun. *I had an extra copy. I thought you might like to have this stunning photo of your Charles, as I know I would were he my son. I saved one for myself as well, so please enjoy it.*

I would so love to hear news back from you, though I understand you will be quite busy in the coming months. Is it difficult not to see Charles after such a dangerous feat? Did he not require much sleep as an infant? Perhaps you don't remember that far back. I had four children of my own, and I cannot remember anything of their first five years, they grow so fast.

Yours truly,

Esther Lipshitz (Mrs. Hersh Lipshitz)
Amarillo, Texas

LINDY'S MOTHER JUGGLES FAME
ALONGSIDE SON

WELL-WISHERS SEND THOUSANDS OF MESSAGES
TO MRS. LINDBERGH

DETROIT, Mich., May 25—Mrs. Evangeline Lindbergh, mother of Captain Charles A. Lindbergh, the intrepid New York to Paris birdman, has learned that there certainly can be too much of a good thing. Today the most famous mother in the world requested that reporters extend her heartfelt gratitude to the people from all over the globe who have sent thousands of telegrams and letters since her son's death-defying transatlantic journey.

"I hope to write a letter to each person who has been so kind as to remember me, but with telegrams still pouring in, I find that it will be extremely difficult to do so," Mrs. Lindbergh said. "Please tell all of these kind souls how much I appreciate their generosity and their admiration for my boy."

A steady stream of newspapermen have been trailing Mrs. Lindbergh ever since her son landed in Paris. Some have asked for photographs and other memorabilia from the boy's earlier years, and Mrs. Lindbergh has reportedly complied in some instances.

Various newspapers have implored the famous mother to write the story of her son's life, but she has responded repeatedly that she wishes to recede from the spotlight. "I would like to rest, for it is my boy's time to be in the sun," she said with a winning smile, which seemed to be filled with unending pride.

June 1, 1927

Mrs. Hersh Lipshitz
Amarillo, Texas

Dear Mrs. Lipshitz:

Thank you kindly for your support. I will be sure to express your sentiments to my son as well, that is as soon as I see him!

Yours truly,

Mrs. Evangeline L. Lindbergh

Amarillo, Tex.

June 5, 1927

Mrs. Evangeline Lodge Lindbergh
Detroit, Mich.

Dear Mrs. Lindbergh:

Thank you for your letter. I understand that you are overwhelmed with correspondence. You are very kind to take the time to send a response to little me in Texas.

Now that I have your ear, I believe I should tell you something that will be difficult to hear. That is how it was introduced to me, so I say the same to you. Something will befall Charles in the coming months, maybe years. I do not know the exact nature of the tragedy, only that it is as certain as I am writing this to you now. It will bring much sorrow to your son's life, but my understanding of the tragedy is that it is something he will endure. I do not know what to tell him to look out for, but perhaps a wary eye might help.

I'm sorry to dampen the aura of celebration, but it would be irresponsible of me not to encourage you to communicate this to your son.

I do look forward to your response.

Yours truly,

Mrs. Esther Lipshitz

(Might you have a photograph of Charles as a child, aged maybe two or three years old? I would so love to see him as he was, blond locks and all.)

The Amarillo Daily Sun, June 5, 1927

TOO MUCH MAIL FOR MOM

MRS. EVANGELINE LINDBERGH FINDS SHE CANNOT KEEP UP WITH HER HOUSEKEEPING

DETROIT, June 3—Mrs. Evangeline Lindbergh, mother of Captain Charles A. Lindbergh, announced to the press today that she simply cannot fulfill the promise she made to herself to respond personally to all of the letters sent since her son's historic New York to Paris flight.

Attired in a green hat and green dress, and with a heart visibly full of regret, Mrs. Lindbergh said, "I have read or will read each and every message with a feeling of reverence. But I simply cannot reply to every single one." She expressed appreciation for the public's kindness because "almost without exception, the letters bear the message: 'I prayed for your son.'" The aviator's mother did add, however, that she intends to respond to a sampling of these letters and telegrams.

Mrs. Lindbergh also admitted that there was one downside to the time spent reading all of the letters of congratulation. "My housekeeping has been dreadfully neglected," she said. "My one ambition is to get my house clean again."

The Detroit Post Office has reported record-breaking amounts of mail in their system. On one day alone, 400 letters were delivered to the famous mother's home or the technical school where she teaches. Approximately 1,100 letters and 500 telegrams have reached Mrs. Lindbergh during the week since the flight which has made "Lindbergh" a household name.

Amarillo, Tex.

June 6, 1927

My Dear Ben:

I believe this letter will be hard for you to read. I have some news that is difficult, but will most certainly bring us all joy. I have not explained this to your father yet, so I ask that you not tell anybody else about this matter.

Charles Lindbergh is your brother. I am certain that you see the resemblance to Reuven. For many reasons, some that I should not explain here for reasons of security, I am certain of this fact. Charles's birthday is exactly that of Reuven's. Well, one day off, but it is very curious. Reuven's, you might remember, is February 3, 1902, and Charles's February 4, 1902. Reuven knew his birth date, I am certain of it, so when he was given to the Lindbergh family, perhaps he communicated this date to them, confusing just one day because it must have been frightening to be with this new family speaking a different language, and separated from us after such a long journey.

Do not tell the authorities yet. I believe that Jonathan at the Hebrew Society must be notified of this first; he will know what to do. I am not upset—I understand why this family might've taken Reuven to raise as their own. He was such a beautiful boy—I thought him to be quite a little American even before we arrived. I am certain this case of confused identity will be set right as soon as the "Lindbergh fever" dies down. But what is troubling me is that I know that something very bad is going to happen to Reuven, and I must find a way to notify him to be on the lookout for strange and tragic circumstances. Again, I cannot tell you here how I know this . . . Just that our desire to clear up the confusion should be amplified by this other piece of knowledge about an impending tragedy.

I do hope you will visit the HIAS office as soon as possible. Cable us back here at the usual address with any urgent news.

And Ben, your family misses you. Since Avi's death. You know, your uncle has finally passed? Since then it is even lonelier. We want you to come home as soon as this matter with the Lindberghs is settled. There will be no more reason for you to stay in New York when your family is in Texas and your brother is all over the world.

Lovingly,
Your mother

NEW YORK PREPARES FOR GREATEST CELEBRATION EVER

8,000 POLICE WILL PROTECT CITIZENS AND PARADE PARTICIPANTS— SAFEGUARDING CHILDREN A PRIORITY FOR CITY OFFICIALS

NEW YORK, June 10—When Colonel Charles A. Lindbergh arrives in New York City the day after tomorrow, he will be met with the largest celebration ever staged for an individual. Millions of people are expected to turn out for the parade, and every citizen, from young child to wizened grandfather, seems to be overflowing with excitement and anticipation for the long-awaited day. The metropolis will virtually shut down on "Lindbergh Day," as private businesses, schools, stock exchanges, and official offices will close their doors in honor of the beloved hero's visit.

Certain details of the day's events are still being settled, but once a version of the program was approved by the Colonel, Mayor James J. Walker stated that, "the city is prepared for what will be a stunning and safe day for all in attendance."

Day to Begin with a Splash

At 10 A.M. or 10:30 A.M. Monday, the flying Colonel will land in an amphibian plane near the Quarantine on Staten Island, which is situated where the very ocean that the flier crossed just weeks before meets New York Harbor. When the flier's plane, the *San Francisco*, splashes down in the harbor, he will be surrounded by another 300 or 400 boats of all stripes, as 200 planes soar overhead. The Colonel will be transferred from his plane to the mayor's dramatically decorated yacht the *Macom*, which will take the Colonel to the Battery while flowers shower down from the heavens, released from planes flying in formation overhead.

It is thought that the aviator's beloved mother, Mrs. Evangeline Lindbergh, will join her son at City Hall, although her precise time of arrival has not yet been determined.

City Explodes in Festivity

In all parts of the great metropolis, Colonel Lindbergh will be greeted with buildings blanketed in brilliantly colored bunting of all colors, as well as thousands of American, and some French flags flapping along the streets. New York's citizens could be seen as early as yesterday morning, balanced on ladders and fire escapes as they tried to make the parade route along Broadway and Fifth Avenue as festive as possible. Taxicabs and newsstands displayed photographs and lithographs of the hero, and already a phalanx of industrious hawkers of Lindbergh souvenirs began setting up shop along the avenues.

Securing the Children

Approximately 5,000 school children will be arranged on the steps of the Public Library to welcome the flier by waving small American flags, and another 25,000 children will await the Colonel near the grandstand in the Mall of Central Park. Dr. William J. O'Shea, Superintendent of Schools, notified the public about the city's plan for its children, who are surely unaccustomed to such a massive display. "The newly-established 'School Committee on Arrangements for the Lindbergh Celebration' deemed it necessary to limit attendance to pupils of the upper grades, as they felt it would be unsafe to risk having the younger children out in the unusual crowds.

"Furthermore, as the length of time the children will have to wait is uncertain, and as the day will most likely be hot, the committee has secured a host of doctors and nurses who will be in attendance at the Library, where a first aid station will be established in case any emergencies arise with the children."

June 12, 1927

NEW YORK CITY

𝕿𝖍𝖊 𝕬𝖒𝖆𝖗𝖎𝖑𝖑𝖔 𝕯𝖆𝖎𝖑𝖞 𝕾𝖚𝖓, June 12, 1927

A FINE DAY IN THE CAPITAL
FOR LINDBERGH

FAMOUS MOTHER AND SON ACCOMPANY COOLIDGES

WASHINGTON, June 11—Colonel Charles A. Lindbergh and his mother Evangeline Lindbergh accompanied President and Mrs. Coolidge first to church and then to a ceremony commemorating the sesquicentennial of the American flag at the Capitol this morning. Nearly a half a million people of all colors and creeds filled the city's streets as the Lindberghs' car passed, and in some locations the throngs broke through police lines to get a closer look at their hero.

At times the Colonel seemed rather languid and not entirely aware of the commotion surrounding his car, but his mother, looking comfortable and rested, waved and smiled at the animated crowds. The Colonel was wearing his blue serge suit and a gray felt hat, while his mother was attired in a gown of flowered chiffon in a pattern of rosena beige background. Her hat was medium-sized, fabricated from black horse hair and trimmed with festive white flowers.

Flier Silent, Mother Smiles

At one point after a visit to Arlington later that day, the Lindberghs experienced a moment of confusion. About twenty young girls of debutante age broke through police lines and rushed to Lindbergh's side as he sat upon the car. Before the guards could control them, the girls begged for his signature and tried to touch the flier's hand.

The shy boy who after landing in Paris was quoted as saying that he "liked girls, but didn't know any," showed himself to be a truth sayer, for when the girls surrounded his car, Lindbergh blushed visibly and hastily pulled his hand away as his mother smilingly looked on. The guards soon controlled the girls, and the embarrassed flier shifted his body so as to be facing away from the commotion, and stared blankly into the distance. Mrs. Lindbergh could be seen chuckling at her son's discomfiture, though neither mother nor son uttered a word as the procession continued.

Mother by Son's Side

Mrs. Lindbergh went almost everywhere with her son today, except she did not accompany him into the wards at Walter Reed Hospital. She did, however, trail behind her famous son as he addressed each in a long line of "chair cases," wounded veterans who had been wheeled outdoors for the occasion. Mrs. Lindbergh smiled kindly at the unfortunates, but she did not shake each and every one of their hands as the flier did. Both mother and son seemed genuinely affected by the visible suffering assembled before them.

When asked if she was proud of her boy's being commemorated on a postal stamp on Saturday night—the first time a living person has been honored in such a manner—Mrs. Lindbergh replied, "I've always been proud of him."

Next stop for the Lindberghs: New York City.

Ben stepped off the streetcar and headed west on foot, toward the mall in Central Park. Three taxicabs with signs on them that read "Welcome Home, Lindy!" passed in front of him—all with the flier's same unsmiling, hard face on them, his mouth fixed in a straight line, hair parted just so. Ben couldn't help but hate him a little. He entered the southeast corner of the park, strolling by the usual crowded benches along the walk. Ben finally decided upon a bench with a view of the empty bleachers set up for the next day's speeches. He sat and watched the people parading by, seemingly enjoying the warm Sunday evening. A mild breeze tickled the trees above him, and Ben took out one of the ready-made cigarettes he'd bought after getting paid last week and lit it.

He leaned back against the bench, inhaling deeply and arching his neck to gain a look directly above him. Some birds fought noisily over a worm, eventually snapping it in half before fluttering off in different directions. He wondered if this was a waste of time, if cruisers didn't come out on such crowded Sundays. *He* was here. Though there was something different—he couldn't quite name it—in the air that day, children hysterical and running in and around the empty bleachers like wild animals loosed on Central Park. A mother, alone, yelled repeatedly at her son to come down from the bleachers, but he would not obey.

Ben flicked his cigarette onto the ground and stepped on it. He strolled over to the young mother, quite distressed by then.

"I can retrieve him if you wish," Ben offered.

She looked at him oddly, the way single women often did.

"Would you like me to?" he asked.

192

"Thank you," she managed. "That would be nice."

It was growing darker, the lamps in the park just beginning to flicker. Ben scaled the skeleton of the bleachers toward the boy. When he reached him, Ben saw that the boy's arm was stuck between two beams, and he was struggling to free himself.

"Hey fellow," Ben said. The boy turned around, startled. His upper lip was a grotesque, tangled web of scars. "What's going on up here?"

"I'm stuck," the boy said softly. He talked strangely too. Ben felt sorry for this boy and knew he would grow up to be a very ugly man.

"Let me help," Ben said, bracing his back against one of the beams and gently pulling the boy's arm. It was stuck pretty good.

"I need to lift you up before we can get you out of here," Ben explained. "Okay?"

The boy did not answer with words, but just nodded slowly, staring at Ben.

"Can you wrap your other hand around my neck?" The boy did as told. "Why didn't you tell your mother that you were stuck up here?" Ben asked matter-of-factly while slowly taking all the boy's weight around his neck.

"She worries too much," he said. "Ow!" And then the boy was free, sliding down Ben's chest to a standing position on one of the benches. He rolled his wrist and extended all of his fingers several times, rubbing his forearm with his other hand.

"You okay?" Ben asked, but the boy was off, climbing down the bleachers, a little monkey.

"Thank you!" the mother yelled, waving at Ben and scolding the boy when he returned.

Ben sat on the bleachers, which grew emptier with the approaching darkness. He looked for the moon, but couldn't see it. He lit another cigarette and quietly smoked it, his feet propped on the bench seat in front of him.

"Nice work," he heard a man's voice say, Ben couldn't tell from where.

"Thanks," he said into the darkness. But soon a tall, thin, dark-haired man appeared, climbing up the seats of the bleachers, taking one with each stride.

"You must have children yourself," the man declared, sitting down next to Ben, but not near him.

"Oh no," he replied. "Cigarette?"

"I don't smoke."

"Me neither," Ben said, tossing his cigarette through the spaces in the bleachers below.

"My name's Carl," the man said, holding out a hand. Ben took it. A warm, soft palm.

"Ben."

"Nice to meet you, Ben," Carl said. "Are you planning on attending the parade?"

"No, I have to work," Ben said. "I just come up here sometimes."

"You come sometimes?"

"Yes, well, somewhat frequently," Ben added.

"My friends in Boston told me about this place; they say the Bitches' Walk is legendary," Carl whispered conspiratorially.

"Yes, the Bitches' Walk," Ben echoed, smiling. "So you're not from here?"

"No, Boston," Carl replied. "Well, Cambridge. I'm just in town for the parade."

"You came all the way to New York for the parade?"

"Yes, well, no," he stumbled. "I study culture at Harvard, so—"

"Oh," Ben broke in, nodding. But he didn't really understand.

"Plus," the man whispered, scooting closer to Ben, "don't you think Lindbergh is handsome as the devil?"

"He's my brother," Ben blurted.

Carl looked at him, confused. "What?"

"No." Ben laughed, and Carl joined in, tentatively at first but then wholeheartedly. There they were, he and a total stranger, laughing at Ben's own dear mother. He wanted it to stop. "I go for the Valentino type anyway," he offered by way of changing the subject.

"Lindy's perfection," Carl cooed, mindlessly. "That blond hair."

"You don't think 'Tino was, as you say, 'perfection'?"

Carl crinkled his nose and curled his upper lip, a gesture that, Ben mused, would have been near impossible for the boy with the harelip he'd just freed from the bleachers minutes before.

"Lindy's okay," Ben added.

"Just okay?" Carl asked, and then punched Ben on the shoulder playfully. The two made eye contact then, and held it for some time before Ben grew shy and looked away, again hoping to see the moon that continued to hide its complicated face from him.

The two men exited the park and strolled down Fifth Avenue to Carl's well-appointed hotel room just off Fifth on Thirty-first Street. The canyon of buildings was lined with banners, bunting, ribbons, and signs of all sorts, vendors setting up carts, police cordoning off certain areas, workers constructing makeshift bleachers on the sidewalks in front of the buildings. But Ben hardly paid attention to anything besides the handsome and sophisticated man striding down the avenue beside him.

In the room, after tea had been delivered on a massive silver tray, Ben tried to sip from the cup the way he'd seen in the pictures. It was the nicest room he'd ever been in, though Ben tried to act as though he visited hotels like this all the time.

Carl spoke of his studies for quite some time, the classes he taught to the younger students at Harvard, his travels abroad—and Ben tried to keep up. His mind, he had to admit, kept creeping into Carl's trousers. He didn't know what else to think, what else might come of time spent with this beautiful man from Boston who spoke so disdainfully of his father, a congressman or some such. Ben had never heard such talk. Never.

And then, after tea was finished: "Join me in bed?" Just like that. Ben took off his coat and necktie, following Carl's lead precisely. "It's okay, come on," Carl added then, sitting upon the bed and unbuttoning his trousers. "Have you not been with many men?"

"Oh, many," Ben answered, also unbuttoning his pants, but they were not clean, and they smelled of the cafeteria where he worked. Ben was embarrassed. "Maybe not like this though."

"Like this? What do you mean?" Carl asked, pulling the bedding back. A few plush pillows fell to the floor, and Ben decided not to answer. "Do you get paid then?"

"No, no," Ben insisted. "Never."

"Okay then," Carl said, crossing to unbutton Ben's shirt. Ben initially smarted at his touch. But soon the exquisite sensation of each button being loosed chilled Ben, his skin rising where the shirt's fabric brushed against it, and then, where the back of Carl's hand did the same.

What followed that evening and into the morning hours was in fact like a first for Ben. Never had a man touched him in that manner. The two had relations, over and over, each taking turns in gaining satisfaction. Sometime the next morning, Carl offered Ben the opportunity to take a bath, and drew one for him. When Ben reclined in the tub, submerged up to his nose in the deliciously hot water and inhaling the steamy air, Carl came into the washroom and soaped Ben's back gently. He had never felt anything like this, not from his mother, any trade, not a fairy, not ever. When Ben toweled himself off and came back into the room naked (for by then they had grown comfortable in this manner), Ben noticed his clothes were missing from the chair he'd piled them on the night before.

"What happened to my clothes?"

"I hope it's okay," Carl said. "I had them washed. They should be delivered in a few hours."

Ben slipped back into the bed and pushed his backside into Carl, who gently stroked the hair above Ben's ear. The sheets were soft against his member, so Ben bunched them between his legs and rolled on his side to face Carl straight on. When Ben opened his eyes after a few seconds, Carl was looking directly into them. Ben felt the shock of this in his chest before closing his eyes again and falling asleep—quite possibly the most comfortable sleep ever.

He woke with a start. Whistles, sirens, bells, shouts, clapping, all seemingly amplified by a tunnel of some sort. Carl stood by the opened window, sticking his head and chest out and straining his neck in the direction of Fifth Avenue. Ben noticed his clothes were now folded neatly over the chair beside the bed. He stretched his legs out under the sheets and extended his toes as far as he could, raising his arms above his head and locking his fingers for one divine moment.

Carl looked back and noticed Ben was awake. Carl was partially dressed in a bright white undershirt and underwear and came bounding toward Ben, launching himself onto the bed. Ben bounced and had to catch himself on the side of the mattress to avoid tumbling off.

"Lindy's coming up Fifth Avenue!" Carl exclaimed. "Can you hear it?"

Ben didn't know what to say. He reached up and pulled Carl into an embrace. At first Carl was stiff, his weight thrown off unexpectedly by Ben's awkward gesture. But soon the two were locked together, Ben rolling on top of Carl and initiating another hour of unbelievable pleasure for both. Afterward, Carl jumped up, his member pink and half swollen, bouncing against his thighs, and ran over to the window.

"Where is he?" Carl asked, pulling on his underwear. "He's late."

The skin on the back of Ben's neck chilled with each swell of the crowd on the streets below their window. Finally he joined Carl and craned his neck out the window for a look at Fifth Avenue. Ben had never seen this many happy people, anywhere at any one time. Also, what seemed like millions and millions of pieces of white paper fluttered down from the sky, swirling among the buildings and blanketing the people below.

"This is so exciting!" Carl said, bumping Ben's shoulder with his own. "Don't you think?" Ben pushed back as a response, for he continued to have nothing to say.

Well, he did have *something* to say. If Ben were to say something, it might be "Tell me everything there is to know about you, and when you are done, tell me more."

Or, "I can't imagine ever spending a day without you."

Or even, "Don't go."

But instead he just stood beside Carl, listening to the overwhelming noises from the street below. Drums and horns could be heard then, thousands of boots marching in time.

"They're coming," Carl said. He was like a child, bouncing up and down in his undergarments with his hands planted on the windowsill. "I can't wait to see him."

Ben pulled his head out of the window and came up behind Carl, placing both hands on his hips and pushing against Carl playfully from behind as he leaned out of the window. Carl looked back and asked, "You don't ever take a break, do you?"

Ben sat back down on the bed, watching Carl, who hollered out the window periodically. He came back over to the bed and located the telephone directory in the table beside the bed. "Want to help?"

Ben shook his head. "I want to watch you."

Carl proceeded to stand by the window and rip and tear the phonebook to shreds like some sort of madman. When he was covered in perspiration, and the pile on the floor was shin-deep, he scooped up the scraps in his arms and tossed them out the window.

"Oh my god, I think it's him," Carl said, a bit of paper stuck to the corner of his lips. The crowd's roar surged even louder. "It's him! It's *him*!"

Ben lay in the bed completely still, hands locked behind his head on the pillow. Who knew a pillow could be so soft? He thought of Reuven, how he hadn't been to the office in well over a year to check on him—even though Ben lied to his mother in letters, assuring her that he still went monthly. Ben tried, but he couldn't picture Reuven's face anymore. The only image he had of his brother was from the file at the HIAS office—Jonathan had given him the photograph of Reuven when Ben told him about Shmuel's death during one of their visits. Jonathan didn't seem to want Ben to be completely brotherless. Ben craved a cigarette then, badly. But he knew not to light one in front of Carl.

"It's him!" Carl repeated. "Don't you want to see? Damn, I wish all this paper wasn't in the air—I can barely see the car."

Sirens blared. Ben thought he might've heard several women screaming. It sounded almost as though they were in danger.

"I think that's his mother in the car behind him," Carl said. "You have to see this, Ben. Get up and see this. I insist you get up and see this."

By the time Ben pulled himself out of bed and popped his head out the window, all he could see was an open black car with a few dark figures on it. One of them Lindbergh. Hats flew up, paper rained down, firecrackers popped madly. What looked like a round woman in a large hat was propped up in the second car, but the white snowy paper-storm obscured Ben's view.

"Now, I've seen it," Ben said, pulling his head back into the room.

"Yes, you have," Carl said. "And what do you think?"

"What if he has to go to the toilet?" Ben asked, half seriously.

"Maybe he went at City Hall."

"Everyone would know," Ben said.

"Well, it didn't seem to be a problem on the trip to Paris."

"But he had a cup then," Ben offered.

Carl turned to him and thought for a moment. "You're crazy," he said, smiling. "But I think I like you."

He shoved Ben back onto the bed behind them. It was a free-falling sensation, Ben letting himself be pushed and pushed backward until he just let go, hoping the softness would be there to catch him. It was. Again, they made love in an even more tender way than before—throughout the rest of the parade, after the steak dinner was delivered and devoured in their room, and well into the next morning.

At some point, Ben opened his eyes when he felt Carl's skin against his own. Carl's back was covered with a layer of cold perspiration. He turned around to face Ben then, intertwining his legs with Ben's under the sheets. "What's this?" he asked woozily, touching a fingertip to the knotted scar on Ben's forehead.

"Oh, nothing," Ben said. "Something from when I was a boy."

Carl's fingers lingered on the scar, and it tingled, verging on unpleasantly, but Ben didn't want him to stop caressing it. Then Carl's hand was heavy on Ben's head, and after a while like this, he closed his eyes, and his hand dropped to the pillow.

"I've never been to Boston," Ben whispered after another few minutes, very quietly. But, it seemed, Carl had fallen back asleep. So too, did Ben.

A thin strip of bright light snuck into the hotel room through the heavy curtains and crossed over Ben's eyelids when he pushed his head deep into the down pillow. A burst of red filled the darkness inside his closed eyes, and Ben opened them quickly. The light burned, though the rest of the room was still dark.

He heard pipes popping on and off in the washroom, also from the floor above them. Ben remembered where he was and immediately reached over to run his palm over the soft, empty sheets next to him. Carl must have been in the bath. Ben fell back asleep then, for who knows how long.

When Ben finally woke up, this time for real, he noticed a chill in the room, where before it had been warm and practically aglow. The bed was still empty next to him, and Ben hoped he'd just napped for a few minutes since the last time he remembered waking up. The pipes were silent.

Ben sat up in bed then, and the room was still fairly dark, considering all the light that was trying to break in around the curtains covering the window. He surveyed the room, which was completely empty, save for last night's dirty plates and Ben's clean clothes draped neatly over the chair beside him.

"Carl?" he called, but he knew it was a stupid thing to do.

Ben stood and opened the drapes. Light shot into his eyes and they ached for a few seconds while he squinted out the window, still propped open from the day before. He poked his head out and looked toward Fifth Avenue. The streets were filled with scraps of all sorts. Three or four street cleaners worked practically silently in the streets below, their work muffled by the snowstorm they waded through.

He dressed silently in the light streaming through the window. His clothes were stiff, but cleaner than ever. Ben knew his boss would most likely fire him for skipping work the day before—especially with all the added business downtown because of Lindbergh.

Ben knew then, picking up *The New York Times* that was resting askew on the dark purple carpet in front of the hotel room door—Lindbergh perched stiffly on the folded top of his car and surrounded by mounted police during yesterday's parade—that it was most likely time for him to head west. He tucked the paper under his arm, straightened his shirt collar, and decided he would purchase a rail ticket for Texas the next morning.

The New York Times, June 14, 1927

ALONG THE ROUTE OF THE BIG PARADE

THRONG JOVIAL BUT HUNGRY

Along Forty-eighth Street, to the east of Fifth Avenue, the paper debris that remained from the Lindbergh parade caught fire close to 5 o'clock, and before the brief run of flame showed signs of expiring, a Fire Department truck had been called out. The truck did valiant work, extinguishing the blaze with one jet of the hose.

September 28, 1927

AMARILLO, TEXAS

The Amarillo Daily Sun, September 28, 1927

DALLAS FINALLY FETES
LINDBERGH TOO

EVER-PROMPT FLIER LANDS AT LOVE FIELD
RIGHT ON TIME

DALLAS, Sept. 27—After a two-hour flight from Ft. Worth via Alvarado and Waxahachie, Colonel Charles A. Lindberg landed today at Love Field, Dallas' municipal airport, at precisely the minute scheduled. Though there was a steady rain, the flying hero deftly landed the "Spirit of St. Louis" as thousands of Dallas' citizens lined the streets and gathered on rooftops around the airfield in hopes of glimpsing their hero.

City officials honored Lindbergh with an elegant banquet and presented him with a scroll of welcome. Two local schoolchildren presented their idol with an oil portrait of the Colonel's mother Evangeline, and then Mayor R. E. Burt introduced Lindbergh to the banquet guests.

"We are honored to add Dallas' name to the growing list of cities of this great country that you have graced with your presence on this tour," Mayor Burt said to the flier before presenting him to the crowd.

When Lindbergh stood to make his remarks, he was met with a roaring applause that lasted for at least five minutes. The flier officially dedicated Love Field in his brief speech, and when he concluded, the audience again cheered thunderously, reluctant to send their hero back up into the skies once again.

Lindbergh is scheduled to leave here Wednesday for Oklahoma City.

Esther dutifully clipped this latest report on the boy and added it to the hatbox on the kitchen table. Normally she kept the box hidden deep in the hallway closet, but Hersh had left early that morning for work and wouldn't be back for hours. It would be a tough sell with him, but Esther knew that if she could just get to Oklahoma City this one time, she would be able to reach Lindy to warn him in person. His silly mother persisted in ignoring Esther's warnings by letter and telegram. Esther hoped something bad didn't happen before he left Dallas on Wednesday, because she didn't know if Dallas would be where the tragedy would befall him—or perhaps it would be Oklahoma City. It could be there, then, or sometime far in the future, she knew. It was an awful burden. Esther looked at the maroon lines in her palms for a few seconds before rubbing them together rapidly in front of her nose, making a little heat.

"Miriam?" Esther called down the hall. The girl didn't respond. "Miriam!" Esther shouted even louder.

Her daughter finally emerged from the back bedroom, half dressed and in the process of tying her hair back. "What, Mama?"

"Do you think you would like to visit Oklahoma City with me?"

"Why?" she asked. "I have to work."

"You never take a day off," Esther said, cursing the department store where her daughter went each day. But in her head she was already trying to conjure another way to OKC if Miriam wouldn't accompany her.

"Yes, I do, I take three days off every week. And there's a sale on winter coats right now. It's very busy," she said before slipping back into her room.

Esther's eyes drifted down onto the story from the paper, folded on top of the pile in the hatbox. There in the first section: *"Lindberg."* *Could it be a mistake?* There never seemed to be mistakes, Esther thought.

This made Esther excited but nervous. Maybe the *Lindbergs* were a Jewish family who wanted a boy who was a Jew, but didn't look like one. Reuven would have been perfect for this. Anybody at Ellis Island would have known it instantly upon their ferry's arrival. They were waiting for a boy just like him. Esther wondered whether Ben had really asked Jonathan at the Hebrew Society about the Lindberghs. Had Jonathan then initiated this line of questioning with the men at Ellis Island? Did they know that Mr. Lindbergh Sr. was a man in the government, a powerful man?

Ben and Esther never spoke of the matter—just that once, shortly after Ben arrived in Amarillo, and the two were finally alone. He had been tired from the journey and told Esther, "Forget it, Mama. This is no good."

"I shall write Jonathan myself," she threatened.

"No, you won't," Ben said sternly. "Mama, *no*!" This was her son talking to her this way, like a dog. A son she barely recognized anymore, after so much time. He was so gaunt and pale.

It was thus useless to ask Ben to accompany her to Oklahoma City. It would have to be Hersh. Esther waited nervously for her husband to return for dinner. When she heard the Wolf's delivery truck engine growling in the driveway, Esther went out to greet Hersh, something she rarely, if ever, did.

"Hello, my love," Esther called to him.

"Is there a problem?" Hersh asked, looking around as though hoping to spot whatever it was on the exterior of their home on Tyler Street.

"Why must something always be wrong?" Esther asked, following Hersh into the house.

"Because there is always something wrong," Hersh said, placing his satchel on the chair in the hallway and going to wash his hands. Esther wondered if there was one time—just one—when Hersh didn't enter the house and cross directly to the kitchen sink to wash his hands. Esther then wondered what he possibly did with those hands throughout the day, but soon shook away the thought and continued pressing on with the topic at hand.

"Hersh," she started. "I would like to go to Oklahoma City this evening."

"What? Why?"

"Lindbergh is landing there tomorrow, and I think it is important for Miriam to see him speak."

"But Miriam works," Hersh said.

"She'll take the day off," Esther lied.

"I don't know, Esther. How will you get there? It's what, six or seven hours?"

"Something like this."

"No, this is a bad idea," Hersh said, shaking his head and wiping his hands on a dish towel. "A very terrible idea."

"Why don't you take me, then?" Esther asked.

"I cannot leave work, you know that," Hersh said. "Mr. Wolf wishes me to go up to Pampa tomorrow."

"Pampa! Perfect," Esther exclaimed. "It's half the distance."

"No it's not," Hersh said. "You don't even know what you're talking about."

"I am going to Oklahoma," Esther tried.

"How? No, you're not."

"I will."

"No," he said again. And that was, Esther knew, that.

November 7, 1927

Miriam turned the squeaky doorknob very gently, so as not to attract the attention of her mother, who was seated in the living room, darning socks that should have been tossed away as rubbish years before. Miriam could get brand-new, very-high-quality socks at significantly reduced prices, though her mother would never hear of it.

Miriam had just poked one foot out the door when she heard, "Miriam?"

"Yes?" she replied, letting the doorknob snap back into place. It made its usual loud noise—usual, that is, when one is not in the process of creeping out of the house undetected. Miriam fancied herself an expert in this arena.

"Will you be home for supper?" her mother asked. "Your brother is coming over."

"I was going to see a picture with some of the girls from the store," Miriam said, but she knew it was useless. *But your brother has been away from us so long, and . . .*

"But your brother has been in New York for so many years, and isn't it so nice when the whole family can be together?" Esther said, practically on cue. Miriam laughed to herself.

"Well, not the *whole* family," Miriam said, hoping to avoid yet another interminable dinner listening to her oldest and most tedious, yet only remaining brother tell nonstop boring stories about New York. But Miriam knew it had backfired when she saw the wounded expression on her mother's face. She felt bad, if only for a moment. Not that her mother didn't deserve it, but still, she caved, "Okay, I'll be back after work."

Esther didn't respond, and so Miriam closed the noisy door behind her and started down the block toward the bus stop. The rain had stopped, Miriam marveled, just in time for her journey to the store. She enjoyed the ride downtown, watching through the open window all the people in their winter clothes, much of which she recognized from the store. As the bus rolled along, Miriam periodically brushed the accumulating dust off the new skirt she had bought with her discount.

When Miriam turned the corner onto Polk on foot, she saw Mr. Levy opening the store's front door and hurried her step. Miriam liked being the first girl to report to work.

"Good morning," she said, scooting in beside Mr. Levy and placing her hat and jacket in the back office. Miriam set about her daily chores of cleaning the display-cabinet windows where the jewelry, perfume, and tonics were housed. Mr. Levy came in then, stomping the dirty wetness from his heavy boots on the front mat.

"How are you, Miriam?"

"Just fine, sir," Miriam answered.

"And your mother and father?" he asked, seemingly just to be nice, for Mr. Levy was a busy man.

"They are well," Miriam said. "Thank you." She knew half of what she reported to be accurate. Since Uncle Avi's death, her mother was much like a coin flipping over and over, Miriam thought. You never knew whether you would get heads or tails, the brightest of sunshine, or something from the other side of the moon.

"Splendid," Mr. Levy said. "Looks like we might be busy today, so let's keep it tidy."

"Yes, sir," Miriam said. She loved folding and stacking the crisp, white men's shirts, fine ladies' shirtwaists, the colorful, silky handkerchiefs.

A few of the other girls scurried into the store then, shaking the rain from their coats in the vestibule before entering.

"It just started *pouring*," Carrie said.

"I'm a mess," added Jenny.

"I got in before it started," Miriam said as they passed.

"Of course, Miriam was early," Jenny said, making a face.

"Not early," Miriam insisted, rubbing a spot on the glass with a white rag. "On *time*."

After about an hour of cleaning and folding, Miriam sold a fur-lined coat to a woman with a chauffeur waiting for her outside.

"Tonight we'll see *Son of the Sheik*?" Jenny asked.

"Oh, I'm so sorry," Miriam said, restraightening the remaining coats on the rack. They were dusty, and Miriam considered taking them outside and beating them, but it was still raining lightly.

"Why? What happened?" Carrie asked.

"My mother wants me to stay for dinner because my brother is coming over."

"Oooh, Ben?"

Miriam ignored this, straightening, straightening.

"He's so handsome," Jenny added.

"Stop!" Miriam demanded, louder than she'd wanted. A customer sitting with one of the salesmen from the jewelry counter turned to look at her. "Stop it," she whispered to Jenny.

"When's he going to marry?" Carrie asked, initiating what Miriam hoped would not become yet another version of the same conversation they had practically every week on the subject of Ben's bachelor status.

"I don't know," Miriam insisted. "Let's get to work."

"There's nothing to do," Jenny said. "Now, back to Ben's rosy cheeks."

"Please, stop," Miriam said again, and this time she meant it. Luckily, the girls' attention was drawn to the ringing bell on the front door.

"Uh oh, look who's back," Jenny whispered to Miriam. "Your fellow."

"He's not my *fellow*."

"Why does he always come in here then?" Jenny asked.

"He needs things," Miriam insisted.

"What's his name?"

"I don't remember." Miriam busied herself with a drawer full of pocket squares and hid behind the mirrored column in the center of the showroom.

The young man stepped up to the counter and asked for Miriam by name. Jenny was happy to point wordlessly in Miriam's direction.

"Oh, hello," Miriam said, pretending to be surprised by him. "How are you, sir?"

"Sir?" he repeated.

Miriam blushed. "I'm fairly busy here."

The man looked around the empty store. The floor creaked under the weight of Jenny and Carrie, both of whom were hurrying toward the front of the store, away from Miriam and the man.

"It doesn't appear to be very busy," he said, before adding, "with all due respect."

"Well, there's still much to do," Miriam said seriously, rearranging the pocket squares in their rows according to color. They were a mess, and she was happy for the disarray.

"Do you remember my name?" he asked.

"No, I'm sorry, I don't."

"Sam Lazarus, of Pampa."

"Yes, that's right," Miriam said.

"Why won't you give me the time of day?"

"I don't understand," Miriam said.

Sam smiled then, but didn't explain. He was dressed in the finest suit, always the latest fashion. His eyes were large and round, very dark, and his fine dark hair was combed back flat against his head, shiny as could be. His full head of hair came to a point in the middle of his forehead, and when he smiled Miriam thought she might fall off her own legs, but she would never let him or anybody else know.

"Can I buy you a soda?" he asked.

"Isn't that a bit forward?" Miriam replied, certain she sounded like her mother.

"How about a walk?" he asked, pulling out his gold watch and checking the time. "I'll wait for you to have your break."

Miriam didn't respond. She turned toward the necktie rack and attempted to look busy straightening it.

"The old geezer gives you a break, doesn't he?" Sam pressed.

Miriam glanced quickly back toward Mr. Levy's office. "I should get back to work."

"I need a tie," Sam said then, reaching up to touch a brownish-yellow one on the rack in front of him.

"What kind of tie are you looking for?" Miriam asked.

"The one you think will bring me success in the important meeting I'm to have in a few hours."

Miriam ran her fingers along the ties, setting them swinging back and forth in a shimmering spectrum. "How about this one?" she asked, pulling a radiant blue one off the rack and holding it up to, but not touching, Sam's suit coat.

He looked at himself in the mirror behind Miriam. "Perfect," he said. "Sold."

Miriam found a box for the tie and folded it in thirds.

"Oh, no need for a box," he said. "I'm going to wear it."

"Wouldn't you like the box for your other tie?"

"No, I'll just leave it in the car."

Miriam rang up the necktie on the register and gave Sam his change, but he didn't leave when the sale was complete. He stood right in front of Miriam and carefully put on his new tie in the mirror.

"Can I help you with something else?" she asked when he still didn't leave after finishing with the tie.

"Your break?"

Miriam laughed and shook her head, trying to busy herself further, but she was running out of things to do.

"Excuse me?" Sam called to the front of the store.

Jenny looked at him. "Yes?"

"I was wondering if you might be able to help me with something?" he asked as Jenny moved closer. "What time does Miriam here go on her break?"

"Oh, she never takes breaks," Jenny said. "She can go any time."

"Thank you," Sam said, bowing slightly to Jenny. "Well then," he said to Miriam.

On their brief walk later—Miriam would grant him only a jaunt to the public library and back—she studied Sam as he talked. His ears were slightly large for his face, but they were of perfect shape. His nose, though not small, had a sort of roundness at the tip, the exact sort of roundness echoed in Sam's eyes. His neck was slender and blemish-free, and the hint of whiskers made the bottom half of his face appear even darker, as though in shadow.

"Are you listening?" he asked when he noticed Miriam staring at him.

"No, I admit, I'm not," Miriam said. "I've a lot on my mind."

"No, no, I apologize for going on and on," he said. "It's just I've been hoping for this with you for many months now, and I am a little nervous it has actually come about."

"Why are you nervous?" she asked.

"Such a beautiful girl," he started. "I don't get to walk with very often—"

"It's cold," Miriam interrupted. "I should get back to the store."

"Okay," he said, but he looked sad.

"Your new tie looks wonderful."

"Have you not had a good time with me?" he asked.

"Of course, I've had a wonderful time," Miriam said. And then, even bolder: "Perhaps we can do it again the next time you come into town."

"I'd like that," he said, brightening. And then they were standing outside the store, the sky threatening to rain down on them yet again.

Miriam looked to see if the girls were watching her from inside, but she could see both of them occupied with customers. She held out her hand and Sam gripped it in his. He wasn't a large man, but it seemed to Miriam that he was strong.

"Thank you," she said, pulling back. "Good-bye."

He watched her enter the store and then checked his pocket watch one more time before heading back in the direction of the library.

December 13, 1927

𝔗𝔥𝔢 𝔄𝔪𝔞𝔯𝔦𝔩𝔩𝔬 𝔇𝔞𝔦𝔩𝔶 𝔖𝔲𝔫, December 13, 1927

LINDBERGH TO MEXICO SOON

WEATHER EXPERTS TRACK CONDITIONS
AS FLIER REMAINS GROUNDED

WASHINGTON, Dec. 12—Colonel Charles A. Lindbergh is geared up and eager to begin his journey south of the border, but unfortunately, the famous flier will not be going anywhere until he receives a promising weather report along his route between Washington and Mexico City.

The conditions over the southeastern United States, and especially Texas, have been less than favorable for the Colonel's intended flight, with an expected duration of twenty-six or twenty-seven hours. In the meantime, the "Spirit of St. Louis" sits with its gasoline tanks filled and valves tightened, until its able pilot is satisfied with the safety of conditions.

R.W. Weightman, the Weather Bureau forecaster, is fashioning regular, special bulletins for the Colonel. Weightman's most recent forecast for the flier was as follows:

From Washington to Alabama, partly overcast to overcast skies Tuesday afternoon, with moderate to fresh south winds up to 1,000 feet and fresh to strong west winds at 5,000 feet.

From Alabama to Tampico, Mexico, via East Texas and the Texas coast, skies growing overcast, with rain Tuesday night, and fresh to strong south winds, most likely shifting to northwest over Southern Texas, up to 1,000 feet, and strong southwest winds at 5,000 feet.

From Tampico to Mexico City, partly overcast skies Wednesday late morning, with moderate south and southwest winds up to 1,000 feet and moderate southeast and south winds at 5,000 feet.

Esther stood in the driveway and peered up into the bright winter sky above her. It was a not-quite gray that went on forever, with many layers upon layers, growing darker as the evening barreled in on her. Everything is never ending here, she thought, and she could see how a body might grow tired of it. The plane against the sky, how can you tell the difference which is which, the plane or the sky? Plane? Or sky? This is maybe why it was able to stay up for so long over the ocean between New York and Paris. The plane and sky as one.

Reuven was flying today. On his way to Mexico City to "mend fences," as they say, with our neighbors to the south. Over Texas he plotted his course—perhaps something draws the boy to this state, Esther thought. Surely he remembers his family was Texas-bound when he was lost. Esther shifted her weight from one leg to the other, inhaling the searing cold and pulling her coat around her. She rubbed her cracked, dry hands together, trying to create some heat. Each year Esther's hands became this way—every winter without fail—so parched they made the sound of dry weeds in a light wind when rubbed together. And they grew red in more places than they did not. Some days, but not today, Esther recalled, the cracks oozed a watered-down sort of blood. Blood, but then not completely blood.

Hersh would be coming home soon, too. She went inside to prepare a quick supper, another variation on leftovers. Hersh never knew the difference—he was equally complimentary of all meals. He was just like that. Over the sink, stealing glances out the kitchen window into the darkening sky, Esther wished Hersh would stay away for just a while longer. Long enough so that she might enjoy the solitary sputtering of her boy's engine in the night sky all alone. Just the two of them, mother and son. She wondered whether the boy might dip his wing, or circle over the city like he did so many times back and forth across the country. There was nowhere else to go but south: Esther understood why he was going. And she would be waiting for him.

Esther finished preparing Hersh's supper and returned to the driveway, listening in the darkness. But the sky remained silent and still, the only sound coming from the pulsing just in front of Esther's ears as she fretted over Hersh's impending arrival. If Hersh would maybe just come across a small boulder in the road on his way home, Esther thought, causing the wheels of the truck to wobble back and forth—maybe he steers himself into a shallow ditch by the side of the road. He is not hurt at all, just a tiny bump on the head that Esther would hold a cold cloth to so it would disappear by morning. Maybe the truck is temporarily stalled, and Hersh must sit on the side of the road for quite some time before a helpful neighbor pulls over to offer help.

And if a kind neighbor does not pass, Hersh would walk the rest of the way home—not too far, just from the beginning of the president-named streets: Washington, Monroe, Jackson, Van Buren, Harrison, and finally to Tyler, their own. She should be so lucky.

Esther's attention was drawn to whispers coming from the weeds along the driveway and in the lot next door to their house. They were flaxen and knee-high in winter, these dry weeds, though she could not see them very well in the dark. They hissed in the breeze, despite the patches of snow blanketing their roots. Esther wondered why they didn't simply disappear entirely under the snow, bent and broken under weight that was not their own. It was strange. The winds were growing stronger, Esther could tell, and she worried what they might be like at 1,000 feet, at 5,000. She didn't like to think of it, the tiny silver plane tossed to and fro, like a child's toy in God's great sky.

The air was knife-like, but Esther decided she would not go inside again until her boy appeared overhead. From which direction might he come? The east, she thought, or perhaps the north, depending on weather patterns. Regardless, she would hear the monoplane's loud engine before she could see it. Esther kept looking up into the sky, by now a complete, purple darkness entirely devoid of stars. The back of her neck, all the way down her spine, ached from so much leaning backward and peering up, but she knew her boy would come soon, and relieve her this burden at least.

Her back became searing fireworks explosions of pain, but Esther continued her vigil. She propped her palms on her hips, but it didn't help to relieve the pain—it hadn't helped all evening. The constant stench of manure, though mild in winter compared to other seasons, had disappeared for a few moments in a brisk easterly breeze. Just a few seconds of reprieve. But then it was back on a strong south wind. Esther could feel it in her bones that it would storm. She hoped the boy would beat the rain (*please don't let it freeze on him*). Esther leaned back some more, her jaw dropping open because she couldn't keep it from doing so. It felt good to let the muscles in her cheeks go slack. Her mouth gaped at the sky, and her tired eyes searched left and right, back and forth over the muffled glow of the tiny city. But they may as well have been closed, her eyes, with Esther searching the inside of her eyelids for something she didn't even know what it would look like after so many years.

It was said that when he flies, he sometimes skims the earth so as to be able to shout to a person on the ground. The astonished villagers in southern Ireland waved and ran beneath the boy and his plane when it materialized out of the clouds on the first flight to Paris. Would Reuven know it was his mother? Perhaps if she stood under the streetlamp, Esther thought, and began crossing into the road. But then she heard Hersh's truck, functioning just fine, clearly having avoided any potential hazardous perils she might've thrown in his path. Here he was as usual, her damn husband, delivered home right on schedule, dependable as the morning paper.

"What are you doing outside?" Hersh asked, putting an arm around his wife's shoulders. "You're trembling."

He guided her inside. Esther did not sleep for even one minute that night, her back aching, ears pricked toward the window Esther insisted they leave open for the duration of the night. The wind whistled through the cracked window, and flicked the curtains wildly against the windowsill like white flames. But Esther would not let Hersh close it, no matter how many times he asked, or how frigid their bedroom became.

TIME Magazine, January 2, 1928 issue

THE MAN OF THE YEAR

HE DEFEATED FAME.

HEROES:

Lindbergh

Height: 6 ft. 2 inches.

Age: 25.

Eyes: Blue.

Cheeks: Pink.

Hair: Sandy.

Feet: Large. When he arrived at the Embassy in France no shoes big enough were handy.

Habits: Smokes not; drinks not. Does not gamble. Eats a thoroughgoing breakfast. Prefers light luncheon and dinner when permitted. Avoids rich dishes. Likes sweets.

Calligraphy: From examination of his handwriting Dr. Camille Streletski, Secretary of the French Graphological Society, concluded: Superiority, intellectualism, cerebration, idealism, even mysticism.

Characteristics: Modesty, taciturnity, diffidence (women make him blush), singleness of purpose, courage, occasional curtness, phlegm. Elinor Glyn avers he lacks "It."

December 29, 1927

Sitting on her parents' floral-printed couch in the living room, Miriam pressed her knees together and tucked her hands between her thighs.

"What time is the boy arriving?" Hersh asked. He read the day's newspaper in his chair by the fireplace, which cast an orange glow through the wrinkled paper clenched in his fists.

"Certainly before sundown," Miriam said, hoping this was the case. She was nervous, though in truth, she didn't know why. It was not as though she would not see Sam any longer if her parents disapproved. There was nothing to disapprove of, and they hadn't the nerve.

A knock on the front door, and Miriam's legs went limp, trembling from pushing them together so tightly. She stood expectantly, but it was only Ben, removing his hat and coat and hanging them on the rack in the hallway. Miriam saw Esther come out of the kitchen to kiss her son on the cheek before returning to the kitchen.

Ben entered the living room and smiled at his sister. She tried to entreat him with her eyes to be good tonight, but she couldn't tell whether he'd gotten the message.

"How's business?" Hersh asked.

"Oh, good," Ben said, sitting down next to Miriam on the couch and crossing his legs. "I think he's opening up another store in Lubbock in the new year."

"Sounds better than just 'good,'" Hersh said, folding the paper and placing it on the stack of newspapers next to him.

Miriam rose then to see if her mother had changed her mind about needing help with preparing supper. Before she got to the kitchen though, there was another knock on the door, three crisp taps, and Miriam knew it was her Sam.

Everybody surged toward the door, but Hersh actually opened it. Sam stood with his hair combed back like Miriam liked it, perfectly filling out his finest brown suit, his overcoat draped over one arm, a bunch of flowers in the other. She could see his finest cuff links peeking out from under his jacket—the onyx ones with his initial in the center. Miriam reached out her hand to him and he took it, bowing his head respectfully and stepping into the Lipshitz house for the first time.

Introductions all around. Sam presented Esther with the fresh-cut flowers, and she blushed while taking his hat and coat and hanging them in the hall closet. Hersh poked his head out into the driveway before closing the door, ostensibly to check the sun's progress in the sky, but Miriam could tell he was also noting Sam's car—a brand-new Model A he'd purchased the day before—the first one delivered to Amarillo after rolling off the line in Michigan.

"Looks like we should light the candles," Hersh said as he closed the door.

"Yes, yes," Esther clucked. "Miriam, did you put all eight candles in?"

"Yes, Mama."

"Sam?" Hersh asked as they gathered around the menorah, the same one that had traveled with them from Kishinev. "Would you like to do the honors?"

"Oh, no, I couldn't," Sam said, stepping back slightly. He was trying to be polite, but he actually meant he couldn't.

"Ben?" Hersh said then.

Ben began, *"Baruch atah, adonoi, eloheinu melech ha'olam . . ."*

"Amen," they all chorused when Ben was done. Everybody embraced, some kissed on the cheeks where appropriate, others shook hands.

At supper, when he thought Miriam wasn't watching, Ben studied Sam from head to toe. He took in Sam's hair color and texture (dark, fine), the color of his cheeks (ruddy), and, when he dropped his napkin to the floor under the table, Ben observed the size of Sam's feet (surprisingly small). He admired the way Sam attired himself. Ben used to put such care into his own appearance when he'd lived in New York, but there was no use for it in Texas. Rare to see such a dapper fellow in these parts, Ben thought, snickering to himself quietly.

In the living room after dinner, Sam sat in Hersh's chair and tried to look around inconspicuously. Esther entered with a tray for tea and coffee, placing it on one of the stacks of newspapers—at least two or three feet tall apiece—that were scattered throughout the room. Some were unruly, yellowed, and threatening to collapse, but Esther chose the newest stack with the most recent papers in it—the one closest to Sam. Miriam soon followed with the kettle, holding it aloft while her mother distributed the cups.

Sam surveyed the scene and wondered about the financial situation of the Lipshitzes. Using the dailies for furniture? He was confused; there was an adequate supply of otherwise average yet functional furniture dispersed throughout what he'd seen of the modest, though comfortable house. The father was a bit disheveled, but what man from the old country wasn't? Sam wondered. His grandfather certainly had been.

"We also use real furniture sometimes," Miriam said, falsely laughing as she poured the steaming water into Sam's cup. It seemed as though she could read his mind.

"I don't understand," Esther said. "Is this supposed to be funny?"

"My mother enjoys clipping the newspapers," Miriam whispered then, though everyone could hear.

Sam placed his cup of tea beside the January 2, 1928, issue of *TIME* magazine, which sat on top of the small table next to him.

"Please!" Esther exclaimed, nearly scaring the pants off of everyone. "Not *there*!"

Sam lifted his cup quickly, though some tea spilled onto the top left corner of the magazine, which boasted a sketch of Lindbergh's face in profile on its red-bordered cover.

"I'm so sorry," Sam said as Esther frantically wiped the magazine with her apron. One of the candles on the menorah in the window burned completely out then, the white wax pooling in circles on the sill beneath it.

"It's okay," Esther said, holding up the magazine and examining it. "I think I got it all before it soaked into the paper."

"I do apologize," Sam repeated. "Perhaps I can—this is a recent issue? Perhaps I can purchase another copy for you at the newsstand tomorrow."

Miriam stood silent and frozen, the steaming kettle by her side, absolutely horrified.

"No, no. There's no need for that," Esther said, sitting on the couch and placing the magazine on her lap. She slowly ran her palms over the cover. "It didn't get on his face."

"I'm sorry," Ben said, standing up suddenly. "I have to be at work very early tomorrow."

"No, Ben," Esther said. Miriam wondered why her mother was always begging her brother for something or other. "Please stay."

"I just have a feeling where this conversation's going," Ben said sharply.

"Ben—" Hersh tried, but it was useless.

"I'm sorry," Ben continued, offering a hand to Sam. "Nice to have met you."

"Indeed." Sam stood and shook Ben's hand, holding it for a moment. Miriam noticed a slight smile forming on the left side of her brother's mouth. Another candle burned out then, and Ben was gone.

The four sat in the living room through a few uncomfortable minutes of silence. Sam sipped his tea a few times, carefully setting the cup back in its saucer each time. Esther still stroked the *TIME* magazine in her lap. "So, what do you think of this direct flight to China for Lindy?" Sam asked suddenly, hoping to start a conversation.

"Yes," Hersh said, "I remember reading something about this. Is it to happen soon?"

"It's just a rumor," Esther offered.

"He's really been everywhere," Sam continued. "Just to Mexico last month, if I remember correctly."

"I don't know about all this far-flung flying," Hersh said. "A dead Lindbergh is not a good Lindbergh—for anybody."

"Hersh!" Esther exclaimed. "How could you say such a thing?"

Sam didn't know whether he should push the matter any further. Esther seemed upset, and whatever you did, Sam knew, you didn't want to upset the mother. Luckily, Hersh suggested, "Miriam, why don't you join your mother in the kitchen so I can have a little time alone with Sam?"

What was this? Miriam was panicked. Her mother carried the magazine into the kitchen, and Miriam tentatively followed. She felt awful leaving Sam alone with her father, but she knew he could handle it. Miriam hoped her mother might rave about Sam as soon as they were alone in the kitchen, but Esther just started on the pile of dishes. She passed the clean ones to Miriam.

"Mother?" Miriam asked after drying a few plates. "What do you think of Sam?"

"Oh, he's a lovely boy," Esther said. "A very lovely boy. And so sweet to bring flowers."

"But what do you *think* about him?" Miriam pressed.

"Well, does he come from a nice family?" Esther asked, because she didn't know what else a mother might say in these matters. What *Esther* thought about Sam didn't seem to be the point. Her own father had suggested Esther marry Hersh, although it didn't seem like a suggestion, as much as a directive at the time.

"Yes, he does," Miriam replied, but it was a lie. Sam didn't really have a family of his own, not one that he talked about anyway. Miriam didn't know why, but she gave her mother one last chance. "He treats me like a queen," she added, dreamily.

Esther dropped a fork onto the floor. "What was that last part, dear?"

"Nothing," Miriam said. Why had she expected it to be any different now than it always had been? "I said yes, he comes from a nice family."

"Good, good," Esther said, furiously polishing the fork. "That's what you should look for—a really solid family."

They continued cleaning in complete silence as the men talked in the other room. It was true: The more she wanted a mother, the less Miriam had one. It would always be this way, because it always had been. *Mrs. Sam Lazarus. Mrs. Sam Lazarus. Miriam Lazarus.* Say it enough times, and it will take you anywhere but this house. Miriam glanced at her mother, once quite beautiful in Miriam's childhood recollections of her. But now she was just plain old—and utterly ugly. Miriam strained to hear what her father and Sam were saying, but she couldn't catch anything over the running water and noisy cookware in her mother's busy hands.

"So what are your intentions with my daughter?" Hersh had asked Sam as soon as the women left. "It seems customary that I do this sort of thing, don't you think?"

"Certainly, certainly," Sam answered, scooting to the edge of his seat and straightening his back. "Well—"

"I mean," Hersh interrupted, "I understand you don't even live in Amarillo."

"No, no, I don't," Sam said, picking a piece of lint off his jacket shoulder. "Not at the present. But I do have a few business opportunities that should make a permanent move to Amarillo feasible very soon."

"And what about Miriam during this time?" Hersh asked, but he didn't know why.

"Well, I hope to present her with a ring sometime soon in the new year," Sam began.

Hersh wondered at such a luxury as this, the way the boy was talking about his life like he could actually plan for it with any accuracy. Such gall.

Sam continued, "I will of course inquire with Miriam at that time, but perhaps she will like to join me in Pampa for a short time before I can bring us back down to Amarillo."

"I see," Hersh said. But he didn't, really. "And what is it, exactly, that you do?"

"I'm in the import-export business."

"I see," Hersh said. "Of what, exactly?"

"Well, ah, many goods from Canada that are popular in the United States . . ." Sam trailed off.

Hersh stared at him. "So you deal in liquor?"

Sam sat back in his chair and crossed his legs. "Well, not exactly—"

"It's okay," Hersh interrupted, "go on, please."

"Basically, yes, I do," Sam said. "But I'm more of the *facilitator* type." He took another sip of the tea and it seared the roof of his mouth. But Sam swallowed anyway, peering over the rim of his cup at what he hoped was his future father-in-law.

Hersh studied the boy sitting in front of him—his suit looked expensive, shoes shiny and new. Like somebody out of the moving pictures, Hersh thought. People like this didn't know the fear of losing. And Hersh knew that Sam would make Miriam forget she ever knew that kind of fear too. Hersh added then, "Well, seems like it's as good a business as any, I suppose."

"Yes, yes," Sam said. "But as I said, I'm hoping to open a retail shop in Pampa and then Amarillo very soon."

"I see. What kind of retail?"

"I'm still working on this," Sam said. "But I can assure you that Miriam will be very happy."

As soon as Sam said this, Hersh wondered if he should truly care whether Miriam was happy. He supposed he should. Hersh was grateful to Sam for calling this sort of thing to his attention.

February 13, 1929

PAMPA, TEXAS

The Amarillo Daily Sun, February 13, 1929

COLONEL LINDBERGH ENGAGED

MISS ANNE S. MORROW THE LUCKY GIRL,
SAYS ANNOUNCEMENT ISSUED AT EMBASSY
IN MEXICO CITY

MEXICO CITY, Feb. 12—While Colonel Charles A. Lindbergh was en route from Belize, British Honduras, to Cuba with a load of airmail today, his engagement to Miss Anne S. Morrow, daughter of the United States Ambassador to Mexico, was announced in Mexico City. Ambassador Morrow simply handed the foreign newspapermen a brief notice which read:

"Ambassador and Mrs. Morrow have announced the engagement of their daughter, Anne Spencer Morrow, to Colonel Charles A. Lindbergh."

The Ambassador would not answer further questions

about a possible wedding date or location, and reporters were asked to vacate the Ambassador's private room at the embassy after the announcement was issued.

Bookish and Domestic

Miss Morrow was born in Englewood, N.J. and is the Ambassador and Mrs. Morrow's second daughter. She is 22 years old and attended the Chapin School in New York City. Miss Morrow then graduated with the class of '28 from Smith College in Northampton, Massachusetts, where she was awarded the prestigious Jordan Prize for writing. Her poetry has appeared in *Scribner's*.

Miss Morrow's friends describe her as a beautiful, gentle girl, who was quite popular with her classmates. She is said to be bookish but also very interested in social activities. She enjoys the arts and literature, and closely follows world affairs due to her Ambassador father. But ultimately, her friends say that Miss Morrow is quite domestic and family-loving.

Which Morrow Daughter?

The names of Miss Morrow and Colonel Lindbergh have long been coupled in newspapers across the United States and Mexico, but all rumors were summarily refuted by both the Morrow family and Lindbergh, who often refuses to answer any question unrelated to aviation.

A recent article in a Mexico newspaper reported that it was Elisabeth, Anne's older sister, who was seen flying with the Colonel in his plane, and that an engagement was imminent. Even family members were unsure about a possible romance.

"Both of my nieces repeatedly insisted that there was nothing to the rumors," said Mrs. J. J. Morrow, the sisters' aunt. "In fact, they both claimed that Lindy isn't even a bit sentimental, and doesn't care at all for girls."

Mexico was Colonel Lindbergh's first stop on his first Central American flight in December of 1927. It was during this stay as the guest of Ambassador Morrow that he and Miss Morrow were first acquainted and subsequently seen together.

Ernestino Calles Robinson, daughter of the former Mexican President, recalled that it was after this visit that the Colonel took off from Valbuena Field in the "Spirit of St. Louis" and completed an impressive nose-dive overhead, which she considered to be a secret tribute to Miss Morrow.

Mrs. Calles Robinson said that the only people truly surprised by today's announcement were "those naive individuals who thought that the Colonel had no affection for any woman besides his mother."

"It's late, I need to be getting home to the missus."

"Oh no you don't," Sam insisted. His tone sounded as though he might be joking with Russell, but he wasn't, not even one little bit. "Sit back down, and let's finish this like we agreed."

Russell loosened the tie around his thick neck and did as he was told, sliding his chair closer to the table. He lit another cigarette and anted up two hundred. "Deal."

Sam added two crisp notes of his own and watched as the cards slid into little piles of five in front of each of the five men at the table. He glanced at his wristwatch and realized he was already late for Miriam, who wouldn't be angry with him—she was never angry with him—but he didn't like disappointing her, didn't like not doing what he said he was going to do. He didn't like when other people did it either.

Sam's hand was solid: two pairs, queens and sixes. He felt like going for it, and he wanted Russell's money, so he opened for two hundred. He was disgusting really, this man drinking, talking, and smoking nonstop. *Get home to his wife?* Sam laughed to himself. *And would that be the "wife" at the brothel in Pampa, or the one in Oklahoma City?* Sam brushed some blowing ash off his shoulder. He hated the way his suits smelled after sitting with these guys for a whole evening.

Everyone called, including Russell, who shifted loudly in his seat. Sam could tell from the way he clenched his jaw that Russell would see this game to its end. He hated Sam too much to grant him the most beautiful wife, biggest house, nicest car, the guy everyone liked even though they thought he was a conniving Jewsie. No, Sam knew that Russell wouldn't let him get away with being the guy with the most money too.

Sam took one card, Russell two.

Sam bet another four hundred. One man called him, and then Russell raised. The next two men folded, and the action was back on Sam, who reraised. The final man dropped out, and now it was just Russell and Sam again.

"I don't have anything to call you with," Russell whined. He stood and pulled his pockets out in that annoying, exaggerated way people do. Sam just stared at him, eyelids at half-mast, feigning disinterest. "I don't. Look," Russell insisted, sitting back down and spreading his empty pocketbook with two fat thumbs.

"Okay, so you're out," Sam said.

"I never said that."

"So what's it going to be?" Sam asked.

"Come on," the last man who folded, Abe, said then. "This is a gentleman's game."

"Exactly," Sam said, "and that's why Mr. Calhoun here is going to be a gentleman."

"I told you I don't have anything else," Russell said, now smiling nervously and seemingly trying to get the other men to join him in the joke.

Sam didn't respond.

"What, you want me to put up my business?" Russell asked, chuckling.

Now everyone was laughing, but not Sam. "Yes, I think that's customary," he said, cold as rocks.

"Okay, okay," Abe broke in again. "We've all been drinking, we're among friends, or at least associates. Maybe this has gone a little too far."

"I don't drink," Sam said, looking at Russell, whose cards formed a messy stack facedown in front of him, a few of their corners hanging over the edge of the table.

"Fine, you sick bastard," Russell spit. "Fine. I call you with my counter in Pampa."

Sam nodded.

"Come on, guy," Abe said then, putting a hand on Sam's shoulder.

"And I'll raise you the shop in Borger," Russell added.

Sam could feel a warm smile coming over him, but not on the outside. This would leave the guy with one jewelry counter to operate out of the Hotel Lafayette in Oklahoma City. "Okay, how much to meet you?" Sam asked.

"Twenty-five hundred," Russell said. He was perspiring more than usual.

"You'll bring the titles over here tonight?" Sam asked.

"You haven't won yet."

Sam wanted to see Russell's hand. "Okay, twenty-five hundred. I can get it tonight," he said.

Russell tried three times to pick up his cards, but the dirty fingernail on his thumb wasn't long enough to do the job. He slid the cards off the table and into his palm, shuffling them in his hand before laying them on the table.

All red, and diamonds.

Sam wordlessly fanned out his hand: queens full of sixes.

"Gentlemen," Sam said, leaning back in his chair. "That, I believe, is that."

"You're not going to do this," Russell whispered.

"Do what?"

"This is my family business."

Sam shrugged his shoulders and stood up. "Keys?"

"This was my father's business," Russell pleaded, still whispering, though everybody else could hear.

"And you still have one of them in OKC, where he started it."

"Sam?"

Sam could feel the guys in the room looking at him differently then. Everyone knew what a crooked cheat Russell Calhoun was, but still.

"You'll bring over the papers tomorrow then," Sam said, more statement than question. "Gentlemen, thank you. Now I need to get home to my lovely bride."

On the walk to his house, Sam mused that nights like these were what legends are made of. His children, and maybe his children's children, would always know this night in intricate, moment-by-moment detail—though in truth what had happened was quite pathetic and almost too easy, beating a fat, pompous bastard who ran his father's five stores into the ground and was best known for slapping up whores after overpaying them for their services. Nevertheless, Sam pictured himself a jewelry shop proprietor. What a strange concept: You go to work in the same place every day, you have people working for you, regular customers who know and trust you. It all seemed so normal. Miriam would be proud.

Inside his front door, Sam stomped the snow off his shoes and removed his coat. He kissed his wife heartily before excusing himself into the washroom. He didn't like her smelling the smoke and liquor on him—especially when he hadn't partaken in either himself. When he came back to the living room, he wore a clean undershirt and freshly pressed trousers. Miriam rose to his embrace. The house was warm, a fire rolling quietly in the fireplace.

Sam tried telling Miriam of the night's developments, but she put her delicate fingers over his mouth and it was clear she would not have anything but more of the very sweet and wonderful lovemaking the couple had gotten in the habit of since marrying and moving into the house in Pampa together. She was beautiful, Miriam, her skin. Each and every place he could reach on it, Sam touched. Little bumps rose under his fingertips, and he held Miriam for quite some time after they made love in their bedroom. The night air whistling in through the cracked-open window was cold, and more snow was on the way. But it was warm inside.

"Can I tell you something?" Sam asked then, rolling onto his side.

"Anything."

"I think we'll get to Amarillo sooner rather than later," he announced, satisfied with himself.

"What?" she asked, propping herself up on an elbow. Sam was momentarily distracted by the now-exposed soft white skin on the underside of Miriam's forearm.

But he continued. "You have just been quite intimate with the proud new owner of two jewelry counters in the panhandle region—one in Pampa, the other in Borger."

"I don't understand," Miriam said.

" 'Lazarus's Diamonds,' or maybe better, 'The Diamond Shop,' " he proposed, hearing it for the first time. He liked how it sounded. The queen of diamonds had been the only one missing from his full house. And even though Russell had had five of those diamonds, it still wasn't enough to beat Sam.

"What happened?" Miriam asked, puzzled.

"Just some business," he said. "But I believe once we get these counters running properly—with your help, of course—we shall be able to open up another store in Amarillo shortly."

Miriam looked at him. "I still don't understand. What about—"

"We are now business *owners*," he pronounced. "And I would like you to manage the store in Pampa at first. That is, of course, if you'd like."

Miriam put her head back down on the pillow, and Sam leaned over her, smiling. She smiled back, wondering if she would ever understand him completely.

"What do you think?" he asked.

"I think yes," she said, closing her eyes and feeling Sam's sweet breath on her cheek. Life was turning out not to be as bad as her mother and father told her it was.

May 28, 1929

AMARILLO, TEXAS

𝕿𝖍𝖊 𝕬𝖒𝖆𝖗𝖎𝖑𝖑𝖔 𝕯𝖆𝖎𝖑𝖞 𝕾𝖚𝖓, May 28, 1929

SURPRISE: LINDY AND ANNE MARRY!

A 'LONE EAGLE' NO MORE

Informal, Spontaneous Ceremony
Attended by Just 20

ENGLEWOOD, N. J., May 27—Miss Anne Morrow, daughter of privilege and society, and Col. Charles A. Lindbergh, prince of aviation, were suddenly married today at the home of the bride's parents, Ambassador and Mrs. Dwight W. Morrow, in Englewood, New Jersey.

The wedding came as a complete surprise to the world, despite the fact that reporters and photographers had doggedly trailed the betrothed couple for the last month. The informal ceremony was witnessed by immediate family only and was performed by the Rev. William Adams Brown of Union Theological Seminary in New York City.

The ceremony combined modified versions of Presbyterian and Episcopal rituals.

Dr. Brown deemed the wedding "a simple, lovely, natural little service." But when a reporter asked whether Mrs. Lindbergh cried, he replied, "How silly! Gentlefolk do not behave that way."

Last Minute Flowers for the Bride

The surprise wedding was so informal and spontaneous that just prior to it, the groom was observed entering the garden of the Morrow home, where he proceeded to pick a bunch of blue larkspur and white columbine to serve as the bride's bouquet.

As usual, the Colonel was attired in the dark blue business suit in which he is frequently seen. The bride wore a simple cream-white chiffon gown with a shoulder-length French lace veil, fabricated for her by Miss Mary Smith, the family dressmaker. She went gloveless and wore blue heeled slippers.

Just after 4:30, Lindbergh, hatless, and his young bride, now clad in a French blue traveling dress with a blue straw and felt hat, were seen leaving the house in an automobile, bound for an undisclosed location. It was presumed that they were en route to Roosevelt Field on Long Island, where Lindbergh's Blue Falcon plane had earlier been ordered serviced and readied for a possible takeoff.

There was no word on a possible honeymoon location.

[advertisement]

FORMAL OPENING
of
"THE DIAMOND SHOP"

THE PANHANDLE'S GREATEST JEWELERS

BORGER, PAMPA & NOW AMARILLO

WEDNESDAY, MAY 29, 1929
AT HIGH NOON

Sam Lazarus and his wife **Miriam** cordially invite you to attend tomorrow's opening day celebration. Inspect our store from the beautiful display windows to the modernistic Gift Shop on the Mezzanine. This great day of celebration, free of commercial interest, proclaims the climax of increasingly prosperous years in Amarillo . . . WELCOME! There will be music and a royal hospitality, but POSITIVELY NO SALES TOMORROW!

"The Diamond Shop" always guarantees:
- *No Interest*
- *No Carrying Charge*
- *No Extras*

Just the nationally advertised cash price—on credit, in weekly, semimonthly, or monthly payments

• 514 POLK, IN THE HEART OF AMARILLO •

Sam held Esther's hand as he carefully led her first through the hotel lobby and then up to the front doors of the new shop. Miriam and Hersh followed a few steps behind them. Sam told Esther to open her eyes.

"Oh my," she exclaimed. "It's quite beautiful, isn't it?"

Sam looked proud. Miriam didn't understand his acute interest in her mother, but she endured it. Perhaps because he hadn't had a mother of his own since he was a small boy.

"It's beautiful," Esther repeated.

"This, this all looks very expensive," Hersh pronounced, leaning over and closely inspecting an empty glass display case with his hands clasped behind his back.

"Oh, but Mr. Lipshitz," Sam began, "everybody knows, one must *spend* big to *make* it big."

"Something like this," Hersh muttered.

Miriam busied herself with inventory while Sam entertained her mother and father in the front of the store. He showed off the custom-made cabinetry, rounded glass display cases, intricate lighting system. Miriam listened to her mother clucking, her father *tsk*-ing and Sam going back and forth in between the two like a hot potato. Miriam checked the safes and drawers—everything just as she'd left it, just as she'd prepared all week long. She had to be forgetting something. Could there really be nothing more to do for tomorrow's opening?

A few workmen on ladders futzed with the wiring above the two longest cases. Sam insisted the lighting had to be just right for selling stones. There was no other way. Some plaster from the ceiling crumbled down on the glass countertop then, and Miriam rushed over to clean it up.

"Don't worry, dear," Sam said.

"What a mess," Miriam fretted.

"They'll clean it up, don't worry."

"I need to get home," Esther announced suddenly from the front of the store, where she was peering into the darkness of the hotel lobby through the window with "The Diamond Shop" logo painted on.

"Is everything okay, Mama?" Miriam asked.

"I need to take care of a few things before starting with supper."

"Mom," Sam began (because this was what he called her these days), "let's all come for a nice meal here in the hotel restaurant tonight. My treat."

"No, no, I won't hear of it," Esther insisted. "I can prepare a silly meal for my family on such a special night." She looked at Miriam and nodded her head expectantly.

"I still have a lot to do here, but I suppose I could come along to help," Miriam suggested, but she would have rather done almost anything than help her mother with supper. She would even climb up the rickety ladder and fiddle with the electric wiring in the ceiling herself. She looked at Sam, hoping he got the message and would rescue her.

"Go, go," he encouraged her, "I've got it covered here." Their wires had obviously been crossed.

"Are you *sure*?" she asked, drawing out the last word.

"Yes, go. You've worked so hard, I feel like a slave-driver husband." Sam laughed, as did Hersh.

Miriam stared over her shoulder at Sam as she and her parents headed out the front doors of the shop. But he was too busy telling the electricians something to notice. Sam didn't see his wife's pleading eyes, nor hear her childlike shuffling as she trailed behind her irritating mother and nay-saying father on their way back home.

It seemed to Miriam that her parents' house was different from the last time she had visited, but she didn't know how or why. Esther rushed directly into the bedroom and shut the door behind her as soon as the two arrived.

"Does this mean I am to start supper alone?" Miriam asked her father, who silently shrugged his shoulders and sat in his usual chair, spreading out the day's newspaper in front of him. There were large squares cut out of it, and Miriam could see half of her father's tired face through the front page of the paper. His mouth hung open slightly, a slack "O."

The house smelled of crusty, dried old paper—that's what it was, Miriam remembered. Burned, damp, mildewed, or just dusty—it didn't matter, Miriam could pick out the subtle traces of paper in all stages of decay. Because it had been a while since she had left Amarillo for Pampa, Miriam hadn't recognized the familiar scent upon walking in the door.

Miriam wandered into the kitchen and wondered what her mother had in mind for the celebration supper. It was, ostensibly, in honor of the shop's opening, but Miriam wasn't feeling very honored. She counted in her head how many would be eating: herself and Sam were two, Mama and Papa, four, Ben, five, Sam's new store manager and his wife made seven. Miriam opened the cupboard and instantly became overwhelmed. Cooking? Not her strong suit. She could cook a book, no problem, but the kitchen? *Ach. Why couldn't they just have a nice supper at the hotel like Sam had suggested?* She marched down the hall toward her mother's bedroom and knocked on the door, squeezing the squeaky doorknob and nudging the door open without waiting for an answer.

"Oh!" her mother screamed, hand to heart. She shuffled papers together and pushed them onto her lap underneath the small desk at which she sat. "You frightened me."

"What are you doing?" Miriam asked, walking over to her mother's side.

"Oh, this?" Esther began. "Nothing."

"It doesn't look like nothing," Miriam said, reaching over and resting her palm on the small stack of newspaper articles that Esther had obviously cut from the paper her father was trying to read.

"I'm just writing cousin Raina in New York," Esther said then, sliding the newspapers from under Miriam's hand and bringing them onto her lap on top of the letter.

"Why are you hiding it from me then?" Miriam asked. She noticed an empty picture frame on the dresser.

"I'm not, I'm not hiding anything from you," Esther insisted. "I don't need to hide anything from my *daughter*." The way Esther spit the word "daughter" made Miriam wonder what Sam was doing at that precise moment. She pictured him in his nice blue suit, with a sprinkling of plaster dust from the ceiling on a shoulder.

"Well, I just wanted to know what you were planning for supper," Miriam said eventually. "I think we should get started, it's getting late. Or maybe we can take Sam up on his offer?"

"No, no," Esther insisted. "I'll be right out if you'll just give me a few moments to myself."

Miriam started to leave but then stopped and looked back at her mother, the empty frame standing up on the dresser, the messy pile of newspapers on the floor, the porcelain figurines on the windowsill that had been knocked down—who knows how long before—by the gritty winds that blew through the house most days.

"Mama," Miriam began, before she could think better of it. "Who is in the picture you are putting into that frame?"

"What picture?"

"The one in your lap."

"There is no picture in my lap."

"Yes, there is, right there under the newspaper," Miriam pointed out.

"Oh, this, this isn't a picture," Esther said. Miriam could see her mother's hands trembling. They had grown spotted, the skin thin and loosely draped over a complicated web of purple veins. "This is just a clipping from the newspaper. I thought it would make a nice little thing to hang up somewhere."

Esther slowly pulled a large combined portrait in profile of Charles Lindbergh and Anne Morrow from the pile of papers on her lap. Anne's face and neck was cut out and pasted onto Lindbergh's cheek. It didn't look like the faces should go together, Miriam thought, at least not in the makeshift portrait. The letter to Raina fell off of Esther's lap and onto the floor then, and Esther quickly bent to pick it up, careful not to send the rest of the papers flying.

"They were married today, you know, it was quite a surprise," Esther reported.

"I know," Miriam said.

"I'm so proud of him for finding such a worthy match," Esther added, holding the picture out in front of her eyes with both hands. She cocked her head left and right, studying the portrait vigilantly. The extra skin under her arms swung gently back and forth as she held the photo aloft.

Miriam watched her mother like this for a moment. She was worried for her. But only for a moment. Soon, Miriam was angry: "Mama, you don't even have a picture of my wedding on your shelf."

Esther looked at her daughter pensively. It appeared as though she was trying to remember a time long ago, a place as different from Amarillo as could be. Miriam wondered what it could possibly be.

"I do," Esther exclaimed then. "I do have a photograph of you and Sam at the wedding. And you're right, this frame will be perfect for it."

Miriam stood there as Esther tucked the letter she was writing safely inside a book on the dresser and then went to the closet and began rifling through the mess inside. Esther made quite a ruckus in the closet and didn't come out for some time, but when she did, she was empty-handed.

"We should start supper now," Miriam said.

"Yes, let's do that," Esther agreed, more bewildered than apologetic.

Amarillo, Tex.

May 28, 1929

Mrs. Anne Morrow Lindbergh
in c/o Ambassador & Mrs. Dwight W. Morrow
Englewood, New Jersey

Dear Mrs. Lindbergh,

Welcome to the family, so to speak. And please accept my deepest, most heartfelt congratulations on the occasion of your union with Charles. He is like a son to me . . . always has been. You two will be quite happy together, I'm sure of it. I believe your love will be most strong if you continue to demonstrate a deep, unwavering interest in aviation, as

I'm sure you know that Charles is a very single-minded young man. Always was. Similarly, respect his mother Evangeline—he dotes on her so.

I struggled with sending this letter to you during such a joyous time, but I believe you shall receive it after returning from your honeymoon. I never had a honeymoon. They do not have these where I am from. They say in the papers you and Charles might travel by Mr. Guggenheim's yacht, this sounds very luxurious.

I have tried for quite some time now to notify both Charles and his mother of some information I have been given about him. It is difficult to hear, but I believe you as the wife of Charles will be sensible and conduct yourself accordingly. The news is this: Something very tragic will befall Charles at some point either near or far in the future. I cannot be more specific than that, but I can tell you that whatever this sorrow shows itself to be, Charles will survive it. I have felt great sorrow in my life, and while I have survived it, I think it better not to have experienced the sorrow in the first place. I believe he (and now you) will be better off without it as well. This is like I am giving you my second chance, or giving Charles my second chance.

I tell you this simply so that you can warn your new husband, so that he and you may be quite aware out in the world, to be on the lookout for strange circumstances with the potential to turn tragic.

I was just interrupted by my silly daughter. Where was I?

Well, I suppose that is all the heaviness I can stand right now. I apologize for the solemn nature of this letter, but now you know, and I have done my duty. I am so happy about your union, my heart swells and my eyes fill with tears of joy when I think of Charles's newfound happiness and see the two of you in the newspaper portrait. He is such a serious boy. He continues to make us proud. I know you will too.

> *Believe me,*
> *Very sincerely yours,*
> > *Mrs. Esther Lipshitz (Mrs. Hersh Lipshitz)*
> > *Amarillo, Tex.*

BABY 'EAGLET' BORN TO
LINDY AND ANNE

INFANT'S ARRIVAL ANNOUNCED ON MOTHER'S
24TH BIRTHDAY

Congratulations Arriving From All Over the World

ENGLEWOOD, N. J., June 22—The prince of the skies will now have a proper heir. It was announced at 3 P.M. yesterday that a son was born to the first couple of aviation, Colonel and Mrs. Charles A. Lindbergh. Coincidentally, the birth of the child occurred on the mother's twenty-fourth birthday, and a small party for the expectant mother had been planned for that day at the Englewood, N.J. home of Mrs. Lindbergh's father, Ambassador Dwight W. Morrow.

A Morrow family representative confirmed to wire services that three physicians and a nurse attended the mother and child, who were said to be healthy and resting comfortably. This announcement was issued despite several scattered, unconfirmed reports that the baby had been born sick, and possibly deformed.

Messages from Around the Globe

Shortly after the 3 P.M. announcement from the Morrow home, radio-broadcasting stations sent word of the blessed event across the nation, interrupting regular programming to do so. Cables buzzed with activity, sending the news across oceans.

Letters, telegrams, flowers, poems, gifts, and songs poured in immediately following the news. Messenger boys could be seen rushing up and down the long road to the Morrow home, laden with envelopes, many from strangers.

A great number of outsiders were turned away by the guards at the gates to the Morrow home. Just a few friends known personally to the guards were actually admitted into the estate.

Recollections of Romance

The couple's nuptials were recalled by residents of the village of Englewood, some of whom had gathered outside the Morrow estate to reminisce about the spring day Colonel Lindbergh and Miss Morrow were suddenly married.

The Lindbergh romance has been one based in aviation. Mrs. Lindbergh has accompanied her husband on approximately 30,000 of the record 50,000 miles he has flown since his legendary nonstop flight from New York to Paris in 1927.

One animated resident recalled the Lindberghs' frightening "one-wheel landing," which occurred on Feb. 27, shortly after the couple announced their engagement. In this harrowing calamity, the Colonel's plane flipped over, and he dislocated his left shoulder. Anne was shaken, but uninjured.

Little Lindy's Family

The Lindbergh heir certainly boasts a notable lineage. On Mrs. Lindbergh's side, he is the grandchild of Ambassador and Mrs. Morrow, the Ambassador coming from generations of Southern ancestry in West Virginia. On Col. Lindbergh's side, the little eaglet's grandmother is Mrs. Evangeline Lindbergh, a teacher, and graduate of the University of Michigan and the widow of Representative Charles A. Lindbergh, who served in the Sixtieth to the Sixty-fourth Congress and had come to the United States from Sweden as a small child.

Amarillo, Tex.

June 23, 1930

Mrs. Anne Morrow Lindbergh
in c/o Ambassador & Mrs. Dwight W. Morrow
Englewood, New Jersey

My Dear Anne:

    Congratulations on the new baby. I simply am beside myself until I know what you will be calling him. Charles would be a fine name, but if not that, may I suggest a name starting with the letter "A"? Andrew, Alexander, something like this for the new prince of the skies. My daughter and her husband, for instance, just had a little boy last month, his name Aaron (borrowing an initial from my recently departed dear brother Avi).

    It has been quite some time since I last wrote. I apologize for this. I am finding it harder to find spare time and change for things like letters and postage. It's hard for all of us nowadays, I'm sure you know.

    But with today's wonderful news I am motivated once again to write. I'm sure you remember I am the one who has been telling you of the impending tragedy that will befall Charles (and now perhaps your entire family). I thought that the accident in which Charles was injured and you were thankfully unhurt (though, I understand, quite frightened), was the tragedy I feared. But unfortunately, I believe it will be considerably more serious than this.

    With the birth of your son, I got a very strong feeling that the tragedy will occur sometime in the near future, say when the baby is four or five years old. This is something familiar to Charles, though he will not know why (you might want to ask his mother Evangeline about this matter, for Charles was just a small child).

    As usual, I encourage you both to be careful at all times, do not assume that all the well-wishers around you are completely worthy of your trust. Perhaps you could refrain from taking the child up into the sky with you until he is past the age of five or six? It seems such a dangerous place for a small child. These are just some suggestions.

Waiting for something you don't know what it is, I understand, is a little like a train with no posted schedule. But it will come, trust me. I just hope I can help you to be adequately prepared when it does.

Please send my love to Charles and pat the little prince on the bottom for me.

Believe me,

Mrs. Esther Lipshitz

February 21, 1932

AMARILLO, TEXAS

The Amarillo Daily Sun, February 21, 1932

[advertisement]

MIRIAM'S BABYLAND
OPENS TODAY

TODAY IS A BIG DAY for the mothers of the Amarillo area, for "Miriam's Babyland," the smartest Baby Shop in the Panhandle, is opening its doors. Here you will find the leading nationally advertised lines of babies' and children's wear. Come in and see where you can outfit your child from head to toe in the season's smartest. If your child is six months to six years of age, you can find what you want at this new shop.

- Shoes in all variety and sizes • Frocks • Playsuits
- Baby Blankets and Comforters • Complete line of Boys' Clothes • Gift Wrapping Free

"FRILLS AND FROCKS FOR TINY TOTS"
High Noon, Next-Door to The Diamond Shop, 516 Polk

With her own son Aaron screeching in his carriage, Miriam fancied she was starting to understand her mother's indifference to most things—namely her. Miriam dug through the last-minute shipments in search of the flannel sleeping suits from Pennsylvania. After a couple years of business-planning with Sam, Miriam's dream shop was to open in less than two hours, but Miriam fretted that after all this, she would still not be ready. If only the baby would stop screaming, the searing pain in her head might cease. Sam came in then, carrying a large cake in a blue cardboard box, cool and collected as always.

"Oh, Sam!" she called as soon as she saw him. She could feel hot pools gathering on her lower eyelids then. Sam placed the cake on the front counter and opened the top of the box: *Congratulations Miriam's Baby-land* was written in blue on a pink-frosted cake.

"Like it?" Sam asked.

"It's beautiful," she said, now crying outright. Finally the baby stopped his wailing when Sam went over to him.

"Hey, my little man," he said, picking Aaron up and holding him aloft. "How's the best-dressed kid in town?"

"I don't think I can do this in time," Miriam said. Finally Sam noticed she was in tears.

"What's wrong?" he asked, propping Aaron on his hip and coming over to Miriam. "I thought this was what you wanted."

"I do, I do want this." Miriam cried some more.

"There, there, honey," Sam said, bouncing Aaron up and down. "You're just nervous. Everything is ready to go, I'm here, your father's coming over, your mother, everything is fine."

"I can't find my invoices for these sleeping suits," she said.

"Okay, it's okay," Sam said, setting Aaron on his own wobbly legs. "We'll find them."

"But I don't know what to charge for them," she continued. Sam hugged her to him then, and she felt a little better.

"It's okay, it's all okay," Sam said, patting his wife on the shoulder.

Just then Esther and Hersh came into the store, the bells on the door startling Miriam. They carried what Sam had requested: napkins, plates, utensils, champagne glasses. Aaron waddled to his grandfather, who picked him up in the air after setting down the boxes he carried.

"*Oy*, he's getting heavy," Hersh complained, putting the boy back down and rubbing his lower back. It seemed to Hersh that this little boy was the only thing that made everything—all of it—worth it. He smiled as the boy toddled over toward his mother and father, who were conversing silently behind the counter.

Sam kissed Miriam on the head before leaving her to greet Hersh. By now both Hersh and Ben were in his employ—Ben general manager of The Diamond Shop, Hersh at the helm of the timepiece department. Hersh felt jittery being around his son-in-law since he'd started working for him. But what was the other choice nowadays?

"How does it look?" Sam asked.

"Wonderful," Hersh said, looking around. Though it seemed ridiculous to have such nice things for children.

"You'll be here for the opening?" Sam asked.

"If that's okay with you—"

"Of course," Sam interrupted. "You can't miss your daughter's grand opening."

"No, I suppose not," Hersh agreed.

"As long as Ben's over there, everything will be fine," Sam added. "Besides, The Diamond Shop is of little concern today. Today, this day is all about babies." Sam scooped up his son from behind, and he wailed until his father put him back down.

"This is pretty great," Sam said again to Hersh, leaning back against a counter and nodding his head slowly.

Hersh didn't respond.

"Don't you think?" he prompted Hersh, but Hersh didn't think Sam really wanted to hear what he thought.

"It's great," Hersh agreed.

"You don't think so?" Sam asked.

"No, I do, I do."

"What?" Sam was used to hearing what he wanted from his people.

"Just seems like a strange time to open more stores," Hersh finally said.

"You think so?"

"Expansion? I don't know if this is so good right now," Hersh said.

"I'm closing the shop in Pampa next month, you know."

Hersh shrugged his shoulders.

"You think those oil fields are gonna dry up?" Sam laughed. "No way."

"You're the businessman," Hersh said then. Sam didn't respond. The two leaned against the display case full of the silver rattles and spoons they'd previously been selling next door at The Diamond Shop.

Esther, meanwhile, was surveying the white and blue sleeping suits stacked on the counter beside Miriam, who was busy counting them. She ran her hand over the top white one. It was unbelievably soft, and Esther imagined it would be quite nice to have something like this against your skin as you slept.

"Do you do shipping?" Esther asked Miriam, who ignored her. Esther repeated louder, "Will you do shipping?"

"What?" Miriam asked, recounting the stacks.

"Shipping?"

"Yes, of course," she answered finally. "Mama, why are you asking this? You can take whatever you want." But Miriam didn't even stop to think what her mother could possibly need with baby clothes.

"Do you want me to take Aaron home?"

"Oh yes," Miriam said. She couldn't believe her mother was being so helpful. For once. "That would be so wonderful. You'll have him back by noon?"

"Sure."

"And make sure he doesn't dirty his suit."

"Of course not."

The Amarillo Daily Sun, March 2, 1932

LINDBERGH BABY KIDNAPPED

STOLEN FROM CRIB AT HOME OF PARENTS IN NEW JERSEY

Americans of All Religions Unite in Prayer for Little Lindy

HOPEWELL, N.J., March 1—Charles Augustus Lindbergh Jr., just 20 months old, was kidnapped tonight from his nursery in the home of his famous parents, Colonel and Mrs. Charles A. Lindbergh, and reportedly taken away in a stolen dark green Chrysler sedan, license plate number "A-1153 N.J."

The Colonel reported details of the crime to authorities himself. He said that the baby had been wearing his blue sleeping suit and was last seen at 7:30 P.M., when he was put to sleep in the crib in his nursery. The youngster had been feverish with a cold, and his mother worried over his condition. When a nursemaid went in to check on him around 10 P.M., the boy was gone.

By 11 o'clock, police in New Jersey and New York established roadblocks on streets and roads within striking distance of the Lindbergh estate. Checkpoints were established on bridges, tunnels, and at all ferry ports along the Hudson River, which borders New York City.

Distraught Parents

When newspapermen reached the isolated Lindbergh home, the Colonel was visibly agitated, though measured and calm. He paced the yard, closely observing state troopers and police detectives as they carefully searched with flashlights for any possible clues left by the kidnapper or kidnappers.

Mrs. Lindbergh was nowhere to be seen, but it was said

that the infant's mother wished to be kept apart from reporters and policemen. A close friend of the family confirmed tonight that Mrs. Lindbergh is expecting another child in approximately three months.

Americans Unite in Prayer

American citizens of all religions united in sending up a common prayer for the safe return of Charles Augustus Lindbergh Jr. Protestants, Catholics, and Jews alike asked a common God to care for the kidnapped boy. In a New York City radio broadcast that interrupted normal programming, Rabbi Avrahim Schwartz of Temple Emanu-El said, "A tragedy such as this affects all Americans, regardless of creed, caste, or color."

Safety Was Always a Concern

Since his birth on June 22, 1930, the 24th birthday of his mother, Charles Lindbergh Jr. has certainly been the most well-known child in the world. News of his birth was carried across the world in a fashion not unlike the day his famous father completed his death-defying, nonstop New York to Paris flight.

The Lindberghs have continued to travel abroad extensively since the child's birth, and Mrs. Lindbergh was frequently quoted as being extremely anxious about the boy's safety—even as he was left in the secure care of his maternal grandmother at the Morrow family's summer home in Maine.

At home too, the Lindbergh heir was well protected. The family's country estate, located in the Sourland Hills of New Jersey, was built for them at a cost of $50,000 while they traveled the Orient. The Lindberghs picked the house's site from the air, specifically with complete privacy in mind. The property is located far from roads and highways, about five miles from Hopewell, and has a private landing field and hangar for the flier's plane.

March 3, 1932

AMARILLO, TEXAS

The Amarillo Daily Sun, March 3, 1932

Local Sports Spotlight:

'PAMPA FLASH' SET TO FACE PUG GRUBBS

TONIGHT IN I. O. O. F. BOXING CARD

Lubbock's "Pug Grubbs" has accepted a challenge from Sam Lazarus's "Pampa Flash." After much anticipation on both sides, the bout will finally take place tonight at 7:00 P.M. in the municipal auditorium's Potter Arena.

"If that's not fighting weight, I don't know what is," joked Mr. Lazarus yesterday at the official weigh-in, where the Panhandle's own "Flash" stood tall on the scale in his undergarments, nose to nose with his hefty opponent.

There was no comment from Pug Grubbs's handlers, possibly still bitter about the call in the fighter's last bout in Amarillo, in which Grubbs was handed his first loss ever in a TKO decision. His record is 20 wins, 1 loss. The young Pampa Flash's record is 12–0.

The Flash-Grubbs fight will be the fourth and final bout of the evening. Tickets are fifty cents general admission, one dollar ringside.

Sam helped Miriam close up shop, and they hurried home to pick up the baby and collect a few of his things. Then they headed over to Esther and Hersh's house to leave Aaron for the night.

Miriam held the boy in her lap as Sam fought with the gearshift and the car coughed and bucked a few times. Miriam hugged the baby close against her bosom.

"Damn this car!" Sam exclaimed.

"The *baby*," Miriam said.

"Well, I'm getting rid of it," he said, continuing to struggle with the long silver shifter, twinkling in the odd streetlamp they passed. Miriam thought it might break from her husband's jamming it into the floor. "You think your father wants this piece of junk?"

"I don't know." The car finally gave in to its master's bidding and it eased into a smoother ride. "We had another good day," Miriam offered after a few moments of silence.

"Yeah?"

"I finally sold that crib."

"Great, that's great," Sam said, looking in the mirror outside the car door. But he was distracted, nervous about the boxing card. There was a lot of money involved. Miriam decided not to bother him the rest of the way to her parents' house.

MRS. LINDBERGH APPEALS DIRECTLY TO KIDNAPPERS

HOPEWELL, N.J., March 2—This is a message to the kidnappers of the Lindbergh baby, from a brokenhearted mother who misses her beloved son. This plea comes directly from Mrs. Lindbergh's lips, and she is asking you to find some shred of humanity left in your heart and follow the diet outlined below. Newspapers across the country are carrying this same message in hopes that you might read the story and at least heed her request, if you don't immediately return the child. The baby has been sick, and if you do not follow this diet, he might grow sicker still. Here is what Mrs. Lindbergh has been giving the baby since he fell ill:

- One quart of milk during the day
- Three tablespoons of cooked cereal, morning and night
- Two tablespoons of cooked vegetables, once a day
- One yolk of egg daily
- One baked potato or rice, once a day
- Two tablespoons of stewed fruit daily
- Half a cup of orange juice on waking
- Half a cup of prune juice after the afternoon nap
- And 14 drops medicine called vioaterola during the day

That is what Mrs. Lindbergh wants you to give the boy.

LINDBERGH WILL PAY $50,000 FOR SON

POLICE REVEAL RANSOM NOTE WAS LEFT IN NURSERY

HOPEWELL, N.J., March 2—While New Jersey state troopers continued to comb the woods surrounding the Lindbergh estate, it was announced that a note had been found in the nursery from which Charles Augustus Lindbergh Jr. was stolen on Tuesday night. The Colonel first found the small envelope containing the note pinned to the sill of the window through which the baby was taken, and it demanded a ransom.

The specific text of the note was being withheld by police, but it has been reported that the boy's safety was threatened if the demands in the note were not met. As of tonight, the Lindberghs stood ready to pay an amount reported to be $50,000. Neither the police nor Col. Lindbergh denied this amount.

Parents Distressed, But Determined

Surely the most heartrending moment since the baby's abduction last night came today when Mrs. Lindbergh, appearing fragile and exhausted, emerged from the house for the first time to make a direct appeal to the kidnappers for the sake of the child's health, (*see* "Mrs. Lindbergh Appeals Directly to Kidnappers," *above*).

Later that evening, as lights blazed from all windows of the Lindbergh estate, Colonel Lindbergh addressed reporters personally. He, too, appeared greatly strained, now attired in a dark gray suit, with a small black dog trotting at his heels. The Colonel had changed out of the mud-stained and wrinkled work garb he had worn while aiding police in the search of his estate during the hours since the boy's kidnapping.

The aviator evenly read a formal request that all reporters and photographers withdraw from his property. He explained that telephone lines had been overburdened, and that a switchboard would soon be installed in the garage to improve communication.

CAPONE WEIGHS IN ON LINDBERGH KIDNAPPING

CHICAGO, March 2—Support for the Lindbergh kidnapping is emerging from a wide variety of places today, including tips from psychics and astrologers, as well as an offer of bloodhounds from a man in Virginia who owns a pack of the scent-tracking dogs.

But certainly the most interesting offer of them all came from the Cook County jail in Chicago today, where Al Capone added his own "two cents" to the Lindbergh baby's kidnapping. Capone was awaiting transfer to an Atlanta penitentiary to begin serving an eleven-year sentence, and in his heartfelt public statement, he offered a generous reward of $10,000 for the safe recovery of the child and the capture of his kidnappers.

Capone said, "It's the most outrageous, atrocious thing I ever heard of. I know how Mrs. Capone and I would feel if our son were kidnapped, and I sympathize with the Lindberghs."

In an ironic twist, it was remembered that Capone himself has been connected to a variety of kidnappings in the Chicago area, among other violent crimes perpetrated against individuals.

"If I were out of jail, I could be of real assistance. I have friends all over the country who could aid in running this thing down," he said.

There is no word as to whether the Lindberghs or police will respond to Capone's offer.

"Hello, my boy," Hersh called out when Miriam let Aaron out of the car in the driveway. Miriam followed the boy as he toddled over to his grandfather. "Who's my little bean?" Hersh asked.

"We'll be by in the morning to pick him up, tell Mama," Miriam said.

"Coming inside?" Hersh asked.

Miriam looked back at Sam, still in the car, engine clicking away. His elbow rested out the window. "The first fight starts in thirty minutes," she said, pushing Aaron along toward the front door.

"Why don't you come in," Hersh suggested, and Miriam knew to do so. She looked back at Sam, by now gesturing with his hands in the air, palms up with one of them sticking out the window. She could tell he was agitated even though his face was mostly obscured through the tiny windshield, more mirror than window reflecting the darkening sky. He cut the engine.

"Where's Mama?" Miriam asked when she entered the house.

Hersh nodded toward the bedroom.

Miriam knocked on the door. "Mama?" There was no answer. "Mama, I'm coming in."

Esther was in the bed staring out the open window, her back facing the door.

"Mother," Miriam began. "The fights are tonight, very important for Sam, remember?"

——

"Remember, Aaron is here for the night," she continued.

Aaron wandered in then, babbling "Na, na, na, na." Hersh appeared behind him. Esther turned over then.

"Everyone wants to see the crying lady?" she said.

"Are you okay, Mama?" Miriam asked, but Esther didn't answer. Her face was red, strained.

"She has taken the Lindbergh thing very badly," Hersh offered quietly.

"I'm right here, Hersh," Esther said, sitting up in the bed and blowing her nose in an already-damp handkerchief. "She this, she that."

"It's very sad about the Lindbergh boy, isn't it?" Miriam said. And then, "But Mother, we need to go to the fights now. Is it still okay if Aaron stays with you?"

"No, no, no. No children!" she yelled.

"Esther!" Hersh scolded.

"No, no, I won't do it," she continued.

"What are you saying?" Miriam asked.

"What is all of this, the parents leaving the kids alone all the time?" she began, a heavy tear leaving a perfectly straight wide line down her cheek before disappearing into the deep wrinkle to the left of her nose. "When I had children, you did not leave them all over the place and go see the men boxing, or go running off all over the world to China, back and forth, here and there."

"Esther, please," Hersh said. He grabbed Aaron's arm and guided him out of the bedroom.

"Mother, what are you talking about?"

"This, this," she exclaimed. "You leaving the babies and running around town and opening businesses and having ladies you don't even know taking care of your baby."

"Mama—"

"No, no. I am not going to do this."

"We have to get going. The Flash is fighting soon, *please*."

"No," Esther insisted, shaking a hand violently in front of her head and closing her eyes. "You'll learn your lesson. I told you this would happen."

"You told me what would happen?" Miriam asked.

—

"You are not taking Aaron for us tonight? You know this is a very important night for Sam. This is business."

"No."

"A boxing match is not a very good place for a child," Miriam threatened.

"I don't care," Esther said, lying back down in bed with her back to Miriam. "You'll learn your lesson."

Miriam left her mother then, closing the bedroom door behind her rather forcefully. Hersh stood, mouth hanging open, out in the hall with Aaron. He shrugged his usual shoulder shrug.

"What? What does *this*," Miriam began, aping her father's posture, "mean?"

"What?" Hersh said.

"She is not well."

He shrugged again.

"What does this mean when you do this with your shoulders?" Miriam asked again. "What, Papa?"

Sam poked his head in the front door then. "All set?"

"We're taking Aaron with us," Miriam said.

Sam looked confused. He looked at Hersh, then back at Miriam. "I don't understand."

"Me neither," Miriam said, collecting Aaron's things. "Let's go."

"Hersh?" Sam asked, stepping entirely through the doorway.

"If you do the thing with your shoulders one more time, Papa," Miriam said, "I will scream. Sam, let's go."

Hersh stood in the driveway as Sam backed his car out onto the street. He watched as the car coasted backward and into first gear before speeding up Tyler and turning sharply at the next corner, neglecting to stop at the sign where the telephone wires ended. One of the taillights on Sam's new car wasn't working—the left one, winking at Hersh like the joke was on him.

Hersh hated the pounding violence of boxing, but he could imagine himself a huge fan of it tonight. Hell, if it meant not having to go back into that house and fruitlessly trying to console the hysterical woman inside, he would even consider getting into the ring himself and going a few rounds.

March 4, 1932

AMARILLO, TEXAS

𝔗𝔥𝔢 𝔄𝔪𝔞𝔯𝔦𝔩𝔩𝔬 𝔇𝔞𝔦𝔩𝔶 𝔖𝔲𝔫, March 4, 1932

HAUNTING SIGHT OF SUFFERING MOTHER

HOPEWELL, N. J., March 3—While much of the nation is focused on the fate of the missing child of the Charles A. Lindberghs, a few New Jersey state troopers are privy to a different side of the ever-developing tragedy. According to trooper Matthew Cobb, every so often a haunting pair of eyes peeks out from the otherwise empty nursery window on the second story of the Lindbergh home in Hopewell.

Cobb described the eyes as "deeply sad and weary," and claimed that they are in fact the eyes of Mrs. Lindbergh, the understandably distraught mother of the stolen child. "Those of us with wives and kids of our own," Cobb said, "well, it's got to be the hardest thing about this whole mess, seeing that lady and thinking what she must be going through."

'PAMPA FLASH' VICTORIOUS IN I.O.O.F. BOUT

Lubbock's "Pug Grubbs" hit the mat hard last night in the third round of his main event fight with the Panhandle's own "Pampa Flash," bringing the young pugilist's record to 13 wins and no losses. Grubbs's record fell to 20–2. The bout took place at the municipal auditorium's Potter Arena.

Sam Lazarus of The Diamond Shop, the Flash's sponsor, experienced a belligerent moment of his own when, after the fight's conclusion, Grubbs's trainer Rod McNeiland hurled a small wooden stool at Sam as he celebrated the victory with his wife and small child ringside. Neither Mrs. Lazarus nor their two-year-old son Aaron was injured in the scuffle. Sam received a small cut on the back of his head, requiring two stitches which were received at Amarillo General a few hours after the fight's end.

Sam declined to press charges. McNeiland and Grubbs challenged the Flash to a rematch next month, this time in Lubbock.

No comment from Sam or the Flash on a possible rematch, but when responding to the question of what's next for the young undefeated fighter, Sam was heard saying, "We're looking to take a step up. I'm thinking of taking him to Dallas next year."

The next boxing card at Potter Arena is scheduled for June 20.

AMARILLO LINK TO LINDBERGH KIDNAPPING?

POSTCARD MAILED HERE 'MOST LIKELY A HOAX,' SAY POLICE

Amarillo Postmaster M.J. Denison confirmed that a postal card addressed to "Chas. A. Lindbergh, Hopewell, N.J.," and carrying a threatening message on the reverse side, was mailed at the post office here in Amarillo about 4 o'clock yesterday.

The typed message read: "Baby safe . . . Do as instructed. Cold weather here . . ." A poorly rendered sketch of a skull and crossbones was drawn below the words in pencil, with the word "beware" printed above it. There was also a thumbprint in ink in the bottom left corner of the card.

Although Amarillo police officers who inspected the card believed it to be the work of a prankster because it was not in fact cold here in Amarillo yesterday, Captain Dean Kent said an investigation would be started immediately, and that every effort would be made to learn the identity of the sender. "It's most likely a hoax," Kent said.

Due to a news story from Dallas Sunday night, responding officers initially took the postcard quite seriously. The Dallas story had reported that a dark green car with New York plates and carrying two men and a baby had been seen in the area and was being investigated. Amarillo police, however, no longer believe the incidents are linked.

Hersh came into the bedroom and asked his wife, "Will you be getting out of the bed today?"

"No," she replied, "not today."

"Okay," he said. "When do you think you might rise?"

"I can't be certain."

"Okay. I'm going to the shop. Will you be needing anything before I come home?"

"No, thank you."

DESPITE NATIONAL TREND, JUST ONE KIDNAPPING IN AMARILLO

BOTH MOTHER AND CHILD DEEPLY AFFECTED BY CRIME

If you are a mother and you are reading this article, then surely you have been following the Lindbergh baby's kidnapping case over the last four days. Surely every mother has asked herself at least once: "What if *my* baby were stolen?"

What indeed?

But while the number of kidnappings has been on the steady rise nationwide, and kidnapping consortiums have been operating in many of our country's major cities, the trend seems to have passed Amarillo by. In fact, in recent memory, only one case of kidnapping has been recorded in the city, and it was carried out by a barren woman who wanted a baby and so stole a 3-day-old youngster by posing as a benevolent Sunday School worker.

Still, with this week's tragic news about the Lindbergh heir, Amarillo mothers and fathers alike realized that a child can be taken from any home at any time. The parents need not be internationally famous. A kidnapper can strike for a variety of reasons, sometimes simply because one parent wishes to gain custody of a child from the other.

Whatever the reason for a kidnapping, it is clear that the visualization of this type of crime is particularly devastating to Amarillo and Panhandle-area parents. In a recent poll conducted by this newspaper during the days since the Lindbergh kidnapping, it was found that a striking number of mothers and fathers said they would prefer their own death to the kidnapping of a child.

When asked to comment on what Mrs. Lindbergh might be experiencing since Charles Jr.'s kidnapping, Dr. Robert Miller of Amarillo said that while he has never treated a mother for kidnapping-related grief, he has read in medical journals that some mothers in this condition have been driven insane by a lack of knowledge of their child's safety. In fact, during her rare appearances in recent days, Mrs. Lindbergh has demonstrated an abiding craving for knowledge about her missing son's care.

Violet Maitland Allsted, who advises parents daily in her newspaper column "All About Your Baby," said of Charles Jr.:

"Babies' memories are not fully set at such a young age. It won't be long before the memories of its extravagant home, generous parents, and comforting nursemaid will slip completely from its mind.

"The experiences of a 20-month-long life could take as little as six months to a year to erase completely. After just a few weeks the baby may begin calling its kidnapper "Daddy" and seeking maternal comfort from whatever woman is aiding the kidnapper in the abduction and ransom scheme. Such is the acquiescence of youth."

"Esther?" Hersh whispered, knocking quietly on the bedroom door and pushing it open slightly. "Esther, the doctor is here for you."

"I don't want to see the doctor," Esther said. "Go away."

"I'm afraid I cannot do that," Hersh said. She wanted Hersh to go away more than she wanted the doctor to.

"Mrs. Lipshitz," the doctor started. "My name is Dr. Miller, and I'm here to see what might be ailing you."

"Nothing is ailing me."

"Okay, well, that's what I like to hear," Dr. Miller said, "but I'd like to determine that for myself if that's okay with you."

"Not with my husband here," she said, sitting up and fixing her hair in a feeble attempt to look presentable.

The doctor looked back at Hersh, who quietly closed the door behind him. Esther heard him talking out in the hall, and she wondered who else was there.

"So, Mrs. Lipshitz, I'd just like to take a few vital signs if that is okay with you."

Esther shrugged, looking out the window as the doctor fiddled with her arm.

"How have you been feeling?" he asked, writing something down in his little book.

"Who sent you?" she asked.

"Excuse me?" he said. "I was wondering how-you-have-been-*feeling*."

"I understand, you don't have to talk like that."

"I'm sorry."

"Who sent you? I know not my husband."

"Well, if you must know, Mr. Lazarus employed my services. He and your daughter are very worried about you."

"There is no reason to worry."

He put the stethoscope in his ears and said, "May I?" pointing to Esther's chest.

He placed the coldness on her chest and Esther breathed for him. This was truly senseless. If everyone would just leave her alone.

"A tragedy what's happened to the Lindberghs," he said then, very casually.

Esther's interest piqued. She worried her heart was beating faster as he listened.

"Just horrible someone would take a little defenseless baby like that," Dr. Miller continued, scribbling something else in his book with a short, mangled pencil.

"It *is* horrible," she echoed. "Why do you say this?"

"Why? I've been reading the papers and listening to the radio ever since it happened. It's very upsetting to me and my wife."

"Your wife?"

"Oh, she's just been, what . . . ? *Distraught* over the whole thing."

"Do you think it's a gang?" Esther asked.

"I don't think a gang would risk something like this," the doctor said. "These people are amateurs."

"I think so too," Esther said, leaning in and whispering conspiratorially.

"Maybe associates of the servants," he added.

"Yes, yes, this is what I've been thinking."

The doctor leaned back in the chair beside the bed and looked at Esther as though she were a fish at the end of his line. Esther saw this immediately, and, smelling a rotten herring, decided to be smarter than that.

"I understand you and your husband lost a child in this manner," Dr. Miller said then, seemingly very pleased with himself.

"No, it was nothing like this," Esther replied, looking back out the window, the curtains blowing slightly.

"I think it is very similar, losing a child at such a young age."

Esther didn't respond.

"Don't you think?" he pressed.

—

"I have been following the case every day."

Esther resisted. It wasn't hard. She hated Hersh for it. After five minutes that would otherwise have been silent if not for the light brushing of curtains against windowsill, the doctor packed up his bag and left Esther alone. A close call, but finally, mercifully, he was gone. She could hear all the voices, trying to keep hushed in the hallway outside her bedroom door.

LINDBERGH BABY FOUND DEAD BY NEGRO

BODY IDENTIFIED FOUR MILES FROM FLIER'S HOME BY COMPARING CHILD'S CLOTHING AND HAIR COLOR

HOPEWELL, N. J., May 12—Just four short miles from the Sourland Mountain estate of Colonel and Mrs. Charles A. Lindbergh, and one mile from Hopewell, the kidnapped Charles Augustus Lindbergh Jr. was found dead in a wooded area, half-buried and partially covered by leaves.

An initial positive identification was made based on the hair on the dead body, which coincided with the curly blond hair of the Lindbergh heir, just 20 months old when he was stolen from the upstairs nursery of his parents' secluded home 72 days earlier. For further identification, fabric and thread from the family home were brought to the site to compare with fragments of the flannel undershirt found on the body.

The items matched, and New Jersey State Police head Colonel H. Norman Schwartzkopf then summoned reporters to the Lindbergh estate's garage, where he read a press release to a stunned crowd of otherwise seasoned newspapermen. Immediately the wires were filled once again with tragic news of the Charles A. Lindberghs, and messages of sympathy began pouring in from all over the world.

Cause of Death Determined

The child's body was decomposed, and in its skull was a hole the size of a 25-cent piece just above the right ear, with another fracture extending from the top of the skull to the left ear. Dr. Charles H. Mitchell, who performed the autopsy on the boy, said that "the cause of death is a fractured skull due to external violence."

Given the condition of the body, Dr. Mitchell's report concluded that death had most likely occurred shortly after or even during the kidnapping. Col. Schwartzkopf added that the body "was in a bad state of decomposition."

Negro Makes Discovery; Nursemaid Identifies Body

The body was found at about 3 P.M. by William Allen, 46, a negro who had gone into the woods after the truck in which he was a passenger stopped on a steep grade of an isolated stretch of road between Hopewell and Mount Rose. Allen explained: "After I got into the woods, I went under a branch and looked down. I saw a skull sticking up out of the dirt. I thought I saw a baby, with its foot sticking out of the ground."

When asked by reporters what punishment should be reserved for the kidnapper-murderer, Allen, visibly shaken, replied, "There's nothing too bad for the man that did it."

Betty Gow, former nursemaid to Charles Jr., positively identified the child's body when state police brought her to the morgue in Trenton, N.J. She made the identification by several undisclosed "characteristic markings" on the boy's body, in addition to the fragments of clothing.

May 25, 1932

AMARILLO, TEXAS

Esther appeared in the kitchen after nearly two weeks of refusing to leave the bedroom, accepting nothing from Hersh the entire time but water, a little food here and there, and the daily paper.

"Feeling better?" Hersh asked, rising to greet her. Sam had suggested Hersh stay at home every day since Esther took to bed. Now maybe he could get back to the jewelry store and do some work, though he knew Sam would still encourage him to stay with his wife—on Sam's dime.

"No, not really," Esther said, pouring a cup of coffee from the pot Hersh had made.

"Would you like me to do that for you?" Hersh offered.

"No, thank you."

"Dr. Miller brought over these pills," Hersh said then, sitting back down at the kitchen table and tapping the little glass bottle with his fingers. "I think you'll feel much better if you take them."

Esther didn't respond. It was exhausting standing up after so many days lying in bed with only a couple of trips to the toilet each day. Her heart pounded, and Esther needed to sit down. But she didn't want to be so close to her husband.

"That coffee's cold. Let me make some more," Hersh said, standing and crossing to the sink. Esther wondered how he could read her thoughts all of a sudden.

Esther sat. "The coffee's fine," she said.

"You're not going to take the pills?"

"No."

Hersh grunted the way he always did and then walked out of the kitchen. "I'm off to the store," he called down the hall. "Do you need anything before I go?"

"No," Esther called back, and then the front door slammed shut, and she was alone—truly alone—for the first time since the news. There had been so many confusing leads, false reports, dashed hopes. And now no chance of finding little Charles alive. Why didn't Anne or Evangeline—or Charles even—listen to her warnings? Perhaps she could've been more clear. She should've known Reuven would have to lose a child of his own in this manner. A hole in his head. A bloody, curly blond mess of hair, buried in the dirt beside the road, and discovered by some negroes who wished to urinate there. It was too hideous.

Whoever was responsible would pay. They would.

Before, when there was hope of a safe return, Esther could forgive—these were, after all, desperate times. But not now. Not after a baby's skull had been pummeled like that. Ditched on the side of the road in nothing but his little soft suit. She wished to see him hang—whoever it was. Hang, or however it was the judges and lawyers punished people in this country nowadays. She would personally see to it herself, if she had to.

LINDY AND ANNE SPEND NIGHT
IN PANHANDLE

'SOMEWHERE NORTH OF AMARILLO,'
SAYS THE FAMOUS FLIER

KANSAS CITY, May 7—After spending the night in their plane on the ground somewhere in the Texas Panhandle, Colonel and Mrs. Charles A. Lindbergh landed in Kansas City at 12:45 P.M. today. Friends and airport officials had worried over the flying couple's safety, since they were to have arrived at 9:30 P.M. the night before. It turns out that one of the trademark Panhandle dust storms had forced the Lindberghs' plane down when visibility was reduced to virtually nothing, according to the seasoned flier.

The Colonel is en route from Glendale, California, to Washington, D.C., where he is expected to testify for the prosecution in the case against Gaston B. Means and Norman Whitaker on conspiracy charges. The two men are accused of defrauding Mrs. Evalyn Walsh McLean of $35,000 by making false promises that in exchange for the money, they would produce the kidnappers of Charles A. Lindbergh Jr.

Fruitless Search

When the Lindberghs exited their plane, both appeared dusty and weary from the experience of spending the night on the ground, but were surprised to hear that friends had been concerned over their fate.

"I'm sorry anybody worried. People shouldn't worry. It's liable to happen any time in the Western country," Colonel Lindbergh said with a smile vaguely reminiscent of the shy boy who became famous the world over on one fateful night in Paris in 1927.

A six-plane search had been sent out the night before, but after hours of fruitlessly crisscrossing the Southwest, the pilots returned with a heaviness in their hearts. When apprised of the frantic search, Lindbergh explained that the landing spot was far north of the Transcontinental and Western Air route, and that he had not been carrying a wireless transmitter on board.

When asked exactly where he had landed his black and red monoplane, the Colonel said, "somewhere north of Amarillo."

Reports from the Panhandle area confirmed that the night was indeed a sandy and windy one. "I couldn't walk more than 100 yards from the ship without losing sight of it," the Colonel said.

No Visit to N.M. Ranch

The Lindberghs' Kansas City arrival debunked an earlier rumor that the Colonel and Mrs. Lindbergh had stopped over for six hours in Moriarty, N.M., last night for a visit with a rancher named Howard.

Lindbergh said he did not know a rancher named Howard, and that he had simply been forced down by the storm about two hours after leaving Albuquerque, N.M., where he had landed in order to refuel his plane. There was no visit to Moriarty or anywhere else for that matter.

Plane Equipped for Sleeping

When asked about the accommodations the night before, Mrs. Lindbergh, attired in a dusty, large man's shirt and gray jodhpurs, informed the gathered crowd that their plane is in fact always equipped for sleeping—precisely for unexpected situations like these—and that she and the Colonel routinely stock thirty days' worth of food aboard the plane.

"We passed a very comfortable night," Mrs. Lindbergh said. She described how the Colonel unfolded a mattress and wedged it into the fuselage of the plane. He then closed the fuselage covering, and the couple was safe and secure for the night.

Well out of sight of any roads or structures, the Colonel and Mrs. Lindbergh dined on both supper and breakfast in the spacious fuselage of their grounded plane. Their only companions, besides each other, were coyotes, jackrabbits, prairie dogs—and a few curious head of cattle.

––––––––

LOCAL ANGLE:

WIDESPREAD SEARCH FAILS TO FIND LINDBERGHS

Before the famous flying couple turned up in Kansas City yesterday, Amarillo railroad dispatchers, Panhandle-area pilots, and airways radiomen searched gallantly for the location in which the Lindberghs spent the night in the Panhandle.

Rufus Diggs of Dumas, an oil worker, claimed to have seen the black and red monoplane taking off around 9 A.M. yesterday, from a dusty strip of land behind his house, approximately ten miles northwest of Dumas. Upon investigation, however, no telltale signs of an airplane's landing or takeoff could be confirmed.

Railroad dispatchers who were on duty in Amarillo throughout the ordeal confirmed that one of the worst sandstorms of the season blew through Dalhart, Dumas, and Channing on the night of the Lindberghs' emergency landing.

May 9, 1933

Esther watched her son-in-law's shoes pushing up and down on the small square pedals on the floor of his car. She noticed the left one squeaked each time he pressed it, very gently up and down, whereas the middle pedal he usually pressed faster, and never at the same time as the small round pedal on the floor to the right.

A dusty warm wind blew through the car and loosed a few strands of Esther's hair from underneath her headscarf. They snaked wildly around her, but Esther didn't bother tucking them back in. As they crossed the Amarillo city limits, she could feel the muscles around her eyes and lips loosen with each wooden post they'd pass by the side of the road.

Sam rambled on and on about the business he was tending to up in Dumas, but Esther wasn't listening. Something about buying up the stock of a man who'd lost his business, Esther couldn't really be sure. Times were hard, yes, but what a perfect time to teach herself how to drive by watching Sam's feet. Esther knew she could do the steering part—in fact she knew all too well where she might steer herself if she ever got into a car and took herself somewhere, but it was the crazy pattern of pushing the pedals up and down she'd have to worry about.

Sam's legs were cramped beneath the steering wheel, and it looked like it might be a little uncomfortable for him. Esther imagined her own legs would fit just perfectly in the same space. Her legs were sore these days more often than they were not, but she believed they would hold up fine for this driving thing. Now that Sam had given Hersh his old car, maybe she could learn.

Who was she fooling? Hersh would never teach Esther how to drive. He thought she was too nervous. Esther didn't know if she agreed with him.

"It helps if you look out the window at the horizon," Sam said.

"What?"

"If you're feeling sick from the motion," he said. "You're looking down, but it feels better if you look out."

"Oh, I'm not sick," Esther said, taking Sam's advice and trying to see the precise line where yellow land intersected with blue sky. It was a gently rolling line, seemingly endless, with black bunches of cattle interrupting every so often.

The wind messed Sam's hair too, Esther noticed, which was a rarity. She wanted to study him, but it was awkward because they sat so close together on the hard, rounded seat. It was quite uncomfortable, but at this moment Esther preferred it to the alternative of a variety of seats in her own home. Sam adjusted the little window sticking out the side of his door, and the wind stopped tossing his hair as much. Esther tried to do the same on her side, but the window was too difficult to budge.

"I'll fix that for you when we stop for gas."

"No, it's fine," Esther said. She could not remember the last time she felt this happy. She knew the day would ultimately end up back in Amarillo, Hersh waving at her in the driveway as Sam pulled in, but for now, the entire day was ahead of them. And it was a crisp, beautiful one, hints of the coming summer on the wind.

In Dumas, Sam parked the car in front of the Canyon Diner and across the street from a small hotel. "I don't know what you want to do during my meeting," he said. "There's a nice restaurant in the hotel over there. I can set you up and then come get you in about an hour. Then we can go do your little thing and head back to Amarillo."

"Okay," Esther said. But when Sam came around to open the door for her, Esther added, "I changed my mind. Is it okay if I just stroll around town for a bit?"

"All right," Sam said. "Are you sure?"

"Yes."

"Okay then. Do you have any money for a cup of coffee?" he asked, reaching deep into his right pocket. It seemed Sam's arm sank halfway down his leg before he reached the bottom, setting coins jingling.

"No, no," Esther insisted, though she had only a dime or two in her purse. She would never take money from her son-in-law—at least not out in the open like this.

"Sure you're going to be okay?" he asked, checking his wristwatch. "I think I'd feel better if I just met you at the hotel."

"Go, go," Esther said, waving him off. "I'll be there when you're done."

Esther stood in the middle of a fairly empty street as she watched Sam stroll off toward a brick building with 117 over the front door and a Coca-Cola sign painted on the side.

A car much like Sam's came up the street, and Esther moved toward the curb to give it room. She saw a young lady step out of the diner with her light-eyed son, the metal door slamming shut behind them, and Esther decided to go inside for a cup of tea. The whole diner was shaped like a train car.

Esther sat in a booth with two upside-down coffee cups already on it. Soon a large woman with an unruly pile of red hair on her head came by her table, flipped over one of the cups, and asked, "Coffee?" after she had already started pouring.

"Thank you," Esther said.

"Anything else?"

"No, this is fine for now, thank you," Esther said. "Oh, excuse me?"

"Yep?"

"Do you know a local man, a Mr. Rufus Diggs?"

"You with the newspaper?" the waitress asked.

"No, why?"

"'Cause they was up here all day yesterday and the day before looking for that damn Lindy plane," she said. "We were nonstop busy all day."

"And so do you know this fellow?" Esther pressed.

"Sure, I know that bastard, what do you want with him?"

"I was hoping to visit him," Esther said. "Do you know where we might find him?"

The waitress looked at the empty booth across from Esther.

"My son-in-law is with me," Esther added.

"I don't know exactly where it is, but if you go up the highway 'bout five, ten miles, you turn off left after a bunch of oil derricks on your right."

"Thank you, that's very helpful," Esther said, but the waitress just looked at her.

Esther sat quietly over her coffee, watching the street through the cloudy window beside her. After some time she saw Sam walking across the street and into the door of the Hotel Dumas. Esther stood to try to catch him, but remembered she had to pay for her coffee first. She fished a ten-cent-piece out of her purse and dropped it onto the table. Esther struggled with the heavy diner door before it released her out into a burst of dry, white sunlight on the street.

Sam came out of the hotel and looked left and right down the block. Esther called to him, and he crossed the street without looking.

"You had me worried," he said. "Where were you?"

"Oh, I was having a cup of coffee," Esther said, pointing a thumb over her shoulder. "A lady told me where this Mr. Diggs's house is."

"Okay, well, I'm done early, so let's get on over there. I also got his address from the phone book."

They headed north out of town. After about twenty minutes, Sam turned off onto a smaller road along a row of ragged trees. At the end, a long, badly maintained path with many holes in it led to the tiny wooden house. The name was on the postbox, although the second "g" in "Diggs" had rubbed off.

"I think it's better if I go in," Sam said, taking in the condition of the house and yard, such as it was. A dusty dog the same color as the land barked at Sam's car when it pulled up. There was all sorts of lifeless machinery on the property, dark black piles of twisted metal and wiry objects of varying shapes and sizes. Half a car, some rotting lumber.

As Sam walked up to the front door, the dog followed a few steps behind, barking the whole way. Sam looked back at it a few times as he approached the door. Esther thanked him in her head for not asking twice about this visit. To Sam it seemed as natural as if Esther had asked him for a ride downtown to Miriam's store.

A man opened the door and Esther watched through the windshield while Sam began talking to him. He was a skinny fellow, very tall and poorly attired. They spoke for some time before Sam looked back to see if Esther was watching. He probably couldn't see her through the windshield, Esther assumed. Sam reached back into his right pocket and peeled a bill off and handed it to the fellow at the door. He tried blocking Esther's view of this by moving behind a small shrub, but Esther could see it all.

With this Sam walked back to the car and Mr. Diggs climbed onto a motorcycle that looked like it hadn't run in ten years. But he jumped three or four times on the side of it and Esther could hear the loud popping of the engine. Sam got into the car and started his engine. They followed the man on the motorcycle out behind the house and into the rocky desert behind it. The man stood on the motorcycle when he went over bumps, and Sam's car rocked up and down, side to side as they crossed the wild terrain. Esther held onto the door with both hands. There were no other structures in sight, and a few small animals scattered out of their path as they traveled.

"He's taking us to the spot," Sam said.

In about five minutes, Mr. Diggs stopped his motorcycle and got off in a cloud of dust. Sam pulled up just behind it, and got out of the car. Esther let herself out and stepped onto the ground. She still clutched her purse because it didn't seem as though she should leave it in the car. Esther nodded a greeting to the man, who was standing with his hands on his slender hips, waiting. He eyed Esther.

They followed him on foot over a small hill beside a little canyon. At the top of the incline, the man stopped and pointed. "That's it right there."

"Where?" Sam asked.

He pointed out at the horizon. "Right 'bout *there*," he repeated, squinting an eye.

The wind whistled around them. "I don't see anything," Esther said.

"Well, the dust's been blowing all night," he said. "I don't know what to tell you." He continued pointing at nothing.

"Can we walk over?" Sam asked. His shoes were dusty, as were Esther's. The whole lot of Mr. Diggs was dusty.

"Sure. You might still be able to see the tracks."

They walked in silence, Esther following Mr. Diggs, Sam following Esther. Every so often when she took a shaky step, she felt Sam's hand on her elbow. The man in front of her stopped. His dog ran by chasing a brown rabbit, which darted into a little shrub and disappeared. The dog poked his nose into the bush. This was the closest Esther had been to Mr. Diggs; she could smell a whiff of alcohol coming off his skin when another warm gust whipped up around them.

The man knelt and pointed to a small line in the dirt. "This is it, right here."

"Where?" Sam asked.

"Right here," he said, moving closer.

"I don't see anything," Sam said. *Bless him,* Esther thought.

"Yeah, I was just getting up that morning. I don't got a job no more, but I was standing in my yard feeding the dog when I heard this loud engine. I knew it weren't no car 'cause don't no one come out here much. I saw a bunch of blowing dust and then off in the distance, coming from about right here," he said, now standing over the tiny line in the dirt, "'bout right here's where this big red plane was trying to get off the ground, real low, then it disappeared, and that was it."

"They said in the paper they couldn't confirm it," Sam said.

"Well, it was Lindy all right," Mr. Diggs insisted.

Esther wandered a bit while the men continued talking. She looked at the ground on which she stood, more sand than dirt. A small brown lizard pushed up and down on a large gray rock a few feet from her.

"Yeah, so I didn't know anything happened 'til I gone into town and them folks from the newspaper were talkin' to everyone," Diggs continued.

Esther squatted, though it pained her knees to do so. She picked up a small, oddly shaped rock and held it tight in her left palm. It was warm from the sun, and Esther thought she might feel the warmth all the way up her arm and into her chest.

"I just told them what I saw, and then everyone come out here all day looking around. I don't know why they say they didn't see nothin'. I showed 'em the tracks clear as day. Must've been the wind blown it over."

Esther rose slowly, but when she was back in a standing position, she grew wobbly and began seeing little white lines on the periphery of her vision. Soon Sam was there, both hands on her arm. "Are you okay?" he asked.

"Anything I can do?" Mr. Diggs asked.

"I'm fine," she said. "I just got a little dizzy is all."

"I think we should get going," Sam said.

"Well, thanks for stopping by, folks."

"Thank you," Sam said, as he guided Esther back toward the car. They walked slowly, the rock in Esther's hand. When Sam opened the car door for her and she sat down, Esther slipped the rock into her purse while Sam walked around the front of the car to his side.

Once back on the main road, Esther turned to Sam. "Thank you."

"Certainly," he said. It seemed to Esther they were driving slower than they had on the way up. Or perhaps she just wanted to.

They sat in silence with the wind blowing loudly through the car, the smell of fuel on Esther's skin, in her hair. She could almost taste it on her tongue and lips, a greasy film that she imagined would require a good scrubbing.

"I hope it's a girl," Sam said.

"Oh?" Esther remembered the time long ago when she had hoped for a girl.

"Don't you?" he asked.

"Either way," Esther said, because truly, nothing ever ended up how you hoped.

"Miriam wants it to be a girl too," he added. "One of each would be perfect."

Esther nodded her head, looking back down at Sam's feet working the pedals, his hand on the thin gearshift. Sometimes Sam reminded her of Avi as a young man.

"Why don't you ever speak of the boy?" Sam asked then. Nobody had been this blunt before—maybe never in her life. "Miriam tells me she doesn't remember much of him, just little bits of the time in New York."

Esther didn't know what to say.

"I hope I haven't offended you," he added.

"You haven't," she offered. It was true.

"What happened?"

"I don't know," Esther replied softly. "He would be about your age."

Sam nodded.

"And Charles's too—exactly," she added.

"Charles?"

"Lindbergh."

Sam took his eyes off the road and looked at Esther with a queer expression on his face. She wondered if he understood, but she couldn't be sure. Perhaps he would be the one to take some of it off of her. Just a little would help so much. But Esther was wary of this prospect too, because it was quite a responsibility, knowing. She had told Ben, but it seemed to destroy him. They hardly spoke anymore.

Sam and Esther rode in silence for another few minutes. The sun sank lower, casting a reddish glow on the yellow plains, making shadows grow. Faces of cattle like big black blocks blurred beyond the side of the road.

"Do you think I might learn how to drive?" Esther asked.

Sam looked at her. "Really?"

"I've always wanted to."

"Want me to teach you?"

Esther couldn't believe what she was hearing.

Sam slowed the car and turned off onto a small road that paralleled a ranch. "Okay," he said, stopping completely, but leaving the car running.

"Oh, I couldn't," Esther said. As a reflex.

"Sure you can," he said, getting out of the car and patting the brown seat. "Scoot over."

Esther put her purse on the seat and did as Sam said. She could feel his warmth in the spot where he'd just been seated. Esther knew she was in the right position then.

She rested her feet in front of all the pedals and waited for Sam to walk around the front of the car. She had been right—her legs fit perfectly under the steering wheel. They trembled.

"Okay," Sam said, exhaling loudly. "I hope I don't regret this."

Esther laughed, and she felt like a girl. She couldn't stop giggling.

"Okay. The little round one on the right makes it go. The square one in the middle is to stop."

"Right, go, left stop," Esther said, concentrating very hard. "What about the other one on the left?"

"That one's the complicated one," Sam said. "Okay, this is the gearshift, and you have to put it in gears to make it go faster and faster."

"Okay," Esther said, putting her hand on the shiny silver stick on her right that disappeared into the middle of the car's floor.

"So in order to move the gears here," he said, placing his hand over Esther's on the shifter, "you need to push down on the left pedal."

"Oh, I see," Esther said. "I've been watching you."

"But the problem is, you also need to push the round one to go while you're letting go of the left one."

"This is too much," Esther said.

"No, no it's not."

"Okay, okay," Esther said. For a moment she thought an almost-sixty-year-old lady shouldn't be doing such things, but there she was, seated behind all of this loud, smelly energy, and she wanted to be the one responsible for moving it.

Sam repeated the directions a couple more times, finally talking Esther through it step by step. The left pedal squeaked when she pushed it all the way in, and she had to struggle a little with the gear to put it into the first one, but she finally felt it lock into place and she let go of the left pedal.

The car jumped underneath them, and Esther's head jerked backward and hit something behind her. When finally the car stopped bucking, Sam was laughing. "This is funny?" Esther asked, terrified, bones rattling. "I think it's broken."

Sam wouldn't stop laughing, and soon, Esther laughed too.

He restarted the car and talked her through the steps again. This time Esther didn't let go of the squeaky left pedal until she was slowly pressing down on the round right one and gently letting out the squeaky one at the same time. The car started moving forward, jerking, but it was moving forward. Esther was thrilled.

After another twenty minutes of one-two-three-two-one gear changing, stopping, starting, and turning up and down the little dirt road, Sam asked, "Want to take her on the highway?"

"Oh I don't know," she demurred, but she wanted to make the thing go faster.

"I think you can do it," Sam said. "Looks like we have another half hour of daylight, maybe more."

Esther looked at him. Then she looked out at the setting sun behind the many distant oil wells silently dipping into the earth, delicate little birds that they were.

Sam talked her through it, and soon she turned onto the asphalt and they were on the road. Esther's palms were sweating on the steering wheel, and she could hear her heart pounding in her ears. A few cars passed them going the opposite direction, and Esther gripped the steering wheel tighter as they did. Loud bursts of wind shook the car at the precise moment the other automobiles passed on the other side. It was strange how even if she held the steering wheel perfectly still, the car didn't always go straight on the road. She would have to turn it a little left and right, back and forth to keep them going forward.

The sky was a light purple now, the ranch entrances growing closer and closer together as the oil derricks and wells grew more scarce. The yellow twinkling glow of Amarillo floated in a haze over the front of the car and to the left. She was bringing them home. This was like nothing Esther had ever felt, much less imagined.

"I think I should take over now," Sam suggested. "It's getting dark." But Esther didn't want to give up the wheel, not now, not ever. She was grateful to Sam for this, for everything, but she didn't know how to say it. There were no words.

"I'm sorry I got you home so late," he said as he steered through downtown. Sam stopped in front of The Diamond Shop and strained to look inside. Things were locked up and seemingly in order. He slowed again in front of Miriam's shop, now with its own storefront, and did the same once-over. Always the businessman.

Hersh was, as expected, in the driveway as soon as Sam cut the engine and set what Esther now knew was the hand brake. He'd parked next to the Model A he'd given to Hersh over a year before.

"Now you can practice on that old thing," he said, smiling and nodding toward his old car. "You did good."

"Thank you," Esther said. Hersh waited, waving dumbly in the entryway of their house. Esther let out a huge sigh and clutched her purse. She leaned over and kissed Sam's right cheek. The boy always smelled so good, she thought.

"Thank you," she repeated, but Sam waved her off.

"Pleasure's all mine."

Esther looked at him then: *Such a gentleman*. She wondered then which of Sam's and Miriam's children would disappear—the one they already had, or the one that was on its way. It was inevitable. She just hoped he would be a little more prepared for it than she had been.

February 14, 1935

AMARILLO, TEXAS

The Amarillo Daily Sun, February 14, 1935

HAUPTMANN FOUND GUILTY!

WILL DIE IN CHAIR FOR LINDBERGH BABY MURDER

FLEMINGTON, N. J., Feb. 13—In the case of the March 1, 1932, kidnapping and killing of Charles A. Lindbergh Jr., Bruno Richard Hauptmann was convicted of first-degree murder and sentenced to die in the electric chair. Supreme Court Justice Thomas W. Trenchard set the execution for some time during the week of March 18, at the State prison in Trenton.

Colonel Charles A. Lindbergh, father of the murdered infant, elected not to be in court for delivery of the verdict. Instead, after attending every single session of the thirty-two court days of the trial, he decided to stay at home in Englewood with Mrs. Lindbergh while the jury deliberated for 11 hours and 29 minutes. The Colonel did, however, hear Justice Trenchard deliver his 70-minute charge to the jury this morning before exiting through a back door of the courthouse.

While the jury stated its verdict and Justice Trenchard summarily pronounced his sentence, Hauptmann stood shackled and handcuffed between two guards, still and mute. His face blanched, and flashes of horror could be seen flickering deep in his stern eyes. Moments later, he was led away to his familiar cell in the county jail. His wife Anna Hauptmann sat still as a statue, her eyes cast down to the checkered floor. She did not weep until her husband's presence had been entirely extinguished from the courtroom.

A Dramatic Verdict

The verdict was returned at 10:45 P.M., and just prior to it, as the jurors were led back into the courtroom, upwards of seven thousand persons swarmed around the Hunterdon County Court House, some chanting "Kill Hauptmann! Kill Hauptmann!" in anticipation of a guilty verdict. The roar of the crowd could even be heard inside the courtroom, until the windows were finally closed by order of the judge.

The scene outside the courtroom was described by one observer as "carnival-like" in nature. Flares from moving-picture trucks eerily lit the scene almost as though it were daytime—when in fact it was a mere hour short of midnight. Men and women thronged around the courthouse, some trying to peer inside from trees, the roofs of cars, and windows in other buildings in the area. The court officers were forced to close the heavy green shades on the windows in order to maintain at least some modicum of calm and privacy inside.

Once the jury had been accounted for and the defendant stood between his personal guards, Justice Trenchard silenced the courtroom with his gavel and asked the jury, "Have you agreed upon your verdict?"

"We have!"

"Who shall speak for you?"

"The foreman."

"Mr. Foreman, what say you: Do you find the defendant guilty or not guilty?"

"Guilty. We find the defendant, Bruno Richard Hauptmann, guilty of murder in the first degree."

A murmur resonated through the courtroom then, as scores of hands quickly jotted notes and shuffled papers. Several eager messenger boys raced to the door, but Justice Trenchard ordered that no person leave the courtroom until each juror was polled individually and the verdict confirmed.

At last: a coda to America's most heinous and colossal of crimes.

Hersh decided to take his lunch alone, without Ben or Sam today. He took the day's paper and tucked it under his arm and walked out into the crisp, cold, sunny afternoon. He carefully avoided the dark ice patches on the sidewalk in front of the Herring Hotel.

"Mr. Lipshitz." The doorman nodded at Hersh as he passed by. Hersh nodded back.

Wasn't it a little strange that Sam lived with his family in one half of the top floor of the Herring? He understood it was easy, right by the stores, with a restaurant downstairs, but what kind of man keeps his family in a hotel? He wondered if Miriam even knew how to cook a proper supper. How was this a home, with all the different people coming and going all of the time? Hersh wondered.

He continued past the hotel and toward the public library. He wished to sit outside to read the paper for a few minutes, but it was just too cold to do so. Hersh looked for a bench in the sun, but shadows covered this side of the big brick building and its surroundings. Hersh walked around the other side of the library, where three or four benches sat in the sun next to the parking lot. A man and woman huddled close together on one of them, the man's arm around the woman's shoulders, holding her tightly.

Hersh sat on the bench farthest from the handsome young couple. He tried to keep from studying them, instead turning toward the library parking lot, half of which basked in sunlight, with all of the twinkling automobiles winking back at him. Hersh noticed what had to be his own car in the parking lot, but no, Esther couldn't have been downtown. She would have stopped by both stores to say hello to everybody, as usual. Though she hadn't done this in a month at least, seeming even more distracted than he'd come to expect. Hersh was puzzled. He opened the paper and leaned back on the bench, but before looking at the paper folded it back up and lay it on the bench beside him. Hersh had to take a closer look at the car.

It was his all right. On the passenger side, spilling onto the floor, there were several thick textbooks from the library. Hersh leaned his head into the car as though it weren't his own—*was it?*—and inspected the spines of the books. Most had long legal titles, "criminal law" this and "forensic" that, such and such statute. Hersh stood back from the car to get a better look. This was definitely the car.

Hersh wanted to find Esther, to see what this was all about. She'd been at relative peace for the last stretch of months, but then he got an idea. He stepped onto a bus at Polk and 3rd and headed home. On the bus Hersh remembered he'd left the paper on the bench. It was probably blowing away by now, cartwheeling along the ground in front of the young lovers and into the street.

Walking from the bus stop, Hersh half imagined Esther would be sitting in the kitchen when he walked in the door—surprised, but mostly a little disappointed to see Hersh home in the middle of the day. Perhaps the car had looked different in the sun, and it belonged to somebody else.

But when Hersh turned onto Tyler and was within view of his driveway, he could see that the car wasn't parked there. He let himself into the house. Inside, the air was cool and still. It was as empty as Hersh could remember it ever being. Now that Ben had moved back in, and they looked after Sam and Miriam's Aaron from time to time, the house was almost never unoccupied. Hersh listened in the hallway. Creaks and sighs normally heard in the dead of night could be heard then, the house probably still trying to settle into its foundation.

Hersh looked into the hall closet, mindlessly fumbling through the coats there. He thought for a moment. Then he went into the bedroom and opened the closet filled with Esther's things. He pushed aside several dresses, folded linens, and other old fabrics. Two hats fell from the top shelf onto Hersh's shoulder. He looked up. There were a few more library books like the ones in the car stacked up there, and behind them, to the left and tucked behind what looked like a little box Avi had constructed for Esther back in Kishinev, there was a large hatbox, brimming with its contents.

Hersh pulled a chair over to the closet and stepped up onto it. He wobbled and the chair tipped onto two legs, but Hersh caught himself on the doorjamb and righted himself. He reached for the box and tried to pull it out, but it was quite heavy. Hersh stepped off the chair and pushed it into the closet. When he stepped back up, more carefully this time, Hersh could slide the box out and get a hand under it. When he pulled it down, the lid fell off and a few papers fluttered to the floor.

Hersh put the box on the bed and bent to inspect its contents. On top he saw some unsealed letters, and several articles and photographs snipped from the newspaper—all concerning Charles Lindbergh and his wife and child—and the trial. Hersh dug deeper and found much more of the same, piles and piles of it, going back in time. He went to retrieve the papers that had fluttered out of the box when he brought it down, one of them having lodged on the shoulder of one of Esther's dresses—a blue one Hersh remembered her having worn many years before. The clipping was a photo of Lindbergh standing under the wing of the *Spirit of St. Louis*, published on the three-year anniversary of his flight. Lindbergh clasped his hands behind his back, his mouth a straight line, turned slightly down on both ends. His light-colored head came up just to the dark underbelly of the wing, and a few men stood talking in a tight circle in the distance, beside the plane's knife-like propeller.

Hersh studied the photograph. It was ripped across the middle, the jagged tear separating both the wing and Lindbergh's upper half from his legs and the grassy ground on which he and the plane stood. Hersh then picked up the other paper that had fallen out—it was an envelope with a letter inside—and was just about to slip the note out when he heard the familiar rumble of his car approaching the driveway. He dropped the papers into the box and stepped back up onto the chair with it, shoving the box back into the corner it came from. He looked for the lid to the hatbox but couldn't find it. He positioned the wooden box of Avi's in front of the hatbox and pulled the chair out of the closet, setting it next to the bed where it usually was. He closed the closet and listened.

The front door opened, and Hersh decided he should sneak out of the bedroom. He opened the window on the other side of the bed and began to step his right foot through it when he wondered why he, an old man, was stealing away from his house like a child, or worse—a criminal. But before he could stop himself, Hersh was outside and pushing down the window to its usual cracked-open position and peering through the kitchen window at his wife.

Hersh could see another stack of books on the kitchen table, next to Esther's hat. Her back was to him and she was leaning over the table, spreading out newspaper clippings across the tabletop and referring to one of the open books. She looked behind her to the other window and Hersh ducked, stepping to the side of the kitchen with no windows and pressing his back up against it. His heart raced. Hersh stood there with his palms against the side of the house, where the wood was still warm from sitting in the sun for the second half of the day.

After a few minutes, Hersh scooted around the side of the house and down the driveway, looking back every few steps. Hersh's back ached, and he knew he would be late returning to the shop. Sam wouldn't mind if he was even there, but Hersh knew Ben would look at him that way he did with his thin little eyebrows raised and his lips pressed together. But he dare not ask his father of his whereabouts. This manager business was just a formality, Hersh knew, the familial hierarchy still safe at home. And truth be told—which it rarely was—Sam's incomprehensibly endless source of money was the only thing staving off the inevitable ruin that awaited them all. These were dark days indeed—and surely the gathering clouds overhead could only be an indication of more darkness to come.

But what of his hopeless, and quite possibly insane wife?

𝔗𝔥𝔢 𝔄𝔪𝔞𝔯𝔦𝔩𝔩𝔬 𝔇𝔞𝔦𝔩𝔶 𝔖𝔲𝔫, August 29, 1941

LINDBERGH IN SOONER STATE

WILL TAKE PART IN TOMORROW'S 'AMERICA FIRST' RALLY

OKLAHOMA CITY, Aug. 28—Governor Leon C. Phillips adamantly defended aviator Charles A. Lindbergh's right to speak on the topic of America's and Germany's "Air Power" as part of the "America First" rally planned for tomorrow night in Oklahoma's capital.

Gov. Phillips, an outspoken adherent of the Roosevelt administration, admitted that he flat-out disagreed with the famous flier's isolationist views, but that Lindbergh "personally thanked me for making the suggestion that he had a right to be heard, and I told him: 'Hell, that's just pure Americanism to me, that's all it is.'

"It has been intimated to me that [Lindbergh] might not be safe. But Lord, I hope we haven't gotten to that," the governor said in a statement to the press. "I want Oklahoma to be recognized as a state of substantial, intelligent, careful people, and my sincere hope is that people here tomorrow night don't bring any disgrace on the state by making any scene out there. All this talk of police protection, God knows we don't want to get to the place in the nation where a man can't be accorded a safe hearing."

Lindbergh Unwanted?

Having resigned as a colonel from the Army Air Corps Reserve earlier this year, Lindbergh has continued to be an increasingly outspoken critic of the Roosevelt administration's foreign policy. Both he and Senator Burton K. Wheeler of Montana, with whom Lindbergh is scheduled to share the stage at the rally, have been made to feel less than welcome on a handful of occasions on which they have spoken on behalf of "America First" across the country.

In fact, tomorrow's rally in Oklahoma City was originally scheduled to be held in the Municipal Auditorium downtown, but the city council unanimously voted to cancel the America First Committee's reservation for the venue after several local organizations lodged complaints about Lindbergh's impending appearance.

Upon being informed of the city council's action, Lindbergh reportedly said, "if we cannot rent a hall, then we can hold our meeting in a cow pasture."

Committee officials, likewise unwilling to cancel the rally entirely, then secured use of the privately owned Sand Lot park, which is normally reserved for semipro baseball games. The lot is located just outside of OKC, and seating for approximately 10,000 persons is currently being assembled there.

The rally is scheduled to begin at 8 P.M.

If Esther left now, she believed she could just make it to Oklahoma City in time for the boy's speech. She thought it would be wise to ask Sam to drive her, but she knew he would never do such a thing without Hersh's knowledge. Hersh would never agree to a trip to OKC, alone or otherwise.

Everybody fussed over her so much these days, it was getting so she felt like a little child, having to ask for permission every time she wanted to leave the house. It was just a little cough. And plus, what the press was saying about her boy lately. What Hersh was saying. They were calling him a Nazi. They had even renamed "Lindbergh Way" downtown—now it was just North Street again.

Esther didn't understand how Hersh could believe all this about their boy. How anybody could. Hersh was confused about what was happening in Europe. Everybody was—even Roosevelt. Especially Roosevelt.

Esther tucked the article from the paper into her purse and went into the kitchen. She took down the aluminum can to which Sam quietly added money each month—for emergencies. There was at least three or four hundred dollars folded deep in the can. Esther checked to see if Hersh was still sitting in the living room and proceeded to fish out four twenty-dollar bills and two tens from the stash. She tucked them into her purse next to the article.

She could say she was going to the grocery, or to visit Miriam, bedridden now awaiting the baby. Esther took a deep breath and walked slowly into the living room. Hersh had fallen asleep in his chair, his gray-whiskered chin jutting into a shoulder. If she woke him, he might worry less. Or she could leave a note. Maybe he was dead. The clock over the fireplace struck ten then, and Esther realized she had to go, now or not at all. She checked to see if the chime had woken Hersh (it hadn't), and headed back to the hallway. Esther found the car key in Hersh's sweater and pulled a scarf and coat of her own out of the hall closet, even though it was so hot out. It would be a long trip, and she often grew chilled with no warning. You never could predict when the weather might change.

She opened the front door carefully—the doorknob normally protesting so loudly every time it was turned—but this time it was silent. Maybe the wet heat in the air had loosened the hardware. Either way, Esther was thankful the house was letting her go. She stifled a gathering cough attack until after the door clicked shut behind her.

Esther pressed the starter three times before the engine whirred and began shaking the seat beneath her. She released the brake and backed down the driveway, praying Hersh was still asleep there in his dingy undershirt, dreaming away of whatever it was Hersh dreamed of. As she pushed the shifter into first gear, Esther checked back through the passenger window to see if Hersh had come out to the driveway. All clear.

Esther looked for signs to Route 66. She had never been on 66 heading in this direction, east, never farther than the fairgrounds. One time they had all piled into Sam's truck and driven the other way to Albuquerque for a weekend. It was the first time Esther had seen a dark, shiny-skinned Indian. There were some Mexicans in Amarillo, and he looked similar to them, Esther remembered, but there was also something different, something more untamed about this man, she'd thought.

She would be seeing her boy for the first time in almost thirty-four years. She pushed down on the accelerator more, but the car couldn't go any faster than it already was. The little needle on the dial vibrated just right of the number 50.

Hours and hours upon hours like this, everything looking the same. Ranches, cattle, windmills, horses with cowboys bouncing along, pushing all the cows somewhere they didn't want to go. The road stretched flat as far as Esther could see. She stopped at a Phillips station for gas in Shamrock. The gentleman who filled her tank said, "God bless you," after giving Esther change, and she pressed a dime into his greasy palm.

It was summer indeed, Esther growing as exhausted as it was hot. She had never driven anywhere near this far in the car alone. But what difference, really, was it from the shorter trips? Just a little more of the same.

Esther's chest ached when she tried to inhale, but it never quite felt like she was getting enough air. The sun was a dry yellow, too painful to look directly into. It beat down on Esther through the windshield. She stopped again for gas, this time somewhere in Oklahoma. The boy who pumped her gas here was silent, possibly mute, Esther surmised. He had that look.

Soon she saw a sign that Oklahoma City was only ten miles away. She couldn't believe it was so. She pressed the pedal to the floor and scooted forward on the hard seat. Esther could see the squat buildings of downtown up ahead and to the left. She didn't know where she was going, so Esther pulled off the road when she saw a sign for "Municipal Auditorium/Downtown." Hersh would be panicked by now. He would never understand. She pressed on, following arrows.

Esther parked her car outside what looked to be a courthouse. There was a small cafe across the street, and Esther went in to get out of the heat. She asked for a glass of water at the counter.

"Are you okay, ma'am?" a young man seated next to her asked.

"Yes, why?" she replied.

"Just wonderin'. You look a little pale."

"Oh, I'm fine, thank you," she said, glancing at the clock over the pie case. It was almost seven o'clock.

Esther ordered some soup and bread, asking the waitress about the Lindbergh event when she brought out the food. She said she knew about it, but didn't know where it was. Esther ate quickly and paid the girl. She stepped out of the cafe and saw a taxi parked next to her own car. Esther went over to the open window. The driver was eating a sandwich.

"You need a ride?" he asked, still chewing his food. He was a big man with a square head, equally square hands.

"Yes, thank you," Esther said. She pulled the article from the Amarillo paper from her purse and skimmed it. "Do you know where the Sand Lot park is, where Lindbergh is speaking?"

"Sure, get in."

"And can you take me back here to my car when it's over?"

"Are you alone?" he asked.

"Why?"

"You just seem a little—"

"What?" Esther interrupted.

"Nothing," he said, finishing the sandwich and wadding up the paper it came in.

Esther retrieved her coat from the car and then got into the taxi.

"You come all the way from Texas for this?"

"Yes," Esther said. "Amarillo."

"You must be against the war then."

"Not really."

"I am," he said. "I think it's terrible what Roosevelt is doing. All because of the Jews, you know."

"I don't really know," Esther said. "I'm just here to see the boy."

"The boy?"

"Charles."

"Not exactly a boy anymore," he said, steering them back onto the highway.

"How far to Sand Lot?"

"Not far at all," he said. "Just outside of town. So, you a big fan of Lindy?"

"Not really a fan."

"What then?"

"I've followed his life."

"Oh boy, then."

"What?"

"Nothing. I'm not sure I should tell you."

"What is it?"

"Well, this friend of mine, he's sort of a collector, he's gonna be out there tonight," he began. "He's sort of hit on hard times and he's got this thing, this, I don't really know how to describe it."

"What is it?" Esther asked, leaning forward in the back seat.

"It's been his most prized possession for years, but he's just run on some really hard times."

"What, *what*?" Esther pressed. She had a good feeling about this.

"You remember when Lindy landed in Paris? Well, a bunch of people, they tore the fabric off of the plane before they could roll it into the hangar," the man said. "This guy, my friend, he got one of these pieces from a friend of his who was there."

"Really?" Esther asked.

"Really."

"It's really from the plane?"

"Oh yes, the fuselage."

"This is amazing," Esther said.

"He's gonna try an' sell it tonight if he can."

"Oh, he shouldn't," Esther said.

"He needs the money."

"Well."

"Would you like to see it?"

"I don't want to miss the speech."

"Oh, he'll be right out there in front."

"Well, okay, if it doesn't take too long," Esther said.

About fifteen minutes later they pulled into what looked like a baseball field. Thousands of cars were parked along the road, everywhere there was space. Lights shot into the darkening sky, down on the red dirt field, all the people milling about. Dust floated through all of it. A small stage with an "America First" banner behind it was set up in the center of the field, with red, white, and blue bunting, ribbons, and balloons. Esther's heart felt like it might stop. She held her chest as she coughed a few more times, but the pesky heaving would not cease.

The taxi driver came around to open the door for her, and Esther tried to get up, but she sat back down on the seat. "You okay?" he asked.

"Oh fine," she assured him. The roar of the crowd, thousands of them, surged when a microphone was tested.

"Hold on, I'll be right back," he said.

"Don't you want me to pay you for the ride?" Esther asked.

"I trust you," he said, smiling. "Besides, I know where to find you."

"Is it okay if I sit here?"

"Sure, give me five."

"Dollars?"

"Minutes. I'll be right back."

Esther watched the lumbering man wander off. She caught her breath as she leaned back in the taxicab's seat. It was considerably more comfortable than that of her own car, another hand-me-down from Sam—for The Diamond Shop and other family business, he'd said, so Hersh would accept it. She closed her eyes and felt a line of perspiration trickling down her cheek. *Perhaps this was a mistake. But how could it be a mistake to see the boy after all?* Finally Esther opened her eyes, and the taxi driver was in front of her, cupping a small leather pouch in the palm of his hand.

"Here it is."

"Oh my," Esther said. "May I?"

He loosened the string around the pouch's mouth and Esther reached in with two fingers. She pulled out a small off-white piece of rolled-up canvas, tied up with a small string that had a little tag on it (much like a piece of jewelry at Sam's shop): *Le Bourget, May 21, 1927.* She slipped the tag through the tiny string and unrolled the piece of cloth. It was roughly the shape of a triangle, with a jagged edge, seemingly more like a thick canvas than cloth. There was a dirt smudge on the widest side. Esther brought the little scrap up to her nose and inhaled. It was the scent of oil.

"Nice, huh?" the driver said.

Esther didn't answer.

"I think he's willing to take a hundred for it," he added. Esther looked up at him, still silent. "Seventy-five?"

"I couldn't take this from him," she said.

"He needs the money. You'd be doing him a favor."

"I don't know," Esther said.

"How much do you have?"

"Maybe sixty-five?"

"I'll ask him." He disappeared again. Esther tried to watch where he went, but the crowd was too thick. Soon he returned. "Make it seventy, and I'll get you a seat right up front."

Esther reached into her purse and pulled out three twenties and a ten, handing them to the man. She figured this would leave her with about fifteen or twenty to get home. Something like this.

"He's going to be so happy," the man said. "I'll take you to the seat and then back to your car after, that sound good?"

Esther rolled the scrap of cloth back up and tied the small string around it. She slipped it back into the pouch and dropped it into her purse, rubbing her thumb in circles over the leather with her hand still in the purse. "Thank you," she said.

She followed the driver behind a long row of filled bleachers on the left side of the field. A lit cigarette flew through the air and landed in front of Esther. It was hard to keep up with the man, though he slowed down every time he looked back and saw that Esther was struggling to keep pace.

At the end of the first row of bleachers, the taxi driver said, "This seat's taken," to a man who was sitting close to the edge of the bench.

"What?"

"I said, move over, this seat's taken."

The man silently pushed himself against the woman seated next to him, who pushed against the woman on the other side of her, and so on with two or three more spectators. The taxi driver pointed at the now-empty seat and bowed his head at Esther.

"I'll be at the car after," he said.

"Thank you, thank you so much."

"You remember where it was?"

"Yes, thank you."

Esther looked at the stage. It was hard to see through the rows of policemen who circled the stage, hands linked in a long, black-clad, human chain.

The crowd roared then, and some booed as several men were led out onto the stage by a police officer. Charles was one of them, Esther was certain when she saw dirty blond hair on the tallest head of them all. It was so difficult to see the stage around the line of policemen in front of it.

Esther thought her boy sat then, but she couldn't be sure because her eyes were not entirely to be trusted. The crowd continued cheering and booing the first man to speak. Esther couldn't hear very well, there was such a persistent echo, and the speakers were set behind her, facing the thousands of people farther out in the field than she was.

The senator from Montana spoke, and was very animated and angry. He garnered much rancor from the crowd. He had a strange voice, though it was hard to tell exactly what he was saying. Esther opened her purse and looked for the pouch, to make sure it was still there. She touched the soft leather and was filled with warmth. She couldn't believe her luck. She coughed again—must be from all the dust.

Esther looked up when the crowd roared once more, this time more than it had before. The tall boy stood at the microphone then, waiting for the crowd to quiet. He was much different from the photographs Esther had from watching him grow up over the years—even different from the newsreels she saw sometimes at the theater. His movements looked a little like Hersh's (though less stooped), a little like Avi's (though slimmer), and there was some of Papa and Ben in him too. He began speaking in what Esther thought was a thin voice, higher than she'd expected. He seemed very excited about the topics he discussed. When he spoke of Germany's air strength, the boy suggested that America could not beat Germany in a war, and the crowd booed, some tossing trash and other objects into the center of the field. Some pieces of rubbish landed on the police officers, while others actually made it to the stage. The officers tightened their circle around the stage, most of them scanning the crowd with fierce eyes. The boy kept on talking passionately through both the jeers and cheers.

Suddenly Esther's view blurred. She worried it was her heart, but then she realized she was sobbing, the tears welling over her eyes—*kvelling*, after all these years? Esther pulled a handkerchief out of her purse and wiped her eyes. When she pulled the cloth down from her eyes, it was covered in brownish-red dirt. Esther imagined streaks of it on her face like the Indians. She didn't want the boy to see her this way.

Esther grew dizzy, the sky completely dark by then. She worried it was late. It was late. The boy talked on, wading through the responses of the crowd almost as though they were obstacles on a road. The next thing she knew, it was done, another man was patting the boy on the back, and the crowd continued its confusing chorus. Esther stood and leaned over the railing toward the stage. A police officer came toward her then, and she saw his blue eyes—like the boy.

"Charles!" she screamed. "Charles!"

But he didn't respond.

"Reuven!" Esther shrieked then, perhaps louder than any utterance had ever crossed her lips. And he turned and looked then, out into the crowd somewhere above where Esther was standing. Maybe he couldn't see because of the lights. But Esther knew he knew.

"Over here," she shouted again, but by now he had turned back to the men on the stage, shaking hands and smiling in that coy way he did—not really a smile at all.

Esther began coughing again as the crowd thinned out around her. She sat back down on the bench, but the coughing wouldn't stop. She hacked and gagged, hoping she could bring up whatever it was and be done with it. Esther fished out her handkerchief and held it to her mouth as her chest spasmed uncontrollably. She clutched her purse to her chest while people stared. When the fit subsided, Esther saw that the handkerchief she'd held to her lips was streaked with blood.

Reuven was led off the stage then, surrounded by policemen, and that was the last Esther saw. The stadium lights swirled in circles around her head, and Esther dropped.

*   *   *

Sam answered the phone on the table between his and Miriam's beds. Hersh and Ben sat across from Miriam, Hersh's head in his hands.

"Hello?"

. . .

"Yes."

. . .

"Yes, yes, is she okay?" asked Sam. Hersh practically jumped to his feet and walked over to Sam, who held his palm up to silence Hersh.

. . .

"Rally? What rally?"

. . .

"Oh my god," Sam said.

"What, what?" Hersh asked.

"She's in Oklahoma," Sam whispered, covering the mouthpiece. "Can I talk to her? Where is she now?"

"Oh, mother!" Miriam exclaimed.

"Shh," Hersh said.

Ben sat in his chair, legs crossed calmly.

"No, no, of course not," Sam said. "Can you stay with her? Please know I'll compensate you very generously for your time, but maybe could you just stay with her until I can get there on the next train?"

. . .

"Yes, I understand, sir. It would be my pleasure to compensate you for your time and help."

. . .

"I insist," Sam said. "Is there a way I can reach you with the train's arrival time?"

. . .

"Okay, okay, how about you call back here at the Herring in one hour, and somebody will tell you when the train will arrive?"

. . .

"I don't know, uh, do you have a wife, might you take her back home with you?"

. . .

"Of course, I'm sorry to hear that. Sorry to be so bold."

. . .

"Yes, thank you, yes, I'll meet you there," Sam said. "Okay, so you'll be calling back here, and somebody will tell you when I'll be arriving. Thank you."

Sam hung up the phone and immediately called the front desk. "Hi, can you get me the train schedule to OKC?"

"What?" Miriam asked, "what is it?"

"The next train," he said into the phone. He waited for a while.

"Oh, Esther," Hersh moaned, "what did you do?"

"Papa, it's going to be fine," Ben said.

"Fine? Fine?" Hersh exclaimed. "What is she doing in Oklahoma? She's a sick lady."

"Shh," Miriam said.

"Okay, 3:08, thank you very much," Sam said into the phone before hanging up.

Sam told them what he knew, that some taxi driver was with Esther, that her car was parked downtown, she had some sort of spell at the Lindbergh rally and he had taken her back to the coffee shop where the car was parked.

"What was she thinking?" Hersh asked, sinking back down in a chair.

"She's not thinking," Ben said then, normally so quiet on the topic of his mother. Sam looked at him, and Ben knew he knew something he wasn't saying. "It's this Lindbergh stuff."

"What?" Hersh asked.

Hersh knew too. He was just choosing not to. "She's crazy," Ben added.

"Ben, please!" Sam said. Hersh looked as though his son had just punched him in the jaw. He sat back down, staring at the floor.

"Why is she doing this to me?" Miriam asked. "She knows I'm not supposed to be agitated until after the baby comes."

"She's not doing anything to *you*," Sam scolded his wife. "I'll get on the first train in the morning and bring her back."

"I should be the one," Hersh said, but everyone knew he was just puffing up his chest like husbands are supposed to. The two of them—Hersh and Esther—out on the road would perhaps be worse than either one of them alone.

"Ben should go," Miriam said. "Sam, you can't."

Ben looked at Sam. He was more than happy to let Sam be the hero.

"No. I'll go," Sam insisted.

Sam left his wife and her family upstairs and stepped into a taxi outside the Herring Hotel. Shortly after, he was on a 3:08 A.M. train for Oklahoma City, which put him into the Santa Fe Depot around 8:30. Esther was sitting in a brown leather-backed chair in the waiting area. Her legs were crossed delicately at the ankles, and her hands were clasped together on her lap. She looked tiny beside the large man with his arms crossed and slumped over in his seat. His head almost touched Esther's, and he was fast asleep.

LINDBERGH DEEMS BRITISH, JEWS AND ROOSEVELT 'DANGEROUS'

AVIATOR TELLS IOWANS THAT THESE THREE GROUPS ARE FORCING AMERICA INTO WAR

DES MOINES, Sept. 11—In an address prepared for an America First rally tonight at the Des Moines Coliseum, aviator Charles A. Lindbergh told a crowd of approximately 8,000 people that America was being goaded into war by three distinct, insidious, and influential clusters of "war agitators."

"The three most important groups which have been pressing this country toward war," Lindbergh said, "are the British, the Jewish, and the Roosevelt administration."

Mr. Lindbergh's speech was preceded by a radio address played over the loudspeakers and delivered by President Roosevelt, who declared to the nation that the Navy was on orders to staunchly defend the American Defense Zone against German and Italian ships.

The crowd cheered the president's words at least ten times during his address. But when Lindbergh took the stage minutes later—the rally having been postponed because of the president's speech—the aviator was met with both cheers and jeers from the vocal crowd.

Two 'Desperate' Positions

Mr. Lindbergh began his delineation of the three groups by describing England as "desperate. Her population is not large enough and her armies are not strong enough to invade the continent of Europe and win the war she declared against Germany—regardless of how many planes we send her."

By now, many in the crowd stood and cheered the aviator, their applause and shouts drowning out the remaining boos. Lindbergh then transitioned from his discussion of England to the Jews. Mr. Lindbergh said that he partially understood their desire to overthrow Nazi Germany.

"The persecution [the Jews] suffered in Germany would be sufficient to make bitter enemies of any race," Lindbergh continued. "No person with a sense of dignity of mankind can condone the persecution of the Jewish race in Germany. However, instead of agitating for war, the Jewish groups in this country should be opposing it in every possible way, for they will certainly be among the first to feel its consequences.

"Their greatest danger to this country lies in their large ownership and influence in our motion pictures, our press, our radio, and our government.

"I am not attacking either the Jewish or the British people. Both races, I admire. But I am saying that leaders of both races, for reasons which are understandable from their viewpoint as they are inadvisable from ours, for reasons which are not American, wish to involve us in the war."

Roosevelt a 'Danger' as Well

Moving on to the Roosevelt administration, Mr. Lindbergh said that, "the danger of the Roosevelt administration lies in its subterfuge. While its members have promised us peace, they have led us to war—heedless of the platform upon which they were elected to a third term."

The aviator concluded by saying that America shall be safe from involvement in the foreign war only when these three groups stop "agitating" for it. After Mr. Lindbergh concluded his remarks and took his seat on stage, most of the crowd continued standing and cheering.

[advertisement]

PROGRAMME

Mr. and Mrs. Sam Lazarus
have the honor to sponsor the debut of the new arrival
Anna _____ ? *
in the sensational success

"IT'S A GIRL!"

Preview: September 11th, 1941
eight pounds, nine ounces (of tuneful harmony)

—

Production under the supervision of
Dr. D. J. Bruno
of Amarillo General Hospital

—

CAST OF CHARACTERS:

Happy Mother .... *Miriam*
Proud Father .... *Sam*
Big Brother .... *Aaron*
The New Arrival ...... *Anna _____ ? **

* A $75 diamond ring will be awarded to the first person guessing the middle name of Mr. and Mrs. Sam Lazarus's new daughter.

(Her first name is Anna.)

Mail all replies to: The Diamond Shop,
514 Polk, Amarillo, Tex.

ARMY OPEN TO LINDBERGH
ADVICE ON WAR EFFORT

WASHINGTON, Jan. 1—In a press conference today, Secretary of War Henry L. Stimson responded to questions about aviator Charles Lindbergh's request to be put on active Army duty. The Secretary began by stating that, "the War Department is open to any helpful advice that might aid in the war effort—from Charles Lindbergh or anyone else."

The Secretary continued, "I want this distinctly understood: Whether it comes from Colonel Lindbergh or anyone else, any advice or suggestion that any American thinks will help the service or improve it will be gratefully accepted and very carefully considered."

There was no word from Stimson as to whether the Army will accept Lindbergh's volunteering of his services to the Army Air Corps. The former Colonel resigned his reserve commission in April after President Roosevelt publicly denounced the aviator's outspoken isolationist activities on behalf of the America First Committee, comparing Lindbergh and others like him to the "Copperheads" of the Civil War era.

Change of Heart

The America First Committee dissolved, and Mr. Lindbergh ostensibly experienced a change of heart sometime during the weeks following the December 7 attack at Pearl Harbor. According to Lieut. Gen. Henry H. Arnold, who first received Mr. Lindbergh's request to be reinstated for duty, the former Colonel's motivations were entirely sincere.

"Lindbergh's act indicates a definite change from his

isolationist stand and expresses his deep desire to help the country along the lines in which he trained himself for many years," General Arnold said on Tuesday upon making public the aviator's offer.

The General's statement came despite many unfavorable accounts in newspapers across the nation, some of which reported that America First was not backing down from its isolationist stand, and questioned Mr. Lindbergh's loyalty and the motivation behind his turnabout.

What of the Nazi Medal?

Also on Tuesday, the Non-Sectarian Anti-Nazi League wrote Mr. Lindbergh with a request that he return the medals he received from both the Nazi and Japanese governments. The same organization requested in September that the Military Affairs Committees of both the House and Senate investigate Mr. Lindbergh on the basis that he was "giving aid and comfort to the Nazi war strategy aimed at the United States."

Professor James H. Sheldon, representative of the league, suggested to Lindbergh that he give up the medals "as evidence of the sincerity of your change of feeling." It is not known at this time whether Mr. Lindbergh intends to honor the League's request.

January 14, 1942

AMARILLO, TEXAS

At least she was home now, in her own bed, Esther thought. Instead of that cursed hospital room. There was her sweet and harmless husband, and not-so-sweet oldest boy Ben, arguing silently in the corner. Or what they thought was silently. Esther could feel their whispered, pointed words drifting in and out of her mind, even if she didn't know exactly what it was they were saying. Her husband's and son's nattering provided a running background against which every memory she had left played— like the first time she saw the talkies.

There was Avi, with the first stringy muscles that announced his impending manhood, learning to cut wood for the first time with their Papa on the shtetl. The shingles on the house, Esther recalled now for some strange reason, were so impossibly large, stacked row after row, overlapping sometimes three and four deep. And yet their roof always seemed to leak right onto Esther's bed when it rained. Mama would push the mattress into the kitchen next to the stove on rainy nights in order to keep Esther warm. But she never was. And she could never sleep because she was too busy worrying that the stove would set her mattress on fire.

Ben raised his voice at Hersh in the corner, and then Esther was back in this bed, in her room in the house on Tyler Street, wishing her son and husband might finally stop arguing once she was gone. Esther half expected the roof to open up above her, to see again the dizzy plane that flew overhead the night before Avi died. Esther remembered thinking each breath was his last. Now she wondered which would be her own last gasp. And would they be sending a plane for her as well?

Esther squeezed the leather pouch in her left hand and silently thanked Reuven for the new life he'd given her that night in '27. Miriam was at her side now—*or had she been there all along?*—and Ben and Hersh had stopped their fussing now that Sam stepped into the room, bouncing the baby Anna-Rose on a hip.

This was the most wonderful feeling ever, Esther thought, closing her eyes with her daughter's hand squeezing her right one, the pouch tucked into her left. More wonderful even than driving with the dusty wind in your hair. She always thought she would be afraid, but this, this was the absence of fear—it was complete control. She could neither speak nor hear very well, or move her body very much, but Esther felt, for the first time ever really, that she could say *where, when,* and *how.*

Miriam was in tears, Sam bowed his sweet, shiny black head, and the baby girl was silent. Hersh rocked slowly back and forth, hugging his slim frame tightly under crossed arms. And Ben? Who knew, but at least she could be sure he would be there when it was Hersh's turn to go. For this at least, Esther was grateful. She detected the faint smell of gasoline coming from the hand on her left side. What a funny thing.

Esther would die the provider of answers to her own questions:

Where? *Here.*

When? *Now.*

And how? *Just like that.*

January 26, 1942

Hersh saw Ben coming in from where the trash was kept on the side of the house. Something wasn't right about him. Hersh took his father's old cane off the hook by the door and waited until Ben came back into the house. Then Hersh snuck outside to inspect the cans, to see for himself what his son had been up to.

On top was Esther's box, topless and overflowing, gaping up at the gray winter sky. Newspaper clippings, letters, a rock, photographs, a small leather pouch tied with a string. Hersh was stunned at his son. He reached down into the can and gently rescued the box as though pulling a baby out of a basinet, and hugged it to his chest. As he lifted, a few clippings fluttered out. Hersh carried the precious bundle back into the house, past the kitchen and down the damp hallway.

"What are you doing?" Ben asked, following Hersh into the bedroom.

"How *could* you?" Hersh asked, setting the box down on the bed.

"How could *you*?" Ben replied.

"She hasn't been buried, what, two weeks, and you want to throw it all away?" Hersh asked.

"I tried to bury it with her," Ben began. "That's what *should've* happened. But that goddamn funeral parlor Sam hired wouldn't let me."

Hersh sat beside the box on the bed, resting a hand on top of it.

"He was a Nazi!" Ben yelled.

"This is your mother's things," Hersh insisted.

"A Nazi bastard," Ben repeated. "You said it yourself."

"No, no. I never said that."

"You said it," Ben said. "And you said it in front of her."

"No, no. I didn't."

"You did!"

"No."

"Papa?"

"No!"

"Papa, listen to me," Ben insisted. "She thought he was Reuven."

"No, no."

"Listen to me, Papa," Ben continued. "She did. She thought Lindbergh was Reuven."

"No, you don't know what you're saying."

"It belongs in the trash."

"No, this is terrible," Hersh yelled. "You have no respect."

"Look, look inside," Ben insisted, pointing to the box. "I put in the letters she wrote me about it in New York. Look."

Hersh looked at his oldest, most strange son and saw what the rest of their lives would look like. Yes, they might have each other. But they would still be acutely alone.

"Look for yourself, Papa, it's in there, all of it," Ben continued. "And it belongs in the garbage."

"I won't," Hersh said. "I won't look."

He never did.

1.

That's not the end.

This is the end.

In yesterday's mail, overnighted to me from my brother back in Texas:

DEAR T:

WE DON'T HAVE A PHONE FOR YOU IN NYC. SORRY YOUR HAVING TO FIND OUT LIKE THIS, IN A ARTICLE. CALL ME, 806-352-2737 YOU SHOULD PROBLY SHOULD COME. CALL ME.

Sonny

The Amarillo Daily Sun, April 6, 2002

LONG-TIME AMARILLO RESIDENTS
PERISH IN TRAGIC ACCIDENT ON I-40

MORRIS AND ANNA-ROSE COOPER of Amarillo died
yesterday evening in a head-on collision with a tractor trailer
while traveling on I-40 in East Amarillo. At press time, state
troopers were still gathering information for their investigation into the accident, which closed the interstate in both
directions for six and a half hours through rush hour and late
into the evening.

According to several witnesses, the Coopers' black, late-
model Chevrolet Suburban truck was not speeding or otherwise behaving erratically while traveling eastbound in the
fast lane. A tractor trailer traveling westbound and carrying
a full load of live poultry crossed the median and collided
with the Coopers' truck, displaying no visible indication that
the driver was braking or taking other preventative mea-
sures to avoid a collision. No other vehicles were involved in
the accident, although there were a few minor collisions in
the backup caused by the crash.

The driver of the truck, whose name is being withheld
until family members can be notified, is in critical but stable
condition at Amarillo General Hospital. It is unclear at this
point what caused him to steer his truck across the median
and into oncoming traffic. Doctors speculated that the
driver suffered a myocardial infarction (heart attack), just
prior to the accident, but tests cannot confirm this theory
until the patient is stable enough to undergo them, or gains
consciousness.

The Coopers were both pronounced dead at the scene.
John Thurgood, an eyewitness, described their car as "a
crushed sardine can with the top peeled off. Never seen anything like it."

Maureen Smythe, who had been driving westbound
behind the tractor trailer, reported, "The road was covered

in feathers. It was just a swirling storm of feathers blowing all around, and there were dead chickens everywhere. A lot of them were still alive though, running around and pecking the ground. [It was] just horrible what happened to those people."

Morris Cooper, 64, was owner and operator of Amarillo's Panhandle Lanes, the largest bowling facility west of the Mississippi. The company, a true Amarillo original, was founded in 1955 by Sam Lazarus, Cooper's father-in-law and owner of several other Amarillo staples, including The Diamond Shop (closed in 1977), and, with his wife Miriam, Miriam's Babyland (closed in 1975).

Anna-Rose Cooper, 60, (née Lazarus), will always be remembered in Amarillo lore as the "Diamond Baby." Her parents, Sam and Miriam, creatively announced Anna's 1941 birth in this newspaper with a contest in which the correct guesser of the baby's middle name (Rose) was awarded a $75 diamond ring from The Diamond Shop.

Anna-Rose and Morris Cooper met at the University of Texas in Austin, relocating to Amarillo after both had graduated. They raised and are survived by two children, Sammy, of Fritch, TX, and T, of New York City.

They are also survived by Anna-Rose's father, Sam Lazarus of Amarillo, and Morris's brother Donald Cooper, sister Amy Cooper Smith, and parents Abe and Natalie Cooper, all of Houston.

Funeral services will be held at The Veterans of Foreign Wars Post 1752, 1887 Georgia St., on Saturday, April 13 at 1 P.M. In lieu of flowers, please send donations to Bowling for Life, PO Box 28259, Amarillo, TX 78104.

So that makes me the last living Lipshitz, genetically speaking. My brother Sammy's adopted, and everyone else either died or is retarded. I know you're not supposed to use words like that, 'cause it pisses off all the retard groups, but I really don't care.

I didn't used to be like this, blurting shit that hurts people. I used to be

a perfect little angel, until I hit thirteen and just snapped, shooting myself
in the foot. Literally. When we were in seventh grade, my friend Jesus
(pronounced *HAY-soos*) and I found my dad's pistol, and I actually shot
myself in the foot with it. Rewind: "Found" is a bit misleading. It was fully
visible and fully loaded on the kitchen counter when we came home from
school one day, next to the peanut butter sandwiches my mom left out for
us. First Jesus picked up the pistol and waved it in the air, cowboy-style.
He aimed at my left eye and said, "I'm gonna kill you, Beaner," but he
didn't pull the trigger. I, infinitely wiser and more firearm savvy, grabbed
the gun from him and aimed it at the ground before pulling the trigger to
see if it was loaded. It was loaded. In a spray of tiny white-orange sparks,
the bullet tore through the top of my foot between the tendons of the big
toe and the next one over. There were orange and brown shag carpet fragments and fibers stuck to the wound when the doctor unwrapped it at the
hospital. I remember that much.

So the Lipshitzes. (I never know how to make that plural.) It's not my
last name (one blessed fucking thing to be thankful for), but that blood,
the same blood that soaked the streets in Kishinev in 1903, eventually
dead-ended in the panhandle of Texas, and became my blood too. And it
either stops or goes on with me.

Toward that end, I have a perfectly nice wife—she's even half-Jewish.
She's half-Mexican too, but that's beside the point. She's beautiful and
sweet, and she wants a baby—"a little you," she says—and she says she
loves me. I don't know why she loves me, but she tells me that she does
almost every day—to the point where if one day goes by and she doesn't
say anything, I'm like, I'm a fucking mess and I want to ask her, "Why
didn't you tell me you love me today? Do you think I'm ugly?" But I don't
ever ask. I just wait, panicked, until the next day, when, usually over toast
and waffles or after the blender goes off from the stinky healthy drinks
she makes, she looks over at me and says, "I love you, baby," or sometimes she'll invert it and say, "Babe, I love you," or something ridiculously
sincere like this. Two or three days a week she'll add, "You're so hand-

some," or, "I think you're so handsome." It's all so sweet and beautiful and kind . . . And I fucking *hate* her for it.

I should probably stop here to say that writing about writers is the most boring fucking thing in the world. The single worst and most boring—no, wait. Actually, after children, writers are the *second* most boring people to write about. That's because nobody cares about writers. Nobody cares about children either; they only pretend they care about children because it's like killing puppies not to care about children. So this is why everyone who wants to write a book starts writing about a fucking child. Like your average fucking adult who can read really sits there and believes that a child of seven can remember all these details, or better yet, that all these witty observations and intelligent analysis of the events in a *seven*-year-old's world is really coming from a *seven*-year-old's perspective. I will say it now, and if you don't like it, you can put my book back up on the rack: NOTHING HAPPENS IN A SEVEN-YEAR-OLD'S LIFE THAT IS ACTUALLY WORTH WRITING OR READING ABOUT.

And no seven-year-old talks like that. Or when writers do write like a seven-year-old would talk, NOBODY WANTS TO READ THAT because it's usually just what an adult *thinks* a seven-year-old talks like. Which is ridiculous because generally, a seven-year-old is just a fucking seven-year-old grabbing his or her genitals at inappropriate moments and, even if he or she went through some really hard stuff, like getting neglected or molested, or a cockroach crawls in their ear and causes encephalitis and irreversible brain damage, or the kid gets beat up a lot for being too girly when he was a boy, or too boyish when she was a girl—even if this is the case, it is still a seven-year-old's voice that is detailing this information, and again, THIS IS JUST NOT INTERESTING.

Okay, maybe there's *something* to be learned from an abused, neglected, molested, and beaten-up seven-year-old with a cockroach in his ear or a rat chewing on his fingertips as he sleeps, but do we have to have three hundred fifty-eight fucking pages of it, and in a seven-year-old via a forty-two-year-old's voice to boot? I'd almost rather hear what the adult that seven-year-old turned into has to say about the events in his or her life when he or she was seven—like are they doing the same shit to their own kids? Or are they therapists helping others through difficult times (*gag*), or are they angry or silent or confrontational, or infinitely acquiescent? Come to think of it, I don't even want to read about the adult the seven-year-old turned into anymore. I just changed my mind.

This whole "Oh, I'm a seven-year-old, and my innocence-lost perspective is really going to teach you a lesson about life even though it's an off-the-cuff lesson that you will have to glean from my precocious voice narrating to you my quotidian experiences that are really more profound than they seem" thing is just *boring*, and nobody really wants to read about it except when they feel guilty that society has done this to seven-year-olds, which brings me back to my original assertion that not wanting to read about children is like killing puppies so everyone is going to pretend they want to read about the raped and murdered seven-year-old even when they really don't.

One amendment to this is Scout Finch. Something happens when Scout Finch talks that makes you not completely care that what Scout Finch has to say is really what Harper Lee had to say. This is the *only* exception. Mostly because it's supposed to be narrated when Scout's older, isn't it? Is it in first person? Whatever, I hate that shit. Regardless, it carefully preserves the youthful squawk of innocence about to be lost, so it feels like a seven-year-old is still telling it. You know what? I feel a lecture on *To Kill a Mockingbird* coming on, and I think it's one that should be stopped right there. Basically, just know that nobody cares about what kids have to say unless it's Scout Finch. That is the only one. No, not even Holden Caulfield. In fact, *especially* not Holden Caulfield.

As I said, the next group that no one cares to read about is writers. Which is why I'm happy I'm not writing about a writer, like every writer has to do at one miserable point in his or her career. I was a writer, but I'm not anymore, so it's not in the story. Or relevant to the story because it's not the writing that's at issue. It's about the fact that no matter what the fuck I do, what I get, how much I'm loved—I'm never happy. I'm always certain it'll all be taken away. And I'm the angriest son of a bitch you'll ever meet, but you'd never know it unless I told you, which I just did. I can hold shit in like you couldn't believe, acting like shit doesn't faze me, but inside I'm all acid-eating my organs, chewing straight through my spleen before starting in on my liver. The way I came up, the Nazis were always marching on El Paso. That's what my mother used to say. And her grandmother Esther used to say the same thing to her, only she'd change it to the Cossacks. They knew of what they spoke. And so how am I supposed to bring a child into this world—a world that has never, not even once, made me or anybody related to me happy?

You don't. You couldn't. It's the simplest answer. The bloodline dies here. It might've so many times before, so what's the difference, really? And you especially don't bring a child into the world when you're "in between careers," like I am. Or, when there are trust issues. And there are always trust issues.

How do you trust a girl who you might love like mad, but who fucked you on the first night and was cheating on some other dude when she did it? I guess that's just what sluts do, but if you ask me, I'll never trust that she's not off doing the same thing to me, even though we've been together something like four or seven years now. I'd kill her if she did cheat on me, but at the same time, you know, I'm pretty much assuming that's what's happening. You have to expect that. And you certainly don't want to have a child thrown into this mix, no matter how much she may beg.

So as I said, I'm "in between careers." How I became a writer is simple, and I feel comfortable relating it because I'm not one anymore. Basically, I barely escaped Texas with my life. When you do this on a boxcar that leads to New Jersey and you hitchhike the rest of the way into the city, people tell you to write about it. Otherwise expensive New York colleges will pay you to attend them because of geographical (and other) quotas, and then you fall in with the most pretentious, annoying, self-obsessed, dramatic, and ultimately boring people, who write about things instead of doing them, and have bad fashion but think they have good fashion, which is the worst kind of fashion to have. And the most terrifying part of it all is that you are one of these people too. You don't know it until years later when you are lucky enough to have your life-story-thinly-veiled-as-fiction published, and then you walk around actually believing the shit you say, that you actually are lucky, and so you say it to everyone around you to make sure they see you rolling over and exposing your belly to them, even though you know you are the most deserving asshole out there, the illest writer—better than any of them at the *very* least. Which I was. I'm also the most insecure, but that's an entirely different story, though completely one hundred percent relevant.

My first review (*Publishers Weekly,* September 4, 2000):

NONE OF THE PARTS

T COOPER, *Random House*

Starred Review. Holden Caulfield in cowboy boots bumps up against and ultimately joins the freak show that is the downtown New York art scene in the 1990s in this stunning, affectingly honest and gritty debut novel from what will certainly be one of the most looked-to voices of the new generation of young writers.

Tough guy Tank Levy narrates most of this rollicking ride through Manhattan's East Village (in the days before cabs would even drop you off there), though a few other denizens pick up the storytelling baton when Tank is otherwise indisposed. Before he's a twenty-something, sometime Coney Island sideshow performer, graffiti artist, and hustler who isn't a stranger to the walls of New York's worst emergency rooms and jail cells, 16-year-old Tank delineates a wide array of small-town disillusions and disappointments served up by all of the adults around him, namely an abusive neighbor who's a high-up officer of a Texas and Oklahoma panhandles-area religious/space cult. Beyond that it's typical suburban glue, helium, and paint huffing, topped off by hours upon hours of premodern video games and rampant experimentation with sex, (more) drugs, and skateboarding. It's no surprise when Tank drops out of high school with nary a note to his parents and hops a freight train outside of Amarillo, somehow managing to land in Newark, New Jersey, before picking up a wealthy trick who houses him during his first month in the big city.

AIDS looms large on the polluted East River horizon. Some of the most poignant and touching moments in the book come as Tank and his friends wade through activist circles, coping with ubiquitous institutional indifference in the face of indescribable loss—not to mention drama in the form of interpersonal relationships of all kinds: straight, gay, and everything in between—as long as they're grounded in art and politics.

Tank meets and falls in love with a young Boho painter named Amanda, who, in the most predictable turn of an otherwise delicious story, breaks his heart and then steals his furniture. The rotating narration is a bit shaky at times—Cooper is most deft when leaving the master-of-ceremony responsibilities to Tank.

A skilled and unafraid writer, definitely worth watching. Contrary to its title, this book has "all of the parts" that point to the kind of writing that gets even better with time.

Like women, reviews are not to be trusted. They will always say one thing and do another. Inevitably, this will happen the very second after you start believing their shit, because you're feeding the same shit to them, too. Only for the first time in your life you actually mean it, which is the fucking tragedy of the whole thing, because it would've been nice. It's the kind of shit that makes you optimistic enough to get some bitch's name tattooed across your chest and do something as stupid as telling her you want to spend the rest of your life with her—and then actually set about doing it.

And optimistic enough to then jump blindly onto the track they place you on, thanks to the almighty dollar, the machine, the man, the "system" (which has its draw, let's be real). At first you are happy, or relatively so—not expecting much, and nobody expects much of you, which is a convenient and advantageous arrangement that, in my opinion, should just be left alone and not tinkered with. But what I think never matters. That is, of course, unless I'm paying some shrink a hundred bucks a week so I can say the same shit over and over and over, week after week. Whatever.

You are nothing, and then someone "out there" thinks you are something, and then your publisher suddenly thinks you are something and acts accordingly. Just up until more somebodies "out there" change their minds like bitches do (see above), and then you're on your own again, limbs dangling from their pulpy stumps, fixing to fall off your torso completely—a bloody, limping leper among a colony of lepers who just don't know it yet.

Yeah, I get nothing from my mother and father for years. To be fair, there was nothing going in their direction from me either. (I'm a big enough man to admit that, now that they're roadkill in a poultry-related accident on the interstate.) But then the book comes out and I'm suddenly invited to family get-togethers again, Hanukkah, Thanksgiving—the last fifteen years recast and newly understood in the context of my struggling to create a middle-America-approved *oeuvre*. I'm finally allowed in my wife's parents' house, questions turning from hourly wages and potential spousal benefit packages to how I like my coffee in the morning. (One sugar and lots of soy milk.)

Bullshit.

Then my mom reads some interview with me on the Web (what the fuck were my parents doing on the Web?), and in the interview I said some bullshit about my next project involving Russian Jews who immigrate to Texas. I didn't even know what I was talking about and had pulled it out of my ass for the interviewer, because it seemed like I should have another project under way. Five days later, UPS Ground, a big recycled box with rolls of tape peeling off it shows up in the vestibule of my apartment building. Inside, a nappy old hatbox stuffed with yellowed newspapers and other stuff. Plus a note:

Dear T,

Paw-Paw Sam gave this to me years ago when we moved him out of his and mom's house after she died. I read that your next book might have something to do with our family, so I thought you should have this. Maybe you can make something of it—I never could figure out what happened to mom's brother Reuven.

Your dad and I miss you. It said you're touring the west in the spring—do you think they might send you out Texas-way? We would love to see you. It's been WAY too long.

We miss you, T. We don't understand. We accept you. Why are you still so mad? We made mistakes—ALL of us did.

Not much news here. We added a dozen more auto-score lanes and a day-care facility to the bowling alley. Brunswick is still pushing to buy us out, but Dad's standing firm. Had to put Paw-Paw Sam in a home because I just couldn't do it alone anymore. I go see him every day. It's sad, but he doesn't seem to know the difference.

Would love to hear from you sometime. Oh, I ran into your old English teacher at the Toot 'n Tote 'Em on Saturday, she said she read your book and was very proud. See, everybody misses you here.

Love,

Mom

When something like this lands, quite literally, on your doorstep—especially when it's true shit that seems like the kind of shit you couldn't even make up if you wanted—you take it. Even considering the source.

So my tour ended, sooner than expected (*without* a visit to the panhandle of Texas, though I did stop in Houston, where my dad's side of the family surprised me by showing up at the reading), and then I set about doing what all first-time novelists do—begin the process of becoming second-time novelists. My agent was mildly encouraging, though significantly less available, thanks to a HUGE sale of a BIG book. He got a swankier office, with a view of the Hudson River and Jersey. Anytime I visited him, the receptionist directed me to the deliveries window, thinking I was a bicycle messenger. And that's when I was wearing my nice clothes. Anyway, the editor at my publisher moved to a different house, and there was, reportedly, a vague, lingering desire to see my next book when the time came. Nothing official, no promises, and then September Eleventh happened pretty much down the block from me, and after that (but not necessarily entirely because of it), I was a nervous wreck, blowing what was left of my advance on therapy, rent, and weed. Thus I was hard at work wading through the crumbling contents of the hatbox and constructing another book out of it. Oh, and completely alienating my wife in the process.

And it's all true. The parts about the lost blond boy (okay, he wasn't entirely white-blond; it was more of a dishwatery, dirty blond thing he had going on), and the part about coming over to America with the Galveston Movement—those were both true. The rest though, I made up entirely. Not one lick is true, though some incidents are true, and others are true, but made up. All facts about real-life, historical figures (like Charles A. Lindbergh)—those are completely, one hundred percent true, including the dates things happened, the articles about them, and what happened. But how members of my family felt about the incidents that the real people went through—all that is also made up, even though it is based entirely on true events, and thus, entirely true as well. Things like my Paw-Paw Sam's winning a jewelry business in a poker game? True. The "Pampa Flash"? True. The faggot great-uncle? He's buried alone, never married. Who can really say about these things?

So what was I going to do? Finish the fucking thing and then slap some bullshit disclaimer "note from the author," or a "note to the reader on historical content and sources" bullshit like most pompous and entitled cocksuckers do at the end of their books? Like I want to read twenty fucking pages of detailed description of the texture of the pavement in front of the Empire State Building in 1935, or hear about the liberties the author took with his meticulous historical research just because he could, and wanted to jerk off all over it? And then everyone just eats this shit up like they're gnawing on enormous, prehistoric-looking turkey legs at the county fair, the crispy brown skin melting in the corners of their lips, stringy pinkish-gray flesh sliding down their arms in pools of fat.

It's as inevitable and predictable as rappers rapping about fame, lawsuits, and bling on their sophomore albums: "Important details have sometimes been dramatized in order to serve my own purposes as an artist." Or, my personal favorite: "You'd be surprised at how much more interesting history is than anything I could actually make up" (*ha ha ha, how witty and charmingly self-deprecating*), and finally, "For a more historically accurate account of such and such, I direct you to so and so's incredible, exhaustive biography, which is more than I could have ever dreamed of writing on the subject."

All this bullshit faux-humility, history-is-mine-and-I'll-do-what-I-want-with-it crap. No way, I was *not* gonna be one of those dudes sticking one of those excruciating, self-indulgent notes on the end of my book. So I quit writing and followed my true calling, which was to be the illest Jewish MC on the earth—and not some fucking washed-up, middle-aged, punk-ass Beastie Boy neither.

This is why I like to say I'm "in between careers," since this one is taking off somewhat slower than I'd hoped or expected. Though you can't call me unsuccessful. By any stretch. I really started off being a DJ for bar mitzvahs—I got tons of work thrown my way via the contacts I made tutoring private school kids around New York. There's like five or ten big bar and bat mitzvahs every weekend in New York City, and soon I was DJing many of them—and making bank. When I started, Eminem's second record *The Marshall Mathers LP* was still going strong, and it was fucking brilliant (no, he won't top it—and there's certainly a lesson in that), and the kids went nuts dancing to "The Real Slim Shady" and pretty much every other track from that record, so I kept feeding it to them like Scooby snacks. After having to sit in a post-hippie, baby-boomer reform synagogue for hours listening to the crackly-voiced torah portion and the fucking eunuch cantor's wailing, these kids would just let go like little psychos, sweating in their little polyester-blend suits and ripping off their ties and going fucking crazy no-rhythm Jew-boy on the temporary parquet dance floors. These little puberts fucking bugged out whenever I put Slim on—they'd be secretly downing the highballs left on the adults' tables, pumped high on carbs and sugar from the cake and whatever disgusting meat- or dairy-filled meal had been served—and these kids would just be out of their gourds, bugging out, and their folks would see this, and their folks' friends would see this, and soon I've got more jobs than I can handle, putting on these "rap"-themed parties for these boys (and some girls) when their parents don't even know what hip-hop is beyond that it seems to make their kids happy. It was fucking crazy.

And I can dance, and I know I can spit an ill rhyme, and so sometimes I'd head out onto the floor with a mic in my hand and rap over Em's tracks, and these kids would just fucking go crazy making a circle around me, all these little shorties waving their hands in the air around me—especially the little girls from all these private rich-girls' schools, who were pretty much being ignored by the boys who thrashed about, jumping all over each other on the dance floor and working out all their homosexual tendencies via some hard-core music that was ostensibly doing the same. So one time I'm out there doing my thing over Slim's song "Stan," and these kids are rushing the stage and trying to touch me like some screaming 'N Sync fans or something, and afterward, this little homely (which is really just a nice way of saying ugly) girl with huge glasses that keep sliding down her greasy nose comes up to me and asks for my autograph. So I sign it, "Dear Katie, thanks for the support. *Slim Lindy*."

Lindbergh's nickname was Slim too.

It hit me the first day I really checked out those articles in my great-grandma's hatbox. So I immediately jotted a chart, just to be sure I wasn't crazy:

	LINDBERGH	EMINEM
HAIR	BLOND	BLOND
EYES	BLUE	BLUE
MOTHER ISSUES?	YES	YES, SERIOUSLY
DAD	DIED WHEN LINDY WAS 22	SPLIT WHEN EM WAS BORN
WORLD FAMOUS	LOVED, THEN HATED	HATED, THEN LOVED
LOVE LIFE	MARRIED FIRST WOMAN HE MET	MARRIED FIRST WOMAN HE FUCKED
CHILDREN	LOST CHILD	ALMOST LOST CUSTODY OF CHILD
BORN/ RAISED	MIDWEST: DETROIT / MINNESOTA	MIDWEST: KANSAS CITY / DETROIT

The next day I'm at the beauty supply store on Broadway where all the trashiest drag queens shop, and I'm buying the strongest bleach I can find—professional salon grade, and I'm back in my bathroom before my wife gets home, buzzing my hair short and brushing that toxic foam into it and just letting it sit and burn for forty-five minutes until I can't stand it anymore. And then I'm staring at myself in the mirror, scalp on fire, red splotches down my cheeks, neck, and forehead. But when I'm done, my hair is practically white, and it looks tight, and not long after that, my clothes grow baggier and baggier, and people start to look at me differently on the subway and walk a circle around me on the street. And I look good. My wife even said so. Well, I was poking the barrel of a .45 into her eyeball when she said it, but still. I trust her opinion.

In this way I became, in one short year, the number one bar mitzvah entertainer (I don't like the word impersonator), in the tristate region, Long Island inclusive—putting on Eminem-themed parties pretty much every weekend, year-round, and raking in dough hand over fist like the

Real Slim Shady. I'm all like, advance-adschmance. Fuck that shit, I was done with that book then and there. I'd gotten up to the beginning of the Second World War or something, I don't really remember—I tied the pages up with string and stuck them in the bottom of a cardboard box in the hall closet of my apartment. What a fucking *mitzvah* not to have to think about that shit ever again. 'Cause I didn't. I still don't. For real.

I probably got that from my great-grandfather Hersh. Or wrote him like that so I could say that's where I got it from. Because some of the things you can inherit aren't so bad. Denial's probably the best one. Inexplicable hyper-responsibility and self-consciousness, even though you try your best to be a flake who could not give a fuck what anyone thinks—not the worst thing to have either, if you hide it well. But a serious case of the crazies? Well, that would have to be the worst. And you can't write that shit out of the story, no matter how hard you try.

Yeah, so the very next gig after I bleached my hair like Em's, that was it: I'll never forget when this other little girl, this one from the Chapin School, who looked at least twenty-two years old (with a fine set of jugs on her, if I might say), she comes up to me all blushing and twisting and says, "I can't *believe* the Horowitzes got Eminem for Robby's bar mitzvah."

Me neither.

Then the party goes late and no one wants to go home to their miserable empty Upper East Side lives, and all the other jealous parents are begging for my business cards like they're food stamps and it's the middle of the projects. Little old bored Jewish ladies are slipping their phone numbers in my pocket and patting my ass. I have more parties than I know how to handle. I'm *hot*—I can feel it static electrical on my skin after every show. Now I'm just trying to maintain this kind of momentum while simultaneously shifting my focus toward making the jump from the bar mitzvah circuit to the mainstream. Or at least the pre-mainstream underground.

In fact, I had to cancel appearances this upcoming weekend at another two bar mitzvahs because of this going-to-Texas bullshit. I sort of feel bad for the kids, plus, it's horrible for my rep. I'm on the plane right now, the fat guy in the seat next to me farting away under his little wool blanket. It's the first time I've gone back in I don't know, something like fifteen years. My brother needed help, the fuckup. He couldn't figure out what to do with our parents' bodies, their business, the funeral—pretty much everything. I swore the day I left with nothing but the bag on my back that I wouldn't come back, but here I am: United flight 1180, LaGuardia to Denver to Amarillo International. *International.* Fuck, they probably have one flight a year to Mexico, just so they can call it that.

I got my headphones on, real loud. I can tell it's bugging the lady on the other side of me, but I don't care. Since September Eleventh, I need a little something to fly. Who the fuck doesn't? I popped a Vicodin at the drinking fountain before getting on the plane. It's left over from my wife's wisdom teeth removal a couple years back. I think they're expired though.

She cried when she dropped me off at the airport this morning. She misses me, she says, sometimes even when I'm home. I don't really know what to say. She keeps pushing about the baby, and it'll probably end up being the death of us, or of me. Ha, now it's my favorite part in the song, where Slim raps that the three things he hates most are women, girls, and bitches. A-fucking-men. I start laughing to myself, bobbing my head to the music like mad in my skinny middle seat. The lady next to me scoots further away than she already was—what, bitch? You gonna wrap yourself around that armrest?

"You can't miss me; I'm white, blond-haired, and my nose is pointy. I'm the bad guy who makes fun of people that die in plane crashes and laughs as long as it ain't happenin' to him." I'm rapping out loud along with Slim, and now the bitch is reaching up and pressing the orange button over our heads, and soon she's leaning over and her lips are flapping at the flight attendant that my ass is being too loud.

The flight attendant checks me out for a while, like she doesn't know how to take me. "Sir, sir," she says then, all white choppers and BOTOX. "Can you turn that music down just a little? It's disruptive to some of your fellow passengers."

I put my headphones back over my ears and crank that shit up even louder than it was before—it's hurting my own head but I don't care 'cause now I'm up on the seat, legs straddling armrests, ripping the tray table from the seat in front of me and bashing the stewardess over the head with it, her gray matter spraying out all over the seatbacks, and the contents may have shifted during the flight, and I am exercising my right to remain violent . . .

"Oh, I'm sorry," I say, shaking off a Vicodin rage and smiling wide, pupils the size of dimes. "I didn't realize just how loud it was."

"Thank you so much, sir," she says, heading back to the galley so she can continue reading last month's issue of *Family Circle* to figure out why her husband doesn't want to pork her anymore, plus ten outrageous things she might be able to do to change that.

I smile at the lady next to me like the perfect fucking little angel I am, and then crank Em's song back up louder than it was before. Don't you know that he only makes this shit up to make you mad, lady? So you can just go and kiss both his and my naked white asses.

2.

When my brother Sammy meets me at Amarillo International on the east side of town, he's idling in the passenger zone in a brown pickup accented by an empty gun rack with room for three rifles, and wearing a cowboy hat, rancher style.

"S'up?" he says, hugging me the way brothers do.

"What's up with you?"

"Nothin'. Nothin' at all."

"Cool," I say, nodding my head and looking at the white concrete barriers on either side of us—Amarillo's defiant nod toward tighter airport security.

"Flight okay?"

"Yeah, fine."

"You dyed your hair," he says then, turning up the radio and steering us onto the interstate while tapping a spastic beat on the wheel with both thumbs. Steely Dan? Steve Miller? Something awful like this.

"Yeah," I say, "bleached it a while back now."

"What's it been, like ten, fifteen years since you were here?"

"Something like that, yeah."

We pass the Big Texan restaurant on the right. The parking lot in its faux-western town is packed with cars, a couple of semitrucks. I remember the time when my parents took us there for some special occasion, and my brother actually finished the seventy-two-ounce steak in under an hour. He got the meal for free, and everyone was real proud of him, just like they always were. For eating half of a fucking dead cow. I remember I couldn't even finish my eight-ounce steak because I was always having stomach problems, and plus, I thought it was fucked-up to eat an animal—and my dad yelled at me for wasting his money and made me take that rubbery thing home and eat it for breakfast the next morning. Sammy teased me and called me a pussy for the next few days. In fact, I was pretty sure he was still beaming over it right now as we drove by. A stupid smiley-faced picture of him in a red gingham bib hung on the wall by the stairs of that place for years. I wonder if it's still there, and I consider asking him, but I don't, because the thought of seventy-two ounces of meat winding its way through his intestines and colon is literally making me throw up in my mouth.

In a minute, Sammy points across the vast dusty dashboard of his truck and says, "That's where they got hit." There's a burnt patch of otherwise dead grass and weeds on the median, and several bunches of dead or dying flowers next to it, a wreath, and a small wooden cross.

"Did the driver live?" I ask.

"Yeah," Sammy says. "Doesn't remember a thing."

"Fuck," I say. So the cross was for them. I wonder who put it there.

"Things are a little tricky," Sammy says soon after. And now we are in Amarillo proper, if you can call it that. "'Cause Paw-Paw's technically still alive."

"Technically?"

"Well, you know what I mean."

"Not really," I say, and Sammy looks at me.

"He pretty much just lies there."

"Do you visit him?"

"No."

I don't say anything, so Sammy adds, "Oh, he don't know the difference. That son of a bitch is gonna be a hundred years old, he's like a fucking vegetable."

I still don't say anything.

"And you know, I moved up to Fritch a couple years back, so I don't get down here too often for that kind of thing."

"What kind of thing?"

"Visiting and stuff," he says, defensive. "*What*?"

"Nothing," I tell him. Other than the fact that the "vegetable" in the nursing home was just about the only not-jacked-up thing about this place for me. Ever.

We pull into our folks' tract-housing development, Quail Run. It's a little weird to have one of these planned community things in an otherwise typical Amarillo type of residential neighborhood, but here it is, and here we are. It's gated, though the only visible threats are three churches, the interstate, and rows upon rows of squat little single-family homes surrounding it. My brother pinches a garage-door clicker clipped to his sun visor, and a wrought-iron gate lets us into the compound, made up of about a dozen town house–style places. There's a lot of seemingly genetically modified or at least accented grass, perfectly bulging lawns like the tops of bread loaves. A kid with punch-stained cheeks playing with a fluffy white dog, a shiny hot-pink tricycle on its side.

"That's right, you haven't seen this place, huh?" Sammy asks, pulling up in front of their house and jumping out of the truck.

"No," I say, but I've pictured it many times. It looked something like this, but also nothing like this. I will admit I hadn't predicted the faux-Tudor façades when my mother wrote that they'd sold the old house and moved here a few years back.

"It's nice, huh? I figured you could stay here 'cause we're sort of in the process of rearranging stuff right now at the trailer," he offered, trying different keys in the front door.

"You're living in a trailer?" I asked.

"Yeah. A double-wide."

"Oh. Cool."

"Sheila inherited it from her folks a few years back."

"Cool."

"You fine staying here?" he asked, opening the door and leading me into the kitchen.

"Sure," I say. But I'm in no way fine to stay here. The white pages are open on the counter to wherever my mother or father left it—Davidson through Donaldson. Dregs in the MR. COFFEE maker. A check on the counter made out to Luz Martin for fifty dollars, a yellow Post-it note that says "Thanks!!!" in my mother's handwriting.

This is just the beginning, I know.

"Well, I'm glad you're here," Sammy says unconvincingly, taking a Caffeine Free Diet Dr Pepper out of the refrigerator and popping it open. "So I guess I'll leave you here to get settled for a bit. I gotta go sign some papers at the lawyer's."

"Will stuff? I thought that was tomorrow."

"No, this is—this is somethin' else."

"What?" I ask.

"Just some other stuff associated with their deaths."

"Oh." I have a feeling not to ask about this. "So, what have you done about the funeral?"

"I picked a time and place, that's pretty much it. I got so much shit to do, I figured maybe now you're here, you could arrange all that stuff."

"Can you leave me the information?"

"There is no information."

"Well, where's it gonna be?"

"The VFW."

"Where are they now?"

"Who?"

"Mom and Dad, them, their bodies."

"Oh, I think the coroner, I'm not really sure."

I look at my brother. He pokes his head into the refrigerator again, this time pulling out a can of Pabst Blue Ribbon. He cracks that open, thrusts it up into the air toward me, and smiles. "Cheers," he says, taking a gulp and burping that way where you hold it in and then let it out sort of silent and hot. His sandy, stringy hair is a mess, looks like it hasn't been washed in days. He's got a belly sticking out over the waist of his Wranglers, but otherwise he's still stick thin. His left leg bounces wildly as he downs the rest of the beer.

I can't believe I'm related by blood to this, I'm standing there thinking. And then I remember: I'm not.

Is that why he seems so free of it?

3.

My mother's keys are hanging on a hook by the door that leads to the garage, so I pick them up and go on in. Her white, typically American-looking car is in the space closest to me. The other space is empty, barring a few cloud-like stains and a sprinkling of oil-saturated kitty litter. There are three wooden tennis rackets hanging on hooks on the opposite wall, beneath the patchy head of a deer my father shot when we were kids. I'd cried when he brought it home in the back of his pickup, blood pooling in the rails of the truck bed, spilling onto the driveway when he opened the tailgate. I click the garage door open and press the alarm fob on my mother's keychain. It chirps, locking the doors and setting the alarm, so I have to press it again to get in.

I have no idea where I'm going, but here I am in my mother's car, which smells like the kind of cheap perfume they used to give for free in airplane bathrooms, and I have detailed directions from the funeral director. I don't want a pill. I *need* one. But I left the last few Vicodin in my bag back at the house. I pass by a drive-in Starbucks in a worn-looking strip mall and think it has to be a mistake. I turn around to make sure. I pull in as a tinny, heavily accented "Welcome to Starbucks, may I please take your order?" streams out of the little brown box.

"Do you have soy milk?" I ask.

"We're out."

"Ice tea?"

"Sure."

"Great, can I, no wait . . . Can I get a McRib Sandwich?"

"Excuse me?"

"Yes, I'd like a—Oh, forget it, I'ma just come in."

"Whatever."

I can't believe I'm buying a Starbucks product, much less that I wouldn't even have to get up off my own ass to fetch it. I decide to forgo the tea and head to the funeral parlor. I have no idea how I'm supposed to pay for all this funeral shit, though I know my parents must have thought about some of this crap before. This—them going like that now—was probably not in the plan. But surely they planned for something. That's just how they were. How I am. It's why I'm here dealing with this shit, though I hate to admit it. We'll know what's what in the morning; Sammy and I are supposed to go to their lawyer's office first thing.

Walking up the creaking steps to the parlor, I realize that here in this town again, I am about as far away from the Real Slim Lindy as I could possibly be. I wonder if, when I break out of the bar mitzvah circuit, I should change my name from Slim Lindy to something a little iller, like Nefarious Means. Or Jewligan. Maybe it'd have to be *Jooligan,* so people got it. Yeah, Jooligan, that's fresh. I'll get it tattooed in gangster script, huge across my rib cage, plus a couple of old-school pirate neck tattoos—and then people will really know I'm fucking crazy and have to take me seriously. Because people with neck tattoos are invariably insane.

Naming, you know—it's always a really hard call because, well, it's no news flash, but your name seriously matters. It sets the tone for everything. Also, I've gained a lot of cred in the bar mitzvah world, and I'd like to carry over some of that energy into when I start battling, but it could also hold me back a little. I don't know, maybe it could still be one of my three personas, like Slim Lindy is my Slim Shady, Jooligan my Eminem, and T Cooper the real me, my Marshall Mathers . . . But the next thing I know, the funeral director comes out and drapes a warm, heavy hand across my shoulder.

"Any trouble finding us?"

"Not at all, thank you."

"I knew your folks. Wonderful, wonderful people," he says. I follow him inside, where rows and rows of shiny new half coffins are sticking out of the wall diagonally. "In from the big city?"

"Yup."

"The *Big* Apple."

"Uh-huh."

"So, I took the liberty of making a few calls after we spoke," he says, motioning for me to sit down on the couch across from him. He's all business, but gentle. "I don't know if you know, but they reserved plots at the Llano Cemetery for themselves already. By your grandparents and some other family members."

"Oh," I say, "great."

"It's in the Jewish section," he adds.

"There's a Jewish section?"

"Well, it wasn't founded until 1935," he says. "The B'nai B'rith organization sponsored it after, you know, the cemetery had already been there for years, so it's kind of, kind of in the back."

"Okay," I say, but this doesn't seem to do much in the way of an explanation.

"And, not to be too morbid, but that's my business," he chuckles a rehearsed laugh. "It looks like they also purchased some space for your brother and you, with room for spouses, for when the time comes."

My spouse? But all I say is, "Oh."

"You know, just so you know." He opens a notebook and flips through it, continuing, "I also contacted the coroner, and I think from the situation he described, it seems as though you might want to consider cremation before burial."

"Oh, okay," I say, then picture my parents' charred, freeze-framed bodies like in the "after" photographs of napalm-blasted villages in Vietnam. Or maybe they were less robot-stiff, more malleable and stringy like the bulldozed masses at Bergen-Belsen in all the Allied footage taken after liberation. These impressions are all I have to go on. It's all a lot of us of a certain generation have as a template for that level of carnage: pictures, movies, museums—all of it once, twice, even three times removed. Sure, I smelled the rotting flesh and stumbled upon the odd body part, but even the bulk of the events of September Eleventh unfolded for me across a television screen.

Then I picture my parents' late-model Chevy truck, which I'd never actually seen, smashed up like a sardine can, the top peeled off like the witness said in that article, and revealing their twisted black and oozing bodies strapped inside. Truth is, I can't really envision what actually happened to them. I know there had to be some sort of blaze—when Sammy and I drove by the median earlier after he picked me up, the grass and concrete were scorched in crazy patterns like fucking crop circles. And of course the feathers. It feels like a century ago now . . . When he picked me up at the *airport,* you asshole. Not the last time with the flames and feathers and all the Jew-barbecuing in Russia . . . See my m.o.? How I can straight-up dis' you in one breath, and then turn around and try to break your heart in the very next?

"So, I don't know if that's what you want to do, like the M.E. suggests— as I said, in these sorts of challenging cases, he suggests cremation," the funeral director prods me again.

"I don't think Jews are supposed to be cremated," I say. I don't know where I'm getting my information, but I do have vague memories of Nanny Miriam's and my Great-Uncle Ben's funerals when I was a kid. I cried only at Ben's—it was in the middle of summer, and I remember my hand felt like it was melting off the bone in my mother's grip. I think I cried because we were the only people at the funeral—just the four of us in my immediate family, plus Nanny Miriam in a wheelchair and Paw-Paw Sam pushing her from behind. Nobody else was there except the old rabbi and the guys cranking the little pine box into the ground. It struck me as pathetic even then—when I was just seven—that he didn't have anybody else. But as I said, who really cares how I felt when I was seven? *Nobody*.

"I don't know the specifics of your people's customs regarding cremation," the funeral director says. But I know he does.

"Yeah, I don't think we should cremate them," I say, and it's meant to be a decision of some sort, though he doesn't look very happy about it. He writes something in his notebook, but I can't tell whether or not the actual decision has been made.

I sit back on the ridiculously comfortable black leather couch with my legs crossed like a dandy as he continues his spiel. Over the next hour I learn more than I ever thought I might about the funeral industry. Like that I could decide to bury their remains in a nice coffin, to give the appearance to mourners that a full, intact body is contained in the box, all peaceful and ready for the big sleep. As we go through the three-ring binders, I look at pictures of coffins of the sort I imagine the king and queen of Thailand being buried in. They are to the pine box what Donald Trump's Taj Mahal is to an outhouse. When I point this out to the funeral director, he doesn't laugh. I think he thinks I think he's trying to screw me out of a bunch of my parents' money. (Which I do, because he is. But that's beside the point.)

I spare no expense on most aspects of the service—the cars, the flowers, the headstones, all this ridiculous stuff. And this seems to make him happy. But I insist on pine boxes. Again, I think that's what Jews are supposed to do, but when I ask him he again claims ignorance and doesn't seem to approve of my choices. Now I can't even do a funeral right, and we can safely add the mortician to the long list of people I've failed in my life in this town. I assure him I will bring a check by for the deposit tomorrow, but it doesn't look like he believes me. He says he has to get busy because the funeral will be in three days.

I want to go anywhere but back to my parents' house. I head up Western and past the bowling alley. The parking lot is half full. The batting cages are gone, as is the miniature golf course that used to take up half of the massive lot. The entire place looks much bigger than I remember it. Up ahead on the left is the place I used to go to trade football cards as a kid—the Hobby Haus. I fucking worshipped the Dallas Cowboys—had every card for every season. I wonder what happened to all those cards, 'cause I could get a ton of cash for them now. I find myself pulling into the parking lot, gravel popping under tires.

Nothing has changed, not even the bell that announced to the crotchety owner when us little brats were in the store. I laugh at the German spelling of "house," something I never noticed as a kid. I wonder why.

The guy behind the counter is decidedly different from the old owner. His head is shaved, and he's got cumulous acne patches on his cheeks and horrible greenish-black tribal tattoos all over his fat arms, not to mention very unfortunately shaped facial hair. He's perched behind the counter on a stool that's clearly too small for him. A small black-and-white TV blares behind him, and a comic book is opened on the counter.

"What's up?" he asks.

"Hey."

I wander the aisles and get a brilliant idea, perhaps the best idea I've had in years—better even than quitting writing. "Do you have the *Spirit of St. Louis*?" I ask.

"What's that, a destroyer?"

"Plane," I say.

"Hold on," he says, and takes down a beat-up olive-green plastic file-card box. It's the same system I remember the old man using to keep inventory of the store when I was a kid.

"Yeah," he says, pulling out a card, "we should have one of them somewhere."

"Can I see it?" I ask.

"Well, that's what I was just gonna go do," he says testily.

I don't say anything. He waddles over to the model plane aisle and bends over, hands braced on knees, studying the rows and rows of boxes. He moves into the ship models section, like I didn't know what the fuck I was talking about that the *Spirit of St.*-fucking-*Louis* isn't a boat. Back when I was trying to write that ass-faced book, I learned just about everything there was to know about Lindbergh and that flight. I don't know; I think it was a second adolescence or some shit.

"Hold on, there's one more place I can look," he says, slowly making his way behind a ratty curtain to the back room. After a while, he comes back. "Here."

It's a small box, covered in cellophane, but it's dusty as hell. I can just barely make out a picture of an already assembled model floating against a blue background with fake wispy clouds.

"Great, how much is it?" I ask.

"Eight bucks."

I'm very excited to get started, but I have no idea how, and I can tell that I'm in over my head, cruising for an education thanks to Mr. Personality. I figure I'll just get it over real quick, ripping-off-a-Band-Aid style. "I've never made one of these things," I say, "so can you just hook me up with everything I need?"

He looks at me like he's real superior, and I have to give it to him. In this arena, he is king. He takes the box back from me and dusts off the back after licking a thumb, reading the spot on the box revealed by the dusting. He silently walks to the paint aisle and pulls down three little paint bottles from a rack—one silver, one black, one clear. He grabs a multi-pack of red paintbrushes, a tube of glue—everything with the name "Flyers." I seem to have a vague memory of this brand, the square, squat shape of the paint bottles—almost like tiny glass grenades—from when I was a kid. My brother must've been into this shit, but I can't exactly recall.

"I can give you every little thing, but if you want to save your cash, you can get pretty much everything else at home," he mumbles. I guess it's safe to assume he's not the new owner.

"What else do I need?"

"Toothpicks for the glue, a file if you want to do it that good, nail clippers to get the parts off the tree, um . . . what else?"

"Okay, so I'm supposed to get all the parts off the tree and then paint them?" I ask.

"No," he says, power-playing. "It's usually easier to paint while they're still on the tree."

I have no idea what the tree is, but I figure I'll figure it out later. Either way, I'm confident it'll be infinitely easier than raising the dead and writing a book. "Cool, so what am I up to?"

"Nineteen dollars, sixty-five cents."

"That's it?"

"You want me to charge you more?"

I give him a twenty and drop the change into my pocket.

"Nice ink," he says, because my tattoos had peeked out from beneath my T-shirt as I paid.

"Thank you," I say. Then I wince and add, "You too."

As I open the door and the bell rings above me, the guy calls to me: "That gray I gave you is aluminum number 1781. They don't make the exact color it asks for on the box anymore."

"Cool, thanks," I say, propping the heavy glass door open with a boot.

"The one I gave you is the closest replacement for the old one."

"Thanks," I say again, and get back into my mother's car.

4.

Back at my parents' house, I can't find any lights, and the sun's just about disappeared in an orange explosion in the sky over the Presbyterian church across the way. The air smells like manure. I promised myself on the day I pulled out of Amarillo on that boxcar that I'd never again get a whiff of that as long as I lived. I guess I got soft or something, because it doesn't smell as bad as I remembered—there's almost something sweet to it. After fumbling around and running my palms along the walls for a few minutes, I finally get some lights on, and I can close some windows against the stench. I put the *Spirit of St. Louis* on the dining room table and head directly to the phone in the living room, in front of a large-screen TV. I call my wife, and it rings six times before she picks up at the same time that the answering machine does. There's the screech of feedback, and then it's just her.

"Hi, baby," she says, her voice unbelievably saccharine. Sometimes it makes me want to bash her face in when she talks like this. Other times it makes me believe in the whole "forever" motif. But tonight it's somewhere in between.

"Hey."

"Uh oh. That doesn't sound good."

"I don't really know where to start."

"Did your brother pick you up?"

"Yeah."

"Where are you?"

"Folks' house."

"Weird," she says. "You okay, baby?"

I want to cry, but I've cried in front of her only once before. Or maybe I could slip this one in because it technically wouldn't be in front of her, in person.

"My folks bought a plot for you in the cemetery," I say.

"What? They don't even know we're together."

"They got plots for me and Sammy and our spouses."

"How thoughtful. They already bought spots for themselves then, huh?"

"I guess so."

"Did you figure out the funeral?"

"Can we talk about something else?" I ask. "Anything."

"You sure?"

"Surer than I've ever been."

"Well, it was nice here today," she says, mindlessly. "They opened up another building down by the pit. One of the hotels or something."

"Great, more people swarming around the neighborhood."

"Oh, this was out of right field . . ."

"*Left* field," I correct her. "Anyway, what?"

"Your agent called this morning after you left. He's sorry about your parents."

"How'd he know?"

"I told him."

"Great, thanks."

"Oh, don't be such a prick, T."

"Thanks. That makes me feel much better, considering I'm sitting all alone in my dead parents' living room right now."

"Don't pull that shit. You know I offered to come."

She's right. She did offer, but I told her not to. I didn't want her to see me here. I didn't want *me* to see me here. "Anyway, what did he want?"

"Just checking on progress," she says. "He even mentioned something about this new stuff maybe being incorporated into the book."

"This new stuff?"

"You know, your parents."

"Someone should probably tell him that the whole two parents dying at the same time thing is way over. He probably just ran through his cut of the huge advance he got for that asshole who chopped off his own leg to save his life—what the fuck's his face."

"T . . ."

"What? He's a prick."

"He was concerned."

"Yeah, concerned about his next advance. He knows I'm done. Over. Finito."

"Well," she says, and I can tell she's watching the TV now.

"What?"

"The packet from the fertility clinic came today," she says after an appropriate pause.

"I can't talk about this right now."

"I'm just telling you."

"Can you do me a favor?" I ask.

"What, stop talking about this topic?"

"No. Send me something overnight?"

"Okay, what?"

"You know the hatbox thing my mother sent? I think it should still be in that big box at the bottom of the closet, under my hockey pads and some other shit. Look inside, I think floating around loose should be a rock. I want that."

"Why?"

"Can you just send it? And there should also be this little pouch thing with a piece of cloth rolled up in it. It's not the pouch with coins in it, make sure you don't send that one. It's the one with the rolled-up fabric."

"What is it?"

"It's supposed to be from the *Spirit of St. Louis* or something."

"What do you mean?"

"I don't know, some brilliant member of my family obviously got bilked for this somewhere down the line. In Paris supposedly everyone was ripping the fabric and other shit off the plane after Lindbergh landed, and he started flipping out."

"I thought you said he was, 'A fucking Nazi'—is the phrase I think you used," she reminds me.

"He's kind of a hero."

"No, he's not."

"He fucking flew for thirty-three and a half hours all alone across the Atlantic in that little flying lawnmower. Nobody does shit like that anymore. There's nothing left."

"Whatever, he was a Nazi."

"Maybe true, but he's still a hero."

"You can't be a hero and a Nazi."

"Yes, you can."

"You're insane. You see how far apart his eyes were on his face? Definitely something wrong there."

"I have to go."

"Come on, babe," she says in her sweet voice, and I then wonder who's going to pay for this long-distance phone call on my parents' line. Who handles this kind of thing? Does it get forgiven when you get pulverized on the interstate?

"I should get some sleep. We have to go to the lawyer's first thing."

"Are you going to be okay?"

"There's satellite TV," I say, but notice there are about fifteen separate remote controls piled in a little basket by the television. "Or I'll read."

"I love you."

—

"Say it," she insists.

"I do."

"Say it."

"I do too."

Then *blah, blah, blah*—something in Spanish I never understand. Probably something about how impossible I am, how I'm a little devil. Then she adds in the language I can understand, "Call me. I mean it. Whenever."

I give her my parents' mailing address and tell her goodnight.

The silence is screaming after I hang up the phone, and I can hear the *click-click* of my skull swiveling on my spine every time I move my head. I can't figure out how to turn on the fucking TV. I grow insanely incensed at my father for this, and I want to smash his fucking golf clubs through the TV screen, one after the other. But then I remember he's dead.

I know that when the wife looks for my great-grandmother's rock and pouch to send me, she'll inevitably find the tied-up manuscript under it. I told her I'd shredded it, deleted the file from my computer's hard drive. I was lying about the first part, but telling the truth about the second. Soon I'll have to endure another serious talk about how I need to finish the book, how I'm an okay DJ and MC, but that it might not necessarily be my true calling, that all this might just be about something else entirely. In her opinion. The opinion of the only person who really knows and loves me on this fucking shit-hole earth.

I start to walk around the house, flipping on lights where I can find them. There are three bedrooms, and I can't decide which, out of the two that aren't theirs, I should sleep in. One is the official-looking guest room, with a queen-sized bed and TV, but it shares a wall with theirs. That won't do. The other seems to be the sewing and storage room with half a twin set and no TV. But at least it's downstairs. I bring my bag in there and sit on the bed. There's a credenza, or at least that's what I think it's called, though I'm certain I've never in my life used or even thought of that word before.

I lay down on my back across the bed and study the ceiling. It's that thick, white cottage-cheesy stucco—looks like it's in the process of crumbling, even if it's not, and will probably outlive me and any offspring that may or may not emanate from me. I hang my head over the side of the bed, and I can see behind me an upside-down box. When I sit up and turn around, the box is, of course, right side up. I open up the flaps: Inside are about two dozen copies of my book—half hardcover, half paperback. I pick up one of the hardcovers and look at the back cover. There's my half-smiling, wholly self-satisfied stupid mug in black and white. I read the bio next to it.

> T COOPER was born in 1972 and raised in the Texas panhandle,
> and has been a writer and activist living in New York City since the
> age of 16. He holds an MFA in fiction writing from Columbia Uni-
> versity. *None of the Parts* is his first novel.

What a load of crap. I toss that shit back in the box and fold the flaps the way you can interweave them and close boxes without the benefit of tape. It's always hardest to bend that last corner under, but I finally manage and sit back down on the bed, staring at the box. Where the fuck did they get it? 'Cause I sure as hell didn't send it to them. Why you would want to keep around multiple copies of something that disses you is completely beyond me. I notice then that the box even has the distributor's logo on it. Hell, they probably got a discount. Cheap Jews.

Eminem's mom sued his ass for ten million dollars after his first single dropped, you know, the one where Em rapped that his mom did more dope than he did. She tacked another million onto the lawsuit before ultimately being forced to settle for just twenty-five grand—and that was before she had to pay legal fees. When asked about his life in interviews, Eminem just rattled off how his mom never worked, popped pills, slept all the time, and filed lawsuits left and right to try to make money. Em had to quit school at fifteen to get a factory job, and when he'd bring his paycheck back home, his mom would take most of it and then kick him out of the house for the thousandth time. And Em didn't back down in subsequent songs either—shit, in one, he rapes his mom and laughs about it. You know, even though he knowingly hides behind his Slim Shady persona when he's saying the craziest shit, I believe every word of it. It's not the kind of shit you make up. But it's also true that without his mom— without that hatred and rage and desire to prove her and everybody else wrong—he wouldn't be a fraction of the rapper he is now.

It could've been worse with my folks. I guess they tried. You know, by pawning off these books on their friends and relatives as some sort of wholesale, prepackaged apology-by-proxy. Nevertheless, I decide I'll be sleeping on the couch and go back out to fumble with the TV until I get a picture, but I still can't figure out how to access the satellite. There are only twelve channels now, but I don't give a fuck, because *Law & Order* is on two of them.

5.

In the morning my brother just walks into the house unannounced through the door from the garage. I'm sitting on the couch in front of the TV amidst the night's blankets, lacing up my boots. The TV hasn't been off since I turned it on, and I'm pretty certain it won't go off until the minute before I leave this house for good.

"Morning," Sammy says. He's dressed in nicer clothes than yesterday, shoes instead of cowboy boots. But his hair is still a mess.

"Good morning," I say. "Hey, do you know how to get the cable turned on?"

"Yeah," he says, going over to the basket of remotes. He fishes one out and presses a button, shaking it at the TV like he's spraying fire starter over charcoals in a barbecue pit. The screen goes black with a green horizontal line, and then the guide channel comes up, serenely scrolling through the TV schedule. It's on channel 400-and-something. Fucking pay dirt, I'm thinking.

"Thanks," I say.

"We should go," Sammy says then, turning off the TV. "I thought we'd get some breakfast at the bowling alley first, if it's cool with you."

"Yeah, that'd be great," I say. "I'm hungry." But I have no idea what I could possibly find to eat there that doesn't involve meat or deep frying—or some combination of the two.

"All righty." He's waiting for me as I finish tying up my boots.

"Actually," I say then, "can you turn the TV back on in case I can't figure it out later?"

He picks up the remote again and the guide channel, sweet Jesus, is back on. "Channels are these buttons up and down."

"Thanks," I say. It is a deep, heartfelt thank-you for the blessing of over a thousand mind-numbing cable channels.

We take my brother's pickup and head down Western past the Hobby Haus as I watch it blast by on our right. My brother seems to have a speed problem. And probably a speed problem too—he's flying.

"You know, they have two guest rooms," Sammy says.

"I know."

"Then why are you sleeping on the couch?" he asks.

"I just fell asleep there."

"Oh," he says, turning left on screeching tires into the massive, mostly empty Panhandle Lanes lot. "I used to stay in the room downstairs. I mean, on and off, between jobs."

We head into the restaurant through the kitchen, and everyone says hello to Sammy. He doesn't introduce me to anyone until we sit in the booth, and people start flooding over to pay their regrets.

"Oh my, will the Lord's wonders never cease?" a large woman in a half apron exclaims, plump tears forming in the corners of her eyes. She hugs me to her voluminous breast. "T baby, I haven't seen you since you were in Little League. What happened to your hair?"

"Hi," I say, extracting myself from her grip. She smells of bacon. "I bleached it."

"You don't remember me?" she asks.

My brother is laughing. She's been waiting tables here since before we were born. She and another leathery guy who I do vaguely remember from the kitchen sit down in our booth and scoot tight up against me, yammering at each other. I can barely understand anything thanks to their accents. Or maybe I just don't want to. They're shaking their heads about the accident, tragic this, unfair that, the Lord working in mysterious ways here, and bless their precious souls there. A few others stand around the table or lean over the backs of adjacent booths, everybody with thin blue strings of cigarette smoke snaking up above their heads.

It's clear everyone, or at least those who are staff, is deferring to my brother in some vague way—as though their jobs depend on it. But it feels a little like their obsequiousness may be directed at me too, and this makes me intensely uncomfortable.

"So, T," the woman begins after our food is served. There is a piece of yellow muffin stuck to the corner of her lips where peach-colored lipstick has rubbed off into small balls. "What was it like in New York on nine-eleven?"

"Oh, I don't know," I say.

"Your mom said you lived right near there."

"I did. I do."

"We were just nervous wrecks about it here," she says. "Those bastards."

"Did y'all have to move out of your house?" somebody asks.

"Just for a few months."

"Where'd you stay?"

"With some friends a little farther uptown."

"We've been praying every Sunday since at church," the woman says. "And my daughter, she works at the Super Wal-Mart, she organized a drive, and they raised around thirteen hundred bucks and sent it to those poor firemen."

"That's great," I say, nodding my head. Because it *is* great. It's just fucking *GREAT*!

"We should get going," my brother says. "We got a meeting at the lawyer's."

Everyone nods knowingly. *The poor orphans. The little lambs.*

I want to tear their heads off their torsos, but some are so thick I'm thinking I'd probably need the help of a chain saw to do the job right.

"Nice seeing all of you," I say. I take out my wallet even though all I had was a slice of my brother's dry toast. He shakes his head at me, like, *No, stupid; we don't pay here.* He doesn't even leave a tip though, and so when he isn't looking, I take out a five and drop it on the table next to the gory remains of his huevos rancheros stuck to a shredded napkin.

At the lawyer's office I learn that my brother has been siphoning as much as he possibly can each month from Paw-Paw Sam's trust. Plus my parents have been periodically contributing to the endless pit that is Sammy. I want to ask him, "What is it you *do* every day?" But he's on his best behavior in front of the lawyer, and plus I don't really care, so I decide against it.

There are no surprises. There's the bowling alley, the house, an apartment building in south Amarillo. Life insurance policies for both of them. Paw-Paw's estate, which is mostly dry from the nursing home and Sammy. Seems all standard to me. We need to empty the house so it can be sold. That is, of course, unless either of us wants it. I certainly don't. Sammy says he's happy where he is up in Fritch. Maybe he'll buy something in town later. The lawyer describes the horrors of inheritance tax, then gives me a temporary checkbook to finish off the bills for the house, funeral payments, incidentals. Sammy eyes me suspiciously.

"You want to do it?" I ask him, offering the checkbook.

"No, no," he says. "I trust you."

The lawyer says he will put the house on the market, asks me to determine what we want from it and what can go. Gives me a card for an estate liquidator who does a glorified yard-sale type of thing at your house. He thinks we should hold onto the apartment building for income. The lawyer, he's telling me all this stuff even though it's clear from looking around at the various pairs of steer horns on the wall, the dress cowboy boots on the lawyer's feet, my brother's red-faced, squinty greedy posture, that *I'm* the freak here and always have been. I keep looking to Sammy for some help with the decisions, but it's a hopeless formality. He just keeps repeating, "Sell it, sell it," because he wants the money and doesn't even pretend otherwise.

The bowling alley is a different thing. It's still in Paw-Paw's name—his and my father's—but it's clear Sammy wants his piece of it. The lawyer asks me if I'm interested in running it, now or at a later time. I laugh, and Sammy is uncomfortable in his chair, shifting several times against the noisy Naugahyde. I assure them I don't want any part of it, but they keep asking the same question in several ways to make sure I'm sure I know what I'm declining. It's coming loud and clear that the son of a bitch is a cash geyser. I can tell by the frantic look in my brother's eyes. I keep assuring them I don't care. They talk of a standing offer from Brunswick, the bowling equivalent of Microsoft, but Sammy assures the lawyer he can run the place. As long as the manager stays ("Give him a raise, a percentage"), and that way my brother won't have to do a thing but stop by every few days, eat some free fried pork-derived foods, and collect the checks. It's determined that he will slowly buy me out of my share of the business, even though I tell him he can have all of it. The lawyer is protecting me, but I keep telling him I don't care. It is finally determined that I'll get my share in the form of monthly payments from the bowling alley. When Paw-Paw dies and thus gives up his share, there'll be a little more.

When all's said and done, I'll have about two hundred thousand dollars more than I ever had or thought I would. I didn't come here for the money, I keep saying that over and over in my head. I might not know exactly why I came, but it sure as hell wasn't for that. There's that line from some book or song where the farther you run, the closer you are. Or maybe I just made it up. I thought I was done with all this, for years this is what I was thinking. I get a rush in my stomach that warms my chest and neck and then realize I haven't had anything to eat since before flying out from New York yesterday morning. Well, there was the toast, but that's it.

I tune out the rest of the conversation, but I have the lawyer's card and my various tasks. My brother seems to have no tasks. Just before we leave, I find out he's pursuing a wrongful-death suit against the truck driver, but with a different lawyer. This one, even with the steer horns on his wall, the ostrich boots, and the ridiculous accent, is strongly advising Sammy against it, one last time.

Back in the car, my brother rolls down the window and smokes a cigarette really quickly before starting the engine—smokes like he drives. Then he lights another one, and I put on my seat belt. "That guy's steamrolling us," he says.

"No, he's not," I say. "He's a good guy. He's known Mom and Dad for years."

"I don't trust him. He don't trust me."

"Well—"

"Well what?" he asks, and I want nothing more than for him to watch the road ahead of us instead of me. We're speeding through the tail end of a yellow light now, and the truck bounces violently through the intersection.

"Don't do this other thing," I say.

"I knew you'd be against me on this one."

"I'm not against you," I say. "I just don't understand it. Did you hear how much money you're getting?"

"I think there's some missing. They had more."

"No, they didn't. You just heard what there is."

"I don't know," he says, all Sherlock Holmesy in a cloud of smoke. "Where are we going?"

"Back to their place. I have all this shit to do now."

We drive in silence.

"Drop the suit," I say again after a while.

"That guy was negligent!" he insists. I wonder if he's ever used that word before the accident.

"Don't you think he's had enough?" I ask. "He's like, retarded or something now."

"It's the trucking company I'm suing, not the guy," Sammy says, flicking his cigarette out the window. "They're fucking billionaires."

"Come on," I say. "If you don't blow the bowling alley, you'll be set for the rest of your life."

"There's talk of him doing drugs," he says, and I laugh. If this isn't the sugar calling the salt white, then I don't know what is.

"He had a heart attack," I insist.

"Mmm-nn, no, not what I hear," Sammy says, looking out the window and shaking his head slowly like he's in possession of a secret. We pull into Quail Run's driveway, and Sammy clicks the garage-door opener three times before the heavy iron gate with "QR" on top slowly opens for us.

"I knew you'd be like this. But you don't know, 'cause you haven't been here," he says. We're idling in front of the garage, silent. "So you're not gonna join the suit?" he tries one last time, popping the truck into gear with his foot on the brake.

"Sorry."

"Fine."

I get out of the truck and go back into our parents' house. I can hear my brother's truck's tires wailing for a few seconds after he goes. They sound a little like sirens.

6.

I finger through some files in the credenza in the second guest room. I find one named "Dad," full of statements and contracts for Paw-Paw's nursing home. I get the address and find it on the map of Amarillo in the middle of the white pages.

The retching in my stomach is getting unbearable, so I look inside the refrigerator for the first time. There's a just-about-to turn smell, and nothing I can eat, except some Skippy peanut butter, jam, and white bread. I make one side of a peanut butter and grape jelly sandwich, pour some apple juice, and sit at the counter, listening to myself chew.

Regis and Kelly are on the TV, but the volume's turned down low. I think I hear her say that Kevin Costner will come on after the commercial. I can't imagine anybody more useless in the world than Kevin Costner, except maybe Alan Thicke. Whose son, incidentally, going by the moniker Thicke, is fixing to put out an R&B/neo-soul/funk/hip-hop album. I heard an advance track from it, and it sounded wacker than the demo tape some skinny little Jewish kid pressed hopefully into my hand after one of my recent bar mitzvah sets. Thicke? Please. I'd rather be nailed to a wall by my ear cartilage and be forced to listen to the official Broadway sound tracks of *My Fair Lady, The Sound of Music,* and *Mamma Mia!* one after the other, over and over, with Vanilla Ice freestyling over it live in front of me.

I finish my meal comprised solely of processed foods and scrape the crumbs off the counter and onto the plate. There is a dishwasher, but for some reason I don't want to open it and see the remnants of whatever my folks last ate stuck to the plates, lipstick stains (hopefully my mother's) on coffee mugs from places they visited on trips cross-country in the motor home, knives with the greasy remnants of butter, various breakfast meats, maybe a starchy string of banana.

I find some dish soap under the sink and clean my plate and glass with a musty sponge. There's no drying rack, so I find a dish towel and lay it out on the Formica counter, and place my dishes on top of it to dry.

I go over to the dining room table and spill the contents of my Hobby Haus bag onto the table. The plastic parts rattle like puzzle pieces as I tear through the cellophane and open the box. It's tiny. Indeed there are two "trees" with the parts connected to them, and one long loose wing, the largest piece in the whole lot—six or seven inches at most. I thought the damn thing would be bigger, like the *Star Wars* X-Wing fighter toy I used to have when I was a kid. You could stick Luke Skywalker in it, for god's sake. But this, this is tiny. Lindbergh would have to be half an inch tall to fly this thing. Literally.

I find a newspaper from the day my parents died on the coffee table and spread it out on the table so I can get started on the model. Let's see . . . *Amarillo Police Department demonstrates the abilities of its first-ever $180,000 bomb-handling robot at the city's old police-training facility.* That shit looks no more technologically complex than Rosie the maid robot on *The Jetsons* cartoons. What else? *Texas Silent Hero awards go to two Amarillo 911 dispatchers. Glenda McRoberts and Dean Smithson will go to Houston to pick up their awards, which honor those whose work behind the scenes during an emergency really stands out.* I wonder whether Glenda or Dean took the call for my parents' accident that

day—or maybe they were already partying it up in Houston by the time
that call came in for the poultry-truck-meets-passenger-car on the interstate . . . I stand up the box with the picture of the assembled plane so it's
facing me and then lay out the directions, parts trees, paints, brushes,
glue—all of it across the newspaper. I start to get that panicked thing,
like I can't do this, it's too overwhelming, but then I realize there's more
I can do to delay the panic.

I go into my mother and father's carpeted bathroom upstairs and find
a nail clipper. It smells like dried blood, and there are a few tiny white
cuticle shards stuck to the inside of one of the blades. There are a few
emery boards with white skid marks from my mother's nails on them, and
several pink-hued nail polish bottles and cotton squares. I pull out the
drawer even farther, and there in the back is a bundle of unused emery
boards, bound by a small rubber band. I take two of these.

Downstairs in the pantry I find a toothpick dispenser and shake out a
few. Everybody in Texas keeps toothpicks at home. I think it's because of
all the stringy steak. In the garage inside my father's bright red toolbox
that looks like it might've been a recent birthday present from my mother
via Sears Roebuck, I find a razor filled with rusty triangular blades. I scroll
them out until the blades become clean and then break off the top four or
five rusty ones, dropping them into the trash can under the sink.

Sit back down in front of the model. Exhale. I'm a nervous wreck.
Let's see what else was going on. *Beef up your freezer for MS.* Excellent.
*The Panhandle chapter of the MS Society will hold its 33rd annual Beef-A-
Thon from noon to 6 P.M. on Sunday. Area cattle feed-yards and ranchers
have generously donated beef that will be sold in both ground-beef packages and in custom-cut quarters. Eden Custom Meats and Skeeter's Meats
will process cattle and also package any beef quarters according to custom
orders. As usual, there will be an additional charge of 35 cents per pound
for custom cutting of the beef.* Perhaps now it's clear what I mean about
the toothpicks.

That's about enough of that. I start reading the directions for the model and then read them again. They are most likely a product of back when they used to make the right-colored paint for the *Spirit of St. Louis* model, and they are practically unintelligible, meant for people (*fucking kids!*) who do this shit all the time. I can't do it. I'm in way over my head. I breathe some more.

I get up to see if there are any more beers in the refrigerator and there are, tons of them stacked on their sides with labels facing the same way in the vegetable bin, all Pabst. I take one out and open it, take a sip and it tastes like shit. Regis and Kelly are spinning some stupid fucking wheel on the TV. The lady on the phone in Missouri has won a Caribbean cruise and she is shrieking. I, on the other hand, would forfeit my entire inheritance *not* to have to go on that cruise. Okay:

1. *Study all illustrations and assembly sequences before beginning to build your model.* How can I study the sequences when I don't even know what all the parts are—left front strut, right front strut, left rear strut, right rear strut, fuselage assembly, stand arm, left landing gear, right landing gear. Fucking fuck. I hate this thing.

2. *Decide if and how much detail you might wish to add to your model, and do you intend to "convert" the basic model in any way?* What the fuck does this mean?

3. *It is suggested that you do not detach the parts from the runner of the parts tree until you actually need them. This will help you keep track of the considerable number of parts in this kit.* When exactly do I need them, before I paint them? After? When I'm gluing them? Now I forget what that guy said.

4. *As you begin to cement parts together, be sure to first check the way in which one part is supposed to fit together with another. This assures an orderly job with no surprises. Keep in mind: It is best to paint most—but not all—parts while still attached to the tree.* I fucking *hate* surprises. How are you supposed to know where parts fit together until you break them off and try them first? And how will I know which to paint on and which to paint off the tree?

5. Always remember to keep your work area very well-ventilated, as plastic cement and paint can be toxic when inhaled for extended periods of time. Now you're talking. I think I'll go close all the windows and at least make this fun.

How can they make these fucking things with no directions that make any sense? It says to read them a couple times. I've read them four times over and I still don't have any idea about how to proceed. For instance: *Insert propeller shaft 8 through engine 6 and* **carefully** *apply cement to the very tip of the shaft only; now gently press propeller 7 onto shaft.* Sounds like the way the director of a gay porn video might instruct his actors.

I read the tips over again, as well as the section on painting, which really has only one paragraph on painting while the rest are about other things, not really involving painting at all. They tell you to paint the whole thing while on the trees—two coats with a full twenty-four hours for drying between each. But then they say that glue doesn't stick very well to painted surfaces, only you can't know which surfaces are to be glued to which surfaces until you break them off the tree, but you can't break them off the tree until they're painted. So what the fuck?

I sit and stare at the parts, directions, and the picture of the plane on the box for at least half an hour. And then I decide to start painting everything with the silver. Just go for it. Do everything but the tires and cylinders, which should be black. The familiar N-X-211 registration numbers are on the decals included with the kit. Mercifully, I can worry about this at a later time.

I open the paint bottle, dip a small brush into it, and start covering the plastic. It's the kind of paint that doesn't come off your skin, unforgiving with mistakes. I get some on my jeans. But damn, I'm getting into this; I'm carefully painting all the minuscule parts, trying to avoid the obvious places where glue goes. I decide you're supposed to file away the places that need glue that accidentally get painted. Or chip it away with the razor. This makes me feel moderately better.

I've done all I can do for now. It has to dry. I set up the trees and wings and fuselage intricately so that no painted surfaces are touching newspaper or each other. I do creative taping, securing the parts in the air on the edge of the table, the box, anything really. The whole dining room table is covered with the plane's guts—looks more like a crack-up after a crash landing than an assembly line.

I go to the sink to clean the brushes in the tiny bottle of paint thinner the guy gave me at the shop. This is the first time I'm getting a buzz from the chemicals. But I'm not sure it's the kind of buzz I like. I go outside and pour the remains of the thinner into the gutter while a neighbor from across the way eyes me and doesn't wave. Then I go back into the kitchen to soak the brushes. Smells like hell, so I open the sliding glass window over the sink. It looks out onto my mother's garden, which is in desperate need of water.

I wash up and take a shit in the guest bathroom, then write down the address for Golden Plains, where Paw-Paw is. I get in my mother's car and head in the general direction, finding the street, but soon I realize the addresses are going the wrong way, and so I turn around in a Sonic drive-thru parking lot. I pass a cemetery, though not Llano, where my folks are to rot in pieces, and then there's the Golden Plains. I don't have to tell you it is neither golden, nor on a plain. In fact, it's in a particularly bleak part of town, by some railroad tracks and a small, dilapidated hospital that looks like it might or might not still be in operation.

I park out front and get directed to the nursing unit by a security guard with a Fuller Brush–like moustache. I approach the desk and the woman says, "Can I help you, young man?"

"My grandfather is here," I say.

"And that would be?"

"Sam Lazarus."

"I've never seen you before."

"I don't really know what to tell you. I don't live here." She stares me up and down as I try to stand defiantly.

"I'm sorry about your parents," she says eventually, but it doesn't seem like she really is. "Follow me. He just had a bath."

Any nursing home anywhere in the world smells exactly like every other one. Unless you've been in one, you don't know the smell. But if you have, you always will—until the day you die in a nursing home of your very own. The nurse takes me to a room with two beds separated by a thick vinyl curtain. Paw-Paw's on the far side, in the bed with a view out the window. His head is turned toward the window, but it's not entirely clear if he knows it.

"Mr. Lazarus," the nurse yells in a sugary voice. It startles me, and the withered old lady in the other bed wakes with a yelp, terrified as I pass the foot of her bed. "Mr. Lazarus, your grandson is here to see you. Isn't that nice?"

Most nursing home employees generally resent the hell out of the family members of their charges, and I can tell from the way she talks to my grandfather that this one is no exception. No matter if you visit your shriveling loved one every day, for hours each day, and bring the nurses donuts weekly and fruitcakes during the holidays, they still resent the hell out of you for making them clean the shit, empty the bedpans, wipe the applesauce from dribbling lips, smell the constant sour stank of death creeping up bleached walls. No matter how much they mop the floors, scrape the corners of all the rooms, toilets, sinks, tubs, bedpans, they can't rid the places of that stench, and they hate you for it even though your ducats keep the dying industrial complex going, and thus, food on their families' tables, cigarettes in their purses.

"Mr. Lazarus," she says again, touching his rubbery thin arm. "Your grandson is here!" She looks at me faux-apologetically, sort of the way she looked when she said she was sorry my parents croaked. Then she leaves.

I look at him in the bed there, foggy oxygen tubes tucked behind each ear, meeting under his nose. I sit in the chair between the window and his bed, in his line of vision.

"Paw-Paw," I say. "Paw-Paw?"

Nothing.

Fucking old people have always killed me. Ever since I was a kid, I don't know, something just makes me go all soft and crazy around them, like when you see an old lady's gnarled knuckles wrapped around a cane in one hand and tiny paper coffee cup in the other, trying to negotiate paying a sighing, snot-nosed kid working some cash register. In these cases I usually pay for whatever it is myself, and help them to a table, or out of a building, up to a doctor's appointment, whatever. I'll be late for whatever it is I'm doing just to help. One time I went and got five bags of groceries for some old lady I held the door for in a friend's building. I'm not trying to front—I'm still the biggest asshole around, but I'm just saying, I don't know, it just makes me want to do something when I see them, even in the face of such complete and utter hopelessness.

Sammy was right; Paw-Paw's a fucking vegetable. I wonder if they told him about his daughter and son-in-law and the accident. I wonder if he remembers how much he worshipped his wife Miriam. I wonder if he remembers that he used to be on the local radio station every week, calling the high school football games. That he sponsored the winningest boxer in Panhandle history. I wonder if he remembers that you're supposed to hold your own prick when you want to take a piss.

He's forgetting all of it quicker than I could ever make it up.

Outside the window there's a little strip of blue sky, but mostly the view consists of a concrete-filled alley where the Dumpsters are. It looks like it gets hosed down very often. An ambulance is in the middle of dropping off another resident, bundled like a tamale on a gurney with its silver scaffolding popping out below as the bored EMTs maneuver her around. Wispy gray hairs peek out of the top of the tamale, waving slightly in an alley breeze.

I look back at my grandfather, and he's staring at me now.

"Hey Paw-Paw," I say. "It's T. Remember me?"

He just looks at me like this, for a full five minutes.

"I'm so sorry," I say, softly. But then he gets all upset, starts like, crying or something, whimpering and shaking. Eyes are hard, set on me, and he's frowning. "What? Paw-Paw, what? Are you okay?"

He's doing his best to push himself farther away from me, so I scoot the chair back from his bed and he relaxes a little. But his expression is still unchanged. He seems like he's trying not to die or something, fighting the good fight, but then I realize it's me. I get up and call down the hall for the nurse.

"What? What's wrong?" she says when she comes in. "Mr. Lazarus, hello, Mr. Lazarus, everything's okay. I'm here."

He calms a little.

"He gets scared of strangers sometimes," she says, caressing his forehead. He closes his eyes then and chills out. "We got a new orderly last month and he nearly flipped out. One of the nurses had to clean the room, but then he was over it by the next time the guy came in."

"Oh, sorry," I say, wondering where they keep the pills. Maybe I could romance this homely nurse a little because she looks like she hasn't seen a loving man in, well, ever. Maybe I can nibble on her earlobe a little and then reach down into her pocket where the keys to the medicine cabinet are.

"Don't think anything of it. I think you're just different-looking to what he's used to seeing around here," she says. Now it seems like she's actually sad for me, and it sort of makes me want to hit her.

"I guess I should go," I say. "I don't want to upset him anymore."

"Okay, I'm sorry." She is stroking his shoulder now, and I'm happy that he at least has this, that even a rough touch from this disaster of a woman makes him feel calm, if not better.

"I love you, Paw-Paw," I whisper, hoping to hell she doesn't see or hear. I touch his foot underneath the pink polyester blanket and head out the door.

7.

The next day the package from my wife arrives. The delivery man peers over my shoulder and into the house when I open the front door to sign for the package, as though you can see death or something.

There's a sweet card from the wife inside an envelope. It's the typical shit: *I love you, Papi,* etc., etc. The rock's in there, as is the pouch with the cloth rolled up inside. Good girl. I put them on the table next to the model, and I sit down to apply another coat of paint.

When I look at the little pieces this time, they look just slightly less boggling to me. I go over them again with the silver, clean the brush outside, and then do the tiny black parts. When I get to the engine block, it dawns on me, the time me and my wife went down to the Air and Space Museum in D.C. a few weeks after I got the hatbox in the mail from my mother. I was all gung ho about the book then, briefly under Lindbergh's spell like my great-grandmother was, and insisting we take the train down to check out the *Spirit of St. Louis* in person. What an asshole.

I forced the wife to pose for a poorly executed photo in front of the real *Spirit of St. Louis,*

and we made out against the railing on the balcony overlooking it after I snapped it. People were staring at us. Then she made me hold her jacket and purse while she stood in line for the ladies' restroom, though I assure you there is nothing restful about a bathroom at the Smithsonian.

While I waited for her I studied the Plexiglas display accompanying Lindbergh's plane. It was the usual stuff—a ball of cord, a rusty needle, fishing line with two hooks, a warped hacksaw blade, an emergency flare, one emergency ration, and a match holder with matches—but on the opposite side was the original nose cone from the *Spirit of St. Louis*. A bunch of folks from Ryan Airlines had painted their names in black inside the cone, underneath the words: "We Are Sure With You." Over forty men and women had signed their names, wishing Lindbergh luck on his flight. It looked like the kind of birthday or get-well-soon cards they pass around at fucking offices when the group honors an individual's special day. I hate that shit.

Anyway, most names inside the cone were unremarkable, but I do recall one, the largest by far, "Adolph Schmidt" (the only name in quotation marks, and written in the same hand and size as the "We Are Sure With You" heading). Presumably it was also Adolph who had drawn a large backwards swastika, dead center inside the nose cone:

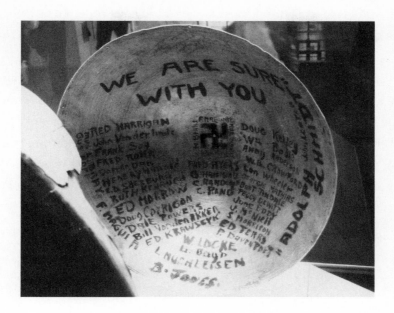

I remembered reading a story in a Lindbergh book about how a crack had developed in the propeller's spinner shroud when the plane was on Long Island, preparing to take off for Paris. Technicians from the Curtiss Company, a competing airplane manufacturer (the Wright Corporation had built the *Spirit of St. Louis*'s engine, Ryan Airlines the body), replaced it for Lindbergh, free of charge. And the displayed signed one was thus left behind after Lindbergh took off into history.

The Smithsonian display briefly mentioned the crack and the Curtiss Company's replacement of it, in addition to identifying two of the key players who had signed the nose cone (B. F. Mahoney, president of Ryan Airlines, and William Hawley Bowlus, Ryan factory manager). But there was no mention of "Adolph Schmidt." The plaque did, however, explain in no uncertain terms that the reverse swastika ("the figure") you see inside the cone was of course not a Nazi emblem, but rather a "Native American good luck symbol."

I don't know about you, but if that motherfucker takes off and I'm looking at it head-on with the benefit of X-ray vision (or just hindsight), that symbol is a straight-up, mirror image inside that cone. And when you look at it this way, that shit ends up looking like a regular, right direction, Nazi-version swastika to me.

I pick up the tree that holds the nose cone of the model, and it's just a tiny little thing, already connected to the engine with no room for anything but a dot. But the inside of the engine block is another story altogether. I hold it up to examine closely. With the smallest paintbrush, I think I can paint a little black reverse swastika in there, just like the one on display at the museum. So I do, hands steady as the surgeon who cut out my burst appendix when I was a kid:

Then I'm as satisfied as Adolph Schmidt was the day he painted what I just did, only on the real thing. So I set the tree down and let the shit dry for another twenty-four hours.

It's only in between stages of building the *Spirit of St. Louis* that I deal with my parents' lives, which seem to be messier in death than they were in life. Makes sense after an accident like that. I certainly don't want to die and go to hell yet—especially not like that—but it feels like I already have a preview of what it's gonna look like. Hell will involve calling estate liquidators, storage companies, and truck rentals, and dealing with real estate agents, sitting on hold with large corporations who provide their region's customers with things like gas and water and light. Hell will also involve going through shit that's not even yours, and feeling like you should always be doing something more. And the kicker will be that you really don't care. Or at least you say you don't, and it then becomes an infinite, self-feeding conundrum where nothing's ever enough and all your second chances and do-overs have been used up before you even realized you got sucked back into the game in the first place.

For instance: photographs, teeming with ghosts. Lindbergh saw them on his flight too; he wrote about it in *The Spirit of St. Louis* book. He described friendly phantoms that floated in and out of the fuselage of the plane behind him, talking to him in human voices over the din of the engine. All the phantoms in the photographs of my family make me tired, and I don't want to look at them anymore. What the fuck do you do with the photographs? Storage. Old letters, legal documents, books, clothes? Storage, storage, Salvation Army, Salvation Army. It might as well be strangers' things I'm wading through, because there's not much I recognize as related or belonging to me. I'm on my third day in Amarillo, and two coats have dried on the plane. But that's the extent of my accomplishments. I should do more. I want to bail after the funeral, I *need* to bail after the funeral, but what of all this shit? Why do I even care? I never have.

Right, time to start separating parts from the trees. I'm still generally panicked when approaching this task, but somehow, after two days of looking at them so closely as I painted, I'm more comfortable with the individual pieces, and I think I can start identifying them somewhat accurately, seeing where they're supposed to go just by looking at them and not the useless, unintelligible directions.

I start snipping the obvious parts—the left and right fuselage, and the wheels. Sometimes when you break off a part though, I notice there's a little jagged bump where it had been connected to the tree—a little umbilical that at one time probably provided nutrients from the rest of the lineage, but that ends up rough and needs careful filing (and repainting) later. Not that they tell you this in the directions. Which is okay, because it's starting to make sense on its own, little by little. I imagine this is what it's like figuring out how an engine works—you're just familiar with all the pieces, have an idea about the whole and what it's supposed to do. So you just figure the son of a bitch out because really, what other choice is there?

I know I'm a nerd, but this makes me calmer, this knowing I'll figure it out because I have to. I am starting to see where some parts are supposed to be glued to others, where I might need to file or chip away the paint for a good connection between them. This comes from just touching them, handling them. There are no directions for this kind of thing. Directions just create the illusion that you can possibly ever know what you're doing before you do it. That goes for everything. Use what you have, and then make up the rest. That's what I did. Because half the time, what you think you have as a starting point, well, that's just as good as made up anyway. By the time I was old enough to appreciate Paw-Paw's stories, he was just past too old to be telling them. Sure, I like to think he treated his wife like a queen—put her in business and slipped a finger on the scale every now and then when some months came out in the red—but for all I know, he could've been beating her ass worse than that boxer he schlepped all over Texas pounded his competition.

You figure it out in chunks—can't have the fuselage without the wings, without the engine, without the wheels, without the struts. So, first things first: I stick the windows in, but you have to be careful because if the glue touches the clear plastic, it's always going to be marred. But I do it perfect. I can see through just fine. Then I chip away at the paint along the insides of the mirror-image fuselage halves. I glue these together and put a rubber band around it tight and set it aside to dry.

Now it's time for the engine assembly. My engine block with the reverse swastika is ready to go, so that means it must be time for the homosexual part of the process: the propeller shaft (8) gets inserted through the engine (6), and then you apply glue only to the tip of the shaft (8) before sticking it into the propeller (7), like this:

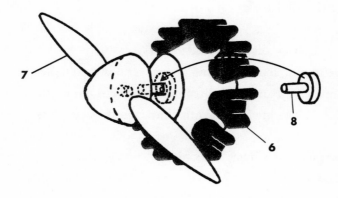

Now it makes perfect sense why you glue only the tip—so the propeller can rotate freely. Duh. I scan the trees. *Shit*. I can't find the shaft (8). I look all over the goddamned trees for the shaft (8), but it's nowhere. Of course, you can't make the shit fly without all of its parts. Plastic, people—whatever. This plane isn't going anywhere without its propeller (7); but you can't have a propeller (7) without the little connector (8). It's nowhere. Disappeared. Or never was. Of course Esther's Reuven grew up to be Lindy. He had to. And now I'm starting to crack up too. They should not be selling these kits with incomplete trees. Same difference with family trees. I keep searching for a long time, repeatedly counting out all the parts one after the other like a retard, but I can't find it. Now I'm pissed at Flyers for selling me this racket that can't actually be made. It's like torture. Or just smart capitalism.

I throw all the parts into the box and get into my mother's car. When I pull into the Hobby Haus's parking lot about ten minutes later, the tattooed guy is just leaving for the day.

"Hey," I say, "I'm glad I caught you."

"We're closed," he says.

"This model, there's a part missing." I hold up the directions.

"So?"

"This is wack man, I've spent a couple days on it already."

"What do you want from me?"

"Well, do you have another one?"

"That was the last."

"What the fuck am I supposed to do?"

"I don't know, man, but I think whatever it is should involve chilling."

I open the box and start spreading the pieces out on the hood of my mother's car. The guy's car alarm chirps and he opens the driver's side door.

"Where are you going?" I ask him.

"Uh, home?"

"Just look at it," I say. "Please?"

He sighs and comes over, stares at the open directions, back at the painted parts, then at the skeletons of the trees. "Nice, man," he says, picking up the engine block with the swastika inside.

"Oh, that's nothing, that's just this thing—"

"Naw man, that's fucking hard-core," he says, nodding his head.

"No, that's just, that's . . ." I'm yammering, but what is there to say?

"You know you did it backwards though?"

"No, I didn't."

"Yeah, man," he says, smiling. "It's two Ss, you've got 'em backwards. It's cool, though. I used to make that mistake all the time."

"What about the missing part?" I say again.

He stares at all the parts for a while, inspects the trees closely. "It's right there," he says.

"Where?"

"There," pointing.

"It's that small?" I ask. I'm so happy I want to jump into this disgusting guy's arms, go to all the fucking monthly meetings of the local neo-Nazi association with him.

"Sometimes they're really hard to see."

"Yeah, well, thanks," I say, quickly gathering the parts off of my mother's hood and back into the box. I leave out the tree with the shaft on it though, slipping it into my front shirt pocket so I can find it later. I'm confident I still won't be able to see it when I get back to my parents' house.

"Sorry to bug you."

"No problem," he says. "Rock on," he pumps a fist at me, then climbs into his car, belly bumping up against steering wheel. It's a red '80s model Mustang. Of course.

Back to the lab again, I got the engine assembled and the wings ready, but now I have to wait until the fuselage is dry before I can stick the engine and wings together. Plus there's tons of paint scraping I need to do with the razor blade on the underside of the wings. Of course they don't warn you not to paint the bottom middle section of the wings. I read the orange glue tube and it says to allow at least an hour drying time. I sit back in my chair and have a sip of the warm beer that's been sitting there since the day before.

I look over and there's the rock and pouch and card the wife sent. I untie the pouch and unscroll the little piece of canvas. There's a faint scent of oil, or fuel of some sort. Plus mildew. I'm holding the little cloth right up to my nostrils and looking at all the parts spread out in front of me, adding up how long I think until I'm done with the plane. But then I notice the little rectangular hole in the top of the assembled fuselage is about the size of the piece of canvas. I roll it up real tight and wrap the little string around it to hold it together. I can just slip it into the plane, and slide it back where it's invisible through the tiny windows. So I do. I was planning to toss this thing in with my mother at the gravesite tomorrow, but this, this seems like a more fitting burial. I pull it out with tweezers, stick a little glue on the bottom, and then carefully guide it back into the fuselage, trying not to touch anything like you do in that kids' game "Operation." When it's all the way back into the tail, I press down with the tweezers, and soon that shit is stuck, and it's not coming out. Now, when the wings are attached, and then the engine block caps it off, there will be two little secrets this plane will have on board that nobody will ever know about until it comes apart again. But it'll have to be broken first.

8.

Most of the parts are drying as I'm watching Saturday morning cartoons from my couch-bed. I have to get up and take a shower and get dressed for the funeral, but as bad as these fucking new cartoons are, I'd rather sit and watch them all day than fucking smile and mourn, smile and mourn with all these stupid motherfuckers.

The shower is scorching hot, and I decide to try to take the whole thing without turning the temperature down. Just take what you give yourself. I have to jump in and out of the stream, and my skin burns. But I'm clean as hell, skin splotchy red when I step out of the shower and towel off. I can't see my reflection when I get out because of the steam—my version of covering the mirrors and sitting *shivah*, I guess. I get dressed in front of the TV, putting on the wrinkled dark gray suit I brought. The wife reminded me to pack it on the morning I left. I don't think about these sorts of things. I put on a thin 1960s tie and slap on some of my father's Old Spice aftershave, though I don't, of course, need to shave. I'm lucky that way.

I call up Sammy because I want to make sure his sorry ass is going to be there with me early to deal with all the people. I don't know any of them. Or, I should say, they think they know me; I don't know them. The phone rings about twenty times with no answer. I hang up and redial, figuring I'd gotten the number wrong. It rings endlessly again, so I hang up and try again. That cocksucker. Maybe he's already on his way.

I sit at the dining room table and survey the plane. Still need the wheels and struts, but it's really starting to look like something that might fly. The wings are on, the engine's mounted, propeller free and able to rotate, and I glued on the tail last night before I fell asleep (it's a little crooked, though I think only I'd know it). I decide I'm too rushed and should wait to finish the struts and wheels until I get back from the funeral. Something to look forward to.

I try Sammy again, and this time he picks up on the tenth ring.

"Sammy?"

"What?"

"What do you mean, 'what?' The funeral's today."

"Who is this?" he asks. He sounds wasted.

"It's T. You gotta get ready."

"Awww, T," he's whining. Sounds like crying. "T, T, T. Sheila's gone. She won't let me in."

"In where? Who's—"

"Sheila, my girl, man . . ."

"Oh, fucking hell. You gotta get down here."

"No, man. Sheila, the bitch kicked me out again."

"I'm coming up there."

"T . . ." He sounds so wrecked I can't even begin to imagine what he's on. Part of me envies him. The other part just swore off drugs forever, including spearmint gum.

"How do I find your place?"

"Aw, T. Mom and Dad, the funeral's today. You *can't* come over."

"Sammy. Listen to me. How do I find the trailer park when I get into Fritch?"

"It's on the left."

"The left of what?"

"Of the trailer park, man."

"Sammy, this is really important, can you do me a favor?"

"What?"

"Go take off your clothes and get in the shower and get dressed. I'm gonna come get you, okay?"

"T, T, T—"

"Sammy, you hear me? I'm getting in the car now. Please get into the shower."

I hang up and look at my watch. I figure I can get up there and make it back just in time for the service. I grab my wallet, keys, the jacket of my suit, and step into the garage. As the door cranks open Batcave-style, I remember the rock, so I go back to get it off the table and slip it into my suit pocket.

Fritch is so damn small it's immediately obvious where the trailer park is. When I pull in, there are a few dogs in the road, the kind of beasts you have to drive around because they don't move for you. A guy is working on an old Corvair, and I lean over to speak to him through the passenger window. "Do you know where Sammy Cooper lives?"

"That asshole?"

Great. "Yeah, that asshole."

"He been shooting off rounds all morning. Sheila took off a couple of hours ago with her kid."

"I wonder why."

"What?"

"Nothing. You know where I can find him?"

"Last one at the end on the left."

"Thanks." I roll up the window and drive around another dusty dog lying in the road. The whole place is a fucking mess, like a storm recently tore through. I drive by one home with a huge dent the shape of a tree branch across its roof, and there's clear plastic taped over it, though poorly. There's an overturned boat that looks like it fell off the trailer beside it.

When I get to the end of the dirt road there are two places, one on either side of the dead end. The trailer on the right is upright, but the one on the left is on its side. I see my brother's truck parked next to the over-turned one. I get out of the car and go up to the trailer on the right and knock on the door. Nobody comes, but I can hear movement inside, the whole thing rocking slightly. The curtains are pulled back on the window next to the door, but it's an old guy with a gray beard looking out, not my brother.

He opens the door and pokes his head out. "What do you want?"

"Uh, Sammy please?"

He doesn't say anything, just points across to the trailer on its side.

Are you fucking kidding me?

"Thanks," I say. "Sorry to bug you."

I go over to the trailer on its side and walk around it, looking in the first window I come across—I think it's the back, but I can't really tell what's what.

"Sammy!" I yell a few times.

He comes out from the other side of the trailer, but I have no idea where from. "What the fuck is going on?" I ask.

"Hey, man," he says, wobbling, barefoot and shirtless in a pair of jeans with a few buttons open at the fly.

"Sammy, what the—?"

"Hey, you little pussy."

"Do you live in there?"

He starts laughing maniacally. "I did, but a tornado came through here a couple months back."

"So?"

"Aw, chill the fuck out, T. Why so fancy?"

"Um, there's a funeral?"

"I know, the funeral, man," he says slowly, rubbing his messy head and growing serious.

"Did you take a shower?"

"It's broke."

I literally can't believe what I'm seeing; I actually think it's possible I drove my mother's car straight through the Panhandle and into a separate universe. In the universe I'm slightly more familiar with, however, I look down at my watch and realize we have to get going.

"Where are your clothes?" I ask.

"At Sheila's," he says, pointing back toward the entrance of the trailer park. "It's locked. She kicked me out again."

"Who lives here?" I ask.

"Me."

"It's on its side."

"I know," he says. "I told you, I've been staying with Sheila since the tornado, but now I'm back here for a little bit 'cause she's such a cunt."

I walk past Sammy around the other side of the trailer, and see that a square has been cut out of the roof with a torch. There's a screen door leaning up against the hole. I move the screen to the side and step inside, ducking because the ceiling, well, the side of the trailer, is so low. All the furniture is set up on the side of the trailer, which is now the floor. There's a mattress, a table and two chairs, a lounger. Shit's on the ground, but in general everything's right side up, like this is how it's supposed to be. I think this has to be a joke, but there's a pile of empty beer cans and meth works on the table by a little TV, as well as a big green bong on its side in a pool of brown bong water. So it starts to make a little more sense.

"Sammy," I yell, rifling through some of his clothes. "Get in here." I'm looking for the outfit he wore to the lawyer's office the other day.

He pokes his head through the hole in the roof (now door), and asks, "What?"

"Put this on." I hold up an only minimally stained white button-down dress shirt. He refuses but steps inside, falling back into a plaid wool recliner pushed up against the end of the twin mattress. "Do it," I say, throwing the shirt at him. He complies, slowly figuring out where his arms go.

I see his shotgun leaning up against the mini-refrigerator, and I go over and open it up, slide out the cartridges, and put them in my pants pocket. I quietly drop the gun to the floor (well, the wall) and kick it behind the table.

I rifle through more of the piles of clothes and see some black jeans with a belt still in them. I throw these at Sammy too, who's now moaning in the chair in the corner. It smells so bad in there, like drug-induced, bilious vomit. Drunken, syrupy piss, cat litter. And *I* was the one who was always supposed to be the fuckup? You know, I remember it well, because it was the last thing I packed to take with me before I left Texas at sixteen: the memory of my mom sitting at the kitchen table in front of a tall bottle of vodka and a tumbler, and her spitting (well, really more of a combination of slurring and spitting), "I wish it had been *you* we adopted instead of Sammy." But this of course was before all of us got clean—well, my brother was, the rest of us weren't. Though things seem to have flip-flopped considerably since then.

But now Sammy is pulling his shoes out from under the bed and starting to put them on with no socks. I open the refrigerator to see if there's any water in it, but it's just beer, and the refrigerator's not even turned on. Back toward the hallway, which is on the ceiling, there's a bathroom that looks like a huge, faux-wood cabinet on the floor. I can see through the swung-open door that, like everything else, the sink is on its side as well. I don't know why I thought it might've been any different.

"YOU FUCKING LIVE IN A FUCKING UPSIDE-DOWN HOUSE!" I yell back at Sammy. Dirty yellow curtains are hanging from the window above his head on the wall of the trailer (now ceiling). Light streams in through the wall above us (again, ceiling). Sammy is mostly dressed, though crying and rocking in the chair, hugging himself. Why does every fucking strung-out loser have to strike this pose at one point or another—usually either at or just before rock bottom?

"Sammy, listen to me. Sam, listen," I'm yelling, but he's just rocking.

"I fucked up, I fucked it all up," he cries. He's slobbering and his lips are cracked, bleeding from the left corner. "I really did it this time."

"Sammy, listen to me. Don't fucking crack up on me now. Don't."

"Maaaa—" he's shrieking, drawing it out so it sounds like cats mating in an alley or some shit. I think I should just go. But Sammy's so fucking pathetic, I sit down on the arm of the chair and put my arm around him. This makes his whole body heave more. He's whining something I can't understand about Mom, and I hold him tighter, though with just one arm. We sit this way for what seems like a very long time. I can hear some dogs fighting outside, a car alarm going off for a few minutes before getting clicked off by its owner. I'm looking around the trailer, trying to remember every little detail, because no one will believe me when I tell them about this back home. And we complain about New York apartments being cramped. At least this one has skylights, even if the ceiling's a little low.

After Sammy calms a little, I say softly, "We gotta go," then lead what's left of him to our mother's car and strap him in.

There's no way we'll make it for the service now, but I think if I drive fast we can get to the cemetery in time for the burial. I stop at a mini-mart and buy a cold bottle of water. I open it for Sammy and make him drink half of it before we're on the road again, Route 136 south, back down to Amarillo. After about ten minutes I see he's fallen asleep, head rolling with the car's motion. His Adam's apple looks like it's about to poke through his skinny neck.

Once we cross Amarillo city limits, I head toward the Llano cemetery, but I get a little lost coming at it from this direction. Finally I find it and drive through the lush main sections toward the far corner, the ghetto. There are squat shrubs, grass, Hebrew-engraved stones with Jewish last names in English, and just on the other side of the fence, dusty industry— a tiny airstrip with weeds pushing up in cracks, train tracks spotted with abandoned rusty cars, a sun-faded tractor stilled for the weekend.

Sammy's still asleep, so I park under a tree and leave him in the car with the windows open. It's probably better this way. At least he can say he was at his parents' funeral. There is the requisite dark huddled circle around the two holes in the ground that will accept our parents once and for all. As I walk toward the crowd, a few people turn to look at me, and I can tell there's been talk. You know how you just know. But they can all just kiss my skinny ass.

It's the end of whatever's going on, and the lady from the bowling alley is crying audibly, her huge chest undulating. She is wiping her eyes with a handkerchief that's wrapped around a plump hand. I stand in the back of the circle and watch as the coffins are lowered into the dark, rectangular pits, almost at the same pace, but my mom is sinking in slightly after my dad: *Yea, though I walk through the valley of the shadow of death, I will fear no evil . . .*

There are tears—not my own. A woman I don't recognize throws some flowers in, others throw dirt—mostly those on my father's side. His sister Amy cuts her eyes at me after she tosses a handful of dirt onto her brother's coffin. And then it is done, and people are beginning to shuffle away, offering hands to the Coopers, some to me. Nobody says anything besides "Sorry for your loss."

The Cooper grandparents come over to me when most of the people have cleared, but they don't say anything. My father's brother Donald slaps me on the shoulder. "You okay?"

"My brother—" I begin, glancing back at my mother's car, but I don't know how I might end the sentence. There is no explanation, no excuse. *Morris and Anna-Rose worked so hard, for this?* I can tell it's what everyone's thinking—about both of us now.

I can tell they see him through the windshield, passed out and oblivious. My grandmother—my father's mom—is crying hysterically now as she and my grandfather stand next to me. I don't really know them—only from visits to Houston every couple of years when I was a kid. And they brought some people to my reading in Houston. We spoke for just a few minutes because it's all I had. They brought some friends, bought some books. They seem like nice enough people.

My father's sister Amy joins us now, and she's clearly determined to break the silence that has enveloped us. "How could you?" she asks me in a tight-lipped whisper.

"Amy," my grandfather says, touching her arm.

"I don't know what to say. I, I'm trying . . ." I begin, but I don't really know what it is I might be trying to do. It's taking everything I've ever had in me not to jump down on top of one of the coffins, do a little jig, and then scream something like "BITE ME!" at the top of my lungs.

"This is trying?" she asks, hugging her mother like I'm the one who steered the semi full of chickens across the median and head-on into my parents' lives. Maybe she doesn't know about the butchery and the barbecue, feathers raining down—all of it preordained on the streets of Kishinev, well before any of us could do anything about the fact that it always comes down to the same thing: blood.

My grandmother sobs even harder then. Probably because she already knows all of this—even if she doesn't know exactly how or why—but she just hasn't told her daughter yet. That somewhere along their own Cooper family line, some sort of commensurate degree of violence seeped in and presaged something like this. Well, that and the whole Jewish conspiracy-for-world-domination thing—including but not limited to the fact that the Jews both planned and carried out the attacks on September Eleventh to trick the U.S. government into declaring all-out war on the Arab world. For this and so much more, my parents and all the rest of them had to die . . . But, um, I decide now's probably not the best time to start goofing on good old earnest Aunt Amy.

"What's *his* problem?" Amy asks then, calming a little and nodding in the direction of my brother, who's slouched over in our mother's car.

I shake my head. I can't begin to imagine I know what his problem is. Probably a whole other slew of shit passed down through another mess of blood, and then acted upon by my mother's and father's after the fact.

"Excuse me," I say, touching Amy's elbow and heading past the open graves with my folks wedged inside. I can feel everybody's eyes, my aunt's especially, burning into the back of my bleach-blond head, boring into my skull, and trying to scrape out my brain. I see some Stars of David on the graves. There's a *Lipshitz*—Uncle Ben, dead in '79—and past him, a headstone with *Lazarus* on it. There's a slab for my grandma Miriam in front of it, with a big empty patch of grass next to her, anxious to swallow up Paw-Paw whole when it's his time. Behind these there's another big stone with just *Lipshitz* on it, and two little squarish slabs in front, like the Lazarus setup, only it's not waiting for anyone to complete the set. On the left: *Hersh Lipshitz, 1872–1951,* and on the right—his left—*Esther Lipshitz,* my great-grandmother of hatbox lunacy fame, *1874–1942.* On her left, her brother *Avi Grodzinski, 1869–1927.*

I stand on top of Esther's grave, between her individual slab and the big Lipshitz gravestone, then kneel in the grass. It's the kind of grass that's always threatening to go brown, mostly because it sort of is, just underneath the green. They don't seem to keep up this part of the cemetery as nicely as the others.

I can still feel the elder Coopers staring at me from behind, so I make it quick, pulling the rock out of my blazer pocket and rubbing it gently between thumb and forefinger before placing it on the corner of the Lipshitz headstone closest to Esther. I wanted so badly for this rock to have been spat out from beneath the Lindberghs' plane's wheels when they made that emergency landing somewhere in the Panhandle, because Esther would've wanted it that way. That's of course the kind of thing we tell ourselves at times like these—that it's the way the dead would've wanted it. *Bullshit.* The dead wouldn't have wanted to be dead in the first place. They wouldn't want some lazy county medical examiner poking at the pulpy mess of their splintered bones and singed flesh and shredded skin, before summarily pronouncing that they should be cremated any further than they already had been.

I let my fingers drop from the rock onto the white marble next to it, and I can tell the gravestone is trying to hold onto a little warmth from the sun for itself. But not much.

9.

I'm gluing the final parts onto the plane. It looked much harder than it was, I'll admit that much. The plane looks amazing though. It's perfect. As soon as I touch up the joints where the glue holds many parts together, I can tell—even before it dries—that this is a job well done. The joints end up looking just like really good welds, and I realize that must be the point, metal on metal, like on like.

I do the decals after the last round of paint dries, cutting them out and dipping them in a cup of water before carefully sliding them into place on the body of the plane. I have a momentary anxiety attack when the right-tail decal—"MFG by Ryan Airlines, San Diego, CAL"—becomes folded on top of itself and thus unreadable. But after deep breathing and Mom's trusty tweezers, all is well again. It looks just like the real *Spirit of St. Louis,* but this one fits in the palm of my hand:

No, there was nothing fun about making this fucking plane, I think, spinning it around in the air in front of my face. But I am good at it, I'm a little in love with it, and I can't seem to stop touching it. One thing I can say for sure is that I will never in my life go near another model airplane again. I don't care if I have a son one day who begs to make a Stealth Bomber or whatever instrument of mass murder they're manufacturing by that time—never again.

Sammy stirs then and wakes up for the third time on the couch in our parents' living room. The first time was on Saturday night after the funeral, when he went to the bathroom and I brought him a glass of water that he guzzled silently before falling back down on the blankets. The second time was on Sunday afternoon, when he woke up in a flurry because he was in the process of pissing himself. And this time? It looks like he's up and actually aware of his surroundings.

"Hey," I say, putting the plane down gently and rising from the table.

"What time is it?" he asks, sitting up and rubbing the back of his head. He's in our father's boxers and T-shirt that I changed him into after he woke up the second time.

"Noon-ish."

"Fuck, I'm tired."

"On Monday," I add.

"What?"

"It's noon on *Monday*," I repeat.

"Oh." He looks confused. "The funeral . . ."

"Yeah, done," I say, getting him another glass of water. He takes it and looks down at what he's wearing.

"Fuck, T."

"I know, dude. You need to do something about this crank shit."

"I just had a bad week," he says, standing up and bracing himself on the coffee table. *Days of Our Lives* is on the TV. He limps off to the bathroom and then I hear the shower go on.

First thing this morning, when Sammy was still sleeping, I'd called the cowboy lawyer. There is no way to keep Sammy's money from him, pending some sort of rehab. Apparently my parents had already paid for several of these—all unsuccessful, even the hard-core, locked-down one in Minnesota that Sammy somehow agreed to a few years back. There is nothing I can do. Or nothing I'm willing to do. If that makes me an asshole, I don't give a shit. He can run through my half of the money too, for all I care.

The bell rings and it's the Salvation Army, picking up the stuff the estate guy doesn't think he can sell. Two guys come in, one big and the other leathery and skinny, with long stringy hair. He's running on years of liquor saturation, you can just tell. I show them the boxes I want them to take, and help them load some into their truck. Then I point out a few pieces of furniture. Sammy comes out of the shower with a towel around his waist while the skinny guy's coming down the stairs with a load of Mom's clothes slung over his shoulder.

"Whoa, what the fuck is this?" he asks.

"Salvation Army," I say, and the big guy follows with a trash bag full of shoes.

Sammy's just standing there, dripping wet in his towel and watching them. And now the skinny guy's standing next to Sammy in front of the

TV and watching *Days*. The big guy comes up to me and gives me a clip-board with some paperwork to sign. "Oh, wait," I say, and run into the bedroom-office. I pick up the box of my books and bring it out. He scratches out the 15 and makes it 16 in the boxes of books column. I sign the paper.

The skinny guy picks up the box of my books but continues watching the soap opera. "All righty," the big guy says, ripping off the bottom carbon copy and giving it to me, "looks like that's everything."

"Thank you," I say.

"Come on," he yells at the skinny guy, who nods silently at my brother and heads out the door with my books. The big guy closes the door behind them.

"I washed your clothes for you," I tell Sammy. "They're in the dryer."

"Thanks," he says, going into the garage to get them. When he comes back out, he's got a shirt over his head and he's pulling it down over his gut. He finishes dressing in front of the couch and pushes the blankets aside to sit down to put on his boots. "When are you taking off?"

"Couple of days," I answer.

"Need any help?"

"No, I got it all," I say. "I'm taking a bunch of shit to storage tomorrow morning, then dropping the car off at some dealership. I don't know, the estate guy's going to get rid of the rest of this shit."

We sit there while the actors on TV are in a tight embrace, where the camera keeps flashing from one face to the other, each behind the other's back. "Why didn't you want the house?" I ask.

"I don't know, I don't know," Sammy says, exhaling. "Maybe I shoulda kept it."

"Maybe it's not too late. You should call the lawyer," I suggest.

"Naw, fuck him."

"Whatever you want."

"What the fuck is that?" he asks, noticing the plane on the table, all the paints and tools I hadn't cleaned up yet.

"Oh, I just made this thing while I was here."

"Why?" He comes over, picks up the plane. "Wow," he says, twirling the propeller. "Does it fly?" he asks, pretending like he's fixing to launch it.

"Please don't," I say, real calm. I will literally, even after nursing him for days, strangle him to death if he throws that plane.

He keeps looking at it closely, turning it every which way. "Why'd you do this?"

"Something to do."

"It's—" He stops, squinting at the tiny writing on the tail decal. "It's *good*."

I want him to put it down, but I know the minute he knows this it will be the end of the *Spirit of St. Louis*.

"We used to make these when we were kids, remember?" he asks.

"I didn't."

"Well, that makes sense."

"Why?"

"Just does." He looks at me. "You didn't really like *anything*." Finally, he puts the plane back down on the table. This near-death encounter with my brother was for certain my plane's equivalent of the death-defying New-York-to-Paris run.

"Sammy," I start, but then chicken out.

"What?"

"You gotta get off that shit," I make myself say. Just because it wouldn't be right not to.

"Just leave it, okay?"

I understand. Completely.

"I gotta go pick up this U-Haul," I say then, granting his wish. "Can you give me a ride over there in Mom's car?"

"I gotta get home." And this strikes me as funny, but perhaps he does not recall the situation in which we last saw Sammy in his natural habitat. "Where's my truck?"

"Fritch."

"Oh, yeah. Shit." It looks like it might be coming back to him, if slowly.

"I'll take you up there after you bring me to get the rental truck. Okay?" I ask.

"Yeah. I need a beer."

"We'll stop at the bowling alley to get something to eat," I suggest. "If you want a drink, you can have one there."

10.

After I drop off the U-Haul, I walk back to where my mother's car is parked. People are staring because nobody really walks around here. Or maybe they stare for another reason, but I like to think it's the former. I slip the keys to the storage unit into my wallet and decide to take both copies home with me. I head to the Golden Plains for the appointment I'd scheduled earlier with the resident director.

I assure the lady in the burgundy business skirt suit that Paw-Paw's rent will be deducted automatically each month from my account in New York. I ask that if there are any problems with money to contact me directly, not Sammy. Likewise with his health. I inquire about a private room, but she convinces me it's better for Paw-Paw to have a roommate so there's more activity around him. We talk briefly about the possibility of transferring him to a facility in the city, but she convinces me it's a bad idea and assures me his quality of care will not change now that my mother won't be visiting every couple of days. I give her two of my bar mitzvah entertainment business cards, asking her to make sure the nurses have one too. It's the least I can do. Too little too late—but it's something you know, selfish, to make myself feel better.

I go in to say good-bye to him, for good. He's sitting under the same scratchy pink blanket, staring out the window at the Dumpsters. You can see the flies buzzing in oval orbits above the overflowing one, which also drips brown liquid from a corner. I stand by the curtain watching him for a moment. I don't want to scare him, but I do want to touch him or something. I want him to know it's me. I want him to remember something, anything, and I'm almost mad he doesn't—but not at him, of course. At that bitch nurse, the whole fucking world, the lady with the daughter at Super Wal-Mart.

Of everyone when I was a kid, he was my one. You know, the one you knew—or at least hoped to hell—that they got it, got you, and always would. Or if they didn't, then it didn't matter because it felt like they did. Get you, that is. Of everyone, he was the hardest to leave, the only one I had to pinch away tears over when I was sitting on that train out of Texas. He wasn't making much sense anymore, but the son of a bitch was still cruising around town the day I took off, when he was eighty-five or so. Every afternoon he'd be strutting along the way-past-its-prime Polk Street shopping district with a cane, tipping his hat at everybody as he passed. There was a dry cleaners and tailor in the old Diamond Shop location by that time, and a twice-out-of-business gun shop in Miriam's Babyland. Even then, he never wore the requisite old-man sweaters, polyester pants, and dopey retirement loafers. He always wore a suit, and if not a jacket, then at least a shirt and tie, polished dress shoes. Always.

I think I learned everything it is to be a good man from Paw-Paw. I'm not saying I always stick to what I learned, but at least I know when I'm not. Like when you get scared because it's too intense with the wife, that the more I love her, the more power she has to leave, and so I want to fucking inflict some pain back and leave her first—but I think of Paw-Paw and how he probably knew that Nanny Miriam was just as scared as he was, and that you can't measure fear anyhow, so why bother.

The guy knew how to treat a lady. My lower lids get a little warm and heavy, thinking of him in one of his fitted vests, courting my Nanny

Miriam at the department store with a fresh flower in his lapel. Naw, he never beat the shit out of her, or anybody else for that matter. The boxer was probably the only way he could get out the anger that all of us get for no fucking reason we can see, but it's there and so you just have to figure a way around it, and hope it doesn't get you into serious trouble.

I keep hiding from my grandfather's view behind the vinyl curtain, all the while being eyed warily by his old lady roommate—his partner in this dying game. I promise myself right then and there that I'll say "bitch" less, and I swear off the word "cunt" forever. As god is my witness.

Damn, it smells even worse in here than the last time—if that's possible. But I don't care if it sticks to me and doesn't wash off for days, weeks, ever. It's all I can do not to climb in bed next to him and cling to the bony sack that he's become. *Don't worry, Paw-Paw. You'll be back in the Llano Cemetery ghetto and hanging with all your buddies again soon—everyone you trusted, who trusted you.* The guy single-handedly held so much shit together, I'd be lucky if I could handle one-eighth of what he did. I step out from behind the curtain for just a second and put my palm on his foot through the blanket, but before he even gets a chance to look over and be scared, I'm gone.

"I can't wait to see you, baby," the wife says on the phone after we've been talking for a while. My parents' house is starting to feel devoid of them, though the liquidator will clean it out once and for all after I leave.

"Me neither," I say.

"I'll meet you at the gate."

"No, don't bother moving the car, we'll never get a parking spot," I say. "I'll just take the bus and subway."

"I'm coming to get you."

"Then don't park," I insist. "I'll meet you outside of baggage claim."

"You okay?" she asks.

"I guess."

"I think the baby boy might've grown up a little on his trip," she says, and it makes me want to call her a bitch. But I don't, because I promised.

"Please," I say instead. "I didn't do anything. It's a fucking mess."

"You did a lot."

"I'll see you tonight."

"I love you."

"Uh-huh. Me too."

We hang up.

I go upstairs to my parents' bedroom and open the door. I'm in search of a shoebox to pack the *Spirit of St. Louis* in for the trip back. I dig in the bottom of both closets, but I can't find any—I'd packed up all the shoes for the Salvation Army. I go downstairs to check the coat closet, and there on the top shelf next to an Eveready flashlight and a can of WD-40 (will the estate liquidator sell these too?), I see a shoebox with "Dad" on it, in my mother's handwriting. *Oh god, what's this?* I think, reaching up and hoping for some sort of mother lode of photographs, notes, secrets. But it's just a shiny new pair of dress shoes it looks like Paw-Paw never got a chance to wear. No need for kicks when you're lying on your back in a mechanical bed. I check the size: eight. He was a little guy. But then so am I. I take the shoes out of the box and tuck them into my duffel bag. Then wrap the *Spirit of St. Louis* and carefully pack wadded-up pages of *The Amarillo Daily Sun* around it in the shoebox. They'd been piling up on the doormat since I arrived. I go back to the closet, where there's a bunch of my mother's wrapping paper and holiday gift-bag type things. There's a blue one for Hanukkah, exactly the size of a shoebox, so I pull it out and pop it open. I check inside the shoebox one more time to make sure the plane's not getting smashed, and as soon as I'm satisfied it's not, I slip the box into the Hanukkah bag and tie the string handles into a knot over it so it won't slip out.

I remember I have to call the lawyer one last time about a few details.

His secretary puts me right through. I make sure he knows I don't mind his calling me with questions, and double-check he has my contact information. I tell him about the arrangement at Golden Plains, and he tries to convince me to keep having Panhandle Lanes pay for Paw-Paw's care. I tell him I'm more comfortable with it this way, coming from my account, and that it'll switch over as soon as the life insurance checks clear.

The airport shuttle shows up and is idling out in the driveway. I've got my duffel bag in one hand, the phone in the other, and I'm about to hang up. But then the lawyer says, "T?"

"Yeah?"

"I just want to say, I know you done the best you could. You know, with all the circumstances."

I don't say anything, because in truth, nobody had ever said something like this to me before.

"I'm proud of, proud to have worked with you on this," he adds. "Your folks, they would, well—it's a proud sort of moment."

"Thank you," I manage. "Uh, thanks for everything." And then we hang up.

I pick up the plane, turn off the TV, and lock the door behind me.

I sit with the shoebox in the Hanukkah bag on my lap for the entire flight. People don't stare at me as much during the Amarillo-to-Denver leg. It's a really short trip, and it makes sense why I might not bother putting it in the overhead compartment. But for the Denver-to-LaGuardia leg of the trip, I guess it's sort of weird when a red-faced, bleach-blond-headed dude blasting hip-hop from his oversized headphones is sitting next to you with a shoebox inside a Happy Hanukkah bag and is being hyper-careful with the thing.

Thus, the lady next to me is staring. I make a concession and turn the music down a little. Hell, I don't even want it that loud now myself, and I'm not listening to Eminem for once. I don't feel like rehearsing. I don't even remember when my next gig is—must be this weekend? Fuck. I decide I'll deal with it later.

"If it were a bomb," I lean over and whisper to the lady next to me after beverage service goes by, "I probably wouldn't be holding it out in plain sight like this."

She is horrified, whispering to her husband or whoever he is sitting next to her.

"Or come to think of it," I continue, "it would probably be a really *good* place to hide a bomb, you know, out in the open."

They are both looking at me now, so I pull off my headphones and leave them hanging around my neck. Some real hard-core shit is still streaming out of them, but it sounds tinny and distant.

"You know, the irony is," I continue, and now both of them are listening. "What I have in here is actually the *Spirit of St. Louis*. Well, a model of it. But don't you think that's funny that it has to sit on my lap inside a plane to get across the country?"

They don't respond.

"Isn't that funny?" I ask again.

"I don't know," the man says.

"What don't you know?"

"I don't know," he says again. "My wife and I would just like to enjoy our flight in peace, is all."

Geez, I was just trying to be nice. Fuck that. "Well it's either funny or it's not funny," I explain, "that a plane, you know, that's known for doing this huge thing, you know, has to sit on my lap inside a United Airlines flight."

"Yeah, I'm not, we're not really interested."

"I'm not trying to sell you anything."

"Sorry, we're just not interested."

"You're not interested in history, or aeronautics?"

"You know what? We'd like to be left alone now," he says, searching up and down the aisle for a flight attendant. "Making off-color remarks about bombs is just not very funny these days."

"Oh, okay, that's not funny. He knows what's funny and what's not funny, this guy," I say, loud. Now I'ma unload my Shady self on their asses. "Off-color. Ha!"

I put my headphones on again, turn it up louder than it was before, and shove them back over my ears. I shift my weight and pull my hood up over my head, tucking myself into the space between the window and my seat. See if I ever try to be a neighborly conversationalist with anybody again.

When we land in New York, I stare at the couple menacingly the whole way down the aisle, and continue my vigil for the length of the Jetway. I know they can feel me, but they keep trying not to look back. They think I'm going to beat them or rob them. Because that's what it looks like I spend a lot of my time doing. Just as we get through the gate and into the terminal, I say, "Want to share a cab into the city?" right up behind the lady, but before I get a response or can do something further about the lack of one, there's my wife, and she's smiling and even more gorgeous than usual and dressed in that tight little black sweater she always wears. It's my favorite.

She's jumping up on me and throwing arms around my neck, and I'm all worried about the *Spirit of St. Louis,* but I think it's fine, and I can see the look on the face of the lady from the plane as she looks back at me like, what's that gorgeous woman doing with that slime-bag thug? I hug my wife closer, and her body feels really good and I can feel her tight belly up against mine, and she puts up with so goddamn much and smells so good, and all I want to do is get back home and fuck. Yeah, that's right: home.

11.

I think women, they hit that age, thirty, thirty-one, and they just go fucking Mom-zilla on our asses. They want a little seed inside them—your seed—and all the feminist bullshit they learned in college just flies out the fucking apartment window, out over the river and then endlessly swirls somewhere over New Jersey or something. And then it's all they can think about, talk about, read about—babies, babies. Their friends are doing it, and look how well it's going for them—they didn't give up their lifestyle. Or their apartment. They still have sex. One is perfect, two, admittedly, would be a huge change. Which is why they never want two. (At first.) Plus you can feel half decent about yourself and the question of overpopulation by leaving one child behind from two people. What about adoption? I always say. There are plenty of kids at the pound who need homes.

"But what about your family, the blood?" my wife asks the next time we have another version of the same conversation.

"I don't care about my family."

"It ends if you don't reproduce."

"Oh really? I didn't know that, thanks," I say. "Why don't the Jews do it like the Catholics, having like ten each generation, and then you don't have to worry about this kind of shit?"

"I think you should be happy you aren't Catholic," she says, speaking from one-half of the experience. She is dressed for work and sitting on the edge of our bed. She has to get on the subway, but I want to mess her up. "Will you go?" she asks sweetly, my fingers tucking the dark hair behind an ear. "Just to get some more information?"

"Fine," I say, agreeing in theory to visit the fertility doctor with her, but in reality I have no fucking clue what I am getting myself into.

She smiles wider than seems healthy or normal. "I love you, baby," she whispers, leaning over to kiss my forehead. She throws her messenger bag over her head and it hangs heavy across her shoulder because of the laptop computer inside. "I made an appointment for tomorrow afternoon," she says. "See you tonight."

I flop back down in bed as I hear her picking up a set of keys and saying good-bye to the dog in the other room. She hollers another good-bye to me, and the apartment door slams behind her, heavy on its spring-loaded hinges. She's gone. Again. The house feels instantly, dismally different. Might I ever reach a place where I'm certain she's always going to come back? Maybe she had a bag packed and grabbed it before walking out the door. It's silent for a few minutes until I hear the dog's nails click-clicking on the floor and heading into the bedroom to join me. He stands there looking at me for a minute before jumping on the bed and curling up against my wife's pillow and letting out a huge sigh.

"I totally know what you mean, man," I say to him, but all he's thinking about is going outside to take a dump.

The *Spirit of St. Louis* sits on its landing gear on the windowsill beside me, the one where if you duck outside and stand on the fire escape, you can lean way over and see some of the work going on around the pit at the Trade Center. I've picked that plane up every day since I finished it (it looks so fucking cool, it practically begs to be touched), but to be honest, once I get it in my hands, there's not really much to do with it. I fly it around my head, blow into the propeller to make it rotate once or twice before it gets stuck. That's about it. Sometimes I try to make it fly at the exact angle it does in *The Spirit of St. Louis* movie with Jimmy Stewart, when it's over Ireland or Newfoundland or wherever the fuck it's supposed to be. I get up out of bed and do this now, flying it the length of the window against the gray sky outside, and then place it back on the sill, in front of its usual backdrop of brick and concrete, and some skeletal, flaking fire escapes on the buildings across the street.

Even with the windows closed and taped, which they have been for the last six or seven months, I can still hear the dissenting wails of heavy machinery down the block. Massive, practically prehistoric cranes picking through twisted, smoking I-beams covered in shreds of clothing, skin, hair—entire lives completely and eternally encapsulated in a swatch ripped from some lady's miniskirt from The Gap.

I throw on some clothes and a hat and walk the dog down toward the site, like we've done every morning since they let us back into our building. He likes to mark the trees along the northernmost police barrier around the pit. The streets here are still coated with a thin layer of gray mud; there are no cars besides emergency vehicles and tractors, ATVs, and the softly whining, dirt-splattered electric golf carts. Tourists flock to the fences all day long, and today is no exception. They line up in a spontaneous, orderly fashion to take turns looking through the green flapping tarps wherever there are holes for air to get out. Or in.

Sometimes people cross themselves after their turn looking through the flaps. Sometimes they kneel, or hug somebody they came with. Sometimes they just unwrap the cellophane from a pack of cigarettes, letting the little strip that opens it float out of their hands as they turn and walk away. Sometimes, depending on the weather, the wrapper floats by their feet, tumbles across the sidewalk, and eventually through the little spaces at the bottom of the fence and, presumably, over the edge.

I wonder if Charles Lindbergh might've imagined something like this when he tried to fill the *Spirit of St. Louis* with as much fuel as possible before making his trip across the Atlantic. You know, cutting out as much as was humanly, physically possible—adequate amounts of food, water, a change of clothes for Paris, his urine and excrement (reportedly dumped along the way, though he didn't like talking about it), a parachute—he didn't even fucking bring a parachute because they weighed something like fifty pounds back then and he figured the trip was mostly over water and he needed the space for fuel anyway. But he was optimistic enough to pack a small raft and hand pump. And his passport. Anal-retentive motherfucker didn't forget his passport.

He called it though, didn't he? Wouldn't take on a copilot like everyone else going after the Orteig Prize was doing at the time: Slim knew all too well that passengers, like a parachute or enough water, were extraneous. Even knowing how to land, when it came down to it, was extraneous. Which is probably why my great-grandmother Esther was so obsessed with the fact that the *Spirit of St. Louis* didn't have any brakes. Or wait, that was just me, making it all up again. Either way, Slim just eased that baby down wherever he landed, and it stopped wherever it stopped. If it ran out of room, then it ran out of room. *Hi, I just slid into a drainage ditch at the end of the runway. But I'm still Charles Lindbergh.* No, he just rolled that ratty thing to a stop, and, even though it may have looked to the contrary, he'd never had any control beyond slight maneuvers in the air just prior to landing. There's a lesson in that, but I'm not really sure what it is. Something about the less stuff, less people, less complications, means more focus, more fuel, all the more to bring down civilizations and/or buildings with you when you fall.

Whatever.

I recently heard Eminem interviewed on a local radio show. The DJ asked Em how he rates himself as a father. His response? "On a scale of one to ten? Like, a twenty." And he wasn't kidding. The guy fucking loves his kid. Sometimes, I can admit it, I tear up when he writes songs to his daughter Hailie. You know, even if he's also, like, brutally murdering Hailie's mother at the same time. And Charles Lindbergh used to make

Charles Jr. wear thumb braces that pinned his hands to the bedsheets so the boy wouldn't suck his thumbs at night. He was wearing them on the night he was kidnapped out of their house in Hopewell. And furthermore, I think he used to call his son "It." And the kid called Lindbergh "It" back. Not the tenderest dude around.

I don't know, but if Eminem and Charles Fucking Lindbergh can do it, so can I. And I'm thinking that if I can land somewhere between stabbing my wife and disposing of her body at the bottom of a lake in front of my own kid on the one side, and then having a son kidnapped and murdered on the other, then I should be in pretty decent shape. I think I'm all set on the former, but losing a kid? Who the fuck knows if I inherited that too.

12.

They're getting ready for the fucking one-year anniversary of September Eleventh next week. There are "No Parking Anytime" signs going up everywhere, bleachers too, a general rush to get things as presentable as possible. What a joke. It's for family members only, though many others, I'm sure, will come. They already have.

Meantime, I have two gigs tonight; one is just a standard performance at an Eminem-themed bar mitzvah party at a hotel in midtown, only I'm not DJing it because I have this other gig later. This second one's at a dark theater that this loaded family rented out around Times Square. I hate when I'm double booked, but it seems manageable. It's hard to get a cab, but I finally hail one a couple blocks over and drive back to my building with the cabbie to pick up my stuff while the wife keeps an eye on it from the fire escape above. I'm loading everything into the trunk of the cab, and my wife is waving down at me, looking all beautiful like she does, and this is the first night in a while I feel like I'd rather be spending my Saturday on the couch with her, watching a movie or something and then fucking. This is the grind, but I can feel the momentum building, so I know I gotta keep pushing through.

The new DJ I just hired seems to be working out okay. Our first gig goes good; the father slaps an extra hundred in my palm when he sees his fucking nerdy pimple-faced kid grinning like mad after my set. The second show has a few glitches because we're not handling the sound system like usual—the pretentious, control-freaky theater people are—but after a while, we're good to go, and I'm up there spitting "My Name Is," and on fucking fire, sweating like I'm on gorilla juice, grabbing at my balls, and stomping around as the DJ eases me into "The Real Slim Shady." I slip in my own moniker every once in a while over the song: "Will the real Slim Lindy please stand up? I repeat, will the real Slim Lindy please stand up?" and the kids go mad. Even some parents are joining in, rocking their corny baby-boomer dancing styles, wiggling and shaking and moving their arms all over like they're filled with helium. I don't think anyone minds when I freestyle my own shit over the regular song—it sounds no different from Eminem—and it feels good to get a little practice in for when I start battling.

After the show, this kid's dad, some investment banker or some shit, gives me a two-hundred-dollar tip and slaps me on the back through my sweaty white T-shirt when I'm packing up my equipment. Most of the kids' parents are here to pick up their offspring, motor-mouthing about how good Eminem was and can they get me for their own bar mitzvahs? I give out a few cards, and some of them try to engage me, but for now I'm anxious to get home to the wife.

My DJ doesn't say much, but he helps me carry the shit out to the curb, and we're waiting for a cab. He's a black man, so I stand out there with my white ass and try to hail a cab while he makes a call on his cell. It's late on Saturday night, and most cabs going by are full. I remember I left my backup mic in the sound booth of the theater, so I tell my man to watch my stuff on the curb for me while I go in and get it. He says okay and I run inside, the air cool against my sweaty skin.

A couple kids stop me on the way out, so I stop and talk with them. But when I get back out to the curb a few minutes later, the cat is gone, and so is my equipment. I look up and down the block, and a I see some red tail-lights making a quick right onto Ninth Avenue. *What the fuck?* I call his name. A couple crosses the street rushing somewhere, the lady's high heels clicking. "Excuse me!" I yell. They keep walking. "Excuse me? Did you see anyone run off with my stuff?" The man turns around and holds up both of his arms in the air.

"Fucking FUCK!" I'm yelling at the top of my lungs. A few bar mitzvah guests are staring. That fucking cocksucker, if he set me up I'll fucking stab him in the gut so hard my fist'll go through his stomach, around his spine, and out the other side. "FUCK!"

I start flipping through my shit—they got pretty much everything. There are a few vinyls left, but my thousands of bucks of equipment's been stripped. And they left some RCA cables. That was nice. I pick them up in my fist and stand there. I don't feel so good.

"It's a white Toyota," some little Puerto Rican dude says to me then. His hands are stuffed into his pockets and he looks like he just got off a job at a parking lot or something. He nods his head in the direction of Ninth Avenue, so I start running, full speed. Tourists are streaming in packs up and down the block. Theater's just let out. When I get to the corner I look north and south, but I don't see anything.

"Fuck!" I yell again.

"Is that Eminem?" a little girl says.

"Oh my god," says another. Then there is screaming.

"Are you Eminem?" a dude walks up to me and asks, taking his Mets cap off his head and handing it to me. "Dude, can I get an autograph?"

"Fuck you," I say.

"It's him, it's him!"

"Yeah, it's him!" I scream. People are gathering. I start wrapping the RCA cables around my neck, tying them so tight it hurts. I yank them up above my head, like I'm hanging myself, jumping up and down and stick-ing my tongue out of my mouth. "I'm *him*. I'm fuckin' Eminem!" I'm screaming.

"Dude, you're wack," the guy says. "But you're shorter than I thought."

"Fuck you," I say again, grabbing his cap and smacking him over the head with it. He laughs the first time, so I do it again. And again. And then some more. He just stands there letting me, with this stupid fucking look on his face, so I deck him in the jaw. It hurts my hand like crazy, but he's flat on the sidewalk with some blood on his lip, and people are circling around him and he's moaning.

"Not so fucking funny anymore, huh, asshole?" I yell, tossing his hat onto the sidewalk beside him.

I see a white Toyota, or what looks like a white Toyota sitting a couple of lanes over, idling at the light. I start running for it. "I got you, mother-fucker!" I scream. Then a horn honks, and it's a deep one so I know it's a truck. Next thing I know my head cracks into a windshield and I'm in the air, horizontal with the pavement. The antenna's flipping back and forth like windshield wipers in front of my face, and my left forearm's searing pain. All my fingers go loose in that hand and I hit the ground, bouncing a few times before it all stops. The lights above me, big signs on the sides of buildings (Britney drinking Pepsi? Something else . . .). After a while, a cop's fat face. I lift up my arm in front of my eyes. It's a filleted salmon, elbow to wrist, pink guts pouring out. *Yes, this is how the story would have to go, isn't it?*

13.

"I murder a rhyme one word at a time. You've never heard of a mind as perverted as mine . . ."

"Excuse me, sir, what?" some faggot's asking me.

"You think I'm not gonna choke you 'til the vocal cords don't work in your throat anymore?"

"Sir, we just need you to calm down, and we need to get a name so we can go ahead and make you feel much better," he continues. It looks like he's wearing a green dress.

"You faggot, stop egging me on," I scream, while the guy's grabbing my hands and feet. "Shut up when I'm talking, you hear me?"

"Stan, I've got his left foot in, can you give me some help with the right?" a female nurse, the regular kind, asks the male one, who seems to be more in charge.

"Yo, my man Stan, I'm your biggest fan," I keep spittin' over the track in my head.

"Okay, we've got the other leg," Stan the faggot nurse says to the black Uncle Tom doctor who's standing by the door of the room, telling everyone what to do with me with his arms crossed and hairy pecs poking out of his V-neck green scrubs. My arms are still free, so I decide to stab him with the first sharp object I can locate, and barring a sharp one, a blunt one will do. I scan the room for something within reach. Uh oh, looks like I'm in the hospital again, and I can't move my legs because these leather straps are cutting into my ankles something fierce. I think they're trying to shock me.

"Sir, what's your name?" Stan asks. There's blood everywhere. Maybe I was successful in stabbing someone. "Sir, I need to know what you've taken. What is it you're on? Is there anything I need to know about?"

"Here we go again, we're out of our medicine, out of our minds, and we want in yours, let us in," I just keep rapping.

Next thing I know the bitch girl nurse leans down close, right next to my ear and in this sexy distracting voice says, "Sir, I need to know your name." I know what this is. It's a trick, and yet it works long enough so that she's got hold of my arm.

"Slim," I say. *Snap,* my right arm goes into the restraint.

"Okay, now is that Mr. Slim, or Slim something?" she coos, real sexy.

"Slim something." *Snap,* my left arm then, real slow and gentle. I can't feel anything below the elbow, can't move my fingers.

"Slim what?" Her voice is sweet, but now I can hear the saliva sticking and smacking to her tongue when she speaks and I want nothing but for her to shut up. Repulsive. "Can you [smack, smack] tell me your last name?"

"Lindy."

"Slim Lindy?"

"Yes." Now I can't move at all.

"Slim [smack] Lindy?"

"That's what I said," I say, and me and this nurse, we clearly have something going. But then *pinch,* and then bubbles, bubbles, and the room spinning slowly, but controlled—not dizzy-jumpy and fast like after you pop a Mini Thin, but real calm spin like you're strapped into a little plane with no windows and it's spiraling down in slow motion through sleet-filled chilly air, and all the canvas airmail sacks are gaping open wide mouths around you, spilling their contents fluttering about in the storm outside your window—love letters, hate letters, Dear John letters, overdue bills, photographs, faxes, eviction notices, marriage licenses, birth certificates, death certificates, newspaper clippings, certificates of naturalization, forged Austrian passports—all spinning around you and your little plane. And you look out the window as a leg that has been crudely severed just above the knee goes by, with a lady's high-heel shoe still on it, but half the panty hose have been torn off, and the rest of her—just a naked torso and head, really—is strapped into the seat in front of you, and the whole lot of her is flying toward Earth in a suspension of jet fuel faster than both you and the mail combined. *It looks like we're going to have a problem here.*

"We're gonna have to call Psych when he comes out," Stan says, real calm, and it sounds like slowing a 45 down to 33 rpm, and my head hits a pillow that has the sound of hay and feel of old canvas.

*   *   *

"Slim? Slim?"

—

"What's your date of birth?"

"What?" I ask, opening my eyes. It's my old buddy Stan. It feels like a year has passed since I last saw him.

"Do you know where you are?" he asks.

"Detroit?"

—

"St. Louis?"

"Do you know where you are?"

"You just asked me that."

"You're in the hospital, at Bellevue, in New York City," he says slowly like I'm some fucking retard. "You were brought in from the street, and you just had orthopedic surgery on your left arm. But you're going to be fine."

"I can't move my legs."

"I know, you were fighting pretty hard when they brought you in. Would you like me to loosen them?"

"I'm not paralyzed?"

"No, this is just so you don't hurt yourself or anybody else."

"Did they take off my clothes?"

"Nobody's going to take off your clothes."

"Why are you talking so slow?" I ask, dragging out each word like he is. "You think I'm cute, don't you? You're just frustrated I won't ejaculate in your ass."

"Well, that's certainly not the case—either the first part or the second," Stan the male nurse says, talking at a normal clip now. "And it's also not the kind of talk that's going to make me want to take off those straps."

"You think I'm ugly, don't you? *Don't* you?"

"I think all of my patients are equally attractive," Stan says, squeezing the IV bag above me. He looks back at the door, where the Uncle Tom doctor from before is whispering with some Jew in a suit under a white coat.

"Psych's here," says the doctor to Stan, who puts some wires next to my strapped-down left arm and recedes behind a curtain in the middle of the room.

"Now can I change rooms?" a middle-aged lady's voice says from behind the curtain.

"Things should be quieter from here on out," Stan answers this lady in his slow retard voice.

"Hi, Slim," the dude in the suit says, standing next to me and placing his hands on the metal handle on the bed. "I'm Dr. Lowenstein."

"A Jew."

"Indeed," he says.

"I'm a Jew."

"This *is* New York."

"Indeed," I say.

"Do you know what happened to you?" he asks.

"Someone stole my shit."

"I see," he says, jotting something down in a notebook. "And what shit is that?"

"My equipment, every last bit of it." My head is pounding.

"I see. And do you know how you were injured?"

"I socked that kid in the face."

"Yes, yes you did," he says, nodding. "Anything else?"

"Not really."

"Do you not remember getting injured?"

"I'm not injured," I say. He looks down at my arm and my eyes follow his gaze. There is a huge white bandage around my forearm, a little oval of blood seeping through on the inside. "Shit."

"You were hit by a truck."

"Oh, man."

"You're very lucky to be alive."

"Yes, that's what they always say. Can you take these off?"

"Just as soon as you tell me what's going on with you."

"You said it yourself. I got hit by a truck."

"I'm thinking more along the lines of maybe why you ran out in front of a truck in the first place."

"I told you that motherfucker ran off with my shit."

"The driver of the truck?"

"No, the one in the Toyota. He took my shit."

"I see. And can you tell me why you might've had some cables tied around your neck? Do you remember doing anything like this?"

I can see where this is heading. "Can you just call my wife?" I ask.

"You have a wife?"

"Yes, well . . ."

"You're married?"

"Well, not actually *married* . . . What, do you think I'm crazy, I'm gonna go get some fucking piece of paper from the city for that shit?"

I begin ranting, but decide to stop in the interest of getting out of this place. "I just call her 'the wife' because she fucking acts like one all the time, and we've been together for like, forever."

"I see. And where might we be able to find her?"

"At our apartment. I'll give you the phone number."

"Okay," he says, looking back at the Uncle Tom doctor, who's nodding his head and watching all this.

"I can't remember it."

"You don't know your home phone number?"

"Fuck, my head is killing."

"You had a pretty serious blow. You were unconscious for some time," the doctor in the doorway says then.

"Can *you* take me out of these things?" I ask him, because maybe a brother will take pity on me.

"We'll take those off just as soon as I can be sure you're not going to hurt yourself or anybody else," the Jew answers as the black doctor just keeps standing there.

"Can you just call my wife—my *girlfriend,* whatever? She's real hot."

He smiles despite himself. We might've been at Yale together. Only I didn't go to Yale. He's a nebbishy fellow, black wavy hair, brown eyes, long face, huge nostrils, eyeglasses more suited to an architect than a shrink. "Can you tell me what's going on with you, a little bit about your life?" he asks earnestly.

"Nurse, I need some water!" the lady from behind the curtain shrieks then. I can literally see the interruption register on the shrink's face. He seems like the kind of guy who literally cannot do two things at once. In other words, a nightmare in the sack. I look at his wedding band and feel for his wife.

"Use your buzzer like everyone else," I yell back at the lady. "And she's complaining about *me*?" I ask the shrink.

He stands up and goes to the other side of the curtain. I can hear a plastic hospital cup of water being poured, and a soft coy "Thank you," from the lady after the trickle stops. With this it's clear the shrink's greener than my great-grandfather was the day he got off the boat from Russia.

"So you're new on this rotation?" I ask as soon as he sits back down beside my bed.

"Yes," he replies.

"Honesty," I say. "This is what they tell you to do with patients like me."

"Yes," he admits, shifting in his seat and switching his crossed legs. "So what seems to be the problem here?"

"Honestly?"

"Yes, honestly."

"Well, sometimes I feel like Mister Understood."

"Is that true?" he asks.

"No."

"Do you want to get better?"

"Do you want to take these things off?" I ask, pulling my arms up as high as they will go, but this ends up being just about level with my chest. My left arm throbs. I notice then how it smells like old lady ass in the room, and I really want to get out.

"Are you using any substances I should know about?"

"Just acid, crack, smack, coke, and dope," I say. "And: *my life's like, kinda what my wife's like . . .*"

"What?"

"*Fucked-up, after I beat her fuckin' ass every night, Ike.*"

"I'm not understanding."

"Will you just call my fucking wife-girlfriend? I remember my phone number now. Fuck!"

"Cursing is really not going to help the situation."

"Will you write it down?" I ask, and then give him the number, and he hands it to the nurse. "Tell her I'm okay."

"She will," the shrink assures me. And then: "So, it seems there are a few discrepancies in your case."

"Discrepancies?"

"Indeed."

"What's with the 'indeeds'?" I ask.

"It appears as though you don't know your date of birth."

"I told that faggot: October 17th, 1972."

"Your driver's license states otherwise."

"What does it say?"

"October *16th,* 1972."

"That's what I said."

"You said October *17th.*"

"Yeah, that's what I said."

"It also appears that you have dark brown hair in this picture, and the license says, Hair: B-R-N."

"Yes, yes. B-R-N for brown." I notice the Uncle Tom doctor isn't standing by the door any longer.

"Did you bleach your hair blond?"

"Frankly, I don't see what this has to do with my getting these restraints taken off," I say. "People dye their hair."

"And there's one other small discrepancy I'm seeing."

Yes.

"Besides your name, there's the whole 'F' in the Sex column on your license."

"Yes, the 'F,' " I sigh.

"So we're looking at quite a few discrepancies, really," he says. "And let me make something *perfectly* clear: As far as we're concerned, there is *nothing* wrong with your lifestyle per se. It's just that when you've assaulted somebody else and caused injury to yourself, well, that's where I come in. And frankly, it's a little worrisome."

"You guys already figured it out, why do you have to torture me?"

"How is this torture?"

"Is my wife coming?"

"She should be coming soon," he says. "Now, can you maybe tell me a little more about what's going on with you?"

I flash on the night me and this doctor might've become official blood brothers, you know, on pledge weekend for the Sigma Alpha Mu fraternity chapter at Yale, when we were assigned to clean all of the fraternity house's toilets and then demonstrate how spotless we made them by licking the porcelain from top to bottom. Only something like this never happened—for me at least.

"Yale, class of 1992, right?" I say to him.

"Yes, were you?"

"No, but—"

"How'd you know?" this little shrinky-dink asks me, looking around the room to see if anybody else heard. I think he thinks I must be some kind of an oracle. Some say that people like me have special powers. Or at least that's the story I heard. He keeps looking at me incredulously.

"Christ on a stick. Do I look like I wouldn't know what Harvard or Yale is?" I ask.

"I'm just trying to figure out what's going on, just trying to help."

"Class of '92?" I prod.

"Ninety. How'd you know?" he asks, but it's obvious he's not supposed to.

"I just knew."

"Doctor, can I speak with you for a moment?" It's Uncle Tom, poking his head back into the room with a bunch of printouts in his mitts. The entire World Wide Web at his fingertips.

The shrink comes back to my bedside, looking further confused. I think he wishes he'd been assigned to the screeching, gang-banged heroin overdose with barbed-wire slices in her arms across the hall.

"So do you believe you are this rapper, Eminem?" he asks.

I start laughing. "This *rapper*?" I say in my best corny-white-guy voice. "Can you take these fucking things off?"

"What do you want me to call you? T, Talia, Slim, Lindy, what?"

"T is fine."

"Okay, T."

"No, Slim."

"Okay then, Slim."

"You can't fucking keep me here. I want to go."

"Well, I actually can keep you here until I know what's going on."

"Fine, fine! You want to know what's going on with me? Fucking *fine*."

"Yes?"

"And then you'll let me go?"

"I can't promise anything, but if I'm satisfied you're safe, then we can get you out of here."

"I don't know," I start, and then I can't stop. "I wrote this fucking novel a couple years ago, and they printed up a bunch of copies, and the bio on the back said I was a 'he,' 'cause I guess some designer or whoever was just going by the picture and it just seemed like, well, I pretty much am a 'he,' and I've always been like this, so we went with it, whatever. Nobody ever said anything. Never bothered trying to change the license. I don't even know if the editor even knew what the fuck I was. Whatever. Done."

"I see. So, you wrote a book."

"Come on, man, I'm telling you the truth," I say. "This is fucking ridiculous."

"Well, I've got to be honest with you, T, or Slim. I don't think I know what the truth is."

"That *is* the truth! I'm not a writer anymore. It was fucking bullshit, that book got all this attention for a while, spilling my guts all over the place. And I know it wouldn't have done shit if it didn't say I was a guy on the back," I yell, but he's not listening.

Look at these eyes, baby blue, baby. Just like yourself. If they were brown, Shady lose, Shady sits on the shelf. Em knows what it is to be given a pass, that if he'd been black, he would've sold half. The shrink is just staring at me while the rhymes are looping rapid-fire through my brain. He exhales loudly through his nose—a high, whiny whistle.

"I'm a professional entertainer now," I add. "You can look at my fucking Web site."

—

"Go look: Eminem-New-York-Bar-Mitzvahs-dot-com—all one word,"
I say. "That's what I was doing tonight when my stuff got jacked."

"You're an impersonator?"

"*Performer*."

"Why are you stating your birthday as that of the rapper Eminem?" he
asks.

"Because it's only one day off from mine, I don't know. I was staying in
character or something," I say. "Obsessions with famous blondes runs in
my family."

—

"Can that kind of shit run in the family? Can you pass it on to a kid?"
I ask then, seriously. I need to know. It's urgent.

"Mental illness certainly can, yes, a propensity toward substance
abuse," he rattles off.

"But what about, like, just fear or something?"

"I don't know," he says, leaning back in his chair. We sit in silence. A
bubble pops inside my IV bag above us, rushing to the surface.

"This was a tough case for your first day, huh?" I ask.

"It's not my first day."

Then Uncle Tom comes in, and mercy of all mercies, my wife is right
behind him.

"Take these off," she says, coming over to my bed and rubbing my
head. "Are you okay?"

The doctor starts unbuckling the straps around my arms. When they
are free he does the same with my ankles, and I hug my wife, but not with
my left arm, which is still throbbing, though in a dull way.

"What the hell is going on?" she asks. *My hero*. "Was this really necessary?"

"Yes," I tell her. "But they could've come off a little sooner."

She smiles at me. "You okay?" she asks again.

"Do you think I'm dying well?" I ask her. Because these were among

Charles Lindbergh's last words to his publisher William Jovanovich when he came to visit Lindbergh in the ICU at Columbia Presbyterian Hospital in New York. This was before Lindbergh made his last flight—though not at the helm—on a United Airlines plane to Maui that had been outfitted with a bed for him to be able to survive the trip. He didn't want to die in a hospital, a judicious instinct. But from the hospital bed before the flight, Lindbergh had pointed to a brown leather bag in the room, and Jovanovich picked it up. The bag contained about half of the memoirs that were published after Lindbergh died, a short time later in Maui.

"You're not dying," my wife says, laughing. She is my Paw-Paw Sam now. The one who gets it. I wish I had a brown bag containing my memoirs to point her toward, for dramatic effect, but I'm sure it would just be getting trampled because now the room is filled with bustling activity. They give you more attention when it's time to leave. But until then, and for all they care, you can just sit and rot. A burly cop appears at the door. "Is this her?" he asks, and she goes over to him.

The cop's whispering, but I can hear what he's saying: "This guy's not gonna press charges. He actually thinks your friend is Eminem and that we're hiding his identity or something, I don't know, but she—"

"He," my wife corrects.

"He. He just, uh, better not pull a stunt like that again," the cop says. He adjusts his dopey hat and leaves after my wife thanks him profusely.

When she comes back to my bed, the wife is rolling her eyes at me the way she does. The Uncle Tom doctor begins telling her about my "case," but I'm barely listening because finally she's here and can take over so I don't have to. He tells her my C-Spine was clear. Same with the CAT scan. Again how lucky I am. How they repaired some tendons in my arm. They were severed when the antenna filleted me, though he doesn't use that particular word. My hand should function normally, though only after consistent physical therapy. She looks worried, and I feel bad she has to come here to deal with the mess that is me.

Then she tells them—and in this moment my boundless love and appreciation for her turns into a venomous icy rage—that I have been taking hormones for a few months, that they have been harvesting my eggs so that she might have my baby. She says she thinks I injected testosterone for a year or more, long ago before she met me, but that she thinks I might've had some health problems related to it. That there was talk of potentially jumbled chromosomes from when I was a kid. She says my moods have been a little crazier than usual since my parents died, and especially since the hormones.

The Jew boy shrink is jotting notes as fast as he can, looking up at me every time there's a pause while my wife's blabbing all my personal business to these assholes. The Uncle Tom doctor keeps prompting her, and there's no way to stop it.

"There won't be another case like mine," I lean over and quietly assure the shrink. But he still looks confused as hell. Though now he's safely sandbagged himself into his comfort zone full of research, notes, pharmaceuticals, patient histories, case studies, verifiable physical realities. I can tell he wants to take a look at what's under my pants, what's not splashed across my chest. This doctor seems to get me just slightly more than I thought my parents ever might. He pushes his glasses up the bridge of his nose, which has become a sweaty, slippery slope. They might have all the facts, but they won't get all of me.

I will be discharged momentarily. Going home with the wife. My dog will be waiting. I can rest my eyes, if only for the moment.

14.

I've been very caught up in what's true and what's a little less than true lately. It's near impossible to tell the difference. One thing I think I'm starting to believe is completely true is that my wife will always be there. She treats me, it seems, the same or better than she treats herself. I know people do this for each other, I just personally have never seen it. She cares about things that happen to me as though they are happening to her. When something goes bad for me, I can see mirrored on her face the precise and intricate way in which it troubles her equally. When things are good—and don't let me fool you into thinking that there hasn't been much good, because there has—she says things like, "I just got chills." In extreme cases, she'll even cry out of happiness. It's downright weird.

I wonder if I'm just the consummate prick, or if I can truly care about another as much as I care about myself. Forget *more than*. First things first. This worries me constantly, because she deserves it. As does any other life we might or might not choose to bring into this addled world.

My arm is healing, though not as fast as things seemed to heal when I was a kid. The fingers on my hand don't move like they used to, but the therapists assure me they will. I'll probably never be able to make a tight fist, but I can move my fingers, and I can place them on my wife's flat, eager belly as we lay in bed together on this lazy weekend morning. I will be turning thirty tomorrow, and my brother Eminem will do the same the day after that. We have nothing planned, and that's how I like it.

Filtered fall light is spilling into our bedroom and across our bodies like we are an average man and wife in a typical American neighborhood—one that just happens to be down the block from the nation's current repository of its collective grief. It's been other places before—in Dallas, Oklahoma City, San Francisco, the middle of the North Atlantic—and it will surely settle somewhere else again soon. From the windowsill next to the bed, the *Spirit of St. Louis* casts a very long and delicate shadow across the wrinkled white sheets wadded up on our bed. Which makes sense, because it is early still, and the light is low. The whole day stretches ahead of us.

Some parts are true, others are made up. Still others are made up, but from entirely true events.

And the last part that is completely true is the part where there's this egg in a dish in a high-tech, stainless steel–swathed laboratory somewhere on the Upper East Side of Manhattan. A dropper full of washed sperm is plopped into the dish, and it wiggles its way dutifully toward the egg. You can't see all the little sperms that represent what's commonly referred to as a drop of sperm, but they're there. Something like a thousand of them, all squirming with fairly good-to-excellent motility toward the egg, which is also in fairly good-to-excellent shape. As far as eggs go. It is in such good shape, I imagine, because it comes from a healthy (generally) genetic female, with many characteristics of a healthy genetic male. This means it will probably really get along with the sperm, since the egg probably, in another life, probably somewhere far, far away, like in Russia or Bhutan, should have actually been sperm instead of an egg. But that's not in the story.

So they're on their way to the egg, all these sperm. They are from someone I don't know. My wife doesn't know him either. But soon, if all this works out, she will be carrying inside her the sperm from this person neither of us knows, and it will have fertilized the egg from someone both of us knows intimately (me), and then in nine months—or probably sooner because this is technically a risky procedure—the wife will squeeze out a baby that looks half like me, and half like this person we don't really know. I say "really" know, because at this point, we will know him—or at least half of him—very well.

Okay, none of that is true either.

But what is, what I can tell you one hundred percent is totally unadulterated and not made up in any way . . . You want to know what it is? It's that that little egg waiting for those little anonymous sperms, well, it is in fact the last of the Lipshitzes. And the truth is, and you probably don't want to hear it, but whether or not it gets successfully fertilized and successfully planted and then successfully carried and delivered by my beautiful half-Jewish wife . . . Whether or not all this happens?

I really don't give a fuck.

And that is the god's honest truth.

I may not end up a famous rapper, or even a semi-famous one. And the literary agent may or may not call several more times, while a hotly deliberated memorial to the dead slowly rises down the block. But one thing I can tell you for absolute certain, this time no fooling or bullshit:

I will never—mark my words—finish writing that fucking book.

* THE END *

STUFF THAT MIGHT'VE BEEN HELPFUL

AND MAY OR MAY NOT HAVE BEEN USED

The Amarillo Daily News, various articles.

Barrington Boardman, *Flappers, Bootleggers, "Typhoid Mary" & The Bomb* (Harper & Row, 1989).

A. Scott Berg, *Lindbergh* (Berkley, 1999).

Anthony Bozza, *Whatever You Say I Am: The Life and Times of Eminem* (Crown, 2003).

David M. Brownstone et al., *Island of Hope, Island of Tears* (Rawson Wade, 1979).

George Chauncey, *Gay New York: Gender, Urban Culture, and the Making of the Gay Male World, 1890–1940* (Basic Books, 1994).

Peter Morton Coan, *Ellis Island Interviews* (Facts On File, 1997).

Eminem, *Angry Blonde* (ReganBooks, 2000).

Zvi Gitelman, *A Century of Ambivalence: The Jews of Russia and the Soviet Union, 1881 to the Present* (YIVO Institute, 1988).

Edward H. Judge, *Easter in Kishinev: Anatomy of a Pogrom* (NYU Press, 1992).

Ava F. Kahn, editor, *Jewish Life in the American West* (Univ. of Washington Press, 2002).

Anne Morrow Lindbergh, *War Within and Without: Diaries and Letters, 1939–1944* (Harcourt Brace Jovanovich, 1980).

Charles A. Lindbergh, *The Spirit of St. Louis* (Charles Scribner's Sons, 1953).

Charles A. Lindbergh, *"We"* (G. P. Putnam's Sons, 1927).

Paul Robert Magocsi, *Historical Atlas of Central Europe* (Univ. of Washington Press, 2002).

Bernard Marinbac, *Galveston: Ellis Island of the West* (SUNY Albany Press, 1983).

Allen Mondell and Cynthia Salzman Mondell, *West of Hester Street* [film] (Media Projects Inc., 1983).

The New York Times, various articles.

Natalie Ornish, *Pioneer Jewish Texans* (Texas Heritage Press, 1989).

Jacob A. Riis, *How the Other Half Lives* (Penguin Books, 1997).

Harriet and Fred Rochlin, *Pioneer Jews: A New Life in the Far West* (Houghton Mifflin, 1984).

Ronald Sanders, *The Lower East Side* (Dover Publications, 1979).

ACKNOWLEDGMENTS

Thanks to:

The MacDowell Colony, where most of this book was written.

The excellent Laurie Chittenden, and everybody at Dutton (including but not limited to Brian Tart, Lisa Johnson, Beth Parker, Amy Hill, and Erika Kahn).

Wunderkind Doug Stewart at Sterling Lord Literistic.

Diane Baldwin, Amy Bloom, F. Scott Conklin, Murray Cooper, Ricki Cooper, Steve Cooper, Michael Cunningham, Jeni Englander, Jay Fenberg, Pudge (Marty) Fenberg, Susan Fenberg, Cary Goldstein, Jennifer Haigh, Brent Hoff, Megan Honig, Johanna Ingalls, Jaime Manrique, Adam Mansbach, Sigrid Nunez, Jay Parini, Amanda Patten, and Johnny Temple of Akashic Books.

Mom and Dad.

And Felicia Luna Lemus.

ABOUT THE AUTHOR

T COOPER is the author of the novel *Some of the Parts*.
T received an MFA in fiction writing from Columbia
University and has twice been a fellow of The MacDowell
Colony. T lives in New York City.